"I MUST ASK ALL OF YOU TO COME WITH ME FOR INTERROGATION."

The Hunter officer could not conceal a triumphant smile.

"Are we under arrest, then?" Morley asked.

"Protective custody would be a better term. Please disarm."

"If you disarm us, you are responsible for our safety," Franke pointed out. "In fact, disarming us could be interpreted as taking us hostage. You know Federation policy on that."

Morley caught the expression on some of the Hunters' faces that showed they understood that if the Federation interpreted taking the humans into "protective custody" as kidnapping, they might be signing their own death warrants. But they'd be doing the same if they disobeyed their officer.

"Disarm them," the officer said to his men. One of the Hunters raised his carbine and fired a burst—into the officer's neck. Humans and Hunters alike froze, all of them certain that the first person to move or speak would be the next to die. . . .

WARRIORS FOR THE WORKING DAY

STARCRUISER SHENANDOAH

WARRIORS FOR THE WORKING DAY

Roland J. Green

A ROC BOOK

ROC
Published by the Penguin Group
Penguin Books USA Inc., 375 Hudson Street,
New York, New York 10014, U.S.A.
Penguin Books Ltd, 27 Wrights Lane,
London W8 5TZ, England
Penguin Books Australia Ltd, Ringwood,
Victoria, Australia
Penguin Books Canada Ltd, 10 Alcorn Avenue,
Toronto, Ontario, Canada M4V 3B2
Penguin Books (N.Z.) Ltd, 182–190 Wairau Road,
Auckland 10, New Zealand

Penguin Books Ltd, Registered Offices:
Harmondsworth, Middlesex, England

First published by Roc,
an imprint of Dutton Signet,
a division of Penguin Books USA Inc.

First Printing, April, 1994
10 9 8 7 6 5 4 3 2 1

 REGISTERED TRADEMARK—MARCA REGISTRADA

Printed in the United States of America

To Frieda, my lady and love

Principal Characters

A. Human

Josephine ATWOOD: Military correspondent for Trans-Rift Media on Charlemagne.

Marshal Emilio BANFI: Federation officer, resident on Linak'h, appointed Supreme Warband Leader of the Administration by the Confraternity regime.

Admiral of the Fleet Wilhelmina BAUMANN, U.F.N.: Commander-in-Chief, United Federation Navy.

His Excellency Aung BAYJAR: Minister of Foreign Affairs, the United Federation of Starworlds.

Colonel Peter BISSELL: Chief of Military Intelligence, Planetary Republic of Victoria.

Captain Pavel BOGDANOV, U.F.N.: Commanding officer, U.F.S. *Shenandoah*.

Ursula BOLL: Wife of Nikolai Sergeyevich Komarov; Federation Intelligence agent. Mother of two children by Nikolai, Sophia and Peter Komarov-Boll.

Leo BUTKUS: Boatswain, R.M.S. *Somtow Nosavan*.

Colonel Malcolm DAVIDSON: Caledonian (British Union) army officer, aide to Marshal Banfi.

Lucco and Teresa DiVRIES: Farmers and intelligence operatives on Victoria.

Major Roger DUBOY: XO, Third Battalion, Linak'h Brigade.

Brigadier General Lev EDELSTEIN: CG, 218 Brigade, Linak'h.

Sergeant Juan ESTEVA: Security & Intelligence NCO for Candice Shores's Third Battalion; also the CO's bodyguard.

Captain Lomo FITZROY, U.F.N.: Chief of staff, Low Squadron, Linak'h Task Force.

Commander Herman FRANKE, U.F.N.: Federation Intelligence officer and Kishi Institute scholar, assigned to Linak'h.

Commander Shintaro FUJITA, U.F.N.: Chief Engineer, U.F.S. *Shenandoah.*

Jeremiah GIST: President, Planetary Republic of Victoria.

Brigadier General Barbara HOGG: CG, Linak'h Brigade, Linak'h Command.

BoJo JOHNSON: Former orphan and stowaway, enlisted in the Victoria Civil Action Group on Linak'h.

First Lieutenant Sergei KAPUSTEV: Officer, Company A (LI), Third Battalion, Linak'h Brigade.

Brigadier General Soliman KHARG: CG, 218 Brigade, Linak'h Command.

Nikolai Sergeyevich KOMAROV: Artist and former Federation Intelligence agent, now art teacher in the Federation Territory. Candice Shores's father.

Warrant Officer Second-Class Mitsuo KONISHI: Candice Shores's assigned command-lifter pilot.

Fumiko KUWAHARA: Wife of Admiral Kuwahara. They have two children, Yaso and Hanae.

Acting Vice Admiral Sho KUWAHARA, U.F.N.: Staff officer at Forces Command, Charlemagne. Commands the Dual-Sovereignty Planet Study Group.

Marcus LANGSTON: Former Federation Army officer assigned to Linak'h; later reinstated with rank of Lieutenant General as CG, Linak'h Command ground forces.

Commodore Rose LIDDELL, U.F.N.: Flag officer commanding the Low Squadron, Linak'h Task Force; pennant in *Shenandoah*.

Charles V. LONGMAN: Chief engineer, R.M.S. *Somtow Nosavan;* affiliate of Joanna Marder.

Vice Admiral Diana LONGMAN, U.F.N.: Admiral commanding Linak'h Task Force and SOPS, Linak'h Command; aunt of Charles Longman.

Lieutenant Commander Brian MAHONEY, U.F.N.: Communications watch officer aboard *Shenandoah*.

Joanna MARDER: Captain, R.M.S. *Somtow Nosavan.*

Major Lucretia MORLEY: Federation MP officer, affiliated with Commander Franke and collaborating with him on intelligence assignments on Linak'h.

First Lieutenant Olga NALYVKINA: Federation Army officer, and gunship pilot, formerly Marshal Banfi's personal pilot.

Colonel Liew NIEG: Federation Army Intelligence officer, assigned to Linak'h.

Lieutenant Colonel Sigrid OLUFSDOTTIR: CO, First Battalion, 222 Brigade, later CO Task Force Olufsdottir, Linak'h Command.

Lieutenant General Alys PARKINSON: Commander-in-Chief, Defense Forces, Planetary Republic of Victoria.

Karl POCHER: Partner in the DiVrieses' farm; Team Leader, Victoria Civil Action Group on Linak'h; later captain, Victoria Expeditionary Battalion.

Captain Lena ROPUSKI, U.F.N.: XO, Dual-Sovereignty Planet Study Group, Forces Command, Charlemagne.

Acting Lieutenant Colonel Candice SHORES: CO, Third Battalion, Linak'h Brigade (formerly the Quick Reaction Force).

Sergeant First-Class Jan SKLARINSKY: Senior sniper, Third Battalion, Linak'h Brigade.

General of the Army Maximilian SZAIJKOWSKI: Commander-in-Chief, United Federation Army.

First Lieutenant Brigitte TACHIN: Division officer, Weapons Department, *Shenandoah;* assigned to the ground party on Linak'h.

Major General Joachim TANZ: Commanding general, Linak'h Command.

Sergeant Major Esther (Eppie) TIMBERLAKE: Battalion sergeant major, Third Battalion, Linak'h Brigade.

Lieutenant Commander Elayne ZHENG: Electronic warfare officer in the 879th Squadron (Heavy Attack).

B. Nonhuman

Fleet Commander Eimo SU-ANKRAI: Baernoi; former commander of the Seventh Training Squadron off Victoria.

BORONISSKAHANE: Ptercha'a Senior Confraternity activist on Linak'h and eventually member of Confraternity regime.

Emt DESDAI: Ptercha'a; agent of Payaral N'an, Confraternity activist, senior member of Isha Maiyotz's staff.

Warbander DRYNZ: Ptercha'a; Confraternity soldier on Linak'h.

Senior Councillor Dollis IBRAN: Merishi; leading member of the Council of Simferos Associates.

Ship Commander First-Class Brokeh SU-IRZIM: Baernoi; Inquirer, assigned to Linak'h.

Warband Leader First Sirbon JOLS: Ptercha'a Leader, Legion Three-Eight, Administration Warband, and opponent of the Confraternity.

Ship Commander First-Class Zhapso SU-LAL: Baernoi; Inquirer, assigned to Linak'h.

The LIDESSOUF twins, KALIDESSOUF and SOLIDESSOUF: Baernoi; elite Assault Force veterans, assigned to the Inquiry mission on Linak'h under Rahbad Sarlin.

Isha MAIYOTZ: Ptercha'a; formerly a leader in the Administration Fire Guard on Linak'h, eventually a leader of the Confraternity regime.

MUHRINNMAT-VAO: Ptercha'a; Great Warband Leader in the Warband of the Coordination.

Payaral NA'AN: Merishi; head of the Trade Mission on Victoria.

Senior Councillor Zydmunir NA'AN: Merishi; a senior leader of Simferos Associates.Father of Payaral Na'an.

Air Warrior First-Class Taidzo NORL: Ptercha'a; Coordination fighter pilot and brother-in-law of Fomin zar Yayn.

Ship Commander First-Class Rahbad SARLIN: Baernoi; veteran field agent of the Special Projects branch of the Office of Inquiry, assigned to Linak'h.

Warbander SEENKIRANDA: Ptercha'a; pair-mate to Emt Desdai; Confraternity activist and senior staff to Isha Maiyotz.

Great Warband Leader Sharfas SHORL: Ptercha'a; senior Ptercha'a leader in the Intervention Force; son of Egobar Shorl, an old comrade of Marshal Banfi.

F'Mita IHR SULAR: Baernoi; commander, Fleet-chartered merchant vessel *Perfumed Wind.*

Fleet Commander F'Zoar SU-WEIGHO: Baernoi; retired but still influential Fleet officer. Patron of su-Irzim and Zeg.

Warband First Leader Fomin zar YAYN: Ptercha'a; Legion commander in the Warband of the Coordination of Linak'h.

Jillyah zar YAYN-NORL: Ptercha'a; wife of Fomin zar Yayn; mother of one son, Ousso, by her first pair-mate.

Ship Commander Second-Class Behdan ZEG: Baernoi; Special Projects field officer, half-brother to Rahbad Sarlin.

Glossary

AD: Air Defense.

AEW: Airborne Early Warning.

afksi: Small carnivorous fish, native to Merish. Schools of them were traditionally placed in the moats of defended posts for additional security.

Alliance: Freeworld States Alliance, principal human rival to the United Federation of Starworlds.

AO: Area of Operations.

AOP: Air Observation Post.

ASI: Air Speed Indicator.

AS & M: Air Supply and Maintenance.

Baernoi: Sapient humanoid race, highly militarized, whose remote ancestors resembled Terran pigs. Refer to themselves as "the People."

balgos: Dense dark wood of a tree native to Merish; frequently used for making ceremonial or religious objects.

BBA: Blabbers Boiled Alive; the Federation's legendary highest security classification.

Big Brawl: Colloquial term in the Federation Forces for the ultimate war; the Federation vs. the Alliance, the Merishi, the Ptercha'a, *and* the Baernoi all at once.

blastwater: Baernoi liquid explosive. If allowed to soak into a permeable object, renders the whole object capable of being detonated.

BSM: Battalion Sergeant Major.

CA: Combat Assault.

CG: Commanding General.

Chadl'hi: One of the older Ptercha'a-settled planets; Seenkiranda's birthworld. Contributed a Legion to the Intervention Force.

Charlemagne: Capital planet of the United Federation of Starworlds and site of Forces Command.

Climb: Merishi term for a subspace transition (see "Jump").

C-cubed: Command, Control, Communications.

CO: Commanding Officer.

Confraternity: A loose-knit, theoretically illegal organization among the Ptercha'a, dedicated (also theoretically) to an independent position for the whole race in relation to the Merishi and humans.

CP: Command Post.

crus: Edible tuber native to Linak'h, often used in appetizers among the Ptercha'a.

dawnfood: Baernoi term for breakfast.

deeochs: Edible bivalve, native to Pterach but extensively cultivated on Linak'h.

E & E: Escape and Evasion.

EI: Electronic Intercept/intelligence.

EOD: Explosive Ordnance Disposal.

E & R: Evaluation and Report (on an officer or NCO).

ETA: Estimated Time of Arrival.

EW: Electronic Warfare.

EWO: Electronic Warfare Officer.

flarebase: High-BTU liquid chemical compound used by Federation armed forces. With appropriate additives or containers, can be used for illumination or as fuel-air explosive.

fmyl: High-protein vegetable, a staple of Ptercha'a crop.

frytinz: Shaman attached to Ptercha'a Tribal units.

goldtusk: Derogatory Baernoi term for an idle aristocrat.

Governance: Most common general term for the Merishi interstellar political community.

grode: High-carbohydrate fruit native to Baer; analogous to the Terran breadfruit.

grumbler: Medium-sized ursinoid predator, native to Monticello, but transplanted to several other Federation planets for game control; named for its call.

Guidance: Baernoi term for Navigation (of a spaceship or ocean vessel).

haltmeal: Baernoi term for lunch.

holosh: Widely cultivated Ptercha'a fruit-bearing bush.

House of Light: Ptercha'a fraternal/religious association, of great antiquity and considerable social significance in Ptercha'a life. Divided into quasi-independent Lodges.

Hufen: Capital city of the Governance of the Merishi Territory on Linak'h.

ihksom: Ptercha'a term for a matchmaker.

inward-eating: Baernoi term for a condition equivalent to stomach ulcers.

IOC: Initial operating capability.

JAG: Judge Advocate-General.

JOT: Jack of all trades.

Jump: Instantaneous transition of a starship through subspace.

kawde: Baernoi war gas; non-lethal if an antidote is administered within eighteen hours.

Khudr: Baernoi term, literally meaning "First to fight," now extending to mean any leader. The Great Khudr is the founder of the planetary unity of Baer.

kirpan: Sacred knife of the Sikhs.

koayass: Ornamental shade tree, native to Merish but highly popular among the Ptercha'a.

kuip: Ptercha'a game, similar to *go*. Originally played with fmyl seed pods, it is now played with carved wooden or molded plastic replicas of the pods.

LI: Light Infantry.

LZ: Landing Zone.

Merishi: Humanoid sapient race, evolved from climbing omnivorous reptiles; ruthless and far-flung traders. Refer to themselves as "the Folk," and are called "Scaleskins" by both Baernoi and humans.

nest-free: Merishi term for being of legally adult age.

N-GB: Federation chemical spray, used to break down residual poison gas.

Och'zem: Ptercha'a capital of the Administration of the Federation Territory.

OECZ: Outward Edge of the Combat Zone.

okugh: Potent Merishi distilled spirit, about 130 proof.

OP: Observation Post.

orgint: Organic intelligence, that obtained by a live observer as opposed to Electronic or other sensors.

Oryng: Ptercha'a-inhabited planet, a contributor to the Intervention Force.

Pass of Gihans: One of the most famous battles of Pek's Fifty.

PE & D: Planetary Exploration and Development.

Pek's Fifty: Semi-legendary Ptercha'a Warband, who liberated their native city from a foreign occupation. Said to have among them possessed every known war skill. The planet Pek is named after the leader.

pelsh: Potent Baernoi amnesiac drug; used for both therapeutic and military purposes.

Petzas: Nearest major Baernoi planet to Linak'h; Petzas-Din (Petzas, the City) is the capital.

p'nris: Large semi-domesticated ungulate, native to Pterarch, resembling the Terran buffalo.

psed: Shrub native to Linak'h; its leaves are commonly used as a seasoning.

Ptercha'a: Humanoid sapient race with strongly feline characteristics, first encountered by humans when serving as mercenaries for the Merishi. They call themselves "the Hunters," and are called "Catpeople" (human), "Furries" or more formally "Servants in War" (Merishi), and Furfolk (Baernoi).

QRF: Quick Reaction Force.

quickgun: Baernoi term for an automatic weapon.

Rhaym: Merishi arsenal planet.

RHIP: Rank Hath Its Privileges.

R.M.S.: Registered Merchant Ship.

ROE: Rules of Engagement.

RTB: Return to Base.

SAR: Search and Rescue.

schwerpunkt: The main offensive thrust in a land battle.

Security: When capitalized, the Merishi term for their armed forces.

senior: Ptercha'a term for a person of high rank; capitalized when used in direct address.

SFO: Supporting Fires Observer.

sgai: Spicy fruit-based after-dinner Merishi drink, nonalcoholic.

skrin: Small, voracious predator, native to mountain regions of Baer.

SOPS: Senior Officer Present in Space.

Special Action Band: In Ptercha'a law-enforcement organizations, elite teams comparable to human SWAT or Hostage Rescue units.

thryne: Small, sometimes domesticated ruminant, native to Pterach.

TI: Training Instructor.

TO & E: Table of Organization and Equipment.

True Speech (also "Language"): Ptercha'a term for their native language.

UC: Federation non-lethal gas, inducing violent nausea.

uhrim: A staple of the Baernoi diet; a tuber resembling the sweet potato.

uitsk: Untranslatable Merishi obscenity.

uys: Fortified fermented Baernoi beverage, resembling sherry.

VEB: Victoria Expeditionary Battalion.

vidis: Ptercha'a obscenity; one who steals milk from the young.

Warband: General Ptercha'a term for a military unit of any size.

War Crafters: Ptercha'a term for combat engineers.

Watch: Baernoi unit of time, equivalent to 5.2 hours. The Baernoi standard day is divided into five watches.

z'dok: Merishi obscenity borrowed by the Ptercha'a; one who defecates in another's nest.

zyrik: Coniferous tree native to Linak'h; sap-loaded and, when dry, dangerously flammable.

Prologue

Linak'h:

The hot blue sky was that of Marcus Langston's native Monticello. He knew that he was *General* Langston. Why wasn't he standing in the reviewing stand as the Musical Ride began?

The massed bands swung into "Washington Grays," a riding march that had been old when Philip Stoneman gave humanity the stars. Some of the bolder riders let their horses prance; they drew bleak looks from the Marshal of the Ride.

Then the whole mass of horses were cantering forward, past the stands, wavering as the cheers and the dust rose together. Looking down at the four columns, Langston saw the packed stands sprout waving hats and scarves, like a hillside of jumper fig after a spring rain. The drink-selling robots vanished, and the bands played louder.

Langston also saw why he wasn't in the reviewing stand. He was a boy of twelve Standard again, seven years short even of signing up. The reviewing stand beyond the river of horseflesh, bay and chestnut, black, gray, and Appaloosa, was crowded with uniforms and riding habits.

Langston wondered who was representing the Briggs family today, and which of Monticello's three resident Marshals of the Federation was doing the honors for the Regulars. He also wondered why the drums in the band seemed to be growing louder. They were light drums, with a tappeta-tappeta-tappeta beat that shouldn't have been heard above the other instruments. Somehow they reached Langston's ears, tickling them, tickling his memory—

Machine guns. Old-fashioned chemical-propellant machine guns.

And the riders were heading straight for them. Not cantering any more, either, but breaking into a gallop, riders jostling for position toward the front until the four columns tangled into two, then into one—

The dust rose thicker. The people shouted and cheered as if this were some wonderful new addition to the old ceremony. Hats now flew from the stands onto the field, to vanish under trampling hooves.

Couldn't anybody see that the Musical Ride had become a battle? The riders were charging into the fire of the weapon that had murdered mounted cavalry—

The machine guns drowned out all other sound. A swirling gray mist seemed to rise from the ground to swallow the riders. Only the lance-mounted pennons of the Marshal's escort thrust above the grayness.

Silence came with the mist, unbroken except for one throat-tearing scream. It had a higher-pitched echo, but Langston stopped wondering about that when he realized that the echo was his own scream.

Linak'h:

Acting Lieutenant Colonel Candice Shores was leaning back in her chair in the corridor outside Marcus Langston's room when he started screaming. She stiffened, the chair's back legs slipped, and both landed with a crash.

Before she could rise, she was nearly trampled by what looked like a dozen medical staff, hurled into action by Langston's cries. Langston stopped as the medics stormed into his room, but the alarms linked to his vital-signs monitors went on whining and beeping. Shores was ready to put her hands over her ears when the charge nurse came out of Langston's room.

"You can go in now, Colonel."

"You didn't give him a soother?"

"No. He woke himself up from what must have been an unusually nasty emergence dream. He was starting to orient himself by the time we reached his bed. Then he mentioned something about 'machine guns'—a weapon, I suppose." The nurse, a captain, looked significantly at Shores's sidearm.

Shores looked back. The nurse frowned. "We really do have secure places for weapons, Colonel."

"I'm sure you do. So secure that it would take much too long to get this back if some serious terrs came through your exterior security." They locked eyes.

"All right," the nurse said. "But we'll have to hold you responsible if the sight of your weapon causes any additional trauma in our patient."

"I was under the impression that I was pulled away from my battalion because I'm the closest thing to a familiar face for General Langston. I'm supposed to be in there helping him orient himself, not out here listening to you."

The nurse gave a satirical imitation of a salute. "Yes, ma'am. Oh, by the way—he's not a general anymore. He resigned his commission before he came out to Linak'h."

Shores decided that she was not hallucinating. "I suppose everybody was in too much of a hurry to pass on that trivial point? Or is it a new approach to starsleep-emergence therapy, to disorient the familiar face as well as the patient?"

She didn't give the nurse a chance to answer. Instead she brushed past the other medics, most of them failing miserably to pretend they hadn't heard the exchange, and strode into Langston's room.

It was definitely bad to look shocked at the appearance of the person you were helping to emerge from starsleep. It was also hard for Shores to do anything else. She'd last seen Langston on Victoria, a bit more than two Standard years ago. He looked as if it had been closer to ten.

Some people took starsleep badly, and there was always fluid loss and tissue shrinkage even in the best starsleep capsule (which Langston would have had). Something else had put the lines about the brown eyes and the gray in the close-cropped dark hair.

Shores stopped and saluted. "Good morning, sir."

"Don't—have to salute—anymore, Captain. I'm a civilian."

Right. With a flag-rank room in the Forces Med Center. And I'm Cleopatra of Egypt.

"Old habits die hard, ah—"

"Mr. Langston, if you don't want to call me Marcus."

"Mr. Langston. I just heard you'd resigned your commission. I'll need a little time to get used to it."

"I thought I was the one supposed to be getting used to—Linak'h, isn't it?" Shores nodded. "And you're a light colonel now. You've been on Linak'h—what, something like half a Standard year?"

She nodded. Langston was orienting himself much faster than the average (or at least the average laid down in the text she'd scanned when they tapped her for this assignment). Something besides a bad starsleep-trip had to account for his appearance.

"Yes. You cut yourself such a piece of the action that we heard about it even all the way back on Charlemagne. Langston wriggled his shoulders. "Could you help me sit up? And did that Mongol khan masquerading as a Forces nurse say anything about fluids by mouth?"

"He didn't say anything against them."

"Good. I've always believed that everything not forbidden is allowed. Can you pour me a cup of water, please?"

Shores knew they were undoubtedly being monitored in six different modes, but if the nurse or anybody else wanted to interfere, let them. What Langston needed from the "familiar face" was not psych witchcraft. He needed a soldier's briefing.

But she would have to probe his memories first, or she would need her sidearm to repel the medical staff who would barge in and tell her what to do. The result of her inquiry would leave her battalion headless and the hospital understaffed, with Linak'h on the brink of war.

One

Linak'h:

Colonel Malcolm Davidson resented taking his morning exercise indoors. His resentment made no more difference this morning than it had the previous ten. Sergeant Major Kinski didn't even have to use the word "sniper." He just looked meaningfully at the estate.

Davidson also looked out at the scarred lawns, the gaps in the trees, and the lowering gray sky. He made some noncommittal remark about its looking like rain, then headed for the basement.

Working out on the climber, Davidson wondered if Kinski was beginning to lose it. Snipers were the least likely form of attack, seeing that every spot within range of Marshal Banfi's house was monitored by sentries, sensors, or both. Heavy weapons from ten kloms away or even a lifterborne CA were more likely tactics for serious opponents, and then it might be safer outside the house than in.

Even a Sergeant Major of Kinski's seniority couldn't bully a full Marshal. Maybe he was bullying the Marshal's aide instead?

The insight didn't improve Davidson's temper, but it improved his morning workout by pumping adrenaline into his system. The showering afterward was a pleasure, and even a breakfast of freeze-dries was more tolerable than it usually would have been. (The Marshal's cook was like the rest of the unarmed staff: long gone into the zone, to Och'-zem, or home, depending on race, politics, and opinions about the Linak'h crisis.)

The good mood even survived the arrival of Colonel Liew Nieg. Not only was the intelligence colonel usually the bearer of bad news (or at least word of further complications), he was not Olga Nalyvkina either, an aesthetic loss at the very least.

But the Marshal's former chief pilot had only been transferred to Linak'h Command's Tactical Air Group ten days ago. She'd still be checking out as a tactical gunship pilot. Also probably still lobbying for an upgrade to light attackers, unless she'd become convinced that the longer conversion period would have her still grounded when the war started. The mutually-agreed-on consummation of her and Davidson's affection would have to wait.

"Where's the timber mill?" the intelligence colonel asked.

Davidson and Banfi exchanged looks. "Didn't you see it on the way in?" Davidson asked.

"If it was there, I didn't see it, and we made three complete circles and two overflights. We had the recording camera live, too."

Davidson knew that the most they could hope for was a copy of the recording. One would have expected more cooperation with the man who made Nieg's operations possible. But secrecy was inbred in Nieg, as much as curiosity. (Even now, Davidson recognized the telltale signs of Nieg's examination of the Marshal's study for any changes since his last visit.)

Davidson was briefly and savagely glad that there were no new patches on the walls, stains on the rugs, missing trophies or holos, or improvised, visible circuitry. Nieg's curiosity and hypertrophied powers of observation would be wasted on this visit.

Davidson also kept his thoughts masked. Marshal Banfi's chances of being able to assume command effectively on Linak'h, if the occasion arose, probably depended on Nieg. Neither officer, Davidson had long since realized, was acting out of pure patriotism or benign altruism.

"Kinski!" Banfi bellowed.

The steward replied by intercom. The screen showed him seated at the master house console. "Marshal?"

"Has the mill checked in yet? Even any of the mill crew?"

"Let me punch up the list they gave us, Marshal, and I'll check with the security watch chief."

That should have taken less than five minutes, even if the chief was out of the house, inspecting the sentry posts.

After ten minutes, one of the last two robots in the house trundled in, carrying a loaded tray.

Davidson recognized tea, coffee, chocolate, and mixed fruit juices. He also recognized a diversion laid on by Kinski. Pouring for the other two officers kept him from wondering what Kinski was diverting them from.

At twenty minutes they learned. Kinski's face was a thunderstorm when he came back on-screen.

"The security chief says nobody has checked in at all this morning, including the brush-clearing crew down by Sweetwater Spring."

"Thank you, Sergeant Major," Banfi said. This time it was three officers exchanging looks, with Kinski adding a frown from the screen.

"Any chance they went to work on the west slope?" Davidson asked.

His whistling in the dark met the fate it deserved. "They were still supposed to land here and sign in before they went to work *anywhere* on my land," Banfi said. "Or if they didn't sign in, the security chief was supposed to report as soon as a scan showed they'd landed."

So either none of the Ptercha'a timber-salvage people had arrived or the security watch chief (also Ptercha'a) was concealing their unregistered presence on Banfi's land. To Davidson, that seemed the perfect prelude to another terrorist attack.

"You gentlemen know Ptercha'a customs better than I do," Nieg said. "Is there any way to move the present watch chief off-duty and bring on an equal or senior human?"

"Not without costing me the cooperation of the Ptercha'a security staff," Banfi said. "That would force me either to move into the zone or to stay here depending completely on humans. Does either seem desirable?"

Davidson saw on Nieg's face the same look that had been so often on his: a devout wish that Banfi would move into the zone. However, Marshals of the Federation did not usually honor the wishes of mere colonels.

"If I might suggest an alternative," Nieg said, "I can offer the recording from my lifter. If it shows nothing, I can order another overflight. Meanwhile, we can communicate with the Low Squadron—see if their EI or satellite sensors have any data."

Banfi nodded. "You do that. meanwhile, I will see to communication with the Administration and our own air-traffic people. Rank may prevail where logic will not."

Rank probably would, when it was like Banfi's, held in both Ptercha'a and Federation forces. However, Davidson suspected that Banfi was taking responsibility for these calls for reasons besides a chance to flourish his rank.

No Federation officer could legally have contact with the Confraternity. Technically, the movement for improving the status of the Ptercha'a had been outlawed for centuries. But Davidson suspected more each day that in the Administration of the Federation Territory on Linak'h, this outlawry was more technical than real.

But it was still harder to punish a Marshal than a colonel for dealing with the Confraternity. It was also easier for a Marshal to get answers about missing timber mills or anything else from Confraternity informants.

Davidson rose. The sky still lowered, but he would have wanted the open even if it had been raining lagoons. He needed hands-on work—if not actually hauling logs, then at least controlling one of the lifters.

"Marshal, with your permission?"

"Where were you going?" Banfi asked.

"Unless Colonel Nieg has to get the recording himself, I'd like to lead out a work crew. If the mill isn't coming today, we'd better consolidate the cuttings and spray-sheet the commercially salable material."

Davidson didn't add that he wanted to try catching the Ptercha's staff off-guard. Banfi's nod showed that he understood, and his feigned gruffness would have deceived anyone who knew him less well than Davidson.

"I suppose if you don't go out, you'll sit, fidget, and dream of Olga. Very well. Go, and take Nieg with you. I doubt that I need a bodyguard every minute, and if I'm wrong I can still force anyone I can't kill to kill me!"

Davidson would have doubted that, if the matter hung strictly on physical prowess (even allowing for the Marshal's body armor and loaded carbine). But sheer willpower also carried weight, and 120 Standard years hadn't weakened Emilio Banfi's.

Aboard U.F.S. *Shenandoah,* off Linak'h:

Commodore Rose Liddell shifted a few millimeters in her chair, to keep the patch of gray hair on her left temple out of the center of the picture. She did not take her eyes off the command display at the right side of her desk.

"Fine, Commodore. Hold that for a second ..." She heard Frank Keegan's camera whispering, the hardly louder purr of the ventilation, her own breathing, the background of mechanical vibration, and the indefinable human sounds inseparable from being aboard a ship. None took her attention from the display.

She had made her hourly check just ten minutes ago, so this on-camera check told her nothing new. The strength and deployment of the Federation's Linak'h command hadn't changed by so much as one ship or one battalion.

High Squadron of the Task Force (two capital ships and escorts), Low Squadron (*Shenandoah* and her escorts), relay ships, satellite security, orbital-debris patrol, and auxiliaries all where they'd been. Attackers flitting about like bugs over a marsh. One cruiser squadron still fifty-five hours out, returning from escorting to their Jump point the last of the transports that had brought 218 Brigade to Linak'h.

(And were taking out five hundred refugees. They could have taken five thousand, but the flow of people leaving Linak'h was still only a trickle, not a flood. Most people with roots in the Federation's Territory were staying, either because they liked Ptercha'a enough to trust them or disliked them too much to appear afraid of them.)

Dirtside, 222 Brigade held the north and east of the Territory; it would be engaged early if the Coordination did invade. The display didn't show Coordination forces, except their four orbiting Merishi-built heavy cruisers. Intelligence said the Coordination's deployments gave them the capability of invasion but didn't commit them to doing it anytime soon. (As far as Liddell was concerned, the Coordination could wait until the heat-death of the universe.)

218 Brigade was still deployed in the south, around the Federation Zone, but one battalion was Command ground reserve. The Linak'h Brigade still provided the Quick Reaction Force (Candy Shores's rump battalion) and now had

three other battalion equivalents. The Linak'h Brigade held the east, the Command's Support Group went about its various tasks wherever it was needed, and nobody knew what would happen next.

No, she did. She would finish this photo session with Frank Keegan, then take a shower, have a cup of tea, and—

"All done, Commodore. Thank you for your patience."

"Blank display," Liddell said, and pushed her chair back. Its power drive had failed yesterday. Fixing it came under the heading of non-essential maintenance. She would have to see that Jensen didn't bribe a tech rating to do the job, or Charbon send somebody up. *Shen*'s XO had too much faith in busywork as a means of maintaining discipline.

"How's your portrait of the rest of the ship coming?" Liddell asked, pressing the signal for Jensen.

"I've got about thirty-five hours of material," Keegan said, checking the displays on his camera. "With the usual ratio of dump-to-show, I *may* have two hours of good stuff."

"Well, if it's any consolation, I liked your work on the Victoria crisis." Chief Jensen appeared, trailed by two robots with trays.

"Help yourself, Mr. Keegan," Liddell said. "I've got to shower, change, and get to the Low Squadron's Intelligence Committee meeting in eighteen minutes." She smiled at Keegan's raised eyebrows. "No, I don't think a scene of me in the shower would enhance the film."

"I dispute that, but I admit the bosses might see it your way," Keegan said. "Here I am, surrounded by mature grace and beauty, and what good do I get out of it?"

Jensen looked carefully at the overhead; Liddell merely pointed at the robots. "Enough goodies to keep your mouth and hands busy for a—"

The intercom chime sounded. Liddell sat down again. Jensen was laying out a tray on the desk as the screen lit up. It was *Shenandoah*'s captain, Pavel Bogdanov.

"Sorry to disturb you, Commodore, but we have two matters I thought you should know about."

Liddell picked up a cup of hot chocolate. "So improve my data base, Pavel."

"Is Keegan still with you?"

"Yes, but—are we talking about classified matters?"

"Not yet." He didn't add "but you know Admiral Longman's whims." He didn't have to. Linak'h Command had acquired a good deal of experience with their SOPS's command style.

"All right. Frank, I'll tell Josie Atwood that you were as healthy and charming as ever the last time I saw you. Anything else that can't wait?"

"No. Thank you, ma'am."

Jensen ushered Keegan out, with a farewell gift of a pot of tea and a napkin-wrapped bundle of pastries and vegetables. By the time she returned, Bogdanov had explained the Case of the Missing Sawmill and moved on to the second matter, heavy low-altitude aerial activity in the northwest part of the Territory.

The display now showed a map of the Territory, with the mystery activity highlighted in yellow. It was right along the border with the Alliance Territory, and Liddell's first thought was that some of the backcountry Ptercha'a were fleeing across the border. Then she read the data on flight paths. Most of the traffic was heading *south*.

"My first thought was refugees," she said. "But they'd be heading north."

"These could be chartered lifters, heading south to make pickup," Bogdanov pointed out.

"True." Liddell leaned back in her chair, and the power adjustment came briefly and violently back to life. The chair nearly dumped her headfirst into the wastebasket. She decided the dignity she needed could be maintained better by standing.

Another look at the display told her that Low Squadron had the real control of the situation. Banfi had undoubtedly informed Longman, but the High Squadron was on the other side of Linak'h. Major ship or satellite movements would be too detectable a reaction to these incidents.

"All right, Pavel. Message to the duty attackers—two at high altitude over the mystery flight, two backing up our satellite search for the sawmill with a low-altitude reconnaissance. Level Three ROE—and I will personally dismember any hotheaded pilot who goes to Two without permission. Also, they stay a minimum of fifty kloms from the border."

"Objectives?"

"Find the sawmill and get us an ID on the mystery lifters. Electronic signature, visual check if possible, where they land if they land, and so on. Nothing a good attacker pilot can't really guess."

"Yes, but there are so many of the other kind."

"It takes one to know one." Bogdanov had been in attackers for eleven years. It was his favorite joke, to regard big-ship people like Liddell as mildly effete.

"What about Longman?"

"We're not crossing the border, so we don't need her authorization. Information copies to both her and Tanz, and tell them that we'll update at half-hour intervals." Bogdanov nodded and blanked off.

Liddell realized that she'd emptied her tray since Bogdanov came on screen, which for her was almost an eating binge. Exercises or yoga before the shower? That would help her digestion, but delay the Intelligence Committee meeting.

Her digestion could look after itself this morning, she decided. What it really needed was the loan of a few staff officers from Longman. Even rejects or spies could take some of the routine details off her shoulders.

The Golden Vanity's letting the Low Squadron function nearly independently flattered Liddell, at the price of her and too many of *Shen*'s key people working eighteen hours a day.

Linak'h:

Seenkiranda had hoped their escort on the flight north would be Drynz, old comrade of battle, party, and secret Confraternity meeting. He was not even present, nor was anyone she knew except her pair-mate Emt Desdai.

At first she had been tempted to ask questions, of her fellow passengers or even of the flier's second pilot, when he came back to see how the passengers fared. But they either knew little or spoke less, and her curiosity drew hard looks.

In time she sat in silence, with Emt gripping her hand comfortingly. The disturbing thought came to her that *he* might know hardly more than she did.

Very well. Their work for the Confraternity had to count, when the time came to ask why they had been awakened in the deepest darkness, driven hastily out of town to an improvised flier field, and bundled like orders of barbecued meat aboard this venerable machine.

She would grant that this was no punishment. But knowledge of what a thing was *not* was only a beginning, and in this case a feeble one. Short of using weapons, she would track this mystery to its lair.

From time to time, Seenkiranda slept lightly. The second time she awoke, she knew that the flier must have landed while she slept. Three of the original passengers were gone; four new ones had taken their place. Two were men, two women, and all armed as if ready to hold the Pass of Gihans.

This happened twice more before the flier reached its destination, or at least the pair-mates'. Each time the newcomers were heavily armed. The last time they wore farmers' and timberworkers' coveralls and heavy footguards, that showed signs of hard wear.

It was well on toward Father-rise before the second pilot came back to warn Seenkiranda and Desdai to gather their baggage. Almost before they could draw a breath, they were standing in the shadow of a Giant's Cloak and watching the flier slide away at low altitude. The Yellow Father had not turned off a low ground fog, which to Seenkiranda still seemed to hold the scent of smoke from the great forest fires.

She told herself that the fires were fifteen days extinct, and the lush forest here had clearly not suffered recently from either drought or fire. Was this the northwest of the Territory, near the Alliance border?

She was ready to ask her pair-mate for counsel when he held up one hand and cupped the other behind his left ear. He frowned in concentration, then turned to her.

"I wish we had just one battle helmet," he said softly. "Either my ears are cursed by the Trickster, or there are fliers on the move not far from here."

"Our own—"

"Too many. Both rising and falling, with something softening the noise." He flattened himself against the trunk until shreds of bark clung to his fur, then slipped around to the far side. Seenkiranda drew her single-hand, as useless as it might be against either her frustration or her mate's consuming curiosity.

"I saw no fliers," Desdai said, returning. "But I saw the

kind of mist that often rises from a river gorge at dawn and nightfall.''

"Yes?"

"Beyond that mist, I saw—or thought I saw—"

"I think I shall pluck your whiskers, and then your ear-tufts, if you are slow in the telling."

Desdai clapped both hands over his ears, grimacing as he accidentally jabbed the lining of one. Seenkiranda firmly gripped both of his wrists and pulled his hands down.

"Beyond, I see what might be the South Peak of Treasure Mountain."

"So?"

"Then the mist is most likely rising from the Silver Gorge by Lake Dolyna."

Seenkiranda tightened her grip. "Are you trying to deepen the mystery or solve it?"

"Beloved, it is not in me to solve it. But I suggest that the Confraternity is using the old mine workings around the lake. If they also are using tunnels through the forest debris layer, as the upcountry bandits did—"

"Sound guesswork, Confrere," came a voice, apparently from the depths of the ground. Then what Seenkiranda had thought was a patch of leaves rose at one side, turning as she watched into a hatch. The leaves were only an eye-deceiving layer attached to woven strips of wood.

The hole now gaping was large enough to pass a Hunter, and it passed six before one of them spoke. It was the smallest who did, a woman who looked hardly old enough to lawfully pair-mate. The others were male, and two of them had clearly been reared in tribal villages, whatever ways they kept to now.

All carried battle rifles and small bulging packs, strapped over protective vests in forest colors. Had they taken their place in the ranks of a Legion, it would have been days before any Band Leader noticed.

"If you are Confreres," one of the tribal men growled. Seenkiranda realized that while she had been studying the newcomers, three had somehow unslung their rifles and formed a triangle around her and Desdai. At a signal from the woman, she and the other two drew back.

Now thoroughly alert, Seenkiranda saw that the Hunters of the triangle could shoot her and Desdai without hitting their comrades. It was comforting to be able to recognize this. It would be more so to know what would keep those rifles silent.

Linak'h:

The "Mongol Khan" head nurse relented enough to let Langston have fruit juice instead of water, and offered to provide Shores with anything she wanted. Suspecting that the man had a long-established scale of bribes for such favors, she rejected a stiff drink and reoriented Langston over several cups of Asok Black.

Not that she needed much help from the tea. Langston had a clear notion about all the major events on Linak'h since it had become a crisis, as well as the background. No surprise, that; Langston's life as a Federation Commander on Victoria had been much more difficult, thanks to the antics of terrorists trained by the Merishi on Linak'h and then nominally hired for work on Victoria by Alliance Field Intelligence.

But he remembered the increase of terrorist activity on Linak'h and the dispatch of Federation reinforcements, including *Shenandoah* with Candice Shores's Light Infantry Company embarked. He remembered various incidents, including a bloody terrorist raid on Marshal Banfi's estate and the release to the Merishi of some captured terrorists who were also invaluable intelligence sources.

Retaliation for this release was a raid across the Braigh'n River, which led to a mass defection of the "terrorists." Hard on the heels of the terrorists came a mob of Confraternity Ptercha'a, whom the Merishi clearly wanted back as badly as the Federation wanted to keep them. Langston also remembered the increasingly strained relations between the Federation's Linak'h Command and the Administration of the Territory over the "refugees." The Coordination of Linak'h, the independent Ptercha'a government on the planet, was threatening the Territory with invasion if it didn't hand the Confraternity people back.

Militarily, the Coordination was perfectly capable of carrying out the invasion, even without the increasingly overt help of the Merishi. In fact, Langston knew that the Territory would have either handed the refugees back or been at war some time back, if it hadn't been for a series of forest fires, which devastated millions of hectares of forest in everyone's territory except the Baernoi's. The fires kept everybody busy for weeks, leaving them no time to think about minor matters like wars, while the fires burned over a good part of the potential theater of operations.

"We'd all be feeling a lot better if the Merishi and the Coordination weren't claiming that we set the fires as an act of war," Shores finished. "Add this to the fact that they haven't demobilized, and we're still keeping our eyes moving and one hand near our holsters."

"Sensible," Langston said, sipping his juice. "And how are you doing? Rank seems to suit you, I'll say that."

"So far I haven't really had to live up to these paper leaves," she said. She'd left out most of the details of her personal life, such as finding her father during the cross-river raid. He'd been living in the Merishi Territory with his new wife and their two children and working as an undercover agent for the intelligence network established by Shores's affiliate, Colonel Liew Nieg. That was not only personal, she wondered if Langston had ever been cleared for it.

Probably he had. After all, the Dual-Sovereignty Planet Study Group had BBA clearances up every mentionable orifice; Langston would have seen everything he had time to read, out of what reached Charlemagne.

That was an important limitation, though. The people who had sweated and bled on the ground could always help even people who came around with a firm grasp of the Big Picture. Anything in that category that she knew and Langston needed, she would pass on.

"Do you have anywhere to go in particular today?" Langston asked, after another sip of juice.

"I didn't think I was that decorative," Shores said, not quite frowning. She actually did have several places to go, all of them in the line of duty. Which one would be the most persuasive—unless Langston's wanting her to stay was an aftereffect of the starsleep . . . ?

She wished the psychs in Hades and nodded. "One job at least can't be put off any longer. The Quick Reaction Force is a bit short of cadre to be a real battalion, although we've got four companies now and some heavy weapons. Tanz has authorized me to see 218 Brigade about transferring anybody they can spare."

Langston smiled. "Sorry, but I can't help you there. I don't know Edelstein from Adam's watchdog. He's the one you'll have to win over."

"Tell me something I don't know," Shores said. "Besides, you'll be here for a few days, and the appointment's at seventeen-thirty today."

"As you said, tell me something, etc." He put his juice glass down. "His Khanship not only doesn't want me to leave the hospital, he doesn't want me talking to anybody except you, and that includes the reporters who came out with me."

Shores frowned. "I can discreetly check if that's part of his orders. If you really want to talk to eight starsleepy mediacrats?"

"Enough to be polite, anyway. Besides, if MedCorps captains think that I can be pushed around, who's next?"

TWO

Linak'h:

Just above the seaward horizon, the Yellow Father drew golden glints from a patrolling attacker. Light or heavy? Herman Franke squinted, then rolled over on his blanket to face his companion.

"Sergeant?"

Jan Sklarinsky replied with a sleepy "Mmmm?"

Franke considered waking her by putting a hand on her pulser. That would go beyond a joke, though. She and Juan might not be willing to play bodyguard again, and that would nearly chain him and Lu to the Zone. They'd be less useful to Nieg and at risk for cabin fever.

"Sergeant," Franke repeated, louder. "Your binoculars, please."

Without opening her eyes, Sklarinsky shot out one slim arm. A hand of long, calloused fingers closed on the binoculars. Franke took them, pressed them to his eyes, waited while the sensors adjusted the focus, and turned toward the horizon.

Light attackers, four of them, with Administration gray-green ripple painting. Newlies on Linak'h practically needed a spectroscope to distinguish it from the Fed temperate-forest scheme, but neither party seemed worried enough about mistaken identity to change it. For the Feds to start repainting over a thousand vehicles would be (a) a logistical migraine and (b) admission that they feared conflict with the Administration.

The attackers turned their noses toward the zenith and climbed almost vertically. Sonic booms cracked across the beach a minute later. Franke handed the binoculars back to Sklarinsky.

"You're welcome," she said drowsily. Then she lay down

again like a disturbed cat, apparently asleep but ready to wake instantly at any further signal.

The com lying on the blanket beeped. Franke and Sklarinsky grabbed for it at the same time.

"Rhubarb Condition High Two, Low Three," they heard, in a voice scrambled out of all humanity.

"Acknowledged," Franke said. "Team nominal. Proceeding to Kicker Blue on schedule."

"Good luck." A little humanity, there, and an inflection that sounded like Colonel Nieg himself.

Sklarinsky sat up and scanned first the water, then the beach. It was almost all humans in the water, almost all Ptercha'a on the sand. Ptercha'a didn't enjoy recreational swimming; humans were subject to skin cancer.

Two heads in the water developed shoulders, then bodies. Lu Morley and Juan Esteva strode out of the surf. Like Franke and most of the humans, but unlike Sklarinsky and most of the Ptercha'a, they wore bathing suits, complete with waterproof holsters.

Franke handed Morley a towel. "We got a progress report and the go-ahead," he said.

"You don't sound terribly enthusiastic," Morley said.

"I keep thinking what Admiral Kuwahara said, the last time you and I put ourselves in danger. We'd be an even bigger intelligence windfall this time."

"This time, however, we're carrying out orders," Morley said. "I know Marshals aren't infallible, but Banfi's a lot closer than Kuwahara."

"Even obeying a Marshal's orders—"

"Herman, just drop the question of what wrecking my career will do to your chances of getting my family's approval for our marriage. It won't affect Grandma Jean, and I give you my word that everybody else is irrelevant."

" 'Everybody' covers a lot of territory—"

"—which I know and you don't."

Franke looked to see if Sklarinsky was listening. She'd risen and was walking Esteva off down the beach, one hand holding her pulser and the other hooked into the waistband of his swimming trunks.

"Where should we go for dinner?" Morley asked.

Franke recognized a peace offering that he'd better accept. His fretting couldn't help matters anyway. The refugees aboard *Somtow Nosavan* were both immobilized and protected, as well as they could be short of docking the merchanter with one of the capital ships. The few left in the camp would soon be under equally tight security, proof against anything except a fuser or chem warhead lobbed in on a short ground-hugger trajectory.

"Loutissharatz's," he suggested.

"Another old customer?" Morley said, but a smile transformed her whole face as she spoke.

Franke patted her cheek. "The name's familiar. Probably a fifth cousin in the adoptive line, though. You know Ptercha'a genealogies."

"If I ever do, I'll resign my commission and set up as an expert in Bi-Species Property Law," Morley said. She took off her holster, pulled on her sunglasses, and lay back on the blanket.

"The Confraternity is supposed to have a secret digest of Ptercha'a inheritance law." He shifted his own weapon to allow a quick draw.

"They're also supposed to have a complete *Book of Pviz*," Morley said, without opening her eyes. "Shall I ask them tonight?"

"If we meet anybody worth asking more than what's the house wine," Franke replied. He lay down beside his affiliate. "Seriously, Lu, that's what's bothering me."

"What?"

"Not the risk we're running, trolling for the Confraternity. I'm more scared for you than for myself, which I hope you won't take as an insult—"

"I won't, but I don't see what there is to worry about. If all else fails, Jan and Juan will shoot us rather than let us be captured."

Franke doubted that he would ever reach that level of cold-blooded detachment, even if that was necessary for Intelligence work. "If they're alive to do it, no doubt," he said. "But what about being killed? Or have you reached the kamikaze stage?"

Morley took longer than usual to reply. "I don't think so. I do think it may need a Federation casualty or two to break things out of this damned stasis, which is working more for the bad guys."

"And you've volunteered us to be the casualties?"

"Why not us instead of some nineteen-Standard girl a year away from home?"

Franke decided that was an admirable concept in the abstract but harder to admire when it was you checking every tree for snipers.

"All right. In for a cent, in for a stellar. But suppose nobody starts shooting? Suppose all we have fired at us is Confraternity *maskirovka*, or at best something that Banfi's own sources could have already learned? I don't mind being killed or court-martialed in a good cause, but is getting data in triplicate that good? And don't tell me Banfi thinks so, and *befehl ist befehl*."

"*Er ist*, and I don't think Banfi's being sloppy. He—"

The drone of approaching lifters drowned Morley out. They both watched as twelve troop lifters slid by overhead. "Legion Three-Eight," Franke said, after a glance through the binoculars. "Weapons racks installed too. Do they know something we don't?"

"Probably."

Franke watched the lifters out of sight. He rather wished he could borrow some of Lu's fatalistic self-confidence, or even better, some of Jan Sklarinsky's. She wore it like a suit of power armor, even when she wore nothing else.

Linak'h:

Candice Shores had never served with Lev Edelstein, CG of 218 Brigade, but Esther Timberlake, her BSM, had been a platoon sergeant when Edelstein had a battalion in 212. The man facing her looked like an older version of the one Eppie had described—"thoroughly nice guy unless he thinks you're trying to smoke him, then he breathes flame."

As for the rest, Edelstein was compact, spring-legged, with a profoundly Semitic nose and thinning fair hair. After the exchange of salutes they shook hands, then he waved Shores to a chair and signaled to the serving robot.

"You want some of my bodies," he said, through the steam from a cup of tea. "Why mine in particular? People from the other brigades would know their way around better."

"The Linak'h Brigade is understrength. So is 222."

"222 is understrength only in LI-qualified people. You don't expect to fill all your vacancies with suit-wearers, do you?"

"In a perfect world, General—"

"Forget any world but the one we have, Colonel. Do you have any reason to believe that somebody doesn't trust 222 Brigade or Brigadier General Kharg?"

Edelstein's face told Shores that hers had given her away. She would still wait until she was asked a direct question by a superior officer before she helped stab Kharg. There was Nieg's position to think about as well as hers.

"I do," Edelstein said. He studied a part of his desk that Shores couldn't see clearly—probably a covert scrambler display. Then he drained his teacup and set it down.

"I think Goerke was involved in whatever has set up this crisis."

"Here or elsewhere?"

"The key people, I suspect, are elsewhere. Goerke was their agent-in-place on Linak'h. I think that after he was killed, 222 Brigade came out because Kharg was either already working with Goerke's bosses or had been recruited."

"That would be awfully close timing. Maybe too close." Shores believed that, and she believed even more in testing Edelstein, to see if he was hopelessly paranoid or was just testing *her* backbone.

"Not impossible, though. Agreed?" Shores nodded. "I also think that Tanz knew what Goerke was up to. He either approved, which I doubt, or he was all for a quiet life leading to a third star and didn't think Goerke was doing any harm."

"I'd bet on the second."

"So would I." That also was telling the truth as far as Shores saw it, and without having to reveal any of Nieg's secrets. She began to think that a working relationship with Edelstein would be easier than she'd expected.

"Good. Now we know where we stand. How many bodies do you want to snatch?"

Shores handed Edelstein a printed list. He pretended to knock over his teacup. "Are you sure you don't want my firstborn daughter, or at least my cat?"

Shores shrugged. "The word I got was that I was to make the QRF walk like a battalion, talk like a battalion, and operate like a battalion if somebody started seriously shooting. This is what I need."

"Minimum or maximum?"

She shrugged. "Anything over what I have will be an improvement. How much improvement can you afford?"

"Quite a lot, if you can wait until at least tomorrow morning. We need a bunch of people from Personnel and Intelligence who are on a special assignment until then. But I can give you and your guards quarters in town, if you don't want to make an extra trip."

This time Shores decided that the general would be an even worse poker player than she was. "My guards have the day off. Also a special assignment."

"Hmmm. Is it by any chance connected with an intelligence operation being conducted by Commander Franke and Major Morley?"

Shores suddenly realized that Edelstein's left hand was out of sight and his right one was hovering over the com panel. She sat down. As soon as she saw her hands weren't shaking, she held them out in front of her.

"Sorry, that was a bit abrupt," Edelstein said. He put both his hands on his desk. "But my Intelligence Sergeant Major used to be a Ranger, under the name of Murtag Singh. He knew Nieg rather well, back when they were both ninjas in uniform. He hasn't forgotten Nieg's fondness for cutting superior offices out of his networks, or some of the methods he used. I can let you talk to him tomorrow, once he's back from the special assignment."

"Would that be keeping an eye on your friends? Maybe with the help of your own private brigade QRF?"

"Medals have been awarded for worse guesses."

"My gratitude is inexpressible, General."

"So don't express it. Have another cup of tea."

"All right. On one condition. Did—Murtag Singh—tell all of the people he's watching?" If he hadn't, she was going to tell Nieg, whatever Edelstein thought. Uncoordinated covert operations were an excellent way of losing field people wholesale.

"He swore on his *kirpan* to tell one. Probably Esteva."

Shores nodded. "He's got the most intelligence experience."

The fresh tea arrived; Edelstein set his aside to cool. "I had the feeling your friend Nieg might not have thought too clearly about my need-to-knows. *Before* Murtag Singh came forward, incidentally. If you want to massacre someone over this when we have a chance, I'm first. The beervine took my mutterings to him, and he came up to fill in my guesswork."

Shores added milk to her tea. Edelstein liked it at a strength that could dissolve hull ceramics. She thought of suggesting that her silence with Nieg would depend on his cooperation with the reassignments, then remembered one of the unwritten rules of service politics: "Always let the senior open the blackmailing."

And another was, "Do not create situations where senior officers you don't trust will have to intervene."

The senior officer, in this case, was Admiral Longman, although she seemed to be avoiding folly if not yet achieving wisdom. She was not an ally Shores wanted to need.

She would pass on Edelstein. Nieg could settle accounts with Murtag Singh. But she would have something to say to Esteva and Nieg about their—call it "excessive discretion." Even with a Marshal on your side, there was such a thing as playing your cards so close to the vest that nobody (including your partner) could tell if you were in the game at all.

Linak'h:

The House of Loutissharatz had an Och'zem address only because the legal boundaries of the city took in territory that would have been independent suburbs in a human community. A broad stretch of mixed but mature second-growth timber ran across the base of the peninsula where the restaurant and its neighbors stood. Wildfowl perched on the roof and nested in the marsh grasses that crowded around the landing stage, except for the channel dredged for the rental boats.

Half a dozen of the boats were out on the river when Lu Morley led her party up the front stairs. Most of the occupants were human. Only those Ptercha'a willing to learn to swim risked boating in deep water. The religious prejudice against dying in water meant that the Ptercha'a built few boats and numerous very strong bridges.

The restaurant's headwaiter met them at the door. She was human, trimly elderly, and not quite able to hide her nervousness.

"We have arranged for a private room, but I cannot say at the moment which one it will be," she whispered.

"All the better." The later any enemies knew where they were, the less time to find them. The same applied to their friends, of course, but any covert security would probably be Rangers, capable of lightning-fast movement. As for the Confraternity, Morley sometimes shared Herman's skepticism about their showing up at all, or being useful if they did.

A Ptercha'a waiter took them to the fourth private room on the right, down a corridor leading off from the main dining room into the hillside. Morley checked both the entrance and the exit. She didn't like it that the corridor's only rear exit seemed to be a locked door.

"What's beyond there?" she asked, pointing at the door.

"A storeroom," the waiter said, in True Speech. "It opens on the freight dock."

Morley looked to Herman, whose True Speech was better than hers. He nodded. They held a brief conversation of blinks and gestures, concluding that they were secure enough unless somebody blocked off the dock as well.

Just the same . . .

"Sergeant Esteva."

"Major?"

"Check exits from the dock. Use the quick-alert signal if you see anything suspicious, then report back here *fast.*"

The quick-alert signal was "RV," clicked out on Esteva's com.

Esteva left. The others sat down, all with their backs to the wall and their holsters unsnapped. Sklarinsky's pulser was under the table, strapped into a peace-bag as the headwaiter insisted. That would not help any enemies. At close quarters, Sklarinsky would be as dangerous with her sidearm, knife, or bare hands, and she could have her sniper weapon free in seconds.

"Menu, please," Morley said. The display in the center of the table lit up. The Ptercha'a waiter materialized with a tray of jugs and glasses, as well as a calligraphed list of the day's specials. By the time Esteva returned to report clear exits from the dock and no suspicious activity, Morley knew she was hungry.

Linak'h:

Candice Shores hadn't planned most of her next few moves. In fact, looking back on them afterward, she realized that she'd failed to keep the initiative to the extend that she would have been in serious trouble if she'd been dealing with enemies instead of friends.

As it was, she agreed to accept enforcements for her escort, from 218 Brigade, and an invitation to dinner from Lev Edelstein for both her and Nieg. If she could find him, that is—he'd said his covert missions were over, but that could be subject to change without notice.

The trip to Nieg's headquarters, her first stop, should have taken less than ten minutes. She wouldn't have worked up a temper in that time.

But she had to report to her battalion HQ that her business in Och'zem might keep her in town until evening. It didn't take as long now for her XO to convince her that he had everything under control, and she was no longer acting to give the man's self-confidence a boost. Major Roger Duboy's diligence and experience compensated for the lack of many flashier qualities.

One of Shores's escorts from 218 Brigade had also taken a com break. He saluted as she left the secure booth and reported that he had orders to accompany her all the way to any destination.

"Whose orders?"

"Ah—General Edelstein knows about them."

That wasn't the same as giving them. It meant almost the same amount of trouble from him if Shores told his people to go diving in a slit trench.

Life would have been much easier if she hadn't been persuaded that she could spare Juan and Jan, without knowing what she was sparing them for. It didn't help that the 218 Brigade people didn't have a need-to-know for Nieg's operation—or hadn't, the last time she checked.

She reached Nieg's little CP angry at him, angry at Edelstein, and not too happy with herself. She stormed into the warehouse with a face that made her escort drop back without orders, and into the office so fast that Nieg's hands darted under the desk by pure reflex.

Then he saw who it was and reason replaced reflex. He

put his hands carefully on the desk, palms down and fingers spread.

"Good evening, Colonel," he said.

Shores stared at him. His face was as blank as usual, but body language said more.

"Did I look that bad?"

"Yes. With your permission ... ?" He jerked a head toward the door. The escort was now pretending not to listen while staying within earshot.

Shores kicked the door shut, hard enough to raise dust, shake files off the desk, and relieve some of her temper.

"How soon can I have Juan and Jan back?"

"Tomorrow morning, at the latest."

"If they're alive."

"I can't guarantee that. But—"

"Everything seems to be 'tomorrow morning' around here. How am I supposed to run my battalion on that basis?"

"Candy, you didn't ask what the 'special mission' was. Don't blame me for your own failure."

Some of her rage eased, as she realized the truth of that. Had she been expecting him to allow their relationship to blunt his tongue? She had certainly never let it blunt hers.

"Fair enough, I suppose. But we have a situation that I think you should know about."

"What is the price for learning about it?" His face was as hard as she'd ever seen it. For all that he said intelligence ran by trading favors, he seemed reluctant to accept her doing it.

Both of us are getting the personal and the professional mixed up today. Can this affiliation be saved?

Or maybe there was another explanation. Something had happened that she didn't know about; her information might save lives. Insisting on trading it could be a bad move, professional as well as personal.

Shores sat down.

"No," she said. "I'll give it to you. Then I have a couple of questions. You judge if I need answers."

Nieg's thin smile hinted that he'd been shaken too. It stayed on his face through her story of the visit with Edelstein. He was silent for a moment afterward, then nodded. "I will have to visit Murtag Singh."

"Not Edelstein?"

"Him second, and after tonight."

"What's going to happen tonight?"

"The mission for which I borrowed Juan and Jan."

"Nothing else?"

"I can't say."

"Can't or won't?" Shores took a deep breath, realizing that an edge had crept back into her voice.

"I swear it's 'can't.' " But I'm in continuous communication with Tanz. He'll upgrade the alert status of the ground troops in plenty of time. Please don't signal our suspicions to anybody by unilateral action with your battalion."

"I should instead leave their arses hanging out on a line, the way you've put Juan's and Jan's?"

"It could be crucial to our security to give no warning."

It would also be fatal to their relationship, his asking her to sacrifice her battalion for one of his intelligence schemes. This was the first time she'd realized how much she wanted to lead her battalion well and how little she cared about anything that might conflict with that duty.

"All right. There's nothing I can do in the time available, I suppose. But there is one more question you can answer." She clasped both hands over one knee and tried to frown the right words onto her lips.

"Banfi had nothing to do with this mission," Nieg said. "He doesn't know any more than you did, unless Edelstein or my old Ranger friends told him. I doubt that Lev would do that, either. He doesn't—"

Shores blinked, not at tears (although she felt her eyes stinging) but in surprise and relief. Nieg hadn't changed. He'd been wrong—Juan and Jan had to be battalion assets now, not part of his intelligence operation—but he'd been willing to take the blame rather than shoving it off on a superior officer.

An order from Banfi to treat her battalion as a reserve of talent for odd little missions would have been hard for Nieg to ignore. Instead it was only his own lack of experience with regular ground units showing again. Banfi had commanded everything from a squad to an army group, many of them in combat. Nieg had gone straight from Ranger Teams to intelligence operations; she would be surprised to hear that he'd ever worked in a unit as large as a company.

Shores drank a glass of water, washing down the lump

in her throat and clearing her eyes. As they cleared, she saw him handing her a face wipe.

Would he have been so honest if he couldn't tell that I was upset? Shores asked herself. Years of trying to mask her own feelings and letting others do the same with theirs left her unsure.

Linak'h:

"What's that in the picture?" Juan Esteva asked, pointing at a cube over the table opposite as if he'd just seen it for the first time Then he dug into his *crus*-filled pasty without waiting for an answer.

Herman Franke decided that the question had been directed at him. With a forkful of his own pasty suspended in air, he shook his head. "Some House of the Light or other. One of the historic ones on Pterach but I'd have to go over and look at it up close to be sure which."

Jan Sklarinsky stared hard at the cube. "Looks like the grandfather of all toilet bowls, turned upside down. That entranceway would be the lever . . ."

She went on in that vein for a minute or two—Franke had given up keeping precise track of time about the third course. By the time she'd finished, all four humans were smiling. Franke suspected that any devout Light followers in earshot might not be amused. Still, not bad for a sniper ordered to be a target instead of seeking one.

Another pair of diners entered the corridor room and sat down at a table toward the rear doors. They were a human and a Ptercha'a, both female, with nothing else unusual enough about them to make Franke suspicious.

That made six other guests in the room with them. The snatches of conversation that Franke overheard (naked-ear, as tempting as it had been to bring along a concealable pickup for his recorder) suggested the three humans and three Ptercha'a were all just what they appeared to be—local business people, combining work with the pleasure of a good meal and not plotting anything except how to salvage a profitable year from the jaws of political turmoil.

The drone of lifters swelled outside, muted by walls and corridors as well as soundproofing but loud enough to suggest a military formation. The sound had just started to fade when the server returned with the next course.

The restaurant's advertising claimed that it used only live servers and cooks. Franke couldn't testify about the cooks, and the waiters he'd seen at least appeared to be organic Ptercha'a.

Their own server, however, could have been an android riposte to all the traditional images of Hunters. He was nearly a meter-seventy, so bowlegged that he walked like a cripple, stump-tailed, and so fat that Franke wondered if anyone at his tables ever got their servings intact.

Methodically he unloaded covered dishes of barbecue—fish and meat mixed, and smoked with *psed* leaves and something Franke didn't recognize—and more *crus*—mashed this time, with an interesting herb sauce. Franke was slicing the fish when a thought crept up from his subconscious to his conscious.

All was quiet outside—too soon. Unless the lifters had increased speed? If they had, the noise would have risen before it subsided.

He looked at his companions and silently mouthed, "Those lifters must have landed." Lu gave a jerky nod, Sklarinsky seemed intent on her dinner, and Esteva seemed to be listening to angelic voices.

Or voices coming through a concealed com unit? Franke didn't bother studying Esteva. A waste of time, when a com unit with a ten-klom range could survive a strip-search.

The sound of a boat's motor running at high power broke in on them. Then a bump as the boat struck the pier, a shout—several shouts, in two human languages and True Speech—and the unmistakable pop of a gas grenade.

At least the four Federation diners didn't mistake it. They were all on the floor and drawing weapons before any of the other diners in the room moved. Then a pulser droned, and a Ptercha'a single-hand replied—four spaced shots—as Jan Sklarinsky got her sniper weapon clear of its "peace" covering.

A standoff or something that produced a lull in the firing followed the initial bursts. A distant whine that might have been a pulser finally broke the silence, just as four Ptercha'a ran into the room. The waiter stood in their path; all four broke right and left to clear him as if they'd been practicing for months. None of them had been overeating lately.

They had definitely been visiting weapons shops though. All four carried holstered single-hands and held stubby human-made carbines. All had waist pouches, bulging to suggest first-aid kits, grenades, respirators, or com equipment.

And speaking of com equipment, . . .

Franke was just about to ask Esteva whom he was talking to when one of the Ptercha'a slung his carbine over his shoulder and made the peace gesture—both hands held out, palm upwards, and eyes aimed at the floor.

"Be calm, all of you," the Ptercha'a said in True Speech. "We are here to guard these warriors—" he pointed in the general direction of Jan Sklarinsky's nose "—from those who seek their lives. If you are no enemy to the warriors, we are no enemy to you."

Then he started to repeat it to Anglic, until Franke interrupted him by returning the peace gesture and following it with an urgent signal for silence.

"I know the True Speech better than you speak Anglic," he said. "I am pair-mate to one of these warriors, and the others are from a Warband oath-sworn to mine. So I can speak and translate for them.

"Who are you, and who seeks our lives?"

Jan Sklarinsky chose the moment to seat the magazine in her pulser. The Ptercha'a didn't miss the motion, or the new burst of firing from outside.

"My name is Drynz, and we are a four of the Confraternity."

"No law or custom binds us to fight you, when you seek to help us. But these—"

Esteva shook his head, the moment he saw Franke pointing at the other guests, then at the rear door. "Negative on that, Commander. Ah—a friend just told me, the bad guys have got people covering the loading area and the landing apron."

"I hope your friends are our friends," Sklarinsky said. Her tone said that Esteva was going to explain his games to her afterward or regret the day he'd ever met her.

"Then go to the end of the room," Franke called to the guests. "Pile tables and chairs in front of you and stay down until the fighting is done."

By the time he'd repeated that in Anglic, Drynz was

giving him the Confraternity salute of hands clasped in front of his chest. As the innocent bystanders scrambled out of harm's way—or at least off the actual target—Franke realized that his command of True Speech had just put him in command of the latest down-and-dirty battle against the terrorists.

Professor Linowitz was right. Learning nonhuman languages does give you opportunities denied to the monolingual.

Franke nodded to Morley, and together they unloaded their table, then tipped it over. Sklarinksy and Esteva did the same with an empty one across the aisle. Franke started mentally revising the guidebook entry for Loutissharatz's— "In the event of terrorist attacks, the well-constructed tables can be overturned and used as barricades. The chairs are light enough to be thrown but heavy enough to hurt if they hit. The carving knives provided with meat and fish dishes—"

This time it was pulsers on both sides that broke the silence. Shouts and screams from both races followed.

Three

Linak'h:

Dinner with General Edelstein was a leisurely affair, leaving Candice Shores thinking that Edelstein's headquarters was casual about housekeeping. She hoped they weren't casual about security.

They were halfway through dessert (some sort of fruit cobbler, the crust tough and the fruit too sweet) when word came of the terrorists at Loutissharatz's. Edelstein nodded and called the Brigade XO and chief of staff. The chief of staff was dining in town; Edelstein ordered out a search-and-escort party for him. The XO already had put out an alert warning.

"Security Red One enough, General?" she asked.

"Red One for Security, Red Two for everything else. Pad alert for our reaction force. Secure our in-town rendezvous points, with local cooperation if possible, without it if necessary. Alert our liaisons with the Administration police and Warband. Medevac for any personnel in out-Zone facilities—not just for Brigade, all Federation personnel."

"Base the medevacs at the rendezvous points?"

"As soon as they're secured."

Meanwhile Shores had been hearing slamming doors, scurrying feet, an occasional squeal or whine of machinery, occasionally a human voice talking urgently but never shouting. She stopped worrying about 218 Brigade's security.

General Tanz came out on the circuit and listened to Edelstein's report. "I've issued the same orders to all other Federation units," he said. "Subject to Admiral Longman's approval, I propose no further action at the moment. I have reports of regular Administration Warband units in the area. Anyone we send into the area should be prepared to cooperate with them."

"I have a company-size force on pad alert now, and we can augment it from the QRF."

"Get your people moving as soon as we have clearance from the Administration. Put the whole QRF on Alert One, but don't have them lift until the situation develops. Do you have enough people, between your Brigade and Hogg's?"

"Short of having to fight the whole Admin Warband, yes."

"Good. Kharg offered to send some of his people down from the refugee camps. I recommended that he wait until we'd evaluated the situation. If the threat is local, we can handle it. If it's general, the camp will be a major target."

Edelstein grinned. Nieg frowned, probably about the same thing that was bothering Shores. *How did Kharg hear of the incident so fast?*

The screen blanked. Edelstein stood. "You people equipped? If not, we can provide just about anything short of a fitted suit of power armor."

"They've got one for me back at Battalion," Shores said. "If I could have a lift—"

"Nine chances out of ten, your reaction force will come through here," Edelstein said. "If you lift back now, you'll be coming or going, out of touch when you're needed."

"Yes, sir," Shores said. Her itch to get back to her battalion didn't seem to be bothering Nieg; *score one for him.*

Linak'h:

During the next lull in the firing, Lucretia Morley crawled down the hall to the civilians. This meant leaving Herman as OTC, but he was a fairly good amateur at the down-and-dirty. His command of True Speech would help him pull his weight (even the several kilos he'd gained since they left Victoria, the Gourmet's Purgatory). The four Confreres didn't seem to need much leading from anybody except Drynz, and the Juan & Jan Show was self-programming. Morley went flat on the rug as the firing rose, then recognized that it was all outside and no closer. She resumed crawling, faster than before.

As she crawled, she noted that the beige rug and green table linens were probably flammable, the wall covering (it looked like Ganger fungus covered with mustard) probably wasn't. The wall covering also wasn't thick enough to absorb rounds; at best it might reduce ricochets.

When Morley reached the civilians, one of the humans had drawn a sidearm, so polished and customized that she didn't recognize the make.

"You're better off disarming and turning the hardware over to us," she told the man. "That won't help you if the terrs break through. If the terrs aren't after civilians, the hardware's more likely to get you killed. If the terrs don't break through, you don't need it at all.

"It damn sure will get you killed if we take any fire from behind. I don't know what side any of you are on and I don't care. If we don't have to treat you as enemies, I'll go on not caring.

"So hand over the hardware now. If the situation gets to where we need volunteers on the firing line, we'll give it back. Otherwise, you're safer all around if you disarm."

Morley had used her flintiest voice and expression. It helped that the humans seemed to have the normal belief that Confraternity Ptercha'a could do anything, and the Ptercha'a looked reluctant to take sides either for or against the Confraternity. In a minute, Morley had collected three slugthrowers, a stunner, and a two-shot sleep-gasser disguised as an aromatic lighter. Two of the humans looked as if they were holding out, and all the Ptercha'a probably had concealed blades, but that had to be most of the long-range equipment.

Morley had just marked each weapon with its owner's name when she heard lifter fans outside. Four lifters at least, and CA'ing, two out front toward the pier and the others back toward the landing pad. The firing crescendoed, with at least one SSW firing from a lifter, then subsided into a silence that still held when Morley returned to the forward position.

She looked at Esteva, then realized that no glaring could draw out information he didn't have. Sharp orders in True Speech broke the silence as Esteva raised his head, then said something into his concealed pickup.

"Admin Warbanders, Eighth Cohort, Legion Three-Eight," he said. "They chased the terrs off the pier, sank one boat, and are pinning down the ones who commanded the landing pad. Our people accounted for three terrs and have one prisoner, no casualties. They're evacuating to concealed OP's."

"Why aren't your buddies coming in?" Sklarinsky asked. "Or do they have orders to trust the Pussies?"

Morley let the language pass, particularly since she wondered the same thing. Franke answered.

"Three-Eight's Leader is a political hack named Sirbon Jols. He wants to be the next Warband Chief so badly he'll lift tail for anybody he thinks can give him that. I don't know who's backing him now, but in your friends' place I wouldn't trust his troopers either."

Somebody among the Confreres must have understood more Anglic than they'd admitted. Before Franke could start a translation, they were all nodding. Drynz and one of his comrades consulted briefly, then Drynz turned to Franke.

The gist of the conversation was that besides his other vices, Sirbon Jols was also violently anti-Confraternity. Four armed Confreres could not wisely allow themselves to fall into the hands of his troops. With their human comrades' permission, they would hide in the storeroom.

"People?" Franke said, looking and sounding a little out of his depth.

Lu gave him a thumbs-up. So did Sklarinsky. Juan nodded, a little reluctantly. "The Warbanders may keep the terrs away from the back door. But if they want to come in themselves, we can't stop them unless we're ready to start shooting at the Warband. We can't do that unless the Warband presents an immediate danger to Federation personnel or citizens."

These sensible Rules of Engagement didn't make it any easier to let the Confreres walk into what might be a death trap. She and Herman had carried out Nieg's orders, to make themselves available for informal Confraternity contacts. Now the problem was to keep everyone alive long enough to exploit those contacts!

Morley crawled back with the Confreres, warning the six civilians that they should *not* reveal the presence of Drynz's four. The Confreres were guilty of no crimes; endangering them would itself be a criminal act, for which Linak'h Command would punish severely.

That was even more bluff than her previous threat. Federation authorities weren't likely to punish anyone for setting up Confraternity members for execution by their own race. The Administration might even reward the Ptercha'a, if Drynz had any sort of a criminal record.

Against jangled nerves, however, the bluff seemed to work. Drynz added a couple of threats in True Speech which Morley understood just well enough to know that they included blood-feud to the seventh generation. Then the four Confreres shorted the lock on the storeroom door and vanished inside.

Two minutes later, the rescuing Warbanders of Three-Eight Legion arrived.

The ones who actually entered the dining room were a sixteen led by the only Ptercha'a officer Lu Morley could ever have described as "foppish." His shorts were embroidered, his boot tops were flared, his tunic was longer than either regulation, fashion, or esthetics allowed, and his sole weapon was an ornate single-hand, all carved wood and silvered metal.

His sixteen were closer to the Ptercha'a norm, if not the highest-grade troops Morley had ever seen. She kept her hands in sight as she stood up, and saw her comrades doing the same.

"We hope none of you bear hurt," the sixteen-Leader—no, his rank insignia was that of a Band Leader—said, in nearly the best Anglic Morley had ever heard from a Ptercha'a. "If so, we urge that you come with us to our Cohort's House of Healing. This is not a safe place."

"The terrorists have fled, thanks to the valor of your warriors," Franke said. "Those same valorous warriors are about us now. We need not depart from this place yet."

"Oh, but you do," the officer said. "Who can be sure that the staff of the restaurant was not in league with the terrorists? Only when we have rigorously interrogated all of them can this place be called safe, and that will take some time."

"Humans too?" Sklarinsky cut in.

"All within are under Administration jurisidiction, by treaties sworn to by both races. Our rights over them in such incidents as this include the most rigorous interrogation."

With humans this would not actually go as far as old-fashioned electrodes, beatings, or needles under the nails. It would certainly involve sleep deprivation, drugs that might be lethal, and bad publicity that would come at the worst possible time.

Morley added "slimy" to her mental file on the officer and waited for Herman Franke's reply

It never came. Instead, a four-Leader hurried into the room. Morley caught only tantalizing hints of the newcomer's report, but Franke's face set in a way that said bad news.

"It seems that there were Confraternity bullies among the terrorists," the officer said. "Four of them, led by a notorious murderer named Drynz. They were last seen heading in this direction. Have you any knowledge of them?"

"They weren't—" Sklarinsky snapped, then froze with her mouth open as Esteva, Franke, and the Band Leader all stared at her.

"They were not what?" the officer almost purred. His hand was conspicuously far from his sidearm, but with Ptercha'a reflexes that meant little. Morley hoped that the sidearm was as useless as it looked. The other warriors around at least seemed less trigger-happy than their leader.

Feet shuffled as both humans and Ptercha'a shifted position, the humans so that none of them had their backs to the Hunters, the Warbanders so that they could shoot at the humans without hitting their leader or each other. The officer spread his hands.

"You have knowledge of the location of the Confreres?" the officer asked. "Or did you mean to say they were not anywhere around here, so you do not know where they might be now?"

Sklarinsky gave a jerky nod. The officer shook his head. Morley now recognized a triumphant smile on a Ptercha'a face. She also recognized fury on Esteva's face—and somewhat to her surprise, on Franke's.

"I must ask you—all of you—to come with me so that this may be confirmed under light interrogation," the Band Leader said. "The law requires it with terrorism, even when Federation humans are involved. That is an interpretation of the law that the courts of both our races accept."

Morley suspected as she had several times this soft-spoken thug's legal knowledge, doubted his interpretation, and was sure he never intended it to stand a court test. "Are we under arrest, then?"

"Protective custody would be a better term. Please disarm."

"If you disarm us, you are responsible for our safety," Franke said. "In fact, disarming us could be interpreted as taking us hostage. You know Federation policy on that—or if you do not, I must ask to speak with a senior who does."

Morley caught expressions on some of the other Warbanders' faces. They might not be seniors, but they understood a bit of Anglic. They also knew that if the Federation interpreted taking the four humans into "protective custody" for "light interrogation" as kidnapping them, they might be signing their own death warrants. They might be doing the same, with dishonor for their kin added, if they disobeyed their officer.

Carefully not turning his back on the humans, the Band Leader stepped away from them, toward his own warriors. When he had opened the distance enough, he raised a hand and said sharply:

"Disarm them." Then he added, "Him first," and pointed at Esteva.

Careful not to turn his back on the humans, the officer had ignored his men. It was one of them who raised his carbine and without otherwise moving fired a burst into the back of the officer's neck. Lu blinked as his blood and brains sprayed her, then blinked again as she stared at the empty space where the officer had stood.

She found him lying practically at her feet, half fallen, half flung by the impact of the bullets. One hand still moved, fingers scrabbling at the rug, then subsided to twitchings, and at last to stillness.

Only then did Morley realize that if the hand had gone on moving, she would have started screaming. Instead, everyone now seemed caught in a stasis field. She would not dwell on the notion that the first person to move or speak would be the next to die.

Aboard U.F.S. *Shenandoah,* off Linak'h:

Liddell was in full-dress uniform and expecting her dinner guests when the news came of the terrorist attack. She'd followed her old custom from when she had been *Shen*'s captain—four to six officers to dinner once a week, and not just because she had only so much tolerance for the loneliness of command. It gave her a chance to evaluate her officers in social situations, and it relieved Pavel Bogdanov of a burden he was glad to leave to the more socially graceful.

It also meant flurry, fuss, and enough wasted food (Jensen's cronies could eat only so much) to make a crater in her entertainment allowance when something happened to cancel the dinner at the last moment.

Twenty minutes after word came, Liddell's table was cleared. The two guests from other Low Squadron ships were shuttling back to their posts. Liddell had changed from full dress into fatigues. *Shenandoah* herself had maneuvered to within a few kloms of Admiral Longman's flagship *Roma,* so smoothly and deftly that Liddell knew Captain Bogdanov must have taken the con himself.

Now Liddell sat at the Flag console in the Auxiliary Combat Center, watching Admiral Longman come up on the screen.

"Recommendations, Commodore?"

One good side of the Golden Vanity's manners: she doesn't waste words.

"Unless you have some indication of Coordination movements—"

"I don't. What about you?"

"Nothing for now."

"Now is when we have to decide. Rose, staff estimates are two stellars a dozen. I want your recommendations because you've been here long enough to have a feel for this miserable planet."

"If the terrorist incident is isolated, leave it to the ground-pounders," Liddell said. "But monitor ground movements as closely as possible. We haven't established that the Coordination is working closely with the terrs. But they might take advantage of an incident being enough to give them a political bonus."

Liddell wished she could be more encouraging. But from thousands of kloms out in space, there wasn't the Hades of a lot the Navy could do to affect either the duration or the body count of the incident itself. All they could do was keep any opportunists from rushing the party while the ground-pounders had their hands full.

"Agreed. Continue monitoring that lifter activity in the northwest corner of the Territory, though."

"Can I have any more air assets?"

"Deal directly with Tanz, if you do. What's in space now, stays there. In fact, I want a full space-to-space load in every heavy attacker."

Longman's face vanished; her voice remained, coming in on another frequency as a scrambler code turned Liddell's display into brief, dazzling pyrotechnics. "This came up by courier this morning. It has Tanz's endorsement, but I think it smells like Nieg, and you know him better than I do."

Unscrambled, the intelligence assessment absolutely reeked of Nieg. Also of major trouble. It was the colonel's assessment that a faction within the Administration, possibly a majority, was planning major action with regard to the "refugees" aboard *Somtow Nosavan.* It was Nieg's further hypothesis that other parties within the Administration might offer resistance to this action, possibly with the support of armed Confreres.

"That might explain those lifters," Liddell said. "Particularly that close to the border with the Alliance Territory." Longman's face returned, nodding silently. Even with a secure com link, they didn't feel like discussing the knowledge they shared about possible Alliance support for the Confraternity. *Alliance Navy, anyway.*

"I agree. But their ID as a convoy of work crews and refugees has held up. They may be Confraternity, but just because the organization is technically illegal doesn't require us to declare war on it."

Liddell tried to control her eyebrows. That was in fact exactly the interpretation a good many Federation officers and politicians put on the status of the Confraternity. The Golden Vanity had certainly come to Linak'h sounding that way.

"I have no problem with that, Admiral."

"Good. Because our major concern right now has to be *Somtow Nosavan.* I want our flagships and a squadron of attackers making a security sphere around her, and a clear space at least five thousand kloms around that sphere. No Fed ships, no Baernoi ships, no neutral merchanters, no inhabited orbital debris, no nothing. If anybody shows up for a kamikaze run on *Nosavan,* I want them ID'ed and killed before they even know they're under surveillance."

"Again, no problem. But—what about ground support?"

Longman snorted. "What about it? It would take the coordination's cruisers to mount a threat that our AD and TacAir couldn't handle, and if they come on we'll have attackers all over them like stink on a grumbler. Have you been getting enough sleep?"

The non sequitur left Liddell barely able to control her mouth, and her eyebrows not at all. Longman gave a wolfish grin.

"Neither have I, but it still ought to be you painting me this picture. The only way we can lose this one big is by ending up with all factions in the Administration against us. The best way somebody could bring that about is by taking out *Nosavan*."

It occurred to Liddell that taking out *Nosavan* was also the best way to guarantee that Longman never got her fourth star. But if the priorities were right, the motives hardly mattered.

"What about creating a second security sphere, built around *Intrepid* and open to any merchanter who wants help?" Liddell asked.

"Fine. Just as long as we put our own depot ship alongside *Nosavan*. I don't want her and *Perfumed Wind* in the same sphere."

Liddell heartily agreed. The last notable thing the Baernoi had done, according to Intelligence, was to have some of their new Ptercha'a mercenaries in the Merishi Territory at the time of the great fires. Since then, the Tuskers had been keeping such a low profile that they might as well not have been on Linak'h. It was against the laws of probability and the nature of the Baernoi for this to last much longer.

Linak'h:

Herman Franke's first thought was that the smell of blood (and other body fluids—the officer had voided bowels and bladder in dying) totally altered the atmosphere of the restaurant. Cooking smells, the ripe dampness of the river, the brisker scent of the forest when the wind was right—none of these was the smell of death.

Franke's own body stayed narrowly under control as his mind raced. His first thought was to dive for the floor. His second thought was to become invisible. His third was for him and Lu to dwindle to submicroscopic size until they passed into another dimension.

The first meant movement, certain to inspire more shooting. The second and third were impossible. Franke focused on trying to guess which Ptercha'a warrior was going to do what next.

All of the Warbanders facing him looked surprised. Some looked frightened as well. Three in particular seemed to be alert. One was the warrior who'd shot the officer—although he also looked the most frightened of all. The other two were a sixteen-Leader and a four-Leader. They seemed to be glaring at each other over the head of the killer, who was about the shortest of the Hunters present.

The sixteen-Leader broke the stasis, whirling on the four-Leader and drawing a combat knife at the same time. The killer whipped his weapon around as the sixteen-Leader threw the knife. It sank into the killer's throat just above the armored vest.

The four-Leader tried to get a safe firing angle on his senior. The sixteen-Leader had no such scruples. He raised his carbine and pumped a burst into the other. It not only ripped his chest open but also hit the Hunters on either side of him.

"Down!"

The voice was half command, half war cry. Franke was on the rug before he recognized Drynz's voice. Then a carbine fired three shots and half a dozen Ptercha'a squalled, screamed, or cursed.

Franke ended facing a Ptercha'a who was clawing a sidearm free. The muzzle rose, and Franke knew the man had to be aiming at one of the humans. He reached for his sidearm, realized that he'd already drawn it, and by sheer reflex pumped two shots into his opponent's face at a range of less than a meter.

Something slammed down on the rug—Lu grappling with a Ptercha'a. She had armor under her uniform, and her opponent was shifting his—no, her—claws to target Lu's throat. Those efforts came to an end when Franke shot the Ptercha'a in the back of the head.

Both Franke and Morley rose to hands and knees, and Lu reached out to trail one bloody finger along Franke's cheek. Then they stood on shaky legs as the remaining

Warbanders threw down their weapons under the baleful glare of Drynz and the steady muzzles of Confrere weapons.

One of the wounded Warbanders finished applying a dressing to a bloody arm, then rose and lifted his good arm to Drynz. Drynz returned the hail. Franke recognized an exchange of Confraternity recognition signals.

"Excuse us for a moment," Drynz said. His voice pretended calm. His ruff, tail, and twitching ears told another story.

"No," Franke said. He forced his brain to catch up with his mouth. "What you have to say to each other can be said before all of us. None go apart until all know what is happening."

Drynz took the other Confrere's arm. Franke signaled to Jan Sklarinsky, and her pulser came up to her shoulder.

"Drynz, the Confraternity may kill you for revealing secrets. Sixteen-Leader Sklarinsky *will* kill you for seeking to leave. You need not remain within hearing, only within sight."

Drynz looked from the Confrere to Franke, then to the muzzle of Sklarinsky's pulser. His tale writhed, and he lowered his ears.

"Come, Confrere."

The conversation that followed wouldn't have told Franke much even if he'd heard every word. Half of it seemed to be code or hand gestures that he recognized as variants of some of the ritual gestures of the House of Light. *So much for the theory that the Confraternity recruited only those who had rejected the Cult of the Light.*

Drynz and the Confrere returned. The Confrere retrieved his weapons and equipment from the floor while Drynz explained the situation. Or at least he tried. Franke didn't think he succeeded, but he admitted that the failure might not be entirely Drynz's fault.

"The Eighth Cohort had orders to arrest us under some pretext and hold us as hostages for the Confreres aboard *Somtow Nosavan*?" Franke asked.

"Not only the Confreres," Drynz said. "The human refugees from the Masters' Territory."

Franke felt mentally slack-jawed and spoke slowly. "Had they forgotten Federation policy on hostages?"

"They had not, as far as I know."

"Then as far as you know, we were supposed to die?"

"Very possibly. But your deaths would have forced the Federation either to fight the Administration or to at least withdraw support from it. Then the Coordination and the Masters would have been free to hunt as and where it pleased them."

Franke felt closer to vomiting at the convoluted, vicious thinking behind such a scheme than he had at the smells of the officer's death. He wished that he could believe Drynz was lying. Unfortunately, his own access to Kishi Institute files suggested otherwise. Humans, Merishi, and Ptercha'a had all conceived and executed worse in the name of the battle against the Confraternity, and sometimes with many more than four victims.

He gave the other humans a condensed but uncensored version of Drynz's report. Nobody seemed skeptical. The bodies on the blood-soaked rug and the tight-faced prisoners were too much evidence.

"Juan, get on the circuit to your friends outside," Franke said. "Exchange situation reports. Drynz, I'd like to send these Hunters back to their comrades. Federation law on hostages—"

A distant burst of firing interrupted him, pulsers and SSW's together, with what sounded like a few grenades and what might have been a scream. Franke couldn't tell if it was human or Hunter.

"Juan, move it!"

The conversation was short and almost one-sided. Juan turned to Franke with his olive complexion paler than Franke had ever seen it.

"The Eighth Cohort's got the whole peninsula cut off. They've posted people nearly shoulder to shoulder in the tree line. That firing we heard was when some of the restaurant staff tried to make a break for it. One of them was killed, and the others were driven back."

Curses in three human languages and several dialects of True Speech echoed around the dining room. "All right," Franke said. "Juan, I assume your friends outside are pushing all this talktalk upstairs."

"Yes, and so far the Warband hasn't jammed. I don't know about intercepts, though."

"They can't break our scrambler codes on a real-time

basis," Morley put in. "Figure that we have communications security, and yell for help loud and clear."

Franke nodded and turned to Drynz. "I'd thought of releasing these people. Apparently we can't do that safely, but we also can't guard them. Do we have enough restraints or drugs to keep them secure without hurting them?"

One of the Confreres made an explicit gesture. A couple of the prisoners cringed. Drynz shook his head and turned to Franke.

"Their fate is a matter for the Confraternity, of which I am senior present."

"The Federation claims joint custody of them," Morley said. "We are obliged to resist by force any executions."

"What force?" Drynz said, then looked at Jan Sklarinsky and said in a different tone, "May I propose a compromise?"

"As long as it leaves the prisoners alive—"

"I will swear for the Confraternity, that we will harm neither their bodies nor their spirits, if you will send a message for us."

"What is the message?"

"It is in Confraternity code. Those who hear will understand."

Those who heard would also be Confraternity, receiving if not recognition, then at least substantial assistance from Federation officers. But too many lives were st stake.

If Drynz and the Confraternity chose simply to opt out of this fight, the 218 Brigade teams outside would be left unsupported or at least without intelligence. If the Eighth Cohort's Leader was shrewd and fast, he could eliminate the remaining human witnesses to tonight's affair, then hope to blame it on the terrorists. He'd be disappointed, but that wouldn't bring the dead back to life or reduce the chaos let loose in the Territory and soon all over Linak'h.

"Swear by whatever you hold most sacred that these prisoners are safe," Franke said. "In return, you have my oath to give you access to our communications for your message."

Drynz swore all the conventional potent oaths as well as two or three that drew sharp looks from the other Confreres. Another hypothesis confirmed: the Confraternity had developed its own quasi-religious aspects. And why should anyone be surprised, when documents of the Confraternity's existence went back to before human contact with the Merishi and their furry friends?

Franke swore five oaths in Anglic, Hispanic, Hebrew, and True Speech, then managed to remember enough Russian to start working through oaths in that. Drynz held up a hand.

"Enough. All these oaths may please Higher Powers, if it is in them to care about what we do. We are bound more by the wish to see Father-rise than by anything else, I think."

Franke returned a grin as tooth-laden as any Ptercha'a's, and Lu Morley joined him. She also had better teeth for grinning.

Linak'h:

Seenkiranda awoke from what she hoped was not a seeing-dream. In it she had been fleeing through the streets of a half-ruined, half-aflame city. Once it had been peaceful, inhabited by both humans and Hunters. Now it was a sacrifice to the spirits of war.

She ran heavily, steering wide of burning buildings and piles of smoking debris. In her arms she carried a child, whom she somehow knew was not hers. Somehow she also knew that to stop was to die, for enemies—she knew only that—were on her trail.

A burst from a battle rifle gouged chips from a wall just ahead of her. The trap had closed; she set the child down and told—him? her?—to hide, while fumbling for a single-hand or even a knife. The fear that swept through her when she realized that she was unarmed was what finally woke her.

She awoke to find the tunnel outside the chamber she shared with Emt Desdai crowded with armed Hunters. Their battle arrays looked to be a mix of older Administration-issue material and new equipment made for Hunters by humans.

The tunnel lighting was low, but she still recognized several acknowledged Confraternity members from Och'zem and other towns, as well as one or two voices she'd heard on speaker links. She also saw that Emt's bed had been slept in but was now empty save for two complete sets of battle gear. She and Emt were clearly not prisoners.

She was inspecting the gear when the murmur of voices outside sank nearly to silence. Then it redoubled. Several times she heard the words "Time of Power."

That was the Confraternity's phrase for the distant day when it would openly rule on one or even many Hunter-held worlds. Seenkiranda had seen some of the debate about how and when. She had also studied some of the human tales about gods coming again, such as the Barbar-oza and the more popular tale of the Christ-lord. She suspected that all alike were dreams.

But here came the woman leader of those who had greeted them when they landed. She wore full battle gear, complete with ammunition pouches, but her weapons were slung or holstered. In one hand she held high a metal bottle that, judging from her red eyes and weaving gait, did not hold vegetable juices.

"Confreres, it has been proclaimed. The Time of Power is at hand for Linak'h!"

The cheering this brought was so loud that the woman was out of sight before Seenkiranda could think clearly. Linak'h, or just the Administration's territory? It would be marvelous if the Confraternity was also going to take power in the Coordination. That would mean peace, except perhaps with the Scaleskins, who had little strength and fewer friends on Linak'h—

Emt Desdai appeared. He also carried one of the metal bottles—in fact, he carried several, slung over one shoulder on cords in place of some of his war gear. From his eyes and gait, however, he had not been sampling their contents. Seenkiranda halted her pair-mate with an embrace and a rubbing of muzzles.

He dropped the bottles with a clang and swept her into an embrace. The warmth of the embrace reminded Seenkir-anda that she wore nothing but shorts. She pulled Desdai inside and shut the door.

"But the drinks—" he protested.

"If it was your work to distribute them, I think that is being done for you." Certainly the cheering outside was louder.

He embraced her again. "Very well. I will call that work done and move on to the next task, which is—"

"Telling me what is happening. As much as you know yourself," she added, when she saw his face at her sharpness.

What he knew was enough to both hearten and alarm her. Legion Three-Eight had either mutinied or been misled by certain among its seniors into cooperating with the terrorists and bandits against Federation Warbanders. When they attempted to capture the Federation people, the assigned cohort faced a mutiny on its own ranks.

Rumors of the Legion and others in the Administration's Warband and civil seniors planning to help the Coordination had been circulating in Confraternity circles for some time. A few days ago, the Confraternity seniors had realized that the only alternative to chaos and the withdrawal of the Federation (leaving the Confraternity at the mercy of the Coordination and its allies) was to proclaim the Time of Power.

"In the Federation Territory only?" Seenkiranda asked.

"I know nothing of our strength in the Coordination itself. The main strength of the Confraternity in the Masters' land has already fled or gone into hiding. In the Alliance Territory, we already have many friends and much freedom. Indeed, what you are about to don came across the border."

Seenkiranda took a deep breath. Emt tried to silence her by rubbing muzzles and running hands up and down her bare back. She pushed him away, nearly extending her claws as she did. He looked as uneasy as if she had truly clawed him.

"What troubles you, dear one?"

"It seems to me that we have more chaos to fear, not less. We are overthrowing the Administration with weapons provided by the Alliance, the greatest human enemy of the Federation?"

"One takes friendship where it is offered."

"An old saying. But is the Alliance offering friendship? The whole Alliance, not just the handful of Navy seniors on Linak'h."

"Our seniors would not tell me that even if they knew." Desdai frowned. "Beloved, you seem ready to accuse me of lying, or at least of withholding truth that I know. I have done neither. All of this knowledge I was given in full only since I was summoned to council at Fatherset. You would not have thanked me for waking you to tell you what you might not have understood. When you are sleep-mazed—"

She held up a hand, then lightly touched two fingers to his lips. "Very well. But you have said nothing about what will prevent the Coordination from intervening."

"Nothing will, other than speed, success, and the threat of the Federation. We hope that after we have saved their Warbanders, the Federation will look at the Confraternity in a new light."

"And if we do not save the Warbanders?"

Emt looked exasperated. "Some will call that defeatism."

"I call those arrogant."

"Hurling harsh names will do nothing." He sighed. "I share your fear. But I have some hope of our success, at least in saving the Federation people. From what I have heard, the Confraternity senior with them is our friend Drynz."

For the first time, Seenkiranda smiled. Drynz would be harder than most to either kill or outwit. If the Federation people swallowed their notions about the Confraternity and followed him ...

Four

Linak'h:

Candice Shores glanced at the display to the left. The three troop carriers were still holding line-ahead formation, 120-km/h speed, and below-treetop altitude. She'd long since decided that flying like this in a heavy carrier with her nowhere near the controls made her nervous and that her nerves were irrelevant to the tactical situation.

She swiveled her chair and looked at the display to the right. "There," Nieg's voice came from behind.

"I see them." She tried to keep her voice level. Nieg's presence was hardly surprising and only moderately welcome, but unlike her nerves it was not irrelevant. Any hostage situation called for real-time intelligence collection and evaluation, the kind best done on the spot.

The display showed eight dots that hadn't been there before; the armored squads had dropped five minutes ago from a heavy attacker, onto the north side of the Sinnis'h River. Their dropper was now running high cover and com relay, while two other heavy attackers rode at medium altitude above the three troop carriers.

Doctrine called for five or six heavies for this kind of operation, if the infantry had no dedicated gunships or organic heavy weapons. The situation left the hastily mounted and still more hastily named Operation Root Canal making do with three.

The Navy wasn't making any secret of keeping upstairs all the heavy attackers it could beg, borrow, or steal. Tanz was as frank about giving priority to Kharg and Hogg. The situation at Loutissharatz's, he said, needed cool heads, already on the spot in ample supply, not airborne firepower.

"Position update and ETA," Shores said. The left-hand display changed. Now she could see a square that was a hundred kloms on a side, with the track of the troop carriers from the Zone unrolling across it. They were already working up the second side of a broad V. At the top of the V was the drop point on the north side of the Sinnis'h, twenty kloms and ten minutes away.

"Hammer One to Huntress," sounded in Shores's ears. The attacker leader's voice had more expression scrambled than in person. "Admin AD sensors have lock on us. IFF interrogation nominal. No weapons signatures."

"Huntress to Victory One," Shores said. "Negative sensor scans for us, so far. ETA nine minutes forty."

"Good luck, Huntress."

Shores turned right again. "Project deployment," she said. The display flickered, then showed the AO as it was supposed to be when everybody was in place.

South of the restaurant, Eighth Cohort, Legion Three-Eight, in a static defense/security position. Inside the restaurant, Herman Franke & Co. with Confraternity—"allies" was accurate, if not legally binding. In indeterminate and hopefully mutually neutralizing positions around the restaurant, Edelstein's improvised but probably reliable QRF and any terrs who hadn't fled to the arms of the "Renegade Legion" (which had probably finished them off to eliminate witnesses).

North of the river, eight of Shores's people in suits, creating a quickly redeployable sensor net. In the middle of that net, was the LZ where two platoons from 218 Brigade and three platoons from Shores's battalion would be landing.

"What happens then?" Shores had asked, when they'd first discussed the plan, if you could call two minutes a discussion. Nieg had raised everybody's eyebrows by saying that he didn't know.

"Or rather, it depends on a lot of factors," he added. "One thing I do know—if we try to CA any significant forces on the south side, we lose either way. Landing behind the cohort could panic them. Landing in front means a small LZ and a target-rich environment for any hothead with an itchy claw on the trigger."

Nieg clearly had some sort of mandate to influence the plan that she didn't know about and Edelstein wouldn't talk about. So they'd be going into battle with a CO from one brigade commanding units from both her brigade and another, according to a plan heavily influenced by an ex-Ranger intelligence specialist.

Shores took some consolation from the last fact. Ranger operations got this large just often enough that Nieg had probably planned or participated in a few. Also, he undoubtedly had political insights that she couldn't match.

The ETA was eight minutes, then seven, six, five . . .

At four minutes, the power-suiters redeployed, to cover the LZ, and two heavy attackers dropped to two thousand meters. Tactically linked to the high-altitude AOP, they should respond to any ambushes or retaliatory fire on the LZ.

At three minutes, Shores and Nieg stood up and locked, snapped, and tightened all their gear. Then they did a quick visual and hands-on buddy inspection, which somehow turned into what was not quite a hug but more than business.

Two minutes. One minute. Thirty seconds, and the troop carrier pilot was counting down.

"Mark! Touchdown in five, four, three, two—"

Rrrummmpppp! Metallic protests and a sort of seismic-wave effect as the deck of the carrier flexed under the lifter. Bow and stern doors opened, revealing dark woodland—cool and nearly lifeless too, not even much showing on the high-gain thermal imager.

The lifter's fans cut in, lost in the metallic whine and whistling air from the other three. Then the pilot eased on the lift field and let the fans push the now-weightless lifter toward the bow.

Two of the carriers had four lifters apiece; they were unloaded in thirty seconds and airborne again in a minute. The third lifter carried unmounted platoons from Shores's battalion, under Lieutenant Kapustev, the new XO of the LI company. They deployed on foot, sprinting for the tree line to set up a security perimeter and get clear of the fan wash.

As the third carrier disappeared from the display showing the LZ, Shores popped the side hatch and scrambled out. Kapustev was already scurrying toward her.

"First Platoon is on the way to the riverbank," he said. "Third will hold the perimeter and Fourth be the reserve."

Nieg started to speak, then looked at Shores. She nodded. "Good enough for now."

She didn't want to ask Nieg "What next?" when he'd upheld her authority. Also, the next move depended on a situation report from the restaurant *and* the ETA of some high-value assets, nature unspecified.

She hoped that ETA was soon. Right now she had nearly two hundred people close enough to the Eighth Cohort to be a vulnerable target and too far from the restaurant to do anything for the people in there except avenge them, if the Eighth Cohort decided to move in hard and fast.

At least the Eighth Cohort's leader was probably as nervous as she was—more so, unless he had nerves that could ride out a mutiny in his ranks.

Linak'h:

Like a good many of Och'zem's modern buildings, Loutis-sharatz's had its recycling suite on the roof. Compressed air or staff with buckets hauled the raw material upstairs, filters did their usual job in the tanks and basins, and a large hose fed the result into lifters that landed on a small roof pad.

Right now, Lu Morley was less concerned about the operation of the system than the amount of cover and concealment it provided. She doubted that any part of it was even fragment-proof, but all of it was opaque, providing good if somewhat smelly concealment for her, Jan Sklarinsky, and a two-man OP from the 218 Brigade QRF.

The two newcomers had infiltrated during the shoot-out inside the restaurant, according to their leader, a buck sergeant named Deloia. Morley now lay under a pipe, a captured Admin carbine resting within reach. It was light enough to fire single-handed, handy if she was caught on the move. Sklarinsky and the other infiltrator covered the perimeter, while Deloia crawled around the roof with a captured scancorder.

Troop lifters—no, heavy carriers—droned north of the river, the sound muffled by distance, hills, and the heavy night air. They still drowned out the desultory firing south of the restaurant for nearly a minute. Clouds now covered the sky, apparently grown in place—Morley couldn't feel a breath of wind.

With no more sound that a snake slithering on sand,

Deloia reappeared. He flexed arms and legs, then leaned back in the V between an airpipe and a liquids tank. His fingers flew as he changed power cells and film cartridges entirely by touch.

"You a Ranger?"

"Need-to-know?"

"You just answered my question."

"Sorry, Major. But—ah, the boss told us to keep a low profile. He—wait one."

Deloia cocked his head, listening, then subvocalized the message onward to Juan Esteva below in the restaurant. "218 Brigade's put in five platoons across the river, under Colonel Shores. They're expecting some special-operations assets in a bit, then they'll warn the cohort leader to stay clear while the assets move in."

"They'll want real-time intelligence on the terrs—" Morley began.

"Already set up, Major," Deloia said. He slipped the exposed cartridge into a socket on his com harness, then twisted around to extend the antenna of his back unit. The single shots from around the landing stage and along the shoreline turned to bursts. They all stiffened, until they heard no rounds passing.

"Either the terrs are breaking contact or the Warbanders are pretending to fight them."

"Could be a real fight," Deloia said. "I wouldn't want a wild card like the terrs lying around, if I was the Admin. Or they could be simulating a firefight to cover *their* infiltration. Remember how good the Pussies are at night fighting, and that some of the Warbander's have to be real hard cases who aren't going to give up easily."

Linak'h:

Ram Daranji and seven other Rangers were the first of Nieg's expected assets to arrive. From what Nieg had said about Daranji, Candice Shores had expected a bearded giant, fit to strangle Death Commandos with his bare hands.

The beard was there, but the rest of Daranji was only a bit taller and broader than Nieg, although obviously in the same superb shape. He flashed a grin at everybody and nobody, then turned to Shores.

"We're ready to move anytime your plan asks it."

Shores did not ask, "What do you mean, *my* plan, Tame Ninja?" because she had one and also because even if she hadn't she'd be cursed if she'd let Nieg see her caught off base. Instead she nodded.

"You have any underwater gear?"

Daranji shook his head. "We came in a civ lifter docked to another heavy." He pointed at the sky. "The heavy's up there, with eight of us in suits and the rest of the bay loaded with non-lethals."

That exchange bought Shores the few seconds she needed to polish her plan. "Never mind about the swim-in. Is the lifter really civ, or just disguised?"

"Long legs, light armor and weapons."

That meant basically transportation, not a CA vehicle, but since she wasn't going to put the Rangers down on top of the Eighth Cohort HQ (at least not for now) ...

"Update deployment display," she told the computer, and added, "Message for Command Group—meeting at twenty-one thirty here."

Nieg seemed to be trying not to meet her eyes. The most likely reason was the non-arrival of some of the other assets he had promised. *Which can happen in the best-run wars.*

"Colonel Nieg. Do we have all the assets in place that we need for securing the restaurant?"

"Short of the Administration launching an all-out attack, yes."

"The non-lethals will buy us time to withdraw across the river," she said. "If they want to chase us that far, we have air superiority and they have to be ready to declare war."

This time Nieg met her eyes, nodded, but maintained silence. Shores began to suspect that one of the remaining assets could be Marshal Banfi. If so, Nieg had nicely impaled himself on the horns of a dilemma.

Hold back on Operation Root Canal, and risk the hostages, Shores's authority, and his relationship with her. Let it go ahead, and risk creating a situation which the Marshal could probably still solve but might not appreciate having to. Unappreciative Marshals were something even the most distinguished and rational covert-operations colonels had to fear.

Linak'h:

Herman Franke was a well-educated Federation citizen and Forces regular. Therefore, he had heard of the Ranger motto "Hours of planning for every second of operation."

He wasn't sure if Operation Root Canal followed that rule, because he wasn't sure how long the actual combat took. Judging the length of a firefight was a demanding job even for seasoned ground-pounders, and he was playing diplomat through most of the actual shooting.

The people inside had all of thirty seconds warning. The code word "drill" came over the com net, then he heard the sonic boom of a heavy attacker coming over low, then the warning siren for a dazzler.

None of the dazzler light reached inside. The cries did—both humans and Ptercha'a caught looking the wrong way without eye protection. They wouldn't be blind, they wouldn't even suffer any permanent eye injury, but they wouldn't be seeing well enough to fight for at least five minutes.

Then lifters from the north and firing from the south met and mingled overhead. Franke had to lean against the wall for a moment, as he realized the two were converging right about where Lu Morley would be.

Then his breath returned, as Morley scrambled down the stairs from the roof, half-leading, half-pushing Sergeant Deloia. He was blinking frantically, as if exercising his eyebrows would restore sight to his eyes.

Morley's uniform had been something less than impeccable even before she went up on the roof. Now it was dripping, stained, and smelly. In the opening seconds of this new stage of the fight, somebody had punched a hole in the liquids tank of the recycling unit.

Deloia groped for the wall, turned slowly, then sat down. "Dazzled, or worse?" Franke asked.

"Just a bit of dazzle," the sergeant said. "There's what looks like a whole bunch of infiltrators on their way across the main pad. Your sniper and my partner are engaging them, but I hope we can get some non-lethals down on them fast. If they're from the Admin cohort—"

The debriefing ended abruptly as both the lifter fans and the heavy-weapons firing stopped. The silence lasted two heartbeats, then the barricaded door to the dining room blew open.

Deloia caught the worst of it—his blindness would now need more than time to heal it. But he jerked his pulser around to fire one-handed at the shouting mass of Ptercha'a and humans who burst through the smoke and wreckage.

Even Franke could recognize a desperate assault. He could also recognize both races from the restaurant staff, humans in ragged clothing, and a few Ptercha'a who looked like regular Warbanders complete with eye protectors.

Deloia was overrun in the next few seconds, and one of the Confreres followed him. Both fighters went out swinging, the Confrere literally. That plus the sheer number of bodies trying to crowed into the dining room slowed the assault.

Slowed it by just enough for Franke, Morley, and the surviving Confreres to sprint the length of the dining room without anyone having a clear shot at them. By the time they reached the storeroom door, several of the newcomers were shooting, but hastily down the full length of a dust-hazed, dimly lit room.

Franke felt a ricochet shred a trouser leg and a straight shot clip a boot heel. That was as close as the enemy came before the people in the storeroom powered up the doors, dragged the retreating fighters inside, and closed the way again. A spatter of rounds clanged into the doors, but only echoes sounded in the storeroom.

As both races caught their breath, Franke heard the scrape of boots and Drynz rose to his feet. He was in combat stance, ruff flared, and looked eager to talk.

Franke waved him aside, keyed on the intercom, and hoped his words reached the dining room outside.

"Attention, those who seek our lives," he said in True Speech. "There are within here warriors of the Eighth Cohort, Legion Three-Eight. You cannot enter swiftly without danger to them, and they are comrades to some of you. Is this well done?

"That should buy time—" he began, to Lu, then Drynz tapped him on the shoulder.

"You are firm in honor," the Confrere said. "So you will understand—"

"I understand that if those people out there don't care

about the Admin prisoners, we're in serious trouble. Praise me some other time."

"I speak no idle praise. You know honor, therefore you will not be surprised that some of our prisoners wish to join us."

"What?" Morley, Franke, and the civilians all said in nearly one voice.

"They wish weapons, so that if the enemy enters first they can fight and if our friends come sooner they will at least be seen as true in honor."

This was one of those situations where Franke's academic knowledge of Ptercha'a customs wasn't enough. It said a good deal, that Drynz was willing to pass on the request—but then Drynz had never seemed a fanatic.

"All right," Franke said. "On my authority as Federation representative and Warband senior, issue weapons to those who ask for them. But understand this. Anyone who betrays us, I will slit their bellies open and my mate will dance in boots on their organs of generation. They will die wishing that they had not changed their minds."

"Understood."

Drynz must have picked out the likely recruits already, or else the danger to the Warbanders delayed the people outside longer than Franke realized. By the time every spare hand had barricaded the door with crates and barrels, Drynz had six paroled prisoners ready to join the defenders.

This left a good many captured weapons to spare. "Any of you want these?" Franke called to the civilians.

"I'm a—" one of the humans began plaintively.

"—damned fool if you think there are any noncombatants now," Morley snapped. "I know what I said, but things have changed. Whoever's pushing the people outside wants a bloody incident. Your blood will do as well as ours. Besides, they don't want witnesses, and the quietest witness is a dead one."

The protester didn't accept a carbine but at least shut up.

Franke wondered what was holding up the rescue operation that was obviously under way. Communications with the outside were gone—jamming, personnel or equipment casualties, or simply the key people being too busy to remember about bulletins to people who were technically the focus of the whole operation but who were also out of sight and therefore too easily might slip out of mind—

Franke was crossing the room to check the lock and seal on the outside door when orange flame jetted into the room from the hall door. He dove out of the path of the flame and fragments, heard the death cry of at least one Ptercha'a who hadn't been fast enough, then swiveled on his belly and raised his sidearm in a two-handed grip.

The doors still stood, but the barricade was half-ruined and a hole the size of a Ptercha'a head gaped in the metal. Yellow gas was pouring through and, as Franke watched, a grenade bounced out of the murk. Juan Esteva dove for it, tossed it back at the hole, and with a little help from Higher Powers hit his mark.

That raised shouts and scurrying feet outside but didn't cut off the gas flow. Apparently the gas wielders had masks, but some of their comrades didn't—a fact encouraging in one way: if they were working with a non-lethal, they still wanted prisoners. And discouraging in that if the attackers thought they still had time to take prisoners, the rescue operation must be going slowly.

The Confrere who had surrendered the Warband sixteen suddenly rolled out from behind his cover. He kept rolling until he was up against the barricade, then scrambled onto the ruins, thrust his carbine through the hole, and emptied the magazine.

Fifty rounds could do a lot of damage even if they couldn't penetrate body armor. Franke didn't recall seeing all the attackers armored. The screaming lasted this time, and the gas stopped. Two grenades came in, but one didn't explode and the Confrere repeated Juan Esteva's act with the other.

It bought more time, but that wasn't going to be enough. Franke's eyes felt as if they were melting out of his head. His vision was just clear enough to make out the nightmare spectacle of Lu sprawled beside an overturned barrel, blood around her head. Each breath was a struggle, and his stomach was ready to reject not just dinner but everything else he'd eaten in the past week—

Fwummppp.

The outside door peeled open at the top and one side. Then tortured metal screamed in protest as metal-covered hands gripped, twisted, and pulled, all in one servo-augmented motion.

Through the open doorway two Federation LI troopers, gigantic in power suits, strode like rescuing gods.

Two more followed them, one hurrying for the inner door with an SSW in one hand. Franke knew he should get up, greet the rescuers, and negotiate the surrender of the doomed attackers outside. All he could do was crawl to Lu, try not to splatter her when his stomach finally emptied itself, then lie beside her.

Relief washed through him as she opened one bleary eye and winked, then groped for his hand. If she said anything he didn't hear it. He was watching Juan Esteva lurching to his feet, stumbling toward the open air with one arm around power-suited shoulders.

Then the sound of a single shot made Franke turn his head. Fuddled as it was by gas, he could move nothing else. He saw the Warband Confrere—whose name he'd never learned, he realized—lying beside a box. Blood was pooled around his head, as it had been around Lu's.

The difference was that mixed with the blood were brains and skull, and the warrior's head had no back. Betraying one band of comrades to aid another was a complex problem but one with a simple solution for a warrior of honor.

Five

Linak'h:

The flier lurched, and Emt Desdai gripped the back of the seat. Outside, the clouds thinned briefly, enough to show the ground. Not being either an experienced air passenger or a Warband pilot, Desdai wondered at the reasons for keeping the fliers in the clouds. With six long-range machines cruising south in formation, collision seemed more likely than detection.

Of course, this depended somewhat on whose sensors might be scanning them and how well their bafflers and maskers might be working. Probably as well as could be expected, if they were improvisations like this air-transport squadron. The long-range fliers had essentially been stolen by their pilots, then flown to pick up the Confraternity forces in the northern wilderness of the Administration. The Alliance Confreres had provided weapons and even flown them across the border, but could not safely join the fighting in the south in their own machines.

Desdai sat down and strapped himself in. If they were staying in the clouds, this would not be the last patch of violent sky.

"I could not even get on the driving deck to see who was there," he said. "It is guarded by four Confraternity warriors about the size and shape of Drynz, but not nearly as polite.

"Anyway," he added, patting Seenkiranda's hand, "it may have only been a rumor. Even if it was the truth, he might have been no more willing to speak—"

"—than you were, when you first suspected the truth, until I decided that it must be dragged out of you?" Seenkiranda finished.

"I did speak," Desdai said.

Seenkiranda tried to look severe, then returned the hand pressure. "I heard something while you were seeking our friend," she said. "Two of the fliers may be carrying ammunition."

"All six loaded in the dark. Who says they saw this?"

"Two who passed on the way to the bath stall," she said. "One said he hoped the ammunition carriers would keep their distance if the weather grew worse. The other told him to be silent."

There seemed to be numerous self-appointed seniors about tonight. Desdai was hardly surprised. The Confraternity drew on every sort and condition of Hunter, so there had to be some for whom the phrase "Time of Power" meant a time for *their* power, even if it was only over their fellow Hunters.

The flier lurched again, and kept on lurching, weaving, rising and falling, and generally behaving as if the crew were witless or drunk. Or as if the wind had grown worse—but looking past Seenkiranda, Desdai saw nothing but gray-tinged black murk.

Then the floor tilted sharply down, the alarms all shrieked in chorus, and every warning sign on every compartment wall flared. As the cabin lighting dimmed, Desdai tightened his belt another few claws and hooked his shoulder harness down to the belt.

He also smelled the first victims of air sickness. In an enclosed cabin, it would spread like a pestilence. In fact, just thinking about the prospect was making Desdai's own stomach twitch—

All the windows on the far side of the cabin lit up like the viewholes of a smelter-furnace. On Desdai's side, the clouds turned from near-black to a sickly yellow. The glare of the explosion was already fading when the blast wave struck the flier.

Desdai had time to realize that the flier had made at least one complete roll. He had time to realize that he was in good company for meeting death. Then the floor stabilized—a floor awash with the fruits of air sickness. Outside Desdai saw the clouds now far overhead, and the treetops whipping past seemed close enough to touch.

The flier was running at nearly full speed, at the lowest safe altitude. The thought of hitting a hilltop did not improve Desdai's mood, but it did distract him from his stomach.

The flier banked into a turn. Out Desdai's window he saw the dim shapes of two other fliers, also flying low, fast, and dark. Far behind them, what looked like the lights of a good-sized town blazed in the forest. The formation must have broken cloud right over the town. Desdai hoped its people were friendly.

Then something soared into the sky, trailing golden fire. It lit up a column of smoke rising, as the forest fires' smoke had risen less than twenty days before. It had been no rumor that one of the fliers had been carrying ammunition.

Aboard U.F.S. *Shenandoah,* off Linak'h:

The alarm caught Commodore Liddell taking a sponge bath. The hostage crisis had been resolved (or at least the hostages rescued), but no one was betting on when the Low Squadron would have another shipment of ground-supplied consumables. Hence water conservation.

One disadvantage she'd never realized about sponge baths was that they weren't nearly as satisfying as regular showers, but you were just as bare, just as wet, and just as slow getting to your post when the alarm sounded. Even though the flag emergency cabin was right next to the Auxiliary Combat Center, the incident was over by the time she reached the ACC, and the playback not yet edited.

Rather than look idle or nervous, she called up Pavel Bogdanov. By luck, he had been on the bridge and seen the incident real-time, as it was relayed up to him from the main Combat Center.

Bogdanov's commentary was as good as the ACC's editing. By the time Liddell had had the benefit of both, she at least knew the limits of her knowledge and what had to be protected from this sudden upsurge of chaos.

She talked with Bogdanov with one ear cocked for an urgent message from Admiral Longman. This was all-theater business, not just the Low Squadron's. Liddell still wanted five minutes of thoughts alone with her flag captain.

"I read it as those long-haul passenger lifters we heard were being 'ferried,' caught in an air ambush," she suggested. "One hit—looks like a big load of conventional ammo, rather than a fuser warhead. The rest getting down and dispersing, fast. No sign of anything that might have intercepted, no beam-weapon signatures."

"The weather could have scrambled those," Bogdanov pointed out. "If somebody synchronized a laser with a close lightning flash, from orbit we would lose it."

"Then we need that formation shadowed, from as low and close as possible," Liddell said. "What happens then will tell us a lot about who is shooting and what they're shooting with."

"Longman wants all the attackers upstairs, except the ones handling the Loutissharatz situation."

"If our data on that formation's course was correct, anything we send to ride herd on them will be heading straight for Och'zem."

At that point Longman did come on the circuit, looking as if she'd just been routed from a shared bed. (She had the reputation for preferring company in bed on a regular basis, but not requiring it to an unprofessional degree.) Liddell kept Longman in play while Bogdanov reviewed the data and the ACC's editing. By the time he came back on, Uehara had joined the conference.

"What concerns me is the position of those Coordination cruisers," he said. Liddell tried not to look too confused as the carrier admiral went on.

"Look." The display split, Uehara in a corner and the rest a basic who-was-where-when diagram. "Two of those cruisers were in easy slant range of the formation at the time of the explosion."

"We'd have picked up any long-range beam or missile work," Longman protested.

"Commodore Liddell—excuse me, Captain Bogdanov—has pointed out the matter of lightning flashes. In any case, I was not thinking of the cruisers launching the attack from their present position. I was thinking of their providing sensor data for a ground- or low-launched missile or beam."

"From Admin territory?" Longman said.

"We have evidence that there is some tension within Administration forces," Uehara said.

"That'll do for Understatement of the Night until something better comes along," Longman said. She now sounded awake but sour. "All right. Tazuo, if the cruisers move, they're your baby. Rose, keeping those lifters safe is yours. You can move anything up to a heavy cruiser down for close escort and scan."

"A light will do," Liddell said. "More maneuverable for close escort at low altitude, less threatening, and tough enough to force the bad guys to either escalate or shut down. But there's something we ought to consider before cuddling up to these lifters."

"There's nothing *I* consider more important than preventing any more incidents tonight. Or better, until we can do some plain talking with the Admin people. You're an odd one to be forgetting Air Victoria Six, Rose."

Liddell bit her lip against both anger and laughter. Anger at being accused of forgetting what the accidental shootdown of a civilian passenger lifter on Victoria had done to escalate the crisis. Laughter at being cut off before she could say things that might have weakened her position and the Low Squadron's autonomy.

"On the way, Admiral."

"Good."

Linked only to each other, Liddell and Bogdanov had their plans made in a minute, moving in two more ships *Weilitsch* from Mad Bill Moneghan's squadron doing the low work, with Moneghan himself in *Cavour* as OTC and relay. They also had an all-units request out for data on any radar scans detected in the relevant areas.

"We may not find the smoking radar set," Liddell said. "But those cruisers haven't been operating in blackdown mode. We may learn more than they want us to."

"Shall I take this one?" Bogdanov asked.

"Please. Mad Bill's going to be busy, and I want to get on the com to Tanz."

"Aye-aye, Commodore."

She shifted circuits and leaned back, in a chair that had suddenly become much less ergonomic. There was no reason to involve Pavel in whatever might come from two of her suspicions.

One was that these "labor-crew movements" involved enough lift to support either an Administration crackdown on the Confraternity or a Confraternity coup. Either was more likely than the Coordination's starting the war with its ships and ground troops deployed as they were.

Both also demanded far more complex responses. The one thing Liddell didn't want was Bogdanov being charged along with her for "failure to support a superior officer in implementing Federation policy." That charge had ended the careers of four-stars, and Longman wasn't the sort of officer to admit that Liddell hadn't answered certain questions because she, the superior officer, had been too much in a hurry to ask them!

There was also the request she wanted to make to General Tanz, to have a strong, preferably armed, observation team on the ground at the crash site, no matter who else investigated it. She didn't trust the Administration, the Confraternity, or, for that matter, General Kharg, whose AO included the site, not to make the "evidence" support a favorite hypothesis that might not be either true or in the Federation's interests.

Linak'h:

A heavy attacker swept low over Loutissharatz's, all its lights glowing and the code for "medical mission" flashing at ten-second intervals. The casualties from the terrorist attack were on their way to Forces Med Center in the Zone, some of them destined for wards that were secure, Ptercha'a-designated, or both.

Candice Shores looked past Lieutenant Kapustev, to where a mixed squad of LI and medics was bagging and laying out the bodies. Fourteen of them so far, but mercifully none were or would be Jan Sklarinsky, Juan Esteva, Lucretia Morley, or Herman Franke.

The last three were in one of the medevac lifters docked to the disappearing attacker. At worst they might miss the war, and that only if tonight's events were the start of it.

She turned back to Kapustev, who by nature or good luck had developed the skill of appearing totally relaxed even while standing at attention. She keyed the command terminal to "RECORD" again.

"The only problem I have is why non-lethal gasses weren't used to clear the restaurant immediately," she said. "That might have saved time over blasting the rear door. I don't say that anybody died because of this, or that this is a culpable failure, but I think we ought to have the cause on record."

Kapustev could not keep up the relaxed appearance now.

He looked around, as edgy as a cat on a hot floor, or as he himself had been the day he appeared before the Medical Assessment Board for their decision on his return to duty.

"We didn't have any non-lethals," he said. "Or rather, we didn't have any that were guaranteed non-lethal to both species, regardless of quantity, confined space, age, health, wounds, and so on. What we had was—"

He had obviously been giving the matter some thought, and not just to get himself off the hook. "It seemed less risky to work room to room with concussion grenades and pulsers," he concluded.

In this case, it was only technically true that Kapustev's decision hadn't killed anybody. A good many Ptercha'a and human terrorists had died, mostly at the hands of their intended victims, but when some of the dead were Warband regulars (even if engaged in mutiny, kidnapping, and terrorism), there would be rude questions asked. Between the lack of reliable non-lethals in front and communications failures and general confusion on top, the break-in and rescue had been delayed by several minutes, during which the defenders had been forced to use whatever came to hand and not worry about lethal force.

"It probably was," Shores said. "I won't give anybody a clean bill of health on the communications mix-ups until everybody's been debriefed. But I won't hang anybody, or allow anybody to be hanged."

"Thank you, Colonel." Kapustev almost saluted before he remembered they were still technically in a combat area, with seven hundred armed Ptercha'a of uncertain disposition no more than five hundred meters away. Ram Daranji and his suited Rangers had retrieved all the Eighth Cohort's infiltrators from the belt of non-lethals (mostly web and foam) and returned them to their own Healers, which had lowered but not eliminated the tension.

In fact, Shores really belonged back on the north side of the river, along with the security platoon at the LZ. She was this far forward, where she risked becoming an early casualty of any Administration countermove, because she wanted to walk the ground of the action. As soon as Daranji's people had sprayed the restaurant with N-6B and brought the ventilation system back on-line, she was going inside and let Kapustev and anybody else available lead her clear through from front to back. After that, she would be a better witness in anybody's defense, her own included.

Daranji himself reported that decontamination still had a good ten to fifteen minutes to go. Shores stood up and nodded to the security squad remaining just out of hearing.

"Let's go check the non-lethals."

Kapustev flinched. There was no way she could give that order without implying that he was capable of lying. There was no way she could be an effective witness for him if she *didn't* eyeball the empties, magazines, and reserve.

From the darkness, a voice spoke softly.

"No need for that, Colonel. I've been inspecting the non-lethals myself. Kapustev's right."

Soft voices in the darkness had acquired a habit of belonging to Liew Nieg. This time was no exception.

"How long have you been eavesdropping?" she said.

"Long enough to save you and Kapustev an unnecessary errand," he replied. His face was hard to make out, as he'd camouflage-creamed it like a member of the assault force, but from his voice it would be showing its maximum lack of expression.

"Thank you," Shores said. She didn't so much as blink at Kapustev before he was suddenly twenty meters away and the security cordon nearly as far.

"How did you—?" she began.

"I rode on the medevac flight and dropped on a trail rope," he said.

"Do you always have to do things Ranger-style?"

"Do you have a professional need for an answer to that?"

"I'm responsible for the security of this area against anything the Eighth Cohort may have up its sleeve," she said. "People sneaking around without telling anybody can cause accidents. I would rather not have one happen to anybody, and you more than most."

"I'm grateful not to be regarded as expendable."

This is a delicate job that also has to be a fast one. "I can't let your evidence on the non-lethals stand alone. The battalion has to keep its house in order. That may not save us, but it won't hurt, and it also won't involve you."

"My involvement won't hurt you."

"Unless I'm accused of hiding behind you."

He actually smiled. "What could you do in that position?"

The innuendo eased Shores's nerves; to make a remark like that on duty, Nieg must be nearly as tense as she was.

Shores's com indicated an incoming call. She switched on.

"Dagobert Alpha to Huntress. We have a situation that I thought you should know about."

"Dagobert Alpha" was Edelstein. Since he did not have a reputation for shorting the chain of command, a call directly from him meant something important coming down. Nieg and Shores listened to the report of the shoot-down and the Navy's response. They listened with even less enthusiasm to the report of an unidentified multi-ship Emergence at minimum Jumping distance, and the indications that two of the Coordination cruisers were about to get under way.

"The Navy's prepared for anything, so far," Edelstein concluded. "They're also staying out of our hair. Colonel Shores, you remain OTC for the Loutissharatz's incident. Anything you need, ask."

"Thanks, General. I'll be back with my want list in five minutes."

"I'll be waiting. Dagobert Alpha out."

It might have made a better impression if she'd been able to rattle off her list immediately, but she needed some private consultation with Nieg first to be sure she asked for everything she needed. She would probably have only one chance to ask.

"Do we have any more special assets coming in?" she asked Nieg.

"The situation has changed. I don't know if—"

Shores resisted the temptation to be sarcastic about Nieg's ignorance, only stepped close and whispered. "Is Banfi coming in?"

"If he changes his mind, he may not communicate, and of course I have no way of affecting his decision. If he thinks he's needed for dealing with their air movement. . . ." Nieg shrugged.

Shores felt both more relief and new tension. That was as much confirmation as she'd expected, that both Banfi and the Confreres were on the move. The Confreres in fact were probably executing a coup, on the basis of a signal that she had authorized Drynz to send, using Federation facilities!

For once, everybody's combined ignorance added up to knowledge, at least of what she should request.

Edelstein must have been leaning over the com operator's shoulder, he came on so fast. He listened as Shores requested the rest of the 218 Brigade QRF and the rest of A Company (the old *Shenandoah* LI's) from her battalion. The reinforcements would go into the LZ in the forest on the north side of the river, making the "security perimeter" live up to its name.

"You can send a LI-qualified field grade if you have one to spare, medical supplies, and some hot food, too," Shores concluded. "I think we have to be ready to outsit the Eighth Cohort, if we don't want to have to outfight them."

"It might be better to outsit them with the Sinnis'h between us," Edelstein said. Shores heard a suggestion rather than an order, saw Nieg shaking his head, and frowned. What was the reason, and could she give it before Edelstein turned request into—?"

Got it.

"We haven't finished getting pix for ID'ing the bodies. If we pull back now, we have to either leave the job undone or take the bodies with us. That could start a rumor that we're desecrating the Ptercha'a dead.

"Four platoons here is enough to discourage the Cohort Leader from trying to move in. Four battalions won't be enough if somebody has a gut feeling about 'human barbarians' and those guts are hooked to his trigger finger."

"You couldn't have taken the bodies out on the medevac flight?"

"No room, and we didn't even have a secure perimeter locked in then. An incident then would have been even worse."

"Very good, Colonel. We'll give you as much of what you ask for as we can, as fast as we can. I'll call you when we have an ETA for the first flight. You call if anything out of the ordinary happens."

"Yes, sir."

In the silence, Nieg and Shores looked at each other, then at Kapustev, who had slipped close enough probably to hear the second conversation. That didn't bother Shores. What did bother her briefly was that Nieg obviously wanted to hug her, she wanted to be hugged, and Kapustev was spoiling it.

"I'll put one squad on security for the bodies," the lieutenant said, "and another thickening up the non-lethals as soon as the colonel authorizes it. Some of the stuff will be safe in the open. Everybody else—Alert Two?"

"Right," Shores said. "See that at least a couple of people in the body-watcher squad are familiar with the basic Ptercha'a vigil etiquette. The people on alert should keep both an eyeball and a sensor watch. Otherwise it's like I said—we're challenging the Eighth Cohort to a sitting contest, and I don't intend to lose."

"No, ma'am," Kapustev said. He was talking into his com unit before he was out of sight. The security perimeter contracted, then froze as Nieg threw his arms around Shores. In spite of his slightness and her battle gear, she felt the breath leaving her.

She wanted to rumple his hair, but his helmet blocked her fingers. Instead she trailed them along his cheek, then gripped him by both shoulders.

"Let's go check those non-lethals, Liew. And if you're afraid to tell Banfi to stay out of an unsecured LZ, will you let me talk to the little bastard?"

Six

Linak'h:

For the rest of a busy night, Candice Shores personally reckoned time from her hugging Nieg. She didn't believe in omens, but Nieg's leaving her only professional problems was encouraging about what to expect from him in the long run.

At H (for Hug) + 11 minutes, they finished the inventory of the non-lethals. They turned over the stock to Kapustev, with the assurance that he was in the clear.

"So are you," Nieg told Shores. "I'm not sure about the people who issued the material. They may have made an honest mistake through lack of time. They may have done something else."

Nieg opened his canteen and drank half of it. "However, we may need some high-level cooperation in investigating the matter. I won't hold out too much hope of actually punishing anybody, but we can force them to lie low."

Translation: be very nice to Marshal Banfi if and when he shows up.

Shores wasn't in the habit of being rude to Marshals, but she now made up her mind to do anything that might earn Banfi's goodwill. Her battalion, including one of her best junior officers and she herself, might have been set up for an incident that could still wreck the Federation position on Linak'h. She definitely wanted the people responsible to be lying low.

Preferably in a nice snug box under two meters of Linak'h soil.

At H + 19, Kapustev reported that the work squad had spotted infiltrators. At H + 21, he reported that the infiltrators had been identified as Healers, trying to retrieve a wounded Warbander overlooked in the initial body-clearing. They had been authorized to give first aid and remove the casualty.

At H + 26, Dagobert Alpha came back on the air. He had ETA's for both sets of reinforcements—twenty and forty-two minutes, respectively. The medevac flight had reached the Med Center, and everybody who had been alive when the flight lifted off was still alive when unloaded.

He also had indications that the final assets group was airborne, but no composition, course, or ETA. Even through a scrambler, Edelstein sounded unhappy about that.

Shores didn't blame him. Marshals wandering around in your AO were a headache that a self-respecting brigadier-general didn't need. One needed it even less when there was a lot of other air traffic also wandering around tonight, one bloody mistake already chalked up tonight, and enough tension that a second mistake might start shooting too serious to stop easily.

At H + 34, word came from On High (the Navy, that is; it was Shores's experience that naval officers only sometimes confused themselves with a Higher Power) that two of the Coordination cruisers were under way at high speed. They were not being shadowed, but a broad-band all-ships warning was being sent out from *Roma*: any ships in the Linak'h system were urged to Jump out immediately, to avoid entering a possible war zone. If they could not do that, they should retreat to Jump distance at maximum speed and be ready to Jump if approached by a hostile or even unidentified ship.

There was nothing about putting the returning cruiser escorts on the tail of the Coordination pair. Shores wondered if this was the silence of security or of inaction— which might actually be the wisest course for Longman.

The incoming ships were unlikely to be Federation or even friendly neutrals; Longman had only minimal responsibility for the safety of anything else. Also, three more friendlies and two fewer—*unfriendly neutrals*—off Linak'h might damp the situation a bit more.

Nieg agreed. "Anything that buys us more time that we can use to find out precisely what is happening is welcome."

"Do we need precision now?"

Nieg stared into the darkness as he spoke. "It would help. Otherwise we might have to choose. Make inquiries to the Confraternity at an official, visible, nondeniable level. Or remain too ignorant of what is happening to be able to protect ourselves, let alone anybody else who may be relying on us for their safety."

Shores thought of the five hundred-odd Confraternity refugees crammed aboard *Somtow Nosavan*, "neutral territory" for now. She thought of her father as she'd last seen him, sitting in the *banya* while Ursula tried to shampoo what seemed an entire tree's worth of soot out of his hair, and talking cheerfully about the talents of some of the refugee children in art class.

She realized that Nieg was looking into the darkness in more than one sense of the term and had the decency to be scared by it.

"I'm going to visit the troop positions," she said. "Want to come with me?"

"I'd better see how the ID's on the bodies are coming." He frowned. "How far forward are you going?"

"Not far enough forward to risk capture," she said, and blessed the silence that replied. "When the next flight arrives, I can go back to being the Old Lady running a tactical unit in the presence of—call them potential enemies. Until then, I have to at least simulate knowing what's going on!"

Linak'h:

Seenkiranda lost track of time soon after she lost control of her stomach. They were out of the storm now but flying low and fast, twisting and turning to stay below the ridge crests and at times, it seemed, below the treetops.

This might spare them the fate of the ammunition carrier, while making them wholly unfit for combat when they reached their destination.

Whatever that was. Desdai had closed not only his mouth but his eyes, and put plugs in his nose. This was equally effective at keeping his stomach under control and keeping him silent. Once her stomach was empty, Seenkiranda was able to think clearly and acknowledge that her mate's need for dignity outweighed her need for information he probably did not possess.

They landed safely, after such a long and rough flight that before it ended a few Hunters were moaning that they would rather be shot down; it was a quicker death. Nobody had the strength to be more than rude to these, even after the ramps went down both forward and aft and fresh hill-night air rushed in.

By the time Seenkiranda had cleaned herself and started on her weapons, she saw that most of the disembarked Hunters were doing the same. Their helplessness in the air was ended. Their helplessness on the ground was ending as they regained their wits and fighting power.

Now, where was she?

The sky was still cloud-covered and the darkness nearly total—not a light showed anywhere. Seenkiranda thought she could make out the shapes of both tents and permanent warriors' quarters. A few steps told her that she was right—the tents new, with the Forest Guard badge on them, and the quarters old, with roughly patched holes in the sheet-alloy roofs, peeling weathercoats, and sagging doors and windows.

It looked like one of the old Warband camps hastily pressed into use during the Great Fire. That told her very little about where they were, as there'd been seven or eight such camps, all the way from the sea to the edge of the High Forest, at least two of them foot-march distance from Och'zem.

She was looking for a high place from which to seek the lights of the city when several sets of feet tramped up behind her in the darkness. Two wore Forest Guard clothing, two civil garb. All wore Confraternity armbands. Indeed, one of the civil-clad—a woman—carried a shoulder bag bulging with such armbands. She and her comrades also carried single-hands, and one of them carried a hunting rifle.

"Our senior wishes to see you," the rifle-bearer said.

Desdai spread his hands to indicate both peaceful intent and total ignorance. "Who is your senior, if that is a question I may ask?"

"You may. I do not—" the rifle-bearer said

"Oh, demons befoul your water," the woman said. "We come from Isha Maiyotz. Best this not be shouted aloud in the camp, but you have the right to know."

Seenkiranda looked at Desdai. *Best go and be done with it?* her eyes asked.

He nodded, then his shrug said, *I am as far out on a too-thin branch as you are.*

Seenkiranda fell in behind her mate, and their escort flanked them. As they did, she saw that one of the uniformed Hunters was not a Forest Guard. He was instead clad in the very similar forest-work Warband garb. All badges and marks of rank had been removed, but tunic, overtunic, trousers, and boots were all too clean to be cast-offs bought on the streets.

The noise of the camp fell behind them, but the sky rained thunder as a heavy flier passed the speed of sound. The other three flinched. Desdai did not, nor did the Warbander.

"Have the humans found us?" Desdai asked.

The Warbander looked up at a sky now silent again, as well as dark. "It might be so. We must talk with Senior Maiyotz before we can say if that makes any difference."

Aboard U.F.S. *Shenandoah*, off Linak'h:

All three flag officers watched in silence a recorded view of Forest Guard Camp Iguidannz (newly renamed after the senior Ptercha'a victim of the Great Fire) transmitted from the low-patrolling light cruiser *Weilitsch* by a relay through Mad Bill Moneghan's flagship *Cavour*. There was really nothing to say, and for once Moneghan's nimble tongue was under the command of his excellent brain.

Admiral Uehara finally broke the silence. "The estimate of the Ptercha'a strength seems high."

Moneghan's voice replied equably, "We had all sensors maxed and then added eyeball scans, both real-time and recording. We've come up with the same figure three different times."

There were a number of explanations of how there could be nearly four thousand Ptercha'a in the camp, and Rose Liddell really didn't care for any of them. Not when that mass of armed or at least armable Ptercha'a was within striking distance of Och'zem.

"We don't have any people left there, do we?" Longman asked.

Did your staff forget to tell you or didn't you ask them?

Liddell thought. "No. Our fire crews have all disbanded, and their southern assembly point was Camp Stogund."

"Which is completely deserted," Moneghan put in. Even on the reduced scale of a divided screen, Longman's glare was noticeable.

"I don't believe that required an overflight," Liddell said. "Slant-scan, Bill?"

"The best we could. Want an overflight now, Admiral?"

Longman's glare faded. It had been an overreaction but not pure bad temper. Longman could be quite legitimately concerned about overflights where the disposition of the Ptercha'a and the threat they could offer were both unknown.

"Do it with an attacker, one medium-altitude pass, and no watch unless you get a positive report *and* I give permission." Longman's words came out with the precision of etchings on glass.

This was cutting Liddell out of the chain of command, but the commodore was willing to chalk that up to nerves too. None of them were enjoying this waiting game—waiting, as Moneghan put it, "for the Pussies to take their dump or get out of the head." And adding to the strain the knowledge that some of the local factions would do neither, and those who finally acted would probably all do so at different times.

The conference call ended without anyone's mentioning the ground investigation of the shootdown. That small victory left Liddell in a better mood. Her display showed a heavy attacker burning sky with Tanz's team aboard, and no sign of anything coming out of 222 Brigade's base at Camp Great Bend. Of course, Kharg could use a regular lifter sneaking so low that it wouldn't show from orbit, but that would open him to a charge of negligent security or at least give Tanz a perfect excuse to watch him night and day—if Longman understood the situation well enough to give Tanz a free hand.

It was a pleasure to see Pavel Bogdanov's face on the screen again.

"Pavel, no changes worth mentioning. The Emergence is still unidentified, our own incomers are still safe, and the Coordination cruisers are still riding their hull limit. I'm going to try for a short nap."

"Aye-aye, ma'am. Shall I send up some administrative work?"

Liddell smiled. It was a standing joke between them, using administrative work as a sleep aid. Not that the Low Squadron was sufficiently autonomous to have as much as a detached force of similar size would have, but there was enough for its part-time staff and to spare.

"Fine, but no F & A reports, please. I want to be able to wake up if anything happens."

Linak'h:

Nieg disappeared into the restaurant to finish his walk-around of the ground at the same time as the first flight of reinforcements arrived. They were on time, at full strength, and sounding rather disappointed that there was no fighting and their position might keep them out of any there was. Candice Shores greeted the last sentiment with a total lack of sympathy that she refused to put into words only because calling people you had to work with that kind of names never helped.

Out of the next twenty minutes she spent two on the circuit giving orders and eighteen listening to them being obeyed, with minor and excusable exceptions. This gave her plenty of time to listen to Nieg's report of the Navy's attack of nerves about the Ptercha'a concentration at Camp Iguidannz.

"Is there any chance we can drive a bargain with the Administration—no unexplained troop movements, in return for whatever they may want the most? Assuming they'll put themselves in a weaker position by admitting that they don't have anything they need?"

"I see you're learning your way around the Ptercha'a," Nieg replied. "I suspect that's been thought of more times than we could count without taking off our boots. But the idea runs into practical difficulties every time.

"Besides, this mob may have nothing to do with the Administration. There's too many for it to be entirely Confraternity, but—"

"Why couldn't some of it be Forest Guard? It's a Forest Guard camp, after all." Shores saw that she had his attention in a way she hadn't expected. "I know that a lot of

Forest Guard reservists came back to Camp Iguidannz after the fires. How many did we see leave?"

"Some, but I admit fewer than we expected. Maiyotz said she wanted to organize the replanting and water-clearance teams while she still had everybody together."

"Isha Maiyotz is a Confraternity sympathizer who virtually asked me to keep her informed of Federation attitudes toward her party."

"Did you?"

"I didn't volunteer any information, and she hasn't asked."

"Yet."

Nieg pinched the tip of his nose between his left thumb and index finger, a gesture that was his equivalent of a screaming fit. A delicate situation was getting more so. Give official status to the suspicions of a coup and risk forcing Federation action that could make matters worse? Or look the other way and risk responsibility for a victory of the technically illegal Confraternity?

"We thought Maiyotz's Confraternity sympathies were purely social, or at least politically marginal," Nieg said. "Your hypothesis means—"

Shores waited until it was obvious he wasn't going to finish for himself. "It means that all kinds of marginal Confraternity sympathizers may be up to their necks in whatever's happening tonight."

He forced a smile. "I won't ask you to transfer to Intelligence, Candy. But I want to write this up as a classic case of new eyes looking over old data and finding something useful. I also want to talk to Banfi about this as soon as possible, preferably with you around."

ASAP in this case was indeterminate; Banfi was still in transit and not necessarily to them. The hypothesis was too hot to be sent over the com circuit, and Banfi's private list of Confraternity sympathizers in high Administration offices might not even exist outside the Marshal's memory.

The com alarm squeaked irritably. Shores gave a bite-switch acknowledgment.

"Ah, Huntress, this is Cumberland Four. We have movement in the Eighth Cohort positions."

"What kind?"

"Looks like a working party with heavy packs. That's

closest to their perimeter. I think we've got some people farther back moving into the forest. That's as far as we can track them with passive. Permission to go active?"

"Negative until I see what our air support can do. The Ptercha'a might be just nervous enough to react to active surveillance."

"They aren't the only ones, Colonel!"

"Don't be nervous on company time, Four, okay?"

"Yes, ma'am." The lieutenant was trying to sound crisp, but her voice came out hoarse.

Shores didn't really blame her. A Warband withdrawal from their forward positions could mean a general pullout. They could also be opening the distance between their own troops and the Federation's, so that they could freely employ heavy firepower.

"Keep an eye out for anybody bunching up or staying in the open too long," she said. "Otherwise watch our furry friends, and I'll get back to you as soon as I hear from the air corps."

"Yes, ma'am."

Linak'h:

It was some time before anything surprised Emt Desdai. He had expected the escort to move swiftly and silently. He was sure they were being taken away for a confidential discussion, which it was logical to hold in a secure, permanent, guarded building.

The guards at the door of what looked like the camp school were the same mix of Forest Guards and other Hunters as the four escorts. So were those lining the hall inside. At the end of the hall was an improvised office, with little furniture but much communications gear and several computers.

One of the pieces of furniture was a desk, with Isha Maiyotz sitting behind it. Standing behind her right shoulder, in the position of honor guard, was a Cohort Leader Second from Legion One-Five.

That was the first surprise for Desdai. One-Five was hardly a full Legion, but its number was no lie; its three Cohorts were the best trained of the whole Administration Warband. If a representative of these three thousand dedicated warriors was going to be present, it meant Administration—or at least Warband—interest in the proceedings of the Confraternity far beyond what Desdai had been led to expect.

Or what he found it comfortable to contemplate, either. "Interest" was a neutral concept. The results might not be so neutral. There were sympathizers with the Confraternity in the Administration's Warband, as there were on most Hunter-inhabited planets. It was another matter for them to learn the Confraternity's secrets.

Desdai reminded himself that under the circumstances it was hardly imaginable that the Warband would have them arrested and interrogated, even less so that Maiyotz would consent to it. Unfortunately this merely eliminated one possible cause for their presence here.

He decided that the moment was at hand for surprises.

"Greetings, Senior Maiyotz," Desdai said. "I am honored to be considered worthy of your attention."

The smile was barely detectable and might have been an illusion or a trick of the dim light. "Under the circumstances, I had no choice. Do you represent Payaral Na'an, Councillor and son of a senior in Simferos Associates?"

"In matters of chartering ships for Victoria, yes."

"In anything else?" Desdai saw the Warbander shift both eyes and feet, searching for a lie and ready to act if he heard one.

Desdai chose the truth as bringing him a cleaner end, if no more. "Officially, no. In fact, I am to observe the situation on Linak'h from many aspects, not only the commercial ones."

"I believe you," Maiyotz said, and the Warbander nodded. Desdai wondered if the warrior was capable of speech or moving any part of his face but his eyes. Even his ears might have been cast in plastic.

"I believe you," Maiyotz went on, "because there are rumors among the Confreres. Some say that you are spying on the Confraternity for Na'an. They do not call this spying for the Masters, or you and your mate would not be alive and free now.

"Also, there are those who believe another rumor, which makes you as precious as your weight in Fates' Eyes. It is that Simferos Associates is the heart of a coalition of Merishi wishing to recognize the Confraternity and thereby give to the Masters all the benefits of peace with it. Otherwise, it is said, humans or Baernoi will be first and the Merishi will end by being last."

Desdai had the distinct impression that the too-thin branch on which he had crawled out too far had snapped. He was falling, and the fall would go on until he reached the bottom of the universe and the end of time.

He stood with feet apart and hands clasped behind his back, and looked at the ceiling. Ropes of dust hung from disused lights, and smoke stains deepened the darkness in the upper reaches of the room.

He felt the light touch of Seenkiranda's fingers on his wrists, then cleared his throat.

"My first thought was to ask who had been saying this, that I might know if they had drunk too long or only of bad liquor. But then I realized that you might not wish to give names."

"We do not," the Warbander said.

One miracle: he speaks.

"Then I would as well do the same," Desdai said.

"If you can tell enough of the truth without names, you may," Maiyotz said.

Did she wish to hear the truth, or only support for decisions she had already taken and would not discuss with him? Guessing in such important matter had always seemed to Desdai rather like leaping into a fast-flowing stream that might contain rocks, but now he was already in the stream and the shore held known enemies.

Best swim as well as I can.

"I know nothing that would take this tale out of the realm of rumor. Indeed, I know nothing to suggest that Simferos Associates has any allies, or what the wishes of such allies might be."

The two at the desk remained silent. As anything besides going on would sound petulant, Desdai continued.

"Remember, the Governance of Merish and the Federation alike have tolerated everything short of Hunters openly ruling in the name of the Confraternity. As long as they need not deal with us under law, they prefer profit and peace to obeying their own edicts.

"Nor does the Freeworld States Alliance much honor that edict at all. If they have approached Simferos Associates, it might have emboldened them as much or more than any friendship from the other Houses and Associations. But I offer this only as speculation. I have no knowledge and doubt that Payaral Na'an has more."

A long silence, in which the two at the desk again stared at each other and Desdai considered whether he had given away too much. He decided that any Warbander fit to be a sixteen-Leader would have detected the Alliance's hand already in tonight's work, down to the very claw marks, and no Cohort Leader Second from Legion One-Five would be that kind of witling.

"So," Maiyotz said. "If we have no friends, do we have enemies? Of course we do, but where?" She picked a pipe from a rack in one corner of the desk, knocked the ashes into a carved-bone tray, and began refilling it.

"Suppose the Time of Power came to—Linak'h, let us say, and the Confraternity banner flew openly? The Governance might seek to suppress it, or at least assist the Coordination in doing so. What would Simferos Associates do in such a case?"

Desdai thought that much would depend on where the Confraternity banner flew. Many Hunters would not care to see it flying where it told all that the Confraternity now ruled and others only served. The old tale of Master and servant was best not repeated. The fewer Hunters content with Confraternity rule, the more force needed to impose it—and the more opposition it would face.

With forthright human opposition in the Federation Territory, the Time of Power would come to an end without Merishi or Coordination action. But if the seniors did not know that already, they were foolish, and if they were foolish it would take more than Emt Desdai to make them wise.

"I would say that if the Governance declared open war, Simferos Associates would be loyal. But they would oppose such a declaration up to the last moment, and might find allies.

"If the Governance made war on us only by aid to the Coordination, Simferos Associates would be free to act. What action they might take, and what allies they would find—I wish I knew. But I would wager much that they will not be our open enemies unless we act to make them so."

"I see," Maiyotz said. "Nor could their friendship be bought by favors to you, I suppose?"

"I am not a fool, and neither is Payaral Na'an," Desdai said, speaking hastily to keep Seenkiranda from saying something much stronger.

"I would not call you that, nor did I suspect your leader," Maiyotz said. "Very well. Leader, it seems to have been settled. You know what orders must be given better than I. Trees at least have no minds of their own."

The Warbander gave his style of salute and departed. Maiyotz now had her pipe drawing well, and she puffed it in silence for a while, making so much smoke that, pleasant-smelling as it was, Desdai was near to coughing.

"Neither of you has any Band duties tonight, do you?" she said at last.

"We both have Band assignments," Seenkiranda said.

"I mean oath-bound duties," Maiyotz said. "Or could I attach you to—call it my Assistants' Band, although it will actually serve several other seniors?"

"Not without keeping us from the fighting," Seenkiranda said.

"Maiyotz looked almost motherly. "Youngling, chances for battle will overtake you no matter how fast you run. It is the way of the universe. Do not think you need to stand still and let battle run over you like a misguided roadcar!"

Maiyotz actually seemed to have embarrassed Seenkiranda into silence, a feat Desdai would have sworn was impossible. "We accept your offer for tonight," he said. "Who knows? It may be a chance to meet Leaders Nieg and Shores again."

Maiyotz's pipe clattered on the desk and scattered hot ashes across several stacks of paper, setting the corner of one sheet on fire. She beat the flames out with a furiously wielded ash plate.

"Who told you that?"

"If you know as much about as you seem to, Senior, you will know how we have dealt with them in the past. Also that they are a curious pair, with depths unplumbed even by their own kind."

Maiyotz finished her cleanup and gave them a sour look. "For that I *should* send you back to your Band. But then, I suppose the same could be said of you two." She reached into her desk and pulled out a box. "Some dried holosh while we are waiting?"

Desdai almost gagged. His stomach had barely settled

from the journey before the stale air of the room had begun to work on it. "A hot drink would be honor enough, Senior."

Maiyotz tapped a button on her desk array. "Grahlis, hot sgai for three in my office, please."

Seven

Linak'h:

By the time the first flight of reinforcements was deployed to expand the secure LZ north of the river, Nieg had disappeared again. "Transmit some of our intelligence about the restaurant" was all Candice Shores could get out of him, although she appreciated the "our."

Nieg was just out of sight when she got reports of two incoming flights—one the second wave of reinforcements and the other five lifters with a friendly IFF signature but not responding to other interrogations. She told the first flight to land and deploy, added her own queries to the second flight and got no answer, then called up the air cover.

"Rendezvous and get a visual ID on the five," she said. "Then interrogate by visual signal or even fiber-link if they insist. Have somebody ride shotgun while you're in close, though."

That meant sending two of the heavy attackers of the air cover chasing bogies, and to make matters worse—

"Be sure one of the attackers has a good load of air-to-air non-lethals."

It turned out that nobody had any, which caused Shores to revise downward her opinion of somebody's staffwork. She had to let intercept-and-eyeball orders stand, though, because at that point she learned the Leader of the Eighth Cohort was trying to reach her.

Shores used up all the True Speech phrases in which she was fluent in the first three minutes, then switched to computer translation. Prestige was less important than speed and precision.

"We do not quarrel with the wisdom of a neutral zone between our units, in principle," she said carefully. "But in practice it would give you an advantage that I am sure you would be reluctant to give us. You have much more room to withdraw than we do."

In fact, Shores's four platoons would be swimming if they withdrew more than a hundred meters. The Eighth Cohort had nearly that many kilometers.

On one hand, cooperating in avoiding incidents. On the other, making her people a dense target, without even a securable LZ for evacuating them.

Play for time, Candy.

"I am the servant of my warriors, and my honor is in loyalty to them and care for their safety," she said, trying not to make the near-ritual phrases sound overblown. "I must guard them and my honor, unless ordered not to do so by one who has the right. Have I time to consult with such a senior?"

Computer or no, the tension in the other's voice came through. "Yes. But please do not delay. There has been blood tonight. When there has been blood some warriors always grow careless rather than cautious."

"I have no fear of that in you," she said.

"Nor I in you," came the reply. "But each of us commands many warriors, responding to we know not what. If their responses can do each other no harm . . ."

"You are wise as well as honorable. What my seniors allow, will be done."

Nieg did one of his materialize-out-of-the-shadows acts as Shores's operator started calling up Edelstein. "That was just right, Colonel. Were you deliberately playing for time?"

Shores nodded to the com operator to continue putting the call through, then led Nieg out of hearing.

"I think that requires an explanation, sir."

The darkness didn't hide a moment's indecision on his neat features. Fortunately the moment ended in speech.

"Playing for time is exactly the right thing to do. We're fairly sure now that a Confraternity coup is under way. The Eighth Cohort is the most reliable unit for suppressing it—Sirbon Jols's hand-picked people."

"Not so great a picker, considering what side some of them ended up on."

"They weren't so much for the Confraternity as against

involving humans. Military common sense, not political conviction."

"So the Eighth might be reliable for fighting Confraternity militia?"

"Yes. Or at least providing security to key installations. We think that at least a couple of cohorts of the Warband have gone over to the Confraternity. But they might not be willing to fight their way through the Eighth."

"Then—a war of attrition?"

"Exactly. One that could continue until the Coordination intervened, possibly at the request of people suffering from the chaos. At best, the Territory would be so battered that resisting the Coordination would be up to us—and Charlemagne still isn't interested in a lone stand in defense of the Territory."

"I see. How long am I supposed to—?"

"Orange Three to Huntress. We have a confirmation that the five lifters are friendly. Inbound to you, ETA four minutes."

"Who—?"

"Ah, Huntress, we've orders not to discuss that."

The circuit went dead, leaving Shores open-mouthed but speechless. Nieg looked ready to soothe her, then seemed to think the better of it.

Aboard U.F.S. *Shenandoah*, off Linak'h:

It took a bit more time and computer capacity to translate the display for Rose Liddell, but the commodore had the time and needed the help. She wasn't one of those rare people who could translate formulae into a comprehensive positional fix in her head. Pavel Bogdanov was, but he was busy.

So she waited under the security hood while her screen writhed in a kaleidoscope of raw colors, then suddenly cleared. *Shen* and the Low Squadron, Linak'h's surface, and the Och'zem area were all neatly arranged for her.

Her first reaction was relief, the first she'd felt since the report of troop movements in the Och'zem area and the evaluation of the movements as an attempted coup. (Maybe more than one, with fanatics in both the Confraternity and the Warband picking the same night and ending on a collision course.)

From where she was, guarding *Somtow Nosavan* and in secure communication with *Roma, Shen* hardly needed to move to command the Och'zem area. With only enough maneuvering to clear her sensor and weapons arcs, she could do anything from passively counting lifters and sex-ratios among the moving Ptercha'a to bringing down fusers on Och'zem itself.

"Met update," Liddell said. The visual display vanished; scrolling statistics and a map compiled from both satellite and ground data replaced it.

More relief. The wind in the southern Territory was rising. Low-altitude flight would be slow and rough, maybe too dangerous if visibility shrank again. Major troop movements outside the city might be forced up to altitudes where they could be detected even from orbit, then engaged by heavy attackers. The air-to-air non-lethals either hadn't been unpacked or hadn't been issued, but good attacker people could always improvise harassing tactics.

The only remaining question was who might need such remedial treatment.

Linak'h:

The Administrative District was legally part of Och'zem, but Och'zem sprawled even by Hunter standards. An arterial link of rail, road, fiber-optic, and power-transmission tunnels, and water and waste pipes linked the District and the Inner Circle of the City, slashing on its way through a belt of forest half a day's steady walking from side to side.

The clouds were creeping lower and the wind rising as Isha Maiyotz's improvised Legion of Fire Guards moved out. Seenkiranda watched the fliers of the scouts lurch into the air and wobble off into the night, as other Hunters lined up beside roadcars of all sizes.

In spite of the sudden chill in the air, she was sweating. Battle was one thing, war another, war against your own kind still a third.

To her surprise, Isha Maiyotz led the way toward four roadcars, heavy-wheeled models that could use unpaved routes. One sprouted an improvised but impressive communications array that seemed at every moment about to blow away on the wind.

Desdai climbed into the back of Maiyotz's own vehicle. When Seenkiranda tried to follow, she found four muscular Confreres facing her. One of them put a hand on her shoulder and turned her toward the third vehicle in line.

No doubt it made sense to divide important seniors among several vehicles. Did that make her an important senior? This was a night for the fantastic; perhaps so.

She had strapped in and reconciled herself to discomfort when the leaders' band started off. Heavily powered and lightly loaded, the roadcar was moving at a run before it left the parking area.

By the time it plunged into an aisle of trees, the pinging of gravel thrown up by the roadcar ahead sounded like a battle rifle in action. She could not tell the interval between cars, because everyone was moving without lights, except for the dim glows of displays in the cab.

An uncushioned bump sent them all floating toward the ceiling. A dip in the road slammed them all back in place. Curses as straps tugged fur nearly drowned out the motor-whine and the wheel-thunder.

Linak'h:

Three of the five incoming lifters made touch-and-go landings while the others flew high watch. Candice Shores kept her attention mostly on the airborne ones. If some incompletely briefed pilot strayed too close to the Eighth Cohort and drew fire, she was personally going to see that his anatomy was also rendered incomplete—if the Warband didn't do the job first.

Nothing happened, except that it was a good five minutes before Shores realized who had walked into her CP. Marshal Banfi, his aide Colonel Malcolm Davidson, and Marcus Langston were all sitting in one corner—waiting, as far as she could tell, for her to notice them and then die of heart failure.

Banfi wore a human-tailored version of Administration Warband uniform, with trousers instead of shorts (he was bowlegged) and the insignia of his Warband rank. His baton lay across his lap, however, which meant he was also here as a Federation Marshal.

Nice to have two high-and-mighties occupying the same body. It might get crowded in here, otherwise.

Davidson wore civilian clothes, with tartan trews and an elegant black jacket bulging with unconcealable concealed weapons. Langston wore a gray coverall, and his face was so nearly the same color that Shores's patience finally snapped.

"What are you doing here, sir? I thought you were still a civilian hospital patient?"

Langston chuckled. "You can agree with Nightingale Khan, because he's not here. But is it wise to question Marshal Banfi?"

Shores could make no sense of that reply, until somebody—Nieg, she suspected—turned up the light. Langston's coverall was Territorial Militia woodland camouflage battledress, with the black field insignia of a full colonel on either shoulder.

If Banfi wanted to make a man who should still be recovering from starsleep a militia colonel, he was obviously taking the bit in his teeth. Temporary light colonels would just have to go along for the ride and hope nobody's neck ended up getting broken.

Speaking of which—

"Gentlemen, I accept responsibility for your security." *State the obvious, when you can't think of anything else to say.* "But I assume you would like a briefing on the tactical situation before you decide whether to execute your mission from here." *Which should hide the fact that I don't have the faintest idea what mission needs these three particular people.*

"Certainly, Colonel," Banfi said. "Colonel Nieg, would you please help Colonel Shores?"

The look on Nieg's face settled any possible account with the man. She turned away to hide a grin as Nieg brought up the display.

The briefing took barely three minutes; Banfi's decision took no time at all.

"We stay here," he said.

"Marshal—" Davidson began,

"Malcolm, if you want to change jobs with Nightingale Khan, go on. Otherwise hold it."

Davidson threw Shores a martyred look but obeyed. Banfi continued. "With five extra lifters, we can evacuate, reinforce, or provide air support more easily than before. Also, Eighth Cohort will be happier to talk with me in the neutral zone than across the river."

That assumed there was going to be a neutral zone, but if a Marshal had made up his mind the question was hardly negotiable, at least with the Marshal. The idea wasn't unworkable, with certain precautions.

"We don't want all five lifters airborne for as long as this may take," Shores said. "So I'm going to shift my people who are north of the river around, to create a larger landing zone." She tapped coordinates into the display control.

"Do that," Banfi said. "But we'll want one more lifter permanently on high watch. Lifter pilots have ground-pounders' eyes, Colonel. Remember that, and put not your trust in attacker jockeys."

"Yes, Marshal," Shores said. "In fact, I was thinking about getting some genuine ground-level eyes into the cohort's rear. If we establish a neutral zone by shrinking the perimeter, we can free up Ram Daranji's Rangers. Then we can infiltrate them into the cohort's rear. We'll have to start soon—"

"We can start now," Banfi said. His eyes raked Shores, and his eyebrows seemed even bushier than usual. "Give the necessary orders, Colonel Shores, and Colonel Nieg can carry them, and no, Liew, you can't go with Ram and his merry band."

"Yes, Marshal," Nieg said.

Ram Daranji must have been anticipating something like this; he and his Rangers were on the pad for a touch-and-go pickup five minutes later. The other four lifters all made touch-and-goes as well; it was as much deception as the Federation forces could offer right now.

The actual insertion might take place with the benefit of decoys, diversions, jamming, and dumped bedpans. It also might take place entirely by stealth, reckoning that a lot of electronic and audible noise might attract more attention than it diverted. Either way, Nieg and Banfi would handle that phase, and as long as Daranji and his people were safe and Shores got her lifter back, she wasn't going to worry.

She was, in fact, unworried enough to be taking one boot off to check a foot for blisters when Marshal Banfi returned. A salute with one foot bare and the saluting hand full of boot took some managing, but the Marshal didn't seem to care.

"You would look better in Ptercha'a uniform than I do," the Marshal said. Shores decided that this was a purely aesthetic evaluation, nodded thanks, and went on with the blister inspection.

Banfi looked around the CP and saw no one within eavesdropping distance. "Colonel, I would like to use your CP com gear for dealing with the Eighth Cohort, but with my own operator."

"Who?" No, he probably wouldn't tell her. *Let's stick to the relevant.* "How long?"

"I don't know. This is a request, incidentally, not an order. I can establish my own communications by bringing one of the lifters over, but that will take time. I don't know how much we have to spare. I won't endanger your people, I swear."

Shore's gut reaction told her she was hearing the truth as Banfi saw it. How clearly did he see?

"Marshal, you can have the CP as soon as we have another lifter over here. I have to retain some C-cubed, particularly if anything you say is likely to get the Administration troopers excited."

"I don't know if it will do that."

So much for the omniscience of Marshals.

Banfi stood up and clasped his hands behind his back, then looked at the floor. "I have been discussing the situation with Colonel Nieg, among other people. We are fairly certain now that two coups are proceeding simultaneously, one Administration and one Confraternity."

At least Shores now recognized that she had a puzzle in front of her, even if she wasn't sure about all the pieces. "If the Eighth Cohort is the backbone of the Administration's efforts, you need to do more than keep it engaged here. You need to learn its strength and morale, so you can pass that information on to the Confraternity."

"You are in a confrontational mood tonight, Colonel."

"Marshal, it's your privilege to remove me from command. Or to ask General Tanz to order Colonel Hogg to do so. It's my privilege to consider the interests of my people as long as I command them."

"I was, and I was trying to prevent your removal from

command, not bring it about." Banfi smiled at Shores's confusion and went on.

"If the whole Eighth Cohort is here, Sirbon Jols and his allies are very thin on the ground. He may not be able to make his coup a *fait accompli* before the Confraternity seizes the Administrative District. Then other Administration forces may accept Confraternity authority. They are certainly likely to oppose Jols."

"Intelligence I collect here tonight is more likely to go to loyal Administration Warband seniors than anybody else. Informing allied commanders is not only legal, it's a duty."

"If it's so damned clean, why do you want me out of the circuit?"

"Because some of the intelligence may go to people who could pass it on to the Confraternity."

Shores thought *Isha Maiyotz,* and also thought that "may" and "could" were unnecessarily delicate. But Banfi was still talking.

"—under Clause Nine of Article Eighty-two, concerning 'aid to all parties contributing to the general welfare and public peace of Federation or friendly planets.' That may get us off. It also may not. But Marshals, Caledonian citizens, and retired-generals-turned-Militia-colonels are fairly hard to court-martial.

"You wouldn't be. In fact, you'd be a perfect scapegoat, if some of the things I suspect are true."

"Colonel Shores, I'd wager a good deal more than I ought to that you'll live to wear stars. This will be good for the Forces and the Federation. Why shouldn't I be prepared to sacrifice myself in a rearguard action? Your rear, to be precise?"

Banfi did not quite pat Shores. She did not quite move away. Instead, she was considering this sudden orgy of interest in her career. She'd wasted a lot of time suspecting Nieg; she didn't have any to waste suspecting the Marshal.

She put firmly into her mind the thought that neither Nieg nor Banfi was her parents. Even they had stabbed her in the back more by accident than by plan.

"All right, Marshal. I'll order the lifter over as a backup. But it would be helpful if I were on-line or at least on-call. The Cohort Leader has been talking with me, and I played on his notions of honor. If I dropped out of the negotiations, he might be suspicious."

"You have a point, Colonel," Banfi said. "Can you play back your recording of the first session?"

"Certainly." Shores raised her voice, to the two communications techs. "You can stop pretending you're not listening now. I want a lifter over here now, and our com net patched through it. I also want a playback of my talk with Eighth Cohort, for Marshal Banfi."

Aboard U.F.S. *Shenandoah,* off Linak'h:

On Commodore Liddell's screen, Admiral Longman looked ready to dig in her heels. Liddell decided to do the same.

"I repeat, Admiral. I can certainly attend a flag officers' conference at oh eight-thirty tomorrow. I can even move over to *Roma.* But I have to put Moneghan in a direct link with you and Tanz. Captain Bogdanov can't handle *Shen,* command the Low Squadron, and hold Mad Bill's hand at the same time."

"Moneghan's another Old Vic," Longman said. She let the silence grow after that, like a crystal in solution. Then she nodded. "You're the best judge of whether he can handle a situation that might become incredibly delicate at any moment."

What do you mean, become? was not Liddell's reply. She nodded in turn. "I'll have a shuttle lined up—"

"Attacker," Longman said briskly. "We'll send one over from the Seven-thirty-second. Rose, you aren't expendable. Remember that."

The screen went blank, though not, Liddell suspected, blanker than her own face. Fatigue made Longman even harder to understand than usual. Her own fatigue, that was—Longman was five years younger than Liddell and looked at least twenty years more resistant to sleep deprivation.

Liddell made her routine checks on tactical and ships' status displays and the regular call to Pavel Bogdanov, while Scherbakova whipped up a sandwich. Halfway through the sandwich (rolled smoked Kaloris on a bagel left over from the batch made for Admiral Uehara), Liddell decided to call *Somtow Nosavan.* If Joanna Marder was awake and coherent, a nice Old Lady to Old Lady chat might relieve nerves at both ends of the circuit.

Marder was awake, coherent, and obviously hanging on to her self-control with both hands and a couple of toes on the off foot. That blazed through her polite chitchat like a fuser in a fogbank, until Liddell finally took pity on the other captain.

"If you're wondering about the rumors of a Confraternity coup—"

The sigh of relief almost blew Marder out of her chair. It did produce a tousled blond head from under the covers of a bed just visible at the corner of the screen.

"Charlie, go back to sleep. Now, Commodore, you were saying something about coups?"

"What I can say over this circuit—"

"It's as secure as anything can be, Commodore. Your people so thoroughly rerigged it that we've been hitting the wrong switches for the last week."

"—or any other, is that *we're* up to our navels in rumors too. The one thing I can say and you can pass on is that nobody aboard *Somtow Nosavan* is going dirtside for a while. They're safer on board than they would be on the ground, and there's *no* way we guarantee anybody's safety aboard a shuttle."

"Some of them may feel they're deserting comrades," Marder said. Liddell heard in her voice the lingering survivor-guilt that Marder felt over being dirtside when the Alliance squadron died off Victoria.

"They can feel that until their hair falls out," Liddell said. "Sorry. I didn't mean it to sound that way, but most of them have already done their share for whatever cause they serve. The best thing they can do tonight is try to be alive tomorrow morning."

"You think it will be over then?"

"I can't see anyone being stupid enough to risk a long civil war that would just hand the Territory to the Coordination on a platter. If anybody is, the other side is likely to ask for Federation intervention."

Marder's face was yearning for reassurance that "the other side" wasn't the Administration. Liddell suspected that Marder's face mirrored her own. There wasn't anything either of them could do except pray, and tonight Higher Powers seemed a long way from Linak'h.

Marder blanked off courteously, and Liddell spent a perverse moment envying the other commander for having

Charles Longman—if only as a shoulder to cry on. The moment had just ended when Communications called up.

It had Brian Mahoney's voice, and for a moment Liddell was sure she was hallucinating. Then she remembered that she'd taken great care to have Mahoney returned to *Shen* as soon as the full-strength Navy communications detail was no longer needed aboard *Somtow Nosavan*.

"We have a message from Coordination cruiser *Lazti*, identifying the incoming ships responsible for the Emergence. It was direct to us, but we've recorded and relayed to the other flagships."

"Good work. Put it on Flag Three."

The display lit up and scrolled Anglic and True Speech texts, augmented by a graphic display of four ships. Somebody aboard *Lazti* had the soul of an artist—or a show-off.

Never mind the motives, they'd given her valuable intelligence. The incoming ships were four large Merishi freighters, chartered on behalf of the Coordination.

How large? Very, the *Jane's* File said. Not quite big enough to be Queen Bees themselves, but large enough to be hauling heavy cargoes, including heavy attackers, shuttles, and other CA-capable craft.

Check weapons capability.

That was somewhat reassuring—the heaviest weapons suite the ships could carry was no match for a Federation heavy cruiser. Unlikely they'd be used for CA'ing, when they'd be large, vulnerable targets. Figure them for cargo carriers, then, and go on from the premise that what limited ground campaigns at the wrong end of interstellar supply links was ammunition.

Unless you had time and the industrial base to produce it locally. The Coordination didn't, not at the rate a really major campaign would empty their dumps and overwork their factories. Cross-reference the maximum load of each of these ships with the known ammo requirements of the Coordination's fully mobilized Warband—

Liddell let out a silent curse. The ships coming in could substantially lengthen the time the Coordination could sustain a war. They already had a serious edge in ground troops; if every one of those troopers could go on shooting twice as long as before, the Administration faced being clubbed to death by sheer brute force even if it had notable superiority in tactics and morale, which it hadn't had before and might have even less after tonight's events.

"Pavel, take a look at these figures."

Bogdanov did, and one eyebrow twitched. The eyebrow, Liddell noted, now contained some gray hair. Pavel's hair was so light that one had to look twice.

"Is there anything we can do to keep the ships from unloading?"

"Any 'incident' big enough to destroy four ships would be impossible to pass off as anything except an act of war, and we're not at war with the Coordination. We have to think of political obstacles to using the ammunition, not physical obstacles to landing it."

"While we're thinking, Commodore, I've just had a message from Moneghan. *Weilitsch* reports small-scale CA operations north of the Bryzol Pass."

Liddell's display produced a map. "The route for the arterial to the Administrative District."

"Yes. He also reports definite signs of ground troop movements and some ground fighting. He can conduct low-altitude visual surveillance if he has to, but says everybody down there's likely to have one hand on a bottle and the other on a trigger, which is no place for honest Feds."

"I'm inclined to agree," Liddell said. "Have him put everything he picks up through to *Roma* as well as us. Also maneuver as necessary to stay out of ground fire, keep the pass and the District under surveillance, and watch the borders."

"The only border close enough to observe is—"

"I know. The border with the Merishi Territory. I rest my case."

Eight

Linak'h:

To Emt Desdai's left, battle rifles snarled. Rockets darted from launchers, orange fire-trails ending in flowers of flame. Desdai counted four explosions. He also counted the magazines left for his own battle rifle.

Not reassuring. It would not have mattered if being in Isha Maiyotz's band of assistants had kept him far from the shooting. But as Caribissalone had said in the first of the Equality Wars (the Hive Wars, as the humans called them):

"War fought defying gravity defies much else as well. One loses the power to predict where is safety and where is combat—or even whether combat may not be the safest place."

"Safety" did not seem a term for any spot in the Confraternity bands moving on the Administrative District. Some of them had faced actual destruction by interception in the air or heavy weapons once they had landed. Isha Maiyotz's own Hunters faced nothing more than an old farmhouse long since turned into a hotel and now vigorously defended by a party of whom some at least were District Guardians.

Desdai crept to the right, tapped Seenkiranda on the shoulder, and exchanged his rifle for her viewer. From under the upthrust root of a far-spreading tree, Desdai watched the corner of the hotel crumble. Smoke swirled up from the wreckage, and more from the roof where the rocket-ignited fire was eating through dry wood.

The main door opened, and three Guardians fell rather than walked out, one hand over mouth and the other raised high and trailing strands of vine or houseplant. That must be the closest that they could come to the traditional bunch of grass as a sign of surrender.

There'd been no choice for Maiyotz's band about joining

in the shooting. The Guardians' weapons commanded the site where the leaders had landed. There was no time to move and much danger from still-active enemy fliers— whoever the enemy might be.

Now that the fighting was done, though, it could be left to others to bring in the prisoners. Desdai kept his viewer on the scene as a pair of fours flanked the Guardians and searched them roughly but efficiently. Meanwhile, Seenkiranda was discussing with someone behind her the latest rumor—that three shiploads of human mercenaries in Merishi pay had been detected, coming in to suppress the Confraternity.

"—relying much on human unwillingness to shoot their own kind," the voice was saying. "Foolish of them. The only race more given to self-slaughter than the Hunters is the humans."

"Do not forget the Tuskers," Seenkiranda said. "But I think they expect us to win and the Federation to stand aside from the suppression of the Confraternity."

"May their young die of the bleeding bowels!"

"Ours certainly will, if we try to fight everyone at once."

Desdai groaned. It was becoming impossible for anyone with the wits of a scalpsucker to believe that the work begun this night would have no consequences off Linak'h. Indeed, he was one of the Hunters responsible for that circumstance, by answering when Maiyotz asked. At the moment Desdai felt like a warrior called on to swim in what has been called clean water but that turns out to be liquid ordure.

Someone lay down beside him, disdaining the cover of the root. It was another of those Warbanders without unit or rank badges or indeed much equipment at all save a viewer and a single-hand.

Desdai's patience with that breed had grown short. "Your faith in the Fates touches me," he said. "What if there are others in the house?"

"What if there are?" the Warbander—a woman of middle years, Desdai saw—said, with a casual flick of her tail. "I do not think any are ready to declare war on the Administration Warband."

"No, but they may be ready to shoot without seeing the uniform, a matter of some slight difficulty even for a Hunter's eyes when darkness and fear enter the picture."

"Do you always talk like Gatsh in *Koylan-Zu*?" the War-bander asked.

"Some shoot Warbanders by accident. I talk too much. Stop putting yourself in the way of accidents, and I will talk more briefly."

"Don't believe him," Seenkiranda said. She had to raise her voice, to be heard over a sudden outburst of firing from behind the house. "We have not yet been sworn a year, and already he has—"

"Whuuu," the Warbander said, raising a hand for silence. She seemed to be listening to something unheard by her companions, and Desdai noticed that she wore a light com rig with earplugs and throat speaker.

He crawled backward out from under the tree and, as soon as he reached the shelter of the road, stood up to brush leaves and dirt off his fur. As Seenkiranda joined him, the firing died again—except that as it did, golden light gushed up into the sky from below the horizon. It was long before the air-blast rumbled by, tossing branches and hurling more leaves down on the pair-mates.

"The battle grows," Desdai said.

"Do you know the case of Jara Glayn?" Seenkiranda said.

"Should I?"

"Perhaps. A woman was found not guilty of killing her pair-mate, because he was always stating the obvious."

Linak'h:

Banfi's communications team appeared at Shore's CP within moments. One was Murtag Singh, Edelstein's Intelligence Sergeant Major. He was large enough to make Shores feel dainty, had a beard bushy enough to stuff a mattress, and looked as if he bench-pressed light cruisers to work up an appetite for breakfast.

His companion was a female warrant officer small enough to ride on his shoulder. She was also equipped with a carbine, a wadgun, and a look Shores knew from associating with Jan Sklarinsky. Banfi's security seemed adequate.

Eighth Cohort's first request after the ceremonial introduction to Banfi was for Shores to appear on-screen. At Banfi's signal she complied, then had to sit through a long computer-translated query as to whether she had authorized Banfi's presence here.

The question made very little sense, unless the Administration officer knew more than the Feds had suspected about the human chain of command and was either trying to buy time for his own cause or cover his furry fundament in a case of negotiating with the enemy. Neither seemed likely; neither seemed impossible. Shores regrouped her knowledge of True Speech and replied.

"The Great Warband Leader is here to speak with you on matters that concern all the warriors of our races on this world. This is his right.

"In matters that concern only our own cohorts, you and I still may speak lawfully."

That exhausted her True Speech, but from Banfi's wink it seemed to be enough. She rose and walked out into the softly windy darkness, feeling an incipient headache recede and blood flow back to her limbs.

What she really needed was as much exercise as Ram Daranji and his people might be getting even now, stalking the Eighth Cohort's rear echelons, hunting the Hunters. They would have to be silent and slow, with long freezes, but they would be moving out to gather data with their own senses rather than sitting and waiting for it to be brought to them.

A two-seat ultralight lifter that Shores hadn't seen around before swept in over the pier and dropped its passenger. The passenger ran up the pier, handed something to a small figure who had to be Nieg, and returned to the lifter.

It was Nieg, and he brushed past Shores as if she'd been a public toilet, vanishing into the CP. Shores was on her way to her own command lifter to order a listening watch, pending Nieg's telling her what was going on, when he reappeared.

His face made his request to find a secure spot to talk superfluous. They finally picked a corner of the boathouse by the pier. It was empty, Nieg had a scrambler, and all approaches to it were under surveillance.

"Some of the surveillance is our Confraternity friends," Nieg said.

"Have they turned against us?" Her first thought was

that it would be too disgusting for words if Kharg and the human street brawlers turned out to be right.

"That has become a possibility. Boronisskahane is missing."

The name meant little to Shores. She was annoyed at the obscure reference, and even more ready to be annoyed if Nieg excused his not telling her by "concern for her career."

"Sorry. I simply forgot to put him in that briefing I gave you, on local Confraternity seniors. My fault. He isn't strictly local, but he is a very senior senior."

Boronisskahane was in fact one of the dozen or so highest-ranking Confraternity leaders on all of the forty-two planets with a Ptercha'a population. He was not a Linak'h native, but had come out nearly sixty Standard years ago, possibly in anticipation of just such a situation as was developing.

Tonight he had been on his way from the north to assume leadership, at least, at the Administrative District. It was currently held by the remaining Warbanders loyal to Sirbon Jols, thin on the ground but with plenty of heavy weapons, which they were using effectively against the lightly armed Confraternity attack.

"We think—"

"We, as in you and Banfi?"

He nodded. "We think Boronisskahane was coming south to be infiltrated into the District itself, and rally Confraternity sympathizers in the Administration. Right now, the anti-Confraternity forces are preventing any orders going out that would stop Jols's little coup. If some do go out, he may not obey himself, but he'll lose too much support to be a threat anymore."

"Which explains why Boronisskahane is missing?"

"Maybe. The Administration's airpower is minimal, but leaks can cut search time. The problem is, who leaked what?"

Shores mentally scrolled a map. She realized that she was biting her lower lip when Nieg frowned. "Exactly. He would be coming through Kharg's area. Kharg has—call them *conventional*—views about the Confraternity."

"Also, one Confraternity senior has already been killed by humans under ambiguous circumstances, and we nearly had riots then." Shores knew exactly how ambiguous the circumstances of Sogan Ba-Lingazza's death had been; it had been partly her call for fire support and partly his being where he really had no business being.

"Exactly, and now we also have a rumor that the incoming ships carry human mercenaries sent by the Merishi to suppress the Confraternity. Add the suspicion that we arranged the disappearance of the senior Confraternity leader on Linak'h . . ."

"Gaah." Shores's throat was too dry to form words. She reached for her canteen. The water cleared her throat and to some extent her mind. She gripped Nieg's shoulder, then headed toward her command lifter.

First move: find and fix the Confraternity people. Second: politely shift any who present a security threat. Third: bring them all in for a briefing from Nieg.

"Colonel?"

"Yes?"

"Message from the hospital. Everybody's out of danger. Sklarinsky's on her way back. Also, a squirt from Ram Daranji. DF'ed, he's on the ground. We're decoding now."

"Good. Copy Nieg in on the message."

"Yes, ma'am."

Nieg probably didn't have to be bribed for ordinary matters anymore. But finding out what he thought Banfi was planning wasn't ordinary; it was possibly life or death for her people.

Linak'h:

Seenkiranda and Emt Desdai reached Isha Maiyotz's leader post just before the three Guardian prisoners did. The Warbander who'd also watched with them the assault on the hotel came in only a moment later.

This made the back of the roadcar even more crowded than before. Seenkiranda's training in handling prisoners made her uncomfortable having them this close to Maiyotz, even if all three were disarmed, with wrists *and* ankles in bond-bars.

"Nothing will happen to you, no matter what you say or don't say," Maiyotz said. She sat down at a console, turned the chair about, and rested her chin on the back, fingers stretched up her gray-furred cheeks. "We do not wish blood debts dividing us when the time comes to fight the Coordination."

"We can avoid that fight," one Guardian said indignantly. "You know how. Tell your leaders that if Sirbon Jols had been allowed to arrange matters as he wished, by now we would have no quarrel with the Coordination."

Maiyotz smiled, or at least her darkening gums twitched faintly. "Young warrior, I lead here. You may earn honor and freedom even more quickly than you suspected, by telling me—"

The eyes of one Guardian rolled up in his head, and he reeled against a console. Lightly secured, it tipped and went over, unplugging itself. Its displays died, as the Guardian seemed to do the same.

Seenkiranda was ready to join the others rushing to help the casualty, when she saw one of the standing Guardians working his jaws furiously. She leaped on him, slammed him to the deck, jerked her single-hand free so desperately that the holster tore, and jammed the grip into the Guardians mouth to hold it open.

"Seenkiranda! What in Fate's name—?"

She didn't know who shouted that. It was still echoing around the cabin when the Guardian's eyes rolled up in his head and he went limp. She left the single-hand in place and pulled the upper jaw up, hard enough to dislocate it.

Three sets of hands dragged her off the body. This time the question came in Desdai's voice.

"Seenkiranda! You'd better have a—"

The Warbander stared at the corpse's open mouth, revealed as the single-hand fell clear. She pointed, not at the hollow tooth whose poison had blotched tongue and mouth a grim blue-black, but at a rear grip-tooth.

"I've seen those in the scouts. That's a burst microtransmitter. Good for position and not much else, but—"

"Position is enough, if it's yours," Seenkiranda said, twisting around to point at Isha Maiyotz. "Somebody wants you dead."

'The signal might not have—" someone began. Desdai cut the fool off with a sharp obscenity. Then all the Confreres were storming the door, half-dragging, half-carrying the last Guardian prisoner with them.

"Disperse, disperse!" Maiyotz shouted, as they burst into the open. Not all those in hearing seemed to understand, let alone obey. Seenkiranda let go her hold on the prisoner and snatched at the arms of two or three of the nearest laggards.

The sky howled in agony as rockets plunged down. Fire-trails scarred the darkness, then three of them ended in fire blooms.

The fourth finished its trajectory on the far side of the tree overspreading the leaders' camp. Fragments gouged bark and flesh. Screams joined the crackling of wood as the tree went over. More screams rose as the crackling ended in a tumult of metal being tortured out of shape.

"My thanks," Maiyotz said. She rolled over and stared at the smoke of the air-bursts now drifting away.

"They must have been using single-unit warheads," the Warbander said. "Greater effect with a direct hit, but not as much from an air-burst if they'd used a cluster."

Seenkiranda wanted to shake the Warbander. But the woman was already looking around for the nearest communications gear, ignoring a Confraternity warrior whose arm was leaving a pool of blood almost at her feet.

"I still think I ought to send GIRUN," she said.

"What's that, a love-gift?" Seenkiranda snarled.

"Ah—it's the signal for the Third Cohort of Legion One-Five to end the observation phase and begin open fighting against Jols's forces," Isha Maiyotz said.

"What does that mean?" Seenkiranda said, then realized how stupid she had sounded. Fortunately Desdai was smiling too widely to care.

"It means victory, love. The Warband is joining us. Jols will not be able to divide the Territory long enough for the Coordination to take advantage of it."

As the Warbander sighted a working communications outfit, fliers whipped by low overhead. A moment later light flickered beyond the trees. Seenkiranda recognized air-to-ground weapons ripple-launching.

She also recognized a monstrous explosion when it lit up the northern sky. She was already hugging the ground and Desdai impartially when the blast ripped through the trees, toppling another one, adding no casualties but more than a little confusion.

The Warbander seemed made of metal, as she darted to her goal. Maiyotz sat up and cupped her hands.

"My friend! I think GIRUN has already been sent, but

there is no law against sending it twice. When you speak, tell your friends to be careful with ammunition, both theirs and ours. We have no ships coming in with fresh supplies."

The Warbander nodded. Seenkiranda lay back with her head on Desdai's chest and looked up at the sky.

Victory? Yes, Legion One-Five's intervention would send a message to Jols's followers, and they would crumble by Father-rise. But the victory that came of that would be the victory of Isha Maiyotz and the Administration's own Warband, aiding the Confraternity. Not a victory for the unaided Confraternity, rallying the people.

It might not make much difference to the Confreres how they won. But it could make a great deal of difference in how they ruled the Territory afterward—and how long.

Aboard U.F.S. *Shenandoah,* off Linak'h:

Commodore Liddell had her screen split. One part was a satellite view of a stretch of the arterial in the Bryzol Pass. It was crowded with Ptercha'a making their way north to join the fighting around the Administrative District.

The other, another of Moneghan's special relays, showed the actual fighting. It was now almost all ground combat, hard to interpret even from twenty thousand meters with poor visibility making half the input from the thermal sensors.

There'd been a brief, savage exchange of heavy-weapons fire about half an hour ago. The attackers had suddenly opened up with both ground and air launchers, the defenders fired back with more vigor than accuracy, and eventually the defending weapons were suppressed or withdrawn.

Now the battle seemed to hang on ground strength, which gave the edge to whoever was bringing in massive reinforcements from Och'zem. Liddell had one channel continuously open for reports from ground observers in the Federation Zone, which was as close to Och'zem as any such observer could prudently be tonight.

Liddell wished she could send Prudence to Hades and somebody into Och'zem. What the devil, she would prefer a report from that Tusker thug Behdan Zeg to the present state of ignorance!

Meanwhile, she had an announcement for the Low Squadron. They'd been on Alert One for hours now. The odors of sweat and tension were beginning to wrestle the air fresheners into submission. She'd been hoping she'd be able to announce some decisive result, Governor-General Rubirosa's finally declaring that State of Emergency. Or *anything* except that they were all waiting for the Ptercha'a to figure out who was in charge.

The sound on the ground-fighting display died, and Captain Moneghan's voice came on. "Unh, Commodore, we have a situation here. No, make that a complaint. One of the Hunter leaders isn't happy about being overwatched."

"Which one? The leader in the Administrative District, or the one outside?" That was the shortest circumlocution Liddell could think of that didn't involve identifying either side.

"The one outside."

"Put him on."

"It's a her."

After that, Liddell was not surprised to see Isha Maiyotz appear on the screen. The slightly wavering image told of maximum scrambling, but didn't hide the Hunter woman's fatigue or earnestness.

Hardly a wonder she's tired. By Hunter standards, she's nearly a generation closer to the grave than I am, and I feel like a used wipe rag.

Maiyotz was brisk to just this side of outright rudeness. She did not like having so many sensors and so much firepower so low overhead, even now when those who followed her seemed to have the edge in the fighting.

"Before long, it will be worse. Those who have tried to seize the District from lawful Hunters will be fleeing. Our warriors will pursue and doubtless shoot. If there is fleeing, pursuing, and shooting in the air . . ."

Maiyotz's Anglic had been better than that in the mediacasts at the time of the Great Fire, but firefighting had been her life. Being the general of what was effectively the Confraternity army was something new.

"This is understood," Liddell said. "But we are not telling anybody else what we learn about your battle. We fear there will be more danger to all lovers of peace if we are ignorant.

"Also, where it is, our ship can watch not only your fighting but the borders of the Territory. We do not know what may happen if they are left unwatched."

"Respectfully, Navy Senior Liddell, that is not the whole truth," Maiyotz said. "The ship cannot watch the most dangerous border, that with the Coordination. Or what would be the most dangerous border if the four ships were not coming in."

Liddell tried not to look blank. "No border is safe if there are fools on one side of it, still less both."

"Which fools do you mean?" Maiyotz's claws were out, and she looked ready to bare well-kept teeth.

"Anyone who thinks to profit from chaos on Linak'h," Liddell said. She tried to remember whether the phrase "If the shoe fits, put it on" would carry the right meaning for a Hunter.

A long, silent struggle of eyepower ended with Maiyotz bowing her head slightly and pointing the claws of her left hand at her throat. That was a perfunctory apology, which Liddell decided to accept.

"No pardon is required when no offense was given," she said. "You seem to doubt that the Coordination is dangerous. Is it permitted to ask why?"

Maiyotz shrugged. "It is simple. If they attack now, you may have to fight them to save your own people, since the Administration's warriors have other business. At the very least, you will prevent those ships coming in from landing their cargoes, surely of value to the Coordination."

Liddell could not tell if Maiyotz was looking smug or not. She certainly had a right to. Intelligence or intelligent guesswork on the loads of those Merishi ships, plus a shrewd interpretation of what Federation doctrine would require if Linak'h became a war zone. The big merchanters would be warned off or at least kept under surveillance, and their precious cargoes made as useless to the Coordination as if they'd never left the Governance.

Maiyotz knew Federation law a little too well for Liddells' comfort. But then, any Ptercha'a of Maiyotz's age probably was a veteran of several inheritance cases, and anybody who could deal with Ptercha'a inheritance laws could probably sell bathing suits to K'thressh.

The optimum strategy for the Coordination right now would in fact be to sit this one out until a victor was declared. Whoever won would have only a tenuous hold on power; if they were Confraternity they might face the hostility of the Federation and Governance as well. Far easier to overthrow a weak Administration after the supplies were available and the Federation had perhaps begun looking the other way.

How to avoid that situation? Anybody who wanted to avoid chaos on Linak'h had to work to avoid it, and Liddell knew anything she did tonight could only be a first step. But—"a journey of a thousand kilometers," etc.

"We cannot abandon all observation of your battle," Liddell said. "But we can give the work to one of our attack fliers, as well equipped to observe but far less well armed. Leader Moneghan's ships will move to positions best for observing those we know to be enemies instead of those we hope will be friends. The attack flier will relay what it sees to his ships, and his to mine.

"Is this within reason?"

Maiyotz's words gave an enthusiastic affirmative; her face gave a more cautious one. That was as much as the commodore had hoped for, and faster. She hoped that her own expressions of gratitude would sound less ambiguous.

Offscreen at last, Liddell discreetly mopped her forehead. She'd just finished when Communications came on, with Brian Mahoney relaying Governor-General Rubirosa's proclamation of a State of Emergency.

"Recorded?" Liddell asked.

"Yes, ma'am," with an overtone of "What sort of fumblewit do you think I am?"

"Play it back on all-hands, for the whole squadron."

"Aye-aye, Commodore."

That wouldn't substitute for her own announcement, but it would buy her time. A State of Emergency gave Federation forces a good deal more authority for moving within the Territory, particularly to rescue Federation citizens. Between the ground party and dirtside friends, quite a few people in the squadron might be worried about somebody down on Linak'h; they could worry a little less now.

Linak'h:

Emt Desdai no longer felt like either a warrior or a leader's assistant. Instead, he felt more like a p'nris-herder in the middle of a stampede.

One-Five's fliers and ground scouts had brutally pounded

Jols's warriors. Maiyotz had her understrength legion of Fire Guards and Confraternity warriors ready to move into the District before the wreckage of the enemy's launchers stopped smoking.

Then the mob from the city arrived. They came by flier, they came on foot, they came in every sort of ground vehicle. They did not come by rail because the defenders' launchers had cut the rail just short of the Kos station in the pass.

They were not as numerous as they might have been, because straggling, exhaustion, and nests of hostile snipers in some of the houses in the pass had all taken their toll. Even after these subtractions, Maiyotz suddenly found herself with five thousand new would-be warriors, more than her whole previous strength. Most were armed, most were determined, few knew either discipline or field conditions. Desdai was not even sure that many of them knew what they were fighting for, other than what seemed to be the winning side.

Almost a greater worry were those determined Confreres who had expected to find Boronisskahane at their head, if not actually carrying the Confraternity banner that would fly over Administration House. Some had heard rumors of his disappearance, and they were ready to blame everybody from Isha Maiyotz to Merishi Space Security.

"About all that is likely to save us is that none of them are blaming the same enemy," Seenkiranda said, after they'd led one particularly loud band into position and fled with more haste than dignity. "Few of the ones they suspect are within shooting distance, anyway."

"We still need to soothe them," Desdai said.

"What about giving them a plausible story?' Seenkiranda said. "Boronisskahane was seeking to enter the District secretly, to meet with high Administration seniors and secure its peaceful surrender. Obviously he did not succeed. He may indeed be a prisoner or already executed. To rescue him or at least give him proper rites, we must overrun the District as swiftly as possible."

"Which means obeying Maiyotz's orders and cooperating with the Warband until the District is ours?" Desdai finished.

"Exactly so."

They spread this rumor among every band of new recruits they led into position, and even among those War-banders they found well forward. (Desdai felt more than a trifle guilty at lying to these warriors; they faced danger from both front and rear, as well as inward doubts that could hardly be a pleasure.)

Over what seemed enough time to bring the land from summer to winter (yet all within one darkness), order emerged from confusion. Three columns formed, each two or three bands wide. The vanguard of each one advanced, with Warband fliers and snipers protecting flanks and engaging the few enemies who showed themselves. Warband communications teams also marched with the vanguards.

When each vanguard reached an agreed-on position, it halted. Warband scouts moved out, studying the best position for the next halt. Sometimes fliers dropped teams of selected warriors, both Warband and Confraternity, on these "halt lines." Then the whole ponderous mass of ground fighters would roll forward again.

Isha Maiyotz now had enough assistants to command three Legions. She sent people like Desdai and Seenkiranda forward with the vanguards, to be sure of having trustworthy eyes, ears, and mouths within sight of the actual fighting. Seenkiranda now had a battle rifle; Desdai had a bomb launcher and a single-hander. It seemed polite at least to appear as if they were ready to join the fighting, even if their orders were to watch rather than shoot.

Such orders meant nothing when they came to the last halt line, in a garden two hundred paces from Administration House. There snipers in the trees were making life difficult for anyone who wanted to cross the open ground between the fountain and the walk leading to the House.

"Launchers up!" came the cry. Desdai decided this meant him, and Seenkiranda decided that where he went she would follow. Both ran to take cover behind the hedge around the fountain, and Seenkiranda raised her viewer and began looking for a safe spot to direct her pair-mate's weapon.

Then Warband fliers slid out of low clouds, four of them breaking into two pairs as they descended. Their heavy-weapons racks were empty, but two had turrets and two more had their rear and side doors open and filled with armed warriors. Streams of fire darted from the sky into the trees on either side of the garden.

Branches, twigs, leaves, and half-ripe fruit fell like hail. One sniper's ammunition exploded, and his sheltering tree became his torchlike pyre. Desdai darted out of cover, Seenkiranda behind him, and they sprinted for the next fountain.

They kept firmly to the center of the garden, to avoid being hit by the fliers, and also kept their eyes firmly ahead. So neither had looked behind them when they reached the next fountain, nor did they look behind them until they were ready to move on to the last.

When they did, they saw what looked like the best part of a cohort strung out behind them, stretching out of sight into the shadows. The Warband fliers were hovering just above the tattered trees, somebody shouting from the rear door of the nearest one.

Desdai grabbed the nearest half dozen Confreres and declared them messengers. One was to go back to communications and report that Warband Desdai was approaching Administration House. A second was to find anybody who had reliable explosives and could be trusted to blow open the House doors. The rest were to stay close to Desdai in case there was anything else he needed.

"A Confraternity flag," Seenkiranda whispered. "We don't have a flag to raise over Administration House."

Desdai looked, and from the look his mate returned he must have rather resembled one dying of a crushed brain. *A Confraternity flag* was echoing in his brain—uncrushed, but with no room for anything else.

A dozen of the secret books of the Confraternity and as many more lawful dream-tales spoke of this climactic moment of the Time of Power. They all spoke of a Confraternity flag.

None of them were going to help Emt Desdai, appointed by the Fates as chief scout for the Time of Power, conjure a flag out of thin air.

He sent out more messengers, but they had barely left when the explosives team came up. They looked like two brothers and the son and daughter of one, all seasoned by Legion or mining experience, with their loads on their backs and single-hands or hunting weapons slung in front.

Desdai decided that he had enough of everything ready to hand, save time to wait for a flag to appear. He resisted the urge to strike a pose on the fountain wall, and waved a hand toward Administration House.

Then he had to run, to keep ahead of those followers who would gladly take his place as leader.

The next thing he knew, he was standing well back as one of the explosives people thrust in the last fuse and set the timer on the whole pack wedged under the House doors. The fuse-setter ran, everyone for a hundred paces around either flattened themselves on the ground or were pulled down by those with more good sense than urge to watch history be made, and the packs went off.

One door flew completely clear and crushed a stand of ornamental bushes under its mass of bronze. The other door dangled like a drunk holding to a lamppost. Smoke swirled about the facade of the House, hiding the whole center section.

Again remembering dream-tales, Desdai half-expected a desperate charge out the door by Sirbon Jols's Warbanders. The enemies of the Confraternity were always supposed to sell their lives dearly at the last, and Jols was certainly molded in the tradition of warriors who did that sort of thing.

It also occurred to Desdai that the concussion of the blast had probably knocked all the would-be death-chargers flat on their tails. If the Confreres behind him could be persuaded to let tradition go fly and follow him up the stairs—

A flag waved from a broken window materializing out of the smoke. Desdai thought at first it was white, the human color of surrender, and that Administration House was being yielded by a human.

But lights from Warband fliers came on, scouring every bit of shadow from the battered facade of the House and showing the flag to be yellow, the Hunter color. Desdai stood up, feeling rather as if he had been carrying a loaded flier on his back without noticing it until now, when it took off and let him stand like a living being instead of a hero-statue.

One of the messengers led a handful of Confreres up to Desdai. "Where is Boronisskahane?" one of them asked.

"I do not know,' Desdai said. "The sooner we secure the Administration House, the sooner we are likely to find him or someone who knows where he is."

The speaker stared long and hard at Desdai. He tried to

do the same at Seenkiranda, who rested a hand on the butt of her battle rifle and met him stare for stare. Then he pulled a small cloth-wrapped bundle out of his belt pouch.

It was such a Confraternity flag as Desdai had never seen in any tale. It might have been someone's old work tunics, sewn together and colored with vegetable dye, then hand-painted. It lacked dignity. It lacked much else, except being of the proper design—red-bronze field, green circle, five black hands clasping one another on the circle—and being the only flag available.

Another of those dream-passages ended with Desdai holding the flag in his arms, while Seenkiranda pulled down the Administration flag from the pole atop the House. All around on the roof stood armed Confreres, weapons at the salute, heads raised.

Then their weapons cracked, rattled, and banged enough for a small battle, as Desdai bent on the flag and Seenkiranda raised it to the top of the pole. Twelve heights above the roof, it stood out in the dawn breeze—definitely dawn, that was not fire or battle on the western horizon.

The Confraternity flag. By whatever circumstances, it now flew over a land of the Hunters. And oh, yes, one more small matter.

"I, Emt Desdai, lawful Confrere, proclaim the Time of Power in the Administration of Linak'h, before these witnesses and shown by this flag."

That was as much as he could remember of the formula. So it did not matter that moments later the Father-rise glow vanished as if a shutter had been closed, and it began to rain.

Linak'h:

A lifter rose from the parking lot. Candice Shores sat on a bollard of the pier and watched it vanish into the dripping gray skies.

It was Administration Warband, with the Confraternity trefoil of bronze, green, and black hastily painted on bow and either side. Probably the one sent for Drynz and the other Confraternity Hunters who'd sat out the night of the Time of Power in what might politely be called "protective custody."

They hadn't been particularly happy at first, and it took Nieg and Banfi together to talk them into giving up their infantry weapons. (A body search for single-hands and knives was something no human was prepared to contemplate.) Then they were at least polite, with Drynz leaning on some of his more hotheaded colleagues.

Happiness had to wait until the news of the flag-raising over Administration House. When that came on the mediacasts, for the first time in her life Shores saw Ptercha'a weeping for joy.

What the Ptercha'a were seeing, not for the first time, were humans in a state of terminal confusion. Except for Banfi, who looked like nothing so much as an old alpha male predator seeing a young rival come to a sticky end, and Nieg, who looked as if he was mentally crossing his fingers and toes.

"Hello."

"This is getting ridiculous. All I have to do is think of you and there you are. No footsteps, no warning, even in daylight. Can you teleport, Liew?"

"I've never tried." Nieg sat down on the pier and leaned back against her knees. "Boronisskahane has reappeared. He was shot down, but crash-landed safely. He won't be taking office for a few days, and if he waits too long he may not do it at all."

"Who will be heading the new government, then?"

"Right now, it's a committee, with Isha Maiyotz as chair."

"A government run by forest rangers? That's absurd!"

"Is it? You've met her."

"True. Sorry. I'm too tired to think straight."

"We can both crawl in after you answer one question."
This is the Hades of a time for a proposal.

"Banfi is forming a Political Advisory Committee."

"His own idea?"

"I detect Admiral Longman's influence. She probably wants to come as close as possible to bringing him into the chain of command without actually doing so."

"Sensible of her, under the circumstances."

"Or sophisticated arse-covering, which I admit can also help others besides the arse's owner."

"Is the question a long one? The buildup is."

"Banfi wants an experienced field-grade ground-pounder on the committee. He is looking for volunteers."

"Try Colonel Olufsdottir, First/222. She has a top-grade XO, and she and Kharg don't see eye to eye. Taking her out of his reach would be a favor to her."

"I see. Is she possibly too prejudiced against Kharg?"

"What is 'too prejudiced'?" Shores frowned and lowered her voice. "Did Boronisskahane—?"

"Only because he went down in 222's AO. There are grounds for suspecting Kharg, but also a good many others. We'll have to investigate discreetly."

"Investigate, and see who tries to sabotage the investigation?"

There was no answer, and looking down, Shores saw that Nieg had fallen asleep leaning back against her legs. She rested a hand on his sleek black hair and thought of picking him up and carrying him to a bed in her command lifter. But his dignity and her muscles would both fail that test.

She sat quietly, listening to the plash of water and the distant whine of lifters, until Jan Sklarinsky came out of the restaurant to provide security.

Nine

The news from Linak'h was couriered swiftly and far.

On Charlemagne, the Federation accepted the Confraternity Time of Power as either a fait accompli or the lesser of two evils, depending on which spokesperson or mediacrat one listened to.

Behind the scenes, Admiral Baumann approved Longman's Political Advisory Committee as long as it was renamed "Civil Action Advisory Group." She also approved Longman's apparent plan to divide the Linak'h Task Force into three squadrons, each capable of going independently into action at once.

Admiral Kuwahara divided the staff of the Dual-Sovereignty Planet Study Group into two sections. Captain Fraziano would head the one handling everything but Linak'h. Captain Ropuski would handle Linak'h, under Kuwahara's personal direction.

On Victoria, President Gist held a press conference. He hinted strongly that it might be in the interests of Victoria to send military as well as civil assistance to the new Administration on Linak'h. They and the Victorians had common enemies.

On Merish, two senior Councillors of Simferos Associates met, Dollis Ibran and Payaral Na'an's father Zydmunir Na'an. They agreed to put more ships than ever at Payaral's disposal and discovered that they had an unexpected ally.

A certain highly placed widow in another consortium had a companion named Ezzaryi-ahd, who had helped save *Somtow Nosavan* from hijacking on the way back to Linak'h from Peregrine. Now Ezzaryi-ahd had vanished, possibly at the hands of Space Security. Would Simferos Associates join in the search for her? It would be made worth their while.

The Councillors accepted the alliance.

On Linak'h, even before courier ships had reached the more distant worlds that were curious about Linak'h's fate, Isha Maiyotz announced an election. The voters of the Territory would have the chance to say whether or not they wished to be led by an Administration in which the Confraternity was represented.

"There has been a time for warriors, and there may be such a time again," she said. "These days, however, are the time for clearheaded Citizens.

"I appeal to you as such. Consider, vote, and expect that this Administration will abide by the verdict of your vote."

When news of the planned election on Linak'h reached Charlemagne, Admiral Kuwahara was at lunch with Admiral Baumann and Foreign Minister Aung Bayjar. They had been discussing the discreet investigation of the Bureau of Emigration, aimed at discovering who might have known about the inability of settlers to emigrate from Peregrine and the shadowy worlds beyond it.

This would not necessarily be guilty knowledge. It might be years before the guilty were identified and punished or at least discouraged from repeating their actions.

Then the bulletin about the election arrived. Kuwahara knew enough German to know that the Empress was describing Isha Maiyotz in distinctly unflattering terms.

"This may prove wiser than I admit it appears at the moment," Aung Bayjar interjected.

"Any positive quantity is greater than zero, I admit," Baumann snapped. "But—"

"No. If the Confraternity wins, at the very least many of the questions over Banfi's and others' work with them will be less pressing. If the Confraternity loses, it will at the very least remove the major reason for the Merishi pushing the Coordination to invade the Territory. Without Merishi pushing, peace might break out at any moment."

"Your faith in the Millennial Merishi Plot is touching," Baumann said. "But suppose the Confraternity loses the election and somebody like Boronisskahane proclaims that the humans intimidated the voters?"

"Then we put Boronisskahane back in the hospital," Bayjar said.

Baumann threw him a grossly unappreciative look. "We'll have to cut orders to make our neutrality as ostentatious as possible, without actually endangering security or stopping training. I suppose Max still owes me a few favors."

"Ah, were you—?"

"Involved on the occasion that won him the name? No, but two housemates were. Let's just say that the mightiness of General Szajkowski is not generally in his mind. He might still grow up, though."

"I doubt that," Bayjar said. "But if working with Confreres becomes legally clean, he may dream of a baton again. Warriors have risen to great heights in the grip of such a dream."

"A few of them have also sunk to great depths," Baumann said.

On Petzas, Fleet Commanders Eimo su-Ankrai and F'Zoar su-Weigho met and agreed to recommend reinforcements for Linak'h, while acting on the assumption that these would be approved by sending the first wave at once on their own authority.

Petzas was a long way from the bright heart of the Khudrigate, and there was not a Fleet or Host commander in light-years who would refuse to listen to the two. No one ever faced the axe over the dispatch of one shipload of weapons and a dozen junior commanders, half of them Assault Force veterans who hardly expected to die in their own beds anyway.

Nor did goldtusk Governors commonly make alliances with such a motley crew, least of all against Inquirers whose work might make such a Governor's name shine brighter than his tusks!

On Merish, messages were loaded aboard courier ships and passed at parties and meetings in a dozen great houses.

On Victoria, Alys Parkinson arranged to disguise an expeditionary battalion as two companies (each doublestrength, with its own weapons section) plus a support group (which held not only supply, transport, and medical units but a reserve for the rifle companies).

Jeremiah Gist celebrated this coup by taking Parkinson to bed, then formally proposing. She said yes.

Payaral Na'an hoped the ships from his father and his

father's unknown friends would hurry. He wanted to discreetly study their suitability for transporting humans. Meanwhile, he would use discretionary funds to contract from local manufacturers some of the necessary equipment for converting the ships if they needed it.

That would remain within his budget, reveal nothing to Space Security (like mites in a blister, not fatal but impossible to ignore), and create goodwill among the Victorians.

Na'an hoped that a combination of goodwill among the Victorians and a Confraternity victory in the Linak'h election would clear his record legally—or at least keep Space Security from looking at it too closely.

On Chadl'hi, Ornyng, and Pek, orders went from the Warband Council of Seniors to Legion commanders, then within the legions. Other directives went spaceward, to Hunter ships in orbit or in-system.

On Chadl'hi, an old Hunter Warband Leader stared past all the other souvenirs of old wars at one in particular. It was a flat picture of the Confraternity banner flying over a ruined wall, with a score of figures slumping in afterbattle weariness before the wall.

Not all of those figures were Hunters. The old Hunter did not look at his own image; he did not care to be reminded of how little it resembled what he saw in the mirror each morning.

Emilio Banfi was another matter. If the comrades of that day had kept their oaths so far, it was in Banfi's hands whether their efforts had been wasted.

Good hands, too. And if they had somehow contrived it that Boronisskahane was in the hospital instead of the Senior Administrator's office—here was one warrior who would declare no feud over it.

Isha Maiyotz was something of an unknown quantity as to her ability to deal with humans. Boronisskahane was no mystery—and no Hunter to be given the task of working with any human, even one whose soul had the fur and tail his body lacked.

On Linak'h, it was a bad time for those of any race who did not like political speeches. At times it seemed that the mediacasts in the Administration held nothing but political news and coded military messages.

Some occupied idle time with recreational sex (Davidson and Nalyvkina), recovering from battle damage (Morley and Franke), or in workshops with the door shut (Nikolai Komarov, while his wife, Ursula Boll, tried not to fume in the presence of the children).

Others had no idle time—Emilio Banfi and the Civil Action Advisory Group, Candice Shores and the QRF (now the Third Battalion/Linak'h Brigade) that she was pulling into fighting trim, Liew Nieg and the covert-action people he was trying to keep out of the election, and anybody in the Navy, on the ground or in space.

Then it was Election Day.

Ten

Election Day, 1430. Aboard U.F.S. *Shenandoah*, off Linak'h:

Rose Liddell swung her eyes from the screen on the right to the printout in front of her and then to her chief of staff on the left. The movement brought twinges to her neck. The last three weeks had abundantly exercised her *sitzfleisch* but not much else.

The screen showed a shuttle undocking from *Somtow Nosavan*, rotating, then sliding away toward a reentry trajectory. It was the last of twenty-three shuttle flights that had unloaded the Victorian merchanter's Ptercha'a refugees and their supplies and reloaded her with human consumables. Passengers and cargo might be waiting on the ground; hauling them lay between *Nosavan's* credit account and the civilian shuttle owners.

Liddell skimmed the printout. It was a meticulous record of all but the last shuttle flight, stopping just short of the passengers' blood types, hair colors, and sexual orientations.

"All right. I recognize somebody trying to make a case. You, *Nosavan*, or the shuttle boss?"

"All three of us," the chief of staff said. His name was Lomo Fitzroy, and he was small, bearded, self-effacing, and a total master of every form of staff paperwork. Just as well, because in his three weeks aboard *Shenandoah* Liddell had yet to hear him speak more than two consecutive sentences.

She pushed the printout back across the desk. "Case made. I would have liked the people down faster, but I've confirmed that the camp was short of food."

"Yes. Hunter children on one meal a day would not have helped keep the peace."

That was the longest sentence Liddell had heard from Fitzroy-Khan. It also confirmed that he was one of the Federation Forces people who would have preferred to use the term "Hunters" for the Ptercha'a, if it hadn't smelled of Confraternity sympathies.

Such people were now coming out in the open in strength and were unlikely to go back into the shadows on the orders of mere superior officers. Another fait accompli to the credit of the Linak'h crisis.

Liddel switched the screen display from *Nosavan* to Incidents. That file was still mercifully short, for seven hours of voting in an election that might decide peace or war for more than one planet. Eight incidents now instead of six, but all of them the same kind—shoving matches, electioneering too close to the voting sites, unregistered voters who had to be asked to leave—plus a few minor outbreaks of graffiti.

Barely one an hour. Of course, nobody knew the progress of the voting—one advantage of a low-tech election, instead of an all-electronic pushbutton one where the files were never as inaccessible as the program designers claimed. Partisans on both sides probably still hoped to win peacefully, and certainly both sides feared either Federation or Coordination intervention and the Territory's becoming a battleground if they tried to sabotage the election.

Both sides also probably had plenty of fighters waiting in the wings, ready to go into action if the election went against them. Today might stay peaceful. Tomorrow could turn bloody even before the victors' hangovers wore off.

"Status report on our ground parties, please."

A map came up, with markers for Navy ground parties sprinkled across it. Fitzroy split the screen, and on half of it the TO & E's of the ground parties sprang to life.

"Gamma Yellow is still in transit," Fitzroy said. "I've shown its destination."

"The human refugees?"

"Exactly."

"No danger of intimidating the voters?"

"Tanz and Rubirosa didn't think so."

Liddell hoped that General Kharg had been consulted and his endorsement obtained. His brigade's AO still included the major refugee camps, but that was scheduled to change in five days.

The official word was that Edelstein's brigade was now sufficiently Linak'h-oriented to be able to expand its AO. Unofficially, nobody wanted Kharg in charge of the refugee camps any longer.

Liddell suspected a Ptercha'a opinion on the subject, conveyed through Marshal Banfi. She knew that the landing of the refugees was the result of Administration claims that keeping them in space until after the election would be unhealthy and also imply lack of confidence in a peaceful election.

Another display Liddell couldn't recall having seen replaced the TO & E's. She raised eyebrows as it steadied.

"Bit generous with the extra supplies, weren't you?"

"We had them to spare, More supplies than storage space, in fact."

Liddell resisted asking for proof of that. It would undoubtedly be available, also irrelevant.

"Was that your only reason?"

"Our ground parties are going to be the best-armed and best-oriented humans in several key positions during the 218 Brigade takeover. I thought they ought to be self-sufficient as well."

Amazing how much Confraternity sympathy one could show by moving a few hundred crates from storage compartments to ground dumps.

She wasn't surprised at Fitzroy's taking this sort of initiative. Longman's overinflated staff might have started off as a way of paying professional debts. Now they'd been distributed among all three flagships and Linak'h Command HQ, and nine out of ten were pulling their weight and more. Any intolerable duds, Longman had to be keeping aboard *Roma* or persuading to take up nude spacewalking.

The Golden Vanity wasn't any nicer than ever. But now Liddell had more confidence that the unniceness wasn't a pose to hide lack of confidence or skill.

Election Day, 1455. Linak'h:

First Lieutenant Olga Nalyvkina had seen the Navy shuttle on final approach as she undocked from Gold One. As she entered her own final approach, she saw a converted light attacker with Civil Action markings join the stack just behind her.

Then reflexive concentration took over. The autopilot was the primary control, balancing lift field, drive fans, wind, weight, and other vehicles. The tower control was secondary. She was only backup, but she would be needed *fast* if she was needed at all.

The gunship settled down on its designated pad number without the lieutenant's hands touching the controls. The field died, the fans spooled down, and her backseat passenger started unstrapping.

"Thanks, Lieutenant."

"Anytime."

Nalyvkina thought Elayne Zheng smiled at that, or even leered. But that was probably doing the older woman an injustice. She only *seemed* to be an android, programmed for electronic warfare and sex to the exclusion of everything else.

With a wave, Zheng vanished toward HQ, the recorded data from Gold One's surveillance flight off the west coast of the Southern Territory in her other hand. Nalyvkina knew she should head for debriefing; the CO was a bit obsessive about that, even when your flight was a twenty-minute courier run almost straight up and then back down. Rank Hath Its Passions . . .

Instead she pulled off helmet, cap, and headband, and unfastened the wrists and neck of her flight suit. Today she'd logged just over three hours in two flights. Yesterday it had been more like ten, nearly all at low altitude, and the sweat-irritated chafing hadn't nearly gone away.

A single glance toward the cloud-specked zenith showed her five liftcraft just in the space over the base. Highest was Gold One, climbing away toward her normal twenty thousand meters—delicately, so as to avoid sonic booms.

That was the one new rule for today—no supersonic speeds without orders. On the ground, boom-bombing might be called harassment.

"What about all the flights being called intimidation?" she remembered someone asking at the Father-rise briefing. (At that point, her breakfast omelet hadn't decided whether it was going to allow itself to be digested.)

The CO must have had a better breakfast or maybe a

quick trip to the heads to get rid of it. He shrugged. "We may be accused of intimidating the voters. If terrs get through and shoot up a line of voters, we *will* be accused of not intimidating the bad guys. The orders are to be quiet, not invisible."

And speaking of the non-invisible—

Malcolm Davidson was climbing out of the Civil Action courier, larger than ever in flight gear. A case chained to his left wrist handicapped his gestures as he talked briefly with a welcoming party. Then he turned in her direction, his grin widened, and he was striding toward her.

Conscious of the number of eyes around, they did not make themselves ridiculous. Also, the case handicapped Malcolm's embrace. Her forehead still seemed to tingle pleasantly after he brushed it with his lips.

"I saw you coming down from Gold One. Was that the recon flight south?"

"Where's your need-to-know?"

"Those recon flights are probably logged in a computer on Baer by now, they've been going on so long. As a matter of fact, we rather hope so. We and the Tuskers have a common interest in the Coordination's keeping a low profile in the south."

That was less than discreet, and she refused to believe that Malcolm Davidson would be indiscreet except by direct orders. His passion was real; his professionalism never lost control of it.

"I only docked and picked up Elayne Zheng and the data."

"Good."

"Being the protective male?"

He turned her so that his body shielded her from the spectators and rested a large hand on her shoulder. "No male here."

"Only the best Farsi silk."

"Is that what it was?"

"I suppose a Scotsman can be pardoned for knowing nothing about underwear."

"Or a man in a hurry. Which I am not, for once, by a miracle."

"Oh?"

"Banfi has me flying around giving Civil Action briefings." He lowered his voice. "If you suspect I'm actually keeping an eye on how people are sweating out the election, you'd be right too.

"Anyway, I'm supposed to wait until that Navy shuttleload has unpacked and had lunch. That gives me time to snatch a bite.

Nalyvkina thought of inviting him to her quarters to snatch more than lunch. But she had three roommates, one of whom was usually around, and her quarters were field buildings with precious little privacy even if the door was closed.

"Officers' mess is over this way," she said, slipping an arm through his. The howl of four jet-assisted attackers taking off jammed further conversation for a moment.

Davidson watched the sleek silhouettes dwindle toward the south. "Strike-loaded, too. Isn't that overkill for showing the flag?"

"I think that's the flight assigned to Third/Linak'h."

Davidson frowned, then his memory kicked in. "Oh. Candice Shores's outfit."

"Right. They've got a battalion field problem today. From what our CO said, the Administration and the media are sending observers. And don't look so confused. I worked for Marshal Banfi too, and if he didn't know about that training run—"

"All right," Davidson said, holding up his hands. "I plead guilty knowledge, but not much and most of it secret. At least for today."

"What about tomorrow?"

"Between today and tomorrow, there is always tonight."

"Is that a promise?"

"Not to babble secrets, if that's what you want."

She punched him lightly in the ribs. "Ye ken verra well what I mane."

"Your Scots accent is worse than my knowledge of women's underwear."

"It will improve. We each have a sleeping dictionary, after all."

Election Day, 1610. Linak'h:

Brigitte Tachin hadn't enjoyed lunch. Brian Mahoney had come down with the Navy people on the shuttle, assigned to communications duty with the ground parties. Tachin thought this assignment was a mistake and was ready to make sympathetic noises.

Instead Brian (looking pale and nervous) kept up a continuous stream of jokes and assurances about how much he liked his assignment. Communications was his specialty; ground ops his experience (even if involuntary). He would do fine.

Tachin wondered if he was trying to reassure her, himself, or some unknown superiors preparing an E & R. She also remembered a comment in a career-planning manual she kept on her ready shelf: "You have to be the first judge of the place of any personal relationship in your career plans. This is particularly true if the relationship is with another person in the Forces."

She looked across the mess to a corner where Colonel Davidson and Lieutenant Nalyvkina were doing everything short of holding hands under the table. Were they as carefree as they seemed, and if they were, was it because they weren't worrying about things being permanent, as she and Brian had to? (Brian at least, and she supposed she didn't disagree with him enough to simply shoot the idea down.)

Of course, it cut both ways. Nalyvkina might be flying combat in three days and dead in five; permanence could be something she was pushing out of her mind. Navy ground parties weren't going to be that close to serious shooting—weren't *likely* to be, as memories of Victoria reminded her to add the qualifier.

Somehow she managed to listen politely to the rest of Brian's rambling, through the dessert (synthetic strawberry flan) and the walk to the briefing hall. Colonel Davidson was already there; the expected Civil Action report was not.

The base CO called everyone to attention, exchanged salutes with Davidson, and turned the floor over to him. From the podium, Davidson pointed at the empty report rack.

"I seem to be hexing the local printers, as usual. So I'll run the basics past you, take a break for the report to arrive, then answer questions after you've all had a chance to skim the paper."

Davidson, Tachin decided, would probably live to wear stars, if only for his deft briefings. He managed to give the impression that he was completely familiar with his subject (which he probably was) and was taking his audience entirely into his confidence (which Tachin somehow doubted, considering the amount of BBA material any aide to Marshal Banfi must know).

The basic Civil Action strength was four self-contained groups, each with medical, engineering, construction, technical support, and other appropriate personnel, plus as much organic transport as they could scrape up. One was Federation Regular, one Federation Reserve, one Victorian, and one drawn from the human civilians, refugees, and still-settled.

"What about Ptercha'a?" somebody asked.

"Any particular kind of Ptercha'a?" Davidson asked. "Their 'Civil Action' is still part of the regular Administration government machinery. If they set up any special groups, we'll inform you if they request any cooperation."

Tachin thought that said enough for most people, but other people hadn't heard the rumors she had. *Now, if I could just be sure how much I can trust Mort Gellis . . .*

At least Civil Action support was not likely to be one of her major responsibilities. Her ground team was mostly communications and logistics, where the groups had organic capabilities, and other Navy people would be lending a helping hand with transport.

Davidson gave a few clarifications and updates, then a ground officer ushered the robocart with the reports into the room. Davidson stepped down from the podium, sidestepped a general rush for the cart, and strode purposefully toward the server console in the rear.

Tachin took three sideways steps toward Davidson's path before a TacAir officer fell in step with the colonel and someone else grabbed her arm from behind. Not looking, hardly thinking, she sidestepped and jabbed with her elbow. The answering yelp was in Brian's voice. He sounded like a hurt puppy. He looked like one, too, when she turned to face him. Neither improved her mood.

"Excuse me—" both Tachin and the TacAir officer—a major, she saw—said together.

"After I have some tea," Davidson said firmly. He led his little following to the server. "Can I get anyone anything?"

Tachin had tried to repel Brian with looks but now gave

up and asked for coffee. When everybody had a cup, Davidson looked at the faces around him.

"Major?"

"If we do wind up hauling Ptercha'a units, what about Confraternity surveillance?"

Davidson frowned. "That's only a rumor so far, at least as far as dealing with non-Hunters is concerned."

"I don't suppose they'd tell us if they did start spying on us," the major put in.

Davidson's face and voice hardened. "Quite possibly they wouldn't. But our duties and our oaths remain the same."

Tachin saw her chance. "Forgive me, Colonel, but I suspect the major has in mind the same sort of situation I've had to deal with. Or at least that I've been told I may have to deal with."

"An unreliable source?" Davidson shot back.

"You might say that, and also that I want to protect him for now." Both were true; Gellis was no better a leader than before, but there was so much hands-on work at which he was the best around that he would be hard to spare. His skill with electronics in particular would make Brian's life easier.

"Some of the enlisted people have been fraternizing with human refugees," she said. "What I hear is that the refugees are putting the blame for their situation on the Confraternity."

"That's hardly new," Davidson said.

"Have there been rumors before about looting abandoned farms?" Tachin said. The major's eyes met hers, and she knew that he now considered her an unexpected but welcome ally.

"Specifically by the Confraternity?"

"Yes." That was a reasonable interpretation of what Gellis had said; he had a knack for doing a lot of talking without saying much.

"There's been some looting, we know—satellite pictures even show some farms burned out. Compensation is being arranged. But this sounds like the old 'Confraternity plot' rumor in a new guise."

"Quite," Tachin said. "You understand, I have no complaints against any of my people's conduct toward the Ptercha'a—"

Davidson's look said, "You'd better not."

"—but I suspect it would affect morale and threaten incidents, if they knew the Confraternity was monitoring them."

"I'll run that past the appropriate authorities," Davidson said. Tachin hoped that was not a euphemism for Marshal Banfi; his influence with the Ptercha'a was balanced by his not being in the Federation chain of command.

Davidson set down his cup. "Thank you for your frankness. Unless somebody is a poor loser, we won't have a situation in which the Confraternity will be doing much spying on anybody. If somebody is a poor loser, we'll have a full-scale crisis and the right to look to our own security without consulting any Hunters."

Which did not mean the leaders of Linak'h Command would have the sense to do it, but the possibility was *some* assurance. Tachin finished her own coffee, contemplated another, and instead stood beside Mahoney as the major and Davidson retreated.

"Does anybody around here know what they're doing?" Brian grumbled. His cup of coffee, Tachin noticed, was untouched and growing cold.

She took it from him, squeezed his hand, then slipped the cup into the heater. "Perhaps not, but we have an advantage."

"Oh?" He sounded determined to be sullen and immune to consolation.

"We are veterans of Victoria. We know what it is like to face fifty factions, who also do not know what they are doing."

That seemed to reassure Mahoney, and when his cup was reheated he drank it down. Tachin was less happy. Brian really shouldn't need so much reassurance. Also, the Confraternity had much more experience in being omnipresent and invisible than any of the Victorians did. Seven hundred years, some history books said.

Eleven

Election Day, 2140. Aboard U.F.S. *Shenandoah*, off Linak'h:

The muted sounds of parties preparing to get under way followed Rose Liddell as she made her way from the Auxiliary Combat Center toward the flag suite. The sounds and the parties were going to stay muted, too, at least aboard *Shen.* Otherwise people were going to find that Captain Bogdanov could be as big a martinet as ever and that Commodore Rosie was not as nice as rumor had it.

Alertness was part of it. The rest was shipboard harmony. She wanted the people who thought the Confraternity meant justice and those who thought it meant anti-human revolution to be able to work side by side tomorrow, whoever won dirtside and whoever was hung over aboard *Shen.*

Not that she anticipated feelings running that high. Even Federation people who didn't like the Confraternity liked the Merishi about as little, or even less. *Shenandoah* in particular had acquired so much experience with Merishi behaving like the Great Galactic Sleaze Factor that her crew might have voted to ship fusers to the K'thressh if they thought it would annoy the Governance.

Right now, though, her job was commanding a squadron of ships with plenty of firepower but, God willing, no prospective targets. She let herself in, saw that Jensen had laid out a bedtime snack, and sat down at the table.

It seemed moments; it was actually half an hour before she woke up, with a cup of cold tea in one hand. At least she hadn't slumped forward and dunked her hair in the sherry.

The display was tuned to a planetside mediacast, a Ptercha'a announcing in True Speech with the ship's computer translating. The announcer's voice proclaimed the heavy turnout, as though it was a surprise that Ptercha'a would take seriously the first-ever election in which the Confraternity was openly running.

Mediacrats, Liddell decided, did not differ that much among the races. They all had the knack for making the inevitable or the trivial sound portentous or cosmic.

She called up the Incidents file and briefly wondered what the announcer would make of it. Twenty-two official incidents at the time the polls had closed; two more since. Most of them intraracial and only one of them fatal. Two humans, both drunk, one falling (or being pushed) off a pier to drown in the Sinnis'h, the other already in custody for negligent homicide.

Almost a peaceful day, for a community of two million people who might awake tomorrow on the brink of war.

And if they did, Rose Liddell would have been awake long before they were, so she'd better get her head down and *now*. Pavel, Mad Bill, or Fitzroy had few inhibitions about disturbing a commodore's sleep when they needed her.

Election Day, 2300. Linak'h:

The woman in the display wore a headband and Forces-issue running gear. Her long face was slimy with sweat where it wasn't caked with dust, her hair whipped out behind her, and her eyes bored ahead like lasers without seeing anything.

Candice Shores swallowed to hide both amusement and embarrassment. "I'd forgotten I could look like that. When did you take that, Father?"

"About six kloms into the final leg," Nikolai Komarov said. "Or was it seven? Anyway, they wouldn't let me onto the rest of the course, but the ten-klom run was in open territory."

Shores counted to ten. "Not really. You were technically an intruder, and somebody condoned a breach of security."

"Me," came a voice from the corner. Shores turned, to see Nieg looking up from the game of Chinese checkers he was playing with Sophia and Peter.

"You?" she said. "On my battalion's confidence course?"

"It's not strictly your battalion's alone, and, anyway, I was playing patron of the arts."

"Yes," Komarov said. He seemed to be more alert to the signs of short temper in his daughter than Nieg. "You see," he went on hastily, "I remember that expression—the win-or-die look. But it was only memory. I wanted to capture it live, from your woman's face, not your girl's face—"

Shores held up a hand. She was tempted to put it over her father's mouth, but Ursula Boll would have started laughing if she did that. Nieg might laugh too, which would be even worse.

I really ought to be with the battalion.

She'd said that earlier in the day, when she learned that her XO had organized a minor mutiny and gone around her to Barbara Hogg to make sure that Shores could spend Election Night with her father. "A Security Two doesn't *require* you, Colonel," Major Duboy said. "You need a break more than we need you."

"I have to be able to rejoin—"

"No problem. We—that is, Lieutenant Kapustev—has arranged for the loan of an air courier." He looked away. "With some help from Top Timberlake and Sergeant Esteva—"

"Who's not supposed to be back on duty yet!"

"I didn't say that he was on duty, ma'am. I just said that he helped arrange it so you can get back here really fast if you have to. If you can do that, Brigade will let you go."

So all her protests had been in vain, and now the courier, a converted gunship, was parked on her father's pad with a security detail watching it and the house. Three troopers only, two humans and a Hunter—the refugees needed all the extra hands they could get, to guard and help unload.

Not that her father expected to need round-the-clock security, which he rather intensely disliked anyway. The house was built over a shelter complex dating from the Hive Wars and entered through the basement. Ursula Boll and Nieg had designed procedures that would let the whole family hide if they didn't have time or lift to flee.

"Which is more than we had across the border for all the years we were there, and we are still alive," Komarov had said firmly. "So what do you fear, daughter? And do not again suggest that I give up my teaching at the camp to move into the Zone."

Shores sighed at the memory and looked at the pictures' background. "It was about the six- or seven-klom mark. I realized that I might break the course record for field grades. I guess it showed on my face."

"As usual," her father said. "Young lady, you have *never* been good at hiding your competitive streak. Not even when you were seven years old and racing Raul to the top of the climber maze."

There wasn't anything to say to that truth, but her father kept the silence from being embarrassing by withdrawing. He was back in a moment, holding a small hand-carved wooden box, with "C. N. Shores" on the lid in Forces-style silver lettering.

Shores saw something in Ursula's face that made her want to lead her father outside. But he was thrusting the box at her so insistently that she couldn't stall gracefully. She took the box and slid back the lid.

Eight silver stars nested there on a piece of soft cloth. They were regulation Federation flag-rank stars, or as close as a flag officer needed to worry about, but obviously handmade.

Shores blinked as she looked down at the hands that had made the stars, then up into her father's eyes. There weren't a lot of men who made her look up that far.

"Just to say—to say—I don't quarrel with that streak," he said uncertainly. Then the words came out in a rush. "I think that when you win what you deserve, something of mine will be with you."

Shores was still awkward at hugging her father, but at least she wasn't in armor, and she neither knew nor cared what Ursula might be thinking. At least she stepped back, tried to slip the box into a jacket pocket, and so nearly dropped it that her father finally took it and popped it in.

"May I join the next game?" he asked Nieg. The children squealed approval, and Shores saw an indefinable look pass between Nieg and Ursula Boll. Then her father was sitting down, and Boll was putting down her empty teacup and coming toward her husband's daughter.

"I could use some fresh air, Candy," she said.

"As long as we use the atrium," Shores said. "The security people will bite their nails off to the elbows if they think we're sniper bait."

"Of course."

The atrium was about the size of a six-seat table and the bad-weather roof was planks laid on from above. It still offered sitting room for two, once Shores wiped off the bench with the sleeve of her jacket.

"So," Boll said. "I wondered if Nikolai was really going to have the courage to give you those stars."

"You may not approve, but do you have to imply that my father might be a coward?"

Boll winced. "Forgive me. That was not what I intended to say. I meant that I think you frighten him a little—or is that even worse?"

"Not really. I—no, you're right. Those ten years changed me a lot, and some of the changes weren't for the better."

"Perhaps. I know Nikolai thinks so, and blames himself."

Then why didn't he tell me?

Shores had the feeling that her father hadn't entirely abandoned his old pattern: do the wrong thing, feel guilty about it, but don't get around to apologizing for months or years. When she'd realized how often Nikolai Komarov did that, Catherine Shores's breaking with him no longer seemed so monstrous, if no less painful for their daughter.

"It won't help matters if you negotiate for him, as if he were a child or a certified incompetent."

It was Boll's turn to look insulted. "I was going to ask about something for myself. If I cannot say a word about my husband—"

Oh, for somebody to fight outside my family.

"Sorry. Really. What can I do?"

"Well, it is perhaps something you cannot do by yourself, but if your friends—particularly Colonel Nieg—"

A small light, about the brilliance of the Red Child on a hazy evening, flicked on in Shores's mind. "You would like to stay in the Forces. On intelligence duty?"

"I can hardly take the children on a Ranger strike!"

"Seriously."

"Yes. Of course. It is all I have done for years, that and the children, and I think I am better than some at it."

"Better than most, you mean." Boll seemed ready to argue; Shores held up a hand. "Seriously, I thought you had to be two-thirds of the team or Liew would never have invested so much in it. My father is the sort of man who can draw confidences from stones and treestumps, but you need more in intelligence work. I figure you had most of the rest."

"Some of it, anyway. I enjoyed the work, too. I think—I think I feared you were going to take away my work, not Nikolai."

Shores decided that she would piece together any logic in that statement some other time. Right now she had one good place to grip Boll's twanging nerves, and she intended to use it.

"Liew would have to be the final judge, but if he asks my opinion you'll have my vote. One thing, though: try to get an assignment on some settled garrison world."

"The children?"

"Partly. You've been lucky with them so far. Don't push it." She decided not to mention her suspicion that Peter might need speech therapy. He was bright, responsive, and alert, but a six-year-old should have a bigger vocabulary and use more complete sentences.

"There's my father too. He needs a planet where there's a market for his art. He can keep going on sheer creative juice for a couple of years, but then he starts worrying about not pulling his weight financially.

"I think that's what broke up his first marriage. Leilia was from Outback and liked to live just as far off-route on Norge. San Lorenzo wasn't even the largest city on Quetzalcoatl, and there were always the *turistas* as well."

"You would know that better than I do. He did not talk much about his first marriage, and only a little more about your mother. About you, yes, but not much about your mother."

If Shores had believed her father capable of tact, she might have thought better of him for that. As it was, it occurred to her that when Ursula Boll met Nikolai Komarov, she must have been not too much older than the daughter Nikolai had left on distant Quetzalcoatl, doubtless crying over her every light-year of his path from there to Linak'h but never letting her know that he was still *alive*—!

This hinted all sorts of things about her father, including the possibility that the separation had come at a useful time for both of them. Also, some of the rumors about her father and his younger models might have been true.

Possibilities only, however, and irrelevant now. Or at least irrelevant as long as the marriage to Ursula Boll lasted, and there she could help. (Liew could help more, and Franke, Morley, and possibly Banfi more still. Shores knew Persons of Consequence; she wasn't quite one herself yet.)

"Oh, there you are," her father's voice came. "A thought just came to me. I am thinking of doing a painting of the Rhinemaidens. You could be the blonde, Ursula, and you, Candy, the dark one. Who is that redhaired colonel from 222 Brigade, the battalion commander?"

"Sigrid Olufsdottir?"

"The one with the bony face?" Boll said. "Nikolai, what if the rest of her is like her face?"

"I don't think it will be, and anyway, the face has such *wonderful* bones. Unless there is some regulation about officers modeling? I seem to recall rumors about your admiral—"

"Her buying up all the originals was her own idea, or maybe her brother's, at least according to what Charlie Longman said." Shores stood up. "The general rule is, if it's legal to display it in public, it's legal to pose for it."

"Good. I will call Colonel Olufsdottir myself, Candy. You need not worry about your name coming up unless she agrees. Now—in ten minutes they will be announcing the election results. Shall we go back in and rescue Colonel Nieg from the children?"

"He does not need much rescuing," Boll said.

"True. They like him very much." Shores knew her father's mouth was twisting under his whiskers. "Are you sure he doesn't have three wives and seven children tucked away on some outlaw colony?"

"His family is from Pied Noir, and the custom there is monogamy. But he's got about fifteen nieces and nephews and a couple of grand ones."

They returned to the living room as Nieg finished packing away the Chinese checkers set. One marble escaped; it rolled across the gouged wood floor to the door just as one of the guards stepped inside.

"Pardon me, sir, ma'am, but when you didn't come out to ask for a report—"

"No security problems in here, thank you, Corporal," Nieg said.

"Nothing outside, neither," the trooper replied. "All calm."

Shores made a Ptercha'a gesture of aversion as her father turned the display to the mediacast.

Election Day, 2320. Linak'h:

The forty Voting Districts were all supposed to report in at the same time. In fact the Voting Commissioners in each district had their own schedule for certifying legal votes, discarding disputed ones, and resolving arguments.

They kept to that schedule even in less controversial matters than the plebiscite. So naturally some districts certified their counts ahead of others, and who could blame Commissioners in a hurry to proclaim to the cosmos that they had done their job well?

Emt Desdai could, for one. The first set of announcements put the Confraternity ahead by twelve thousand votes out of just under a hundred thousand recorded. This news spread rapidly; as rapidly Confraternity militia began shooting into the sky.

"Go out and stop that nonsensical noise," Isha Maiyotz said firmly. "No, not you," she said to the Legion One-Five Band Leader, who divided security and assistance work with Emt Desdai and Seenkiranda. "Drynz."

Drynz looked as if he would rather join in the joy-shooting, but he obeyed. Being a hero of the Time of Power (or the Transition, as it was called by the tactful) had raised his rank and taught him discipline.

"It would have been better, Senior, to mix the Warbanders and the Confreres," Drynz said.

"Anyone can be wise afterward ..." the Warbander began, then his voice trailed off as he realized that a Confrere warrior had just supported the official Warband position, in front of the Senior Administrator. He had not closed his mouth or focused his vision before Drynz departed.

As the firing died, Maiyotz looked at the screen. The results were from ten districts only. "Do not be so joyful at this goodwill," she told the Warbander. "Yes, the militia would learn discipline from the Warband. But the Confreres would also keep better watch on the Warband through integrated units. Drynz was quick to see that."

Desdai exchanged glances with Seenkiranda. Both doubted that Drynz had the mental sharpness to have done as Maiyotz said. They also doubted the wisdom of such plain speaking.

"We have made our choice," the Warbander said stiffly.

"I am sure you have. But making a choice does not make one unable to regret it later, and when there are resources to tempt those who regret . . ."

"You trust no one!" the Warbander snapped, with a gargling note of anger and confusion.

"Not truly," Maiyotz conceded. "And the most I can do about it is to leave no one in any doubt that I suspect their motives. They will not think me a dupe, at least, and on that foundation something can be built."

If the voters cooperate, perhaps.

Desdai had not dared ask, but it seemed to him that Maiyotz was wagering on a generous victory for one side or the other. Not that she was the only one, of course—much of the last fifteen days' peace had come from the widespread belief that good behavior beforehand would reap a large reward on the day of voting.

But what if the margin of victory was so slender that the losers might plausibly cry, "Foul kick!" and refuse to accept the results of the game? Then the humans would be all that stood between the Administration and chaos. (They would be willing. Would they be able?)

Fliers had been whining, hissing, and occasionally booming supersonically overhead since Desdai reached Maiyotz's office. No one of any race or conviction could act the fool tonight without fearing an airborne watcher over his shoulder.

Now a flier—no, three of them, all light civilian models—were landing outside. Desdai heard a burst of cheering, quickly cut off, no shots, then a Confraternity war cry. The warriors outside—not all of them militia—began a ragged chorus of "Banner of the Free."

It grew louder as the outer door of the building opened and Hunters in the outer rooms joined in. Then the office door slid open and Boronisskahane entered.

He walked slowly, with canes in both hands and his eyes cast down on the floor until he was almost to Maiyotz's desk. Then he lifted his head, and Desdai understood in a moment some of the power he had exercised within the Confraternity for longer than Desdai had lived.

"I had not heard you were this well," Maiyotz said. "I rejoice in my error."

"It is not so great an error," the man said. His voice seemed thinner, like his fur, although he did not seem to have lost weight. Desdai heard the office door slide shut, realized that Seenkiranda had closed it, and saw that she made no move to depart.

Then he would stay too. If his part in raising that Banner of the Free on Administration House had earned him anything, it was a place here tonight. (Although he hoped that Maiyotz would not mention, unasked, his ties to Simferos Associates, the other reason Desdai wished to stay.)

"The humans treated me as if I were Banfi's long-lost child rediscovered," Boronisskahane said. "So if any of them had a hand in my accident, it was none with friends in high places."

"Consider how many observers were placed about you and how hard it would have been for anything to happen to you even if human seniors had wished it."

"I did. I also wondered how many of them were yours. Truly, that concerned me as much as the possibility of human treachery."

Maiyotz's teeth flashed. "You suspected me capable of your death?"

"My death could not have served your purposes. If it had—truth, in such a situation you could not have altogether trusted me. At least not to the point of my facing danger to save you."

The teeth-baring faded. "I am glad not to think that you have suddenly become overtrustful of the humans. That would argue either madness or untruth. In you, neither would strengthen our cause." She sat. "Our Warband days are behind both of us, but not so far that we have forgotten there are no tribes where the rockets burst."

The screen proclaimed another six districts reporting, the Confraternity lead holding at the same modest percentage with about one-third of the votes in.

"It will be a frail victory if that is our final margin," Boronisskahane said. "The remaining twenty-two districts were said to be largely on our side. If they are not—"

"They are not likely to turn enough to cast us down completely," Maiyotz said, more sharply than Desdai cared to hear. "If they do not, we still have the power to take steps to make our enemies think twice before acting. All our enemies."

Desdai was halfway through a mental list of the various Merishi factions when Maiyotz turned to him.

"Confrere Desdai. You remember what we said the night of the Transition?"

"It would be hard to forget it." *And impossible for me to crawl, Senior, so change your tone.*

"I hoped as much. Do you think that in fact as well as in law, the Supreme Warband Leader Banfi could lead both races. If so, what would the Masters—" she made the word an obscenity "—do about such a combination?"

Desdai rejoiced that he'd been thinking of the Merishi, regretted the continued presence of the Warbander, and took a deep breath. "That depends on how thoroughly we and the humans accept him, and also on which Merishi are likely to come against us in arms."

"Would it help to see our file on Marshal Banfi?" Boronisskahane said. He sounded as if he did not understand what Maiyotz intended but wished to help it regardless. Perhaps also he had seen in the Warbander's face the same as Desdai now observed—a desperate effort not to smile, cheer, or dance. There was one group in the Administration that would not doubt Banfi.

As for the rest—

"We have the same file," Maiyotz said. "Do you have yours in your flier?"

"No."

"We have ours in my computer. Do not fear, it is secure and equipped for self-destruction. Confrere Desdai, let it be transferred to your machine and then read in a secure place. Confrere Seenkiranda and Leader Birrinnssagga, you guard Desdai while he reads."

"I do not need that much guarding," Desdai protested, which earned him grateful looks from his appointed security team. Neither of them wished to be sent out of the room like children on a transparent excuse.

"Perhaps he does not, but that is because he has will, courage, and weapons," Boronisskahane said. "The data has none of these and cannot destroy itself if threatened with capture.''

Desdai looped his tail resignedly. It was some consolation to see that the lovefeast between the two seniors was continuing. He would have been happier if it had not extended to exiling him and Seenkiranda into the outer darkness, even if passing judgment on Marshal Banfi was a responsible task.

Three more districts reported before the data was transferred, increasing the Confraternity lead but not by enough to ease the tension. Desdai set the anti-tamper devices on his machine and formed up with the Warbander ahead and Seenkiranda behind.

Alerted militia and Warbanders (a mixed unit, or at least paired fours) led them to Maiyotz's own command flier. Then Desdai deliberately shut out the rest of the world as he called up the data on Marshal Banfi and threw the whole force of his mind into absorbing it.

He had not yet finished the file when the cheering began, on all sides of the flier and all around the command post. There was no firing, or at least he heard none from outside, only the thunder of rockets and bombs on long-ago and far-distant battlefields where human and Hunter fought side by side under Banfi against enemies to all that either race held to be just and reasonable.

Then a red glare, hued like the Red Child but a thousand times brighter, gushed through the windows. Someone was letting off signal rockets, and when he realized that, he let the cheering drown out the old battles, at least briefly.

Before he turned back to the file, he saw that Seenkiranda was weeping, and that the Warbander was trying very hard not to do likewise.

Election Day + 1, Midnight. Linak'h:

Brokeh su-Irzim concluded that the Governor could never have been much of a field fighter. Too-small incidents threw him into much too great a panic—such as the Wild Continent Ptercha'a celebrating the Confraternity election victory making him suspect an uprising contrived by Behdan Zeg!

Su-Irzim spent nearly a fifth-watch persuading the Governor that they knew of no rebellion in the Wild Continent, had not contrived one, and did not have one as part of their plans. The first two were entire truths; the last only partial.

After the last ritual phrase, su-Irzim rose from before the blank screen, thought of beer and bed, then thought more realistically of a brisk walk in the open air and then back to work. The faster he prepared his report for the Governor, the better.

Su-Irzim had forgotten the Ptercha'a party going on all around the house. The office soundproofing had kept it out while he spoke with the Governor. As he stepped into the dining room, the din assaulted his ears once more. He sat down on the foot of a dining couch to consider his next move.

As he did, Behdan Zeg entered through the other door.

"You the only one up?"

"The others were *trying* to sleep, the last I heard," su-Irzim said.

Zeg cocked his head and smiled wearily. "Half of them are Confraternity, and most of the rest like a good party with friends. Why shouldn't they be noisy?"

"Who complained about noise? Just as long as they do not start letting off weapons. The security systems will react, and possibly living People as well." He summarized his conversation with the Governor.

Zeg looked ready to curse or murder before the tale was half done, then subsided as su-Irzim concluded. He spat into a trash box, then shrugged.

"For that goldtusk, not bad. My thanks. And that give me an idea. If the Governor believes there's going to be trouble over there, can we suggest that he offer asylum to refugees?"

"As long as the Coordination and the Merishi don't officially protest, he might—" Su-Irzim broke off and stared at Zeg. "Will they be genuine refugees?"

"Do you think they would tell us if they were not?"

"Commander, there are various agreements about not abusing refugee status. They all prohibit infiltrating soldiers disguised as civilian refugees. The humans, the Merishi, and the Ptercha'a are all parties to those agreements, or most of them."

"The People are not party to any of them that I have heard."

"I trust your hearing, but what the People have done is not so important here. The standards by which your—ah, stratagem—will be judged are those of the other three races."

Zeg suggested an obscene fate for those standards. Su-Irzim invoked the Governor's habit of caution and concern for the law. Zeg strongly urged an even more obscene fate for the Governor.

This was the point, su-Irzim suspected, at which many despaired of sensible dealing with Behdan Zeg. But su-Irzim had come to know the man better than most, and in this matter he understood Zeg's reasoning, even if he did not altogether agree with it.

With more weapons to become available, Zeg's plans for his Ptercha'a mercenaries had grown. No longer did he think merely of surveillance of the Coordination's Southern Territory, lest it be used for air operations that might endanger the People's Territory. He was thinking of strength sufficient to enter the Merishi Governance or the Coordination itself, or at least to guard every square march of the People's Territory.

Su-Irzim offered his own thoughts. "I won't ask for details on moving the recruits, but you do have reliable people on the ground over there by now?"

Zeg's jerk of the head might have been mistaken for a nod by an optimist. Su-Irzim chose to be one.

"Then spread the word discreetly—"

"That's a contradiction, friend."

"So I'm in a contradictory mood tonight. Let it be known, if you prefer that phrasing, that we will urge the Governor to accept refugees. Hunters of military age who expect to flee the fighting, however, should organize fours and sixteens ahead of the day. We may even give preference to those so organized."

Zeg frowned. "That isn't the same as bringing them over ready to move out."

"I've told you what the laws say about that, and what the Governor will say. Also, the new Administration is hardly going to want to repudiate all previous agreements. They'll protest just to keep the Smallteeth out of their fur."

"What about arranging assignments in advance and having equipment ready for issue?"

"If it is available and your Hunters here can teach the newcomers to use it, I won't interfere."

"Why do I think you wouldn't stand between me and my mother's son, if he protests?"

"Because I won't. Commander, I know enough to keep my tool out of the scissors."

"There's something in that," Zeg said. "And something between your ears besides baby's mush!" He punched su-Irzim lightly in both shoulders, then tapped the ends of both tusks. "Want to join the party? I think they're about to tap the uys."

Su-Irzim decided that the Governor could wait another day for his report. Besides, the party might die down before he himself was too drunk to sleep through the morning.

Election Day + 1, Father-rise. Linak'h:

The screen in front of Marshal Banfi was blank. So was Colonel Davidson's voice on the intercom.

"Malcolm, are you there?"

"If I wasn't, Olga would kill me." Suppressed annoyance now in Davidson's voice, not-so-suppressed female laughter from close at hand. At least they weren't making any secret of it.

"I think I called at a bad moment. Call me when you're free to talk." Banfi was tempted to add a couple of sentences describing the new situation, but fought down the urge. The young folk did not need *any* distractions.

Banfi went out into the garden, remembering to attach his personal IFF chip just in time to keep from setting off the alarms. The transparent roof over the garden and the sensors under every third bush were the alternatives to having sentries posted everywhere except in the bathroom and possibly even there—which would have spoiled Malcolm and Olga's little rendezvous at least.

His knees creaked less than the bench as he sat down. Easy to think of both the colonel and the lieutenant as the young folk; at a hundred twenty Standard the difference between forty and twenty-five was barely visible. Banfi's physical eyes were as sharp as ever; his mental vision gave him more concern.

At least he could see one thing clearly. This was a last

chance at command, even if it would be largely exercised from offices and through committee meetings. (No danger of being killed at the head of his Hunters, like Sam Briggs.)

No, two things. It was also a chance to supremely irritate Di Longman, by stepping into the Theater's chain of command as an Allied Commander-in-Chief. Or maybe not. Short-tempered she was, but no fool.

Give her a veto, certainly, as little as the Hunters might like it. (And if they didn't, he was going to know why. They might know things about Longman that he did not. Their file on him proved that the Confraternity was as capable in intelligence as Banfi had believed, more so than most in the Federation were ready to accept.)

Other things could wait for breakfast and Malcolm.

Banfi had finished muffins, a pear, and two cups of coffee when Colonel Davidson appeared. He looked pleasantly rumpled. Banfi felt a brief pang of jealousy—not over Olga, but simply over the colonel's being young enough to have both the opportunity and the ability. Banfi did not regret his sterilization; by his third campaign he'd been a poor prospect for fathering a normal child. But all the rest had also vanished with the years, and at times like this he wished he could call it back.

"Coffee?"

"Thank you, Marshal. Olga's taking a shower."

'Invite her down for breakfast. Kinski has misprogrammed the cookers as usual. He still thinks I eat as much as he does."

"She has to be back on base by ten three oh. Also, I had the feeling this is BBA."

"Right now it is. By the time Olga's flying missions, it will be in the newsprints they use to wrap barbecue at the streetside stands." He crumbled a fragment of muffin between thumb and forefinger. "I've been offered command of the Administration's Warband."

"Congratulations, Marshal."

"Is that all you have to say?"

"Marshal, I can tell a superior officer who's made up his mind. I can't tell him much."

"You always were a realist."

"I still am. What about Harkorissim and Delo Ba-Kryda?"

"Harkie has resigned his commission. Delo has also resigned, but he's going to be the new Administrator of the Warband."

"I thought that was going to Boronisskahane."

Banfi shook his head and poured the colonel a cup of coffee. "Wrong man to control either the Warband or Security, in a coalition Administration. He's taking External Affairs. He can use his network of off-planet Confreres, be close to the center of things if there's a crisis, and not scare anybody in the meantime."

"So where do I come in?"

"Nowhere, until after the Golden Vanity approves. Baton and dual commission don't count for nearly as much as tact, in dealing with her.

"If all goes well, though, I want you to take over Civil Action. Maiyotz has a list of Hunters I can look over for my chief of staff, and you won't need a dual commission."

"It would serve Florence—"

"Malcolm, you are too damned determined to annoy your sister."

The colonel grinned. "So my parents tell me. So do my uncle, my three cousins, and my niece Kate."

"Has it occurred to you that they may be right?"

"I consider that possibility at least once a month."

"Consider it more often."

"Yes, Marshal."

"Consider that a friendly suggestion, not an order. It has occurred to me that we may still get through this situation without too many dead bodies. The fact that the election went off as smoothly as it did encourages me to optimism.

"I'm not so optimistic about careers surviving. A certain number of those are going to wind up on the casualty list. I don't want yours or Olga's among them."

"All right, Marshal."

"Good. Now, we need a secure line to *Roma* or—how long to lay on a shuttle flight?"

"Fed or Warband?"

"Better go with Fed, until I've talked with Longman."

"I'll get on both."

Twelve

Linak'h:

The day after the election, Great Warband Leader Muhrin-nmat-Vao visited the leader's post of Six-Seven Legion. Fomin zar Yayn had about as much notice of Muhrinnmat-Vao's arrival as he would have needed to slow-heat a packet of soup.

The Warband Leader remedied all the minor deficiencies in his uniform and prayed that the Great Warband Leader would overlook the major ones (there was hardly a shined pair of boots in the whole Legion). Then he went through the rituals of greeting with half his mind on them, the other half on the reason for this visit.

Muhrinnmat-Vao dismissed his guards and pointed to the scrambler set in zar Yayn's command panel. "Maximum discretion, please. What we are to discuss must remain between us. If the Fates themselves ask, lie."

"If the holy words about them are true, then you may need a new leader for the warriors here."

"If the secret gets out, I *will* need a new leader for them. Also, your excellent lady will need a new father for her new son."

Zar Yayn decided that this was the wrong time to jest about Jillyah's wanting a daughter. Or indeed, to make any sort of jest. Death-secrets did not grow on bushes, even on those high slopes of the Warband peak of command inhabited by such as his unexpected and not altogether welcome visitor.

"My duty is silence." Zar Yayn hoped the traditional phrase would satisfy all requirements and open the other's mouth.

"My duty is knowledge." The traditional reply—was it meant seriously? "A general map, please." *Never since maps were devised have Warband leaders talked to any purpose without them.*

"We are sending your warriors into the Merishi Governance," Muhrinnmat-Vao said. "If war comes, they will move against the Territory from there."

Relief that the man was not wasting time warred in zar Yayn's mind with doubt that he had heard rightly. 'I presume that much of the Merishi-given supplies survived the human raid across the Braigh'n in the spring. Otherwise my warriors will either go scantily armed or be supplied by much traffic that the enemy can detect."

"We reckon that about seventy parts in a hundred of the supplies survived. The humans did not penetrate deeply, and the Confraternity rebels were too busy running to search for them."

"Were they too busy running to leave spies and demolition teams behind? Also, how many of those supplies were in the path of the Great Fire? The Merishi seem to have been rather busy evacuating their secret operations warriors and not caring much about anything else."

"Do you suggest I ask the Masters for the privilege of an eye-and-hand inspection?" The senior sounded more bewildered than indignant.

"You are a better judge of the Masters' truth-telling than I, and likewise have more rank to gain answers from them. One of us must guard against their lying, to keep faith with our own warriors."

"I am not asking you to do anything foolish or dishonorable. You will learn this if you hear me out."

Zar Yayn listened and had to admit that the supply problem was at least not being ignored. Two cohorts at least would move openly, with all their equipment and supplies. The reason: the Merishi were requesting assistance in relieving survivors of the Great Fire and in keeping their Territory neutral in the event of war.

"That much is the truth. We can add at least one cohort and a reasonable number of supply convoys. Our food stocks are good and the harvest promises well. A bulk-cargo flier can be loaded with either ammunition or grain without any distant observer being able to tell which."

There would be no "refugee' flights. The Coordination intended to honor the agreements governing disguising soldiers as refugees, at least as long as the Confraternity rulers of the Territory and their human allies did so.

"Also, we do not want it thought that our people lack courage," the senior added. "It has always been wise to brandish your warriors and hide your cowards."

Before zar Yayn's warriors could do any serious brandishing, they would have to cross the Braigh'n River. Nowhere along the Merishi-Federation border was the Braigh'n less than two thousand paces wide, except where it ran through canyons. A formidable obstacle to ground-level travel, it was also a fine watch-line for anyone with a reasonable supply of modern sensors.

"Pek's Fifty will rise from their urns if we go straight across the river," Zar Yayn said. "But I presume that you have some solution to that also?"

"You presume rather much on your warriors being chosen for this work," Muhrinnmat-Vao said. Zar Yayn heard fatigue as well as sober anger in the senior's voice. More of his hair was white than when they last met.

"Forgive me. But you have not spoken against my care for my warriors yet. I pray that you do not begin now."

"Even a senior can grant that prayer. What do you need for a safe crossing of the Braigh'n? Granting that the war requires it at all?"

The bargaining took them through an early lunch. Zar Yayn wondered if he was being allowed this much freedom because he was genuinely trusted or, once again, because his seniors could then scrape from their claws and teeth any shame over his leading Legion Six-Seven and the Tribal Cohorts to disaster.

They agreed on an extra cohort to Six-Seven, plus having Legion Two-Six on zar Yayn's northern flank stretch its scouts southward. If they could strike down any hostile sensors or distract hostile troops along the Braigh'n, the crossing could be opposed only from the air.

"I also suggest that we leave our reserve supplies with Two-Six. Or even move some of the Merishi gifts—"

Muhrinnmat-Vao held up both hands, fingers spread. "The Masters will never allow that. And if you ask what good are they then, I doubt I could give a pleasing answer. But that is the truth."

Zar Yayn had no quarrel with any part of that speech.

"As long as we may move them as we wish when the fighting starts, I will ask no more while peace lasts."

"Your seniors will be grateful." Zar Yayn could detect no irony. "The Masters also, if that matters to you." How little it mattered to the senior before him hardly bore doubting. "But there is one circumstance that might force the Masters to give us anything we ask."

"Which is—?"

"One I would have thought you knew better than I."

Another oblique reference to zar Yayn's Confraternity sympathies (which now had questions being asked in his home Lodge of the House of Light, questions that would need forceful answers when he returned to give them). A reference which also gave him not the slightest hint of which of a score of rumors the senior meant.

No. It is something that the Merishi fear above everything else.

"You refer to the stories of Confraternity Legions space-borne on their way to Linak'h?"

The other nodded. "If they are stories. The Folk believe. I doubt."

"As do I. Or at least, I doubt that the Legions are instruments of the Confraternity. If they are coming, they are not coming from worlds so distant that the Confreres rule openly. They are coming from planets where many Hunters doubt the wisdom of a war merely to expel the Confraternity from a patch of land."

As do I.

Zar Yayn briefly wondered what reply to make if Muhrinnmat-Vao asked about those doubts—or even confessed that he shared them. The senior's reputation was that of one who wished above all peace within the Warband, a peace that would be fragile indeed if it was ordered to carve a path through Hunter flesh to strike down the Confraternity.

He looked at the map again and saw an opportunity to guard that peace, or at least diminish the war.

"I'm going to put a Warband and a Tribal Cohort straight onto guard duty," he said. His forefinger sketched out an area running along the whole border and stretching back two days' march into the Governance. "If we remove any remaining Confraternity sympathizers from that area, the Administration will have no eyes or ears in that area."

It was not only Confraternity sympathizers who would be zar Yayn's target. He'd wager that a good part of what was left of the Merishi's secret warband was in that territory. It might not prove feasible to eliminate them entirely but he could give the Merishi and their human and Hunter tools sleepless nights, wearying treks from one hiding place to another, empty bellies, and scanty arsenals. That should much reduce their power to start a war in which the Coordination would be fighting for the Merishi instead of for itself.

Linak'h:

The whine of a large formation of low-flying lifters drowned out Nikolai Komarov's recitation of "The Building of Yeltsinsk." He looked irritably at the eight bulky shapes bobbing and weaving over the treetops until they were lost in the low clouds. Half the fun in the poem for the children was their father's miming, but Sophia liked to hear the words and Peter needed to.

The whine died away, leaving an empty sky and a world silent except for the song of wind and birds. Komarov tried to remember where he'd left off. Oh yes.

> "Mud, mud, mud! Everywhere you looked,
> nothing whatever that could be cooked!
> Shuttles sank, the marshes stank, the
> sapling birch grew damp and lank!

"What's a birch?" Peter asked.

"It's a kind of tree," Sophia said patiently. "Father will show you a picture of one when he's done with the poem."

"Better than that, we'll go into Och'zem and I'll show you a whole avenue of them, if we can get into the Zone," Komarov said.

"Will Candy be there?" Peter asked.

"She might be with her soldiers out in the country," Sophia said. "She can't come in to see us anytime she wants."

No question about you being Ursula's daughter, Komarov thought. Candy could probably arrange for someone to escort them through the gardens, but it was long odds against her coming herself.

Or was it? Linak'h Command had relaxed since the election, to Alert Three or even Four. (Alert Two was supposed to be hard on people and equipment if you kept it up for more than a few days.) It had certainly begun to look like silly posturing to intimidate an enemy who wasn't there.

Almost a week now since the election, and nobody dead except from natural causes or ordinary crimes. The Confraternity's margin of victory must have helped there. So did the open media coverage of the formation of the new Administration. Isha Maiyotz and Boronisskahane couldn't have hidden what kind of brush they used for their morning grooming, let alone a plot to impose police-state rule on the Administration and throw non-Confreres into some sort of gulag!

If anybody was keeping secrets, it was the Federation. (Also probably the Coordination, but Komarov was convinced that the Coordination would only react to a direct threat of a kind that the Administration alone could hardly present. Another good reason for shaking the dust of Linak'h from their heels: the Federation now needed diplomats on this planet, not soldiers or spies.)

Komarov stood up, brushed at a damp spot on his shorts, and continued reciting. Sonic booms broke in twice, but he raised his voice over their rumbles and went on.

Komarov was doing his best imitation of the statue of Yeltsin that stood in his namesake city's Narodny Prospekt when Ursula came out. She wore shorts, a strap top that threatened to come unstrapped, and a face that strangled a bawdy greeting in her husband's throat.

He still made quite a business of kissing her, until the children shouted to stop being silly, then ran back into the house. He finished the last kiss, then sat down on a stump and pulled her down on his lap.

"Niko, this is no time—"

"Ssh. I saw your face."

"Your eyes weren't aimed at—"

"Ursl, something frightened you. I'm not so big a fool I won't ask what it is. You're not so big a fool you'll frighten the children."

"The Federation guards have left the refugee camp. Those lifters were from 222 Brigade. I used the 'scope on the security compound, and there's nobody there at all."

"So? I thought 218 Brigade was taking over today anyway. Maybe their first flight got delayed, and the CO of 222's last one had a date with someone even better-looking than you are—"

She batted his hand away. "Be serious. There's no one at all guarding the refugees now."

"Except the Confraternity militia units, which are now legal."

"Legal, but weak. Don't you remember? Healer Kunkuhn told me that the refugees hadn't been reissued their weapons after they came down from orbit."

"He may have told you. Are you sure you told me? And is it the truth?"

"I told you when I was posing for one of your Rhinemaiden sketches—"

"Ah. The woman told me. She also tempted me."

This time she did not push his hand away, but her face seemed cast in a frown.

"Nikolai. I'm going to slave the telescope to the com gear. You call up Candy, about showing the children the garden. Then I'll show her a picture of the empty security compound. We can ease it into the conversation somehow, so that nobody who may be intercepting us will understand."

She had better stay in the Forces, Komarov thought. *There's nowhere else so much paranoia is any good.*

Komarov saluted, as well as one could with a woman on one's lap "*Zum befehl, Frau Oberst.* Now—"

"You great infernal hairy *scheisskopf,* we have *work* to do!"

"It will be embarrassing if all we send Candy is a picture of 218's advance party setting up and distributing the militia's weapons."

"I am willing to be embarrassed in a good cause."

"Is that a promise?"

"Oh, you—yes. On my virginity, I swear it!"

She slipped off his lap before he could grab her and darted for the house.

Linak'h:

Candice Shores was sitting out a confidence-course exercise by the Reservists of B Company when her father called.

She'd been doing a bit more sitting with each day after the Election that passed without war, rebellion, or even a self-respecting riot. She'd been doing quite a lot more sitting since Longman and Kharg (presumably with Rubirosa's consent) had scaled the alert level down, until it was Alert Three for Security and the standard Alert Four in everything else.

Federation units wouldn't be easy targets, but they wouldn't be sweating all around the clock keeping watch for so-far-nonexistent threats. The terrorists hadn't shot or blown up so much as a household pet, the Coordination had neither demobilized nor attacked nor even issued any official statements, and the Merishi and Baernoi were pretending to be even more mysterious than they usually were.

This was either an outbreak of peace or the calm before the storm. Regardless, the reduced alert status was allowing a lot of housekeeping and maintenance and a bit of R & R. Not to mention an orderly transfer of several thousand square kloms of Territory from Kharg's AO to Edelstein's—

That was the point at which her father's call came through. It took her about fourteen seconds to sense tension under the pleasantries, but she kept her voice in friendly-chat mode and waited for the other shoe to fall.

It came—a wavering picture of a refugee camp with nothing standing between threats outside and the thousand-odd Ptercha'a (no, not so many now that some of them had found roofs with friends or relatives) inside, except a perimeter wire and its sensors.

Not so many sensors as she remembered, either, and no one monitoring them. Unless Kharg's people left a satellite relay from the sensors to some reaction force elsewhere, and even if they had, how forcefully could it react?

She kept up the charade until her father blanked off, wanting desperately to tell him to run like the Devil and sure that anyone intercepting the call would notice her eye movements and sweaty forehead. Then she played back the call, to make sure that the empty camp hadn't been a hallucination.

It hadn't. Juan Esteva described the same thing she'd seen when she called him in to watch the recording.

"It could be a mistake," he added. "But people sometimes get killed from that kind of mistake."

"I was thinking along very similar lines, Sergeant, believe it or not." She made a copy of the recording and handed it to Esteva. "Run this to Nieg. That's the unofficial but critical copy. I'll do the official thing with Hogg, and recommend it go on up to Kharg and Banfi."

"Banfi?"

"Yeah. Allied Commander-in-Chief, remember?"

Esteva called himself several Hispanic bad names. Shores grinned. "Are you not getting enough from Jan? Or maybe too much?"

"And how is your love life, *mi coronel*?"

"What love life?" Time to sit down did not logically imply time to lie down, except (occasionally) to sleep.

"Exactly. Launching."

Esteva disappeared as the screen glowed again. It was Eppie Timberlake, taking a vacation from paperwork by bossing the confidence-course security detail.

"We have a couple of unconfirmed sightings of intruders in the Secure Area," she said. "I tried to reach the company CO, but he's on the course."

"Picnickers?"

"Not down by the Almais Marsh. Too wet and too buggy."

Also too close to one of the battalion's depots for Shores's peace of mind.

"Mount up and get between them and Depot Two," Shores said. "I'll give you a blank check on calling for reinforcements. Oh, do you have a working biosensor?"

"Don't know if we're looking for hair, scales, or fur?"

"Exactly. I'll make sure that any air support you have also carries one. Good hunting."

"I hope it's a false trail, but thanks anyway."

"Add prayers to the thanks."

"Can do."

Now, back to the first move, which was reaching Barbara Hogg—

"Huntress calling Persia. Huntress to Persia. Security Situation Yellow. Points 34 and 65."

That woke somebody up enough to tell her that Persia was unavailable.

"Make her available. Or the XO. One of the two, and now. I don't care if you have to exhume them. *Now*, and—oh, Hades!"

"Ah—?"

"Not for you." By sheer reflex she'd switched her tactical display to a general map, then overlaid it with a met update. A major thunderstorm formation was moving in on the area of the refugee camp from the northwest, packing enough wind, rain, and poor visibility to seriously affect flying conditions.

It would be a while before the storm affected the Linak'h Brigade or the Zone. But anyone coming north to the camp from 218 Brigade would be even later than they already were.

Linak'h:

Brigitte Tachin hadn't planned to be flying point for 218 Brigade's takeover of security for the refugee camp. But downchecked lifters, communications failures, and a couple of what she hoped were honest navigational errors had taken their toll on the rest of the convoy.

One airborne part of it was now a good forty kloms behind Tachin. Another had just left the Zone. Between them was a section of three lifters, one grounded by accident and two providing security until somebody else could fly out and free them to proceed to the camp.

Forty kloms wasn't an unbridgeable gap, except for the thunderstorm. On the radar it had stretched one long tentacle of rain and turbulence into that forty-klom gap. Tachin and her people had been shaken like beans in a rattle passing through it, and it was worse now. Their backups were going to have to swing well to the east, or if that took them too close to the Merishi border, they might be grounding too.

To add insult to injury (at least for a Navy ground team heavy on communications), the weather was playing the devil with the radio. They needed no scrambling; the lightning bolts to the west and north were doing that very nicely. What they needed instead was a couple of telepaths, so that they could learn what might be going on in the rest of the world.

"Never mind the rest of the world," Mahoney grumbled. "I'll settle for the AO."

"I'm praying."

"Is that all?"

Gellis piped up from the back. "Human sacrifice, anyone?"

"Are you a virgin?" Tachin shot back. Gellis gave a strangled grunt.

Mahoney grumbled on. "After five hundred years, can't somebody make a weatherproof radio?"

"God can still send the lightning."

"You say He's a bigger flasher than any man?"

"No, you said that," Tachin replied.

"We have the camp in sight," the pilot interrupted. "ETA about four minutes. The homing beacon is coming through four by three. Circle and call?"

That last question was aimed at Brian, the senior officer present. Tachin carefully looked the other way. It wouldn't help if he needed to be reminded to lead, not grumble.

"Go ahead."

The two lifters of the Navy team went into a circle three hundred meters up and ten kloms in diameter. The green-clad hills dipped and rose like frozen tsunamis under the lifters. The Great Fire had stayed well to the north of this area, and the rain since had it glowing with life.

In fact, there was more life in the forest than there was in the camp. A few Ptercha'a waved from the camp streets as the lifters droned by, but most of them seemed to be inside to wait out the rain. The security compound on the far side of the ridge from the camp gate was completely empty, not even a sentry posted.

Tachin turned that image over in her mind for a moment, then another. After that she started praying that Brian had seen the same thing and would come to the same conclusion.

"Looks like 222's bugged out ahead of schedule," Gellis said. Tachin gritted her teeth at Brian's glare. The glare faded into a frown.

"Try to raise the camp on the radio," he told the pilot. "They can't see the security area from where they are, and—"

"Urgent, urgent, to Federation lifters. This is Ursula Boll. The refugee camp has no security and no radio. Try to warn them."

"Jerusalem Four to Ursula Boll. We read you and will comply. Do you need security yourself?"

Static drowned out the reply. "Overwatch right above the camp," Mahoney said, and pulled out his notepad.

Tachin warmed to Brian's brisk tone but was only half-listening to him. Most of her attention was outside, on the ridge revealed as the lifter banked into the new, tighter circle.

The ridge was partly wooded, and now she saw moving figures under the trees. When they weren't under the trees, they were low-crawling. Trying to hide? Yes. Also probably human, dressed in what might have been Militia uniforms (she fumbled for her binoculars), and even at this distance, clearly armed.

The binoculars came up; one blink focused them, another cleared Tachin's eyes. Clear eyes revealed long—bundles, boxes, tubes?—some of them held by two people.

"Commander!" she called. "Report unidentified people on the ridge, with personal and probable crew-served—"

One of the tubes gushed fire. Tachin blinked. She didn't wait to see the gush of fire turn into a trail climbing toward the lifter. She saw it only for an eyeblink in any case, as the pilot cranked field and fans together for max-G evasive action.

"Confirmed hostiles on ridge at Point 65, with crew-served AD weapons. Hostiles now—"

The missile chopped into the lifter's rightside skirt, where its light metal joined the tougher ceramics of the belly. A fan died with a scream and the lifter whipped up nearly on its side. Everybody who wasn't strapped down crashed against the right side of the crew compartment.

The pilot let the lifter drop a hundred meters, then cranked in another evasive turn. The lifter tilted back and spun at the same time. Tachin felt she was in a runaway motion-sickness tester. At least not so many people went flying this time; a hundred-meter fall gave time enough for trained people to lock belts and harnesses.

Then they were down, striking too hard but with the belly almost parallel to the slope. Tachin now felt as if she'd been thrown into a plas pourer filled with rocks. She heard cries and expensive noises as kinetic energy overcame careful packaging to ruin communications gear. They ended only when the lifter stopped, at the bottom of a wide swath cut in the brush.

From somewhere high overhead a lifter's turret cannon

raved. They still had a companion, it seemed. Tachin wrestled herself out of her straps and groped for comrades, needing human contact as much as she wanted to help.

Mort Gellis was already unstrapped, so he was the first to reach her and Brian Mahoney. The copilot scrambled up into the turret as the pilot slapped control plates, switching the turret to manual control and unlocking the weapons rack.

"Navy team, out the back," Mahoney said. Tachin could hear nerves fighting to turn the briskness to shrillness but not quite succeeding. That was no great matter; she thought she'd be lucky to get through this little *affaire* with dry pants.

"Which side of the ridge are we on?" Mahoney called.

The turret gun still worked; its hammering swept away the pilot's answer. Tachin read the man's lips and cupped her own hands to shout almost in Brian's ear:

"Security side!"

"Rendezvous at the camp CP." Mahoney called. "Stay paired up, keep your heads down, and don't try to be heroes. Can you people give us covering fire until we're inside the camp? We'll do the same when we're in position."

The pilot gave a thumbs-up and handed over an armful of carbines. Tachin was running through the weapons-check drill as her feet carried her toward the rear without the help of her mind.

The other lifter was still airborne, still firing, and she hoped squalling for help like a treetiger in heat. That was one consolation: they might not be alone for long.

Second consolation: thanks to the shootdown, the fighting might have started sooner and gotten louder and more visible than the terrs had planned. The refugees would *have* to know something was wrong, even if their radio was still out (and was that sabotage?).

Ursula Boll—and Holy Mother, that was Candice Shores's stepmother!—she would also be warned, unless she was deaf and blind. And if she was not, or crippled either, she and her husband and children would be heading for the best hiding place they could reach in five minutes and staying in it until the terrs were dead or running.

She and Brian weren't anywhere near their "loved homes"—two hundred light-years to Killarney, four times that to Charlemagne. But they were certainly standing between a lot of people and "the war's desolation."

This was supposed to be inspiring. Today all she hoped it would do was improve her marksmanship, if she had to shoot somebody.

Though she would do well enough today if her pants stayed dry and she hit what she aimed at.

Thirteen

Linak'h:

The crashed lifter had held eight of the Navy ground party. All of them made it to cover in the security compound; seven of them were in one piece except for cuts and bruises.

A slug gouged Mort Gellis in the leg halfway through the gate. Brian Mahoney grabbed one arm, somebody else another, and they hustled him the rest of the way so fast that neither his wounded leg nor his good one touched the ground.

By then Tachin had the rest of the team armed, organized, and ready to cover the lifter crew's retreat. It was long range for pulser carbines in inexperienced hands, but it beat giving the terrs a chance at undisturbed target practice.

All the firing from the ridge seemed to be anti-vehicle weapons, though, and most of them aimed at the second lifter, still airborne and therefore a more difficult target. Meanwhile visibility shrank as clouds swept across the sky, thunder mounted from every direction except the east until it drowned out most of the shooting, and somebody finished giving Mort Gellis first aid. The first Tachin knew of that was when she heard him shout, "Hey, Commander. Let's hold off getting inside. Ever heard of booby traps?"

Tachin thought the petty officer might have been significantly more tactful, and Brian's face said the same thing. His words came out, "I don't think our own people would have left anything."

"No, but we don't know how long this camp was unsecured and how long the terrs have been around. Lord knows if *I* could think of sending a squad in to plant a few traps, they could have."

Tachin wondered how Brian would react to being told his business in front of his subordinates. Before his reply could give her a hint, something heavy scored a direct hit on the grounded lifter. A moment later, ammunition in the turret detonated.

The turret flew into the air in the middle of a cloud of smoke and fragments that trailed more smoke. One of the crew—Tachin thought it was the pilot—flew out the rear door like another fragment. He struck the ground, rolled twenty meters, then lay still. Dry grass blazed up around him.

Then the airborne lifter slid down out of the sky, flying backward, bow and turret aimed at the ridge, the turret pumping out short bursts. The lifter managed to reach the rear of the next building to Tachin's left before its field generator died. It came down from fifteen meters with a crash, bow smashing through the roof of the building, rear digging into the ground.

Tachin grabbed Mahoney's arm as he rose, looking toward the probably dead pilot. *If Brian's reaction to being corrected is stupid heroics—?*

Or was it stupid, and would she want to be left there in the pilot's position?

This time the thunder didn't roll, it crashed. From a tongue of cloud two kloms wide and ten high, rain spattered down on the battlefield. The view toward the ridge turned into a gray murk. Tachin saw several more rockets sailing off toward the east and heard what sounded like distant small-arms fire from beyond the ridge.

Linak'h:

When the rockets came in, Nikolai Komarov was standing at the foot of the back stairs. He'd just heard Ursula say she was shutting down and joining him, when the nightmare ripping-cloth sound began.

It ended in two thunderous crashes. One of them caught Komarov halfway up the stairs and his wife halfway down. She lost her footing, toppled into his arms, and gripped him like a suckerflower as he turned to leap back down.

Then the second rocket hit. For seconds in objective time, hours in subjective, he had the sensation of falling, while being choked with dust, stabbed with knives, and hammered from his lower ribs down to his ankles with enormous clubs, some of them padded, others jagged and splintery.

Then the sensations organized themselves. He was half-choked and tried to cough his lungs clear. This made his chest hurt and brought up blood. He also discovered that he couldn't move anything below his rib cage.

He looked down and saw that part of the immobility was caused by his being pinned by several large timbers from the stairs. The second rocket must have brought them down, along with a good part of the second floor. The rest of the immobility—and now he realized, the lack of sensation—must have other, more unpleasant explanations.

"Ursula?" he called. He was not sure what he would do if she didn't answer or answered only with a dying woman's moan.

"Niko? Are you all right?"

"I doubt it," he said. '*Liebchen,* I think you had better take the children and the survival kit out of the shelter and run with them."

Ursula loomed through the dust, her face severe, then twisting as she saw him. He laughed and somehow kept the laugh from turning into a coughing fit or bringing up more blood, even though he could feel the blood in his throat. *Internal injuries, as well as a broken back.*

"I forbid you to cry. That is an *order, Frau* whatever rank you'll be commissioned in."

"You aren't my superior. You are—" She swallowed hard, was silent for a moment. "You need first aid. It's still true what we agreed, that in the shelter the children—"

Both of them started as thunder crashed overhead. Komarov thought the house had been hit again. Little gray pockmarks appeared in the dust on the floor as the first raindrops found their way through the gap in the roof.

"It's not the same now," he said. "They used rockets, so they may not have ground units close to us. Even if they do, the rain changes things. If they won't have time to search the house, they'll have even less to search the forest."

He hoped she wouldn't simply refuse to leave him at all. Then their last words would be another fight over the children—and, adding insult to injury, the fight would be over their *own* children, not Candy.

*Who really isn't a cause for trouble between us any more,
thank God.*

"You still need first aid," she said. "I won't go without
giving you at least one of the multipaks."

He had to admit that would help him die less painfully.
Shock, loss of blood, and damage to vital organs were still
going to kill him before serious medical help arrived.

He reached for Ursula's face, misjudged the distance (*artist's eye going already*?), and touched her breast.

"Nikolai—" Her face was dusty except where tears had
cut clean paths down each cheek.

"I've kept my promise, Ursula. You're the last woman
I'll ever look at."

She bent over and kissed him. "You stay right there—
ach, what am I saying? You—oh, let me get the pack."

"Bring the children, too!"

She started to shake her head. He wanted to tell her it
wasn't for good-byes but to save time. They might not
enjoy their last sight of him, but they would live to remember it.

But the shock was wearing off and the pain was setting
in. His words were lost in his first scream.

Linak'h:

The other lifter's Navy people included the EOD team,
which was one piece of good luck. Another was that they
all survived unhurt. In fact, except for one yeoman with a
fragment in her leg and the copilot with a serious concussion, the other lifter's people were all fit and ready to fight
as soon as a target offered itself.

That might take a while, Tachin realized. By the time
the EOD people had gone in to the security CP to delouse
at least one building and its gear, the storm was in full cry.
Puddles two meters wide and ten cems deep stood on firm
ground; unfirm ground was turning into the primordial
ooze.

Meanwhile, the thunder sounded like a fifty-tube barrage,
and the rain made a gray wall apparently just beyond her
nose. An entire battalion of Light Infantry in parade order
could have marched past fifty meters away undetected, except when lightning lit up the whole scene. Sometimes after

one of the bolts, the air stank of ozone and Tachin heard sizable trees going over, long cracklings and crashings always drowned out sooner or later by the rain or the thunder.

Tachin would have liked to know if the bad guys on the ridge were human, Hunter, or mixed. Humans couldn't see as well in low light but could stand heavy rain better. At least the Navy party's survivors weren't making enough of a thermal signature to stand out except on fairly high-powered sensors. For the moment, the battle would be personal weapons guided by the Mark I eyeball.

No booby traps turned up, but the CP's com gear left a lot to be desired. "Also several key components," Gellis said. "I don't know whether some bright type thought they could cannibalize and get away with it, or what."

"Sabotage?" Brian said, and Tachin wanted to kick him, but he seemed to read her mind in time to shut up.

"Give me a shot at the rig in the second lifter," Gellis said. "Two can play cannibal with com gear."

"Your leg—" Tachin began.

"I can do this stuff sitting down, remember," Gellis said.

"Nothing left in—?" Mahoney pointed out into the rain that hid their own wrecked lifter and its crew.

"Nothing worth the risk of crawling out there and bumping into an enemy patrol. Or even a sightseer."

"Just don't start yourself bleeding again," Tachin said. "Even Chief Nakamura might be unhappy if he had to send a lock of your hair home to your family."

She slung on her carbine, tucked a few strands of sodden hair under her helmet, and stood up. "Brian, I'm going to—what is it called, inspect the outposts?"

To her relief, he didn't even think a protest very loudly. "Carry on, Lieutenant. Now, Mr. Gellis, let's see what we can do. At this point even a homing beacon would help."

As Tachin stepped out into the rain, she realized that this somewhat depended on who homed in on the beacon. The terrs might not have any lift anywhere close at hand; they had probably infiltrated the area on foot. Even this close to Och'zem, enough virgin forest stood tall and thick to cover the approach of a battalion, at least from people who might not be looking for it too carefully—

As if her thought had conjured it out of the rain, she heard the whine of a lifter's fans approaching the camp. It was possible that somehow word of their situation had reached across the light-years to the convoy and a point flight was bringing in reinforcements.

It was also possible that the bad guys' support had heard of their situation and was either reinforcing or evacuating by air under cover of the weather. Satellites couldn't see much under this kind of storm, not enough anyway to let the higher-ups evaluate the threat until it was too late for the people on the ground.

"Red One Alert!" Tachin shouted into the rain. Thunder rolled, for once not loud enough to drown out the approaching fans, her order, or the acknowledgments.

Linak'h:

Ursula Boll left the children in the shelter after all. She realized as she unpacked the first-aid gear that the same rain which would cover their tracks once they were out of the house would also cover the approach of terrorists. If the children were out of sight of any unwelcome visitors, the visitors' haste might save them.

If I can make sure the terrorists don't learn anything from me. The thought made her uneasy, as it would not have ten years ago—which she supposed was a tribute to Nikolai and the children. She would have her old survival reflexes if she lived to be a hundred and fifty, but now she had to consciously plug them in.

She still hugged the children more tightly than usual. Sophia knew that something was wrong and either didn't want to learn what or had already guessed. She made soothing noises at Peter, who could barely speak a coherent word.

As an afterthought, Boll had picked up one of the spare survival suits, and it turned out to be a good idea. The rain was pouring in through the roof and sluicing down the ruined stairs onto Nikolai. He already lay in a rusty puddle, but he was also mercifully unconscious.

She stood for a moment with the multipak in her hand. One of the things it would feed into his system was painkillers, but he was already feeling nothing. The boosters might just wake him up.

No. She wasn't going to let him go without a fight. That meant having him awake, so that he could help her or at least himself when she got to the point of moving the timbers off him. They weren't too heavy to move, and if she had time she could go back to the shelter and get a cutter—which she ought to have brought with her this time, fool that she was—!

The front door flew open so violently that she thought it was another rocket hitting. Instead of smoke and flying debris, though, what came through was pounding feet. Boll dropped the multipak—no point in exposing it to battle damage, when Niko might wake up and be able to use it—and headed for the front of the house.

She reached the kitchen in time to see three people fanning out across the living room, with a fourth guarding the door. They wore sodden Militia fatigues, carried issue pulsers, and were groomed in regulation style, but weathered, gaunt faces and boots that had covered too many kloms of wilderness ruined their cover. They also looked more nervous than she was. Crouching and listening told her why.

"Damned fools with the rockets must have scared them off," said the point, a woman who might have been Boll's age. "Nobody here."

"A lot of fancy pictures, though," another said.

"Komarov's an artist, if you'd listened to the briefing," the door guard said. He seemed to be in command. "The briefing also said search thoroughly and no looting. So start searching, and keep your hands off the good stuff."

The three people didn't look too happy about the order or sure of how to execute it. "One pair and a single. Single into the kitchen—I can cover you from there. Pair toward the left. Bedrooms that way, I think."

No mention of the kids, Gott sei Danke. *Either the briefing had been sloppy or maybe even the leader was—* "nervous in the service"?

Boll drew her pistol. She would have dearly loved to have a few grenades—even two thrown quickly would clear the living room. Also bring in reinforcements much too fast to let her help Niko, then escape with the children. It would be mostly the pistol, because she'd need to be very lucky to use the knife. She hadn't kept in practice with that; Niko didn't like it around the children.

Even with the pistol, she was on familiar ground. This was like those fights in abandoned houses where she'd started. Good sense there kept her alive, made her a leader, got her off the pesthole after her parents died.

Linak'h:

The storm blurred the sound of the approaching lifters so that Tachin couldn't learn a thing about their approach except that they were flying low. So would any sane pilot trying to navigate by sight in this murk.

Two sets of fans whined almost directly overhead and flung spray over her. She blinked water from her eyes, pulled her goggles down, and looked up to see the receding shapes of two Ptercha'a-designed lifters. Both showed the Confraternity trefoil, both had their rear doors open, and both had armed Ptercha'a crouched in the openings.

At the same moment one of the crouching Ptercha'a spotted Tachin. He raised his battle rifle. Two comrades grabbed it and him, pulling them both to the deck. A fourth Ptercha'a leaned perilously far out and made the standard hand signals for "Friend" and "Permission to land?"

For a moment the weight of command seemed to squash Tachin into the mud. At the end of the moment she concluded that the Hunters probably were friends, because the refugee camp had a couple of old lifters very much like these. If so, they were blessedly welcome, and if they turned out to be hostile at least they'd be shooting at people who could shoot back.

Tachin stepped into the open, body taut against the possible impact of bursts, and hand-signaled the affirmative. The lifter's field cut so suddenly that its landing was almost a fall. A wave of mud and water swept ankle-deep away from it. The other lifter swung back out. Fifteen Ptercha'a piled out of the two lifters. The second one promptly took off again, just in time to spray Brian as he came out, gaped at the newcomers, and turned his dripping face to Tachin.

"What the bloody—?"

"Friends, I think. Probably from the camp."

"Ah—yes, camp. Healer Kunkuhn send. Not come—"

"Do you have any messages from Healer Kunkuhn?" Tachin said, switching to Commercial Merishi. At the moment they needed communications, not etiquette, and she didn't know enough True Speech or have a translation computer on hand.

The Hunter's fur didn't bristle, possibly because it was too wet, or maybe because—she, Tachin thought—also knew this was an emergency. "We are defending the camp and have the old and the babes as safe as possible," she said. "The Healer thought we could send help to you under the cover of the rain."

"He has the heart of a warrior," Tachin said. She understood more Commercial Merishi than she spoke, and hoped the tactical situation could be covered in her vocabulary.

"With your permission?" she asked, nodding toward the lifter.

"Gladly," was the reply.

Tachin scrambled in. The lifter's last cargo might have been organic fertilizer, and its communications gear belonged in a museum, but one item warmed her like a hot shower. It was a brand-new Federation Forces issue survival radio, modified for Ptercha'a hands but otherwise standard.

She leaped for it so fast that the Ptercha'a pilot whirled into her path with a drawn knife. A shout made them both turn, to see Mahoney with his pistol drawn and the first Ptercha'a frantically signaling for peace.

Tachin wiped rain and sweat off her face with the back of one hand as she switched the radio to one of the continuously monitored emergency frequencies. Technically this was a tactical communication rather than a distress call, but she was not going to worry about legal niceties right now.

"Red, Red, Red," she called. "Point Six Five to any Federation units. Points Six Five and Three Four under attack and needing assistance. Hostile units on the ridge between us and the refugee camp—" *does it have a number?* "—with friendly units in the camp and with us."

Linak'h:

Ursula Boll waited behind the utility stack for the terrorist to enter the kitchen. The woman was thoroughly alert, bigger than she was but not nearly as fast. Possibly Boll also had little more adrenaline in her system.

However it came about, what happened was that Boll

took the visitor entirely by surprise. She clamped one hand over the woman's face from behind and stabbed her in the kidneys. The woman died without a sound, then slipped out of Boll's grasp and thumped to the floor.

That had to warn the others. Boll dropped to the floor, rolled to give herself a clean shot at the guard and leader, and hit him twice in the throat. He dropped, but not before getting off three shots. One of them shattered Boll's left knee.

Shock damped pain but seemed to speed up her thoughts. *No getting clear now.* Her plan had been to get behind the other two, probably with the couch for cover, and pin them down. It might have worked, too—the dead man had grenades on his belt that she could have used.

Boll was searching her first victim as the pain hit and the other two terrorists burst out into the living room. They were trained enough to dive for cover, but not enough to do it by instinct. Boll had the instinct, in spite of the pain, and she also had the dead woman's carbine.

She might have hit one of the terrorists and certainly chopped bits out of the walls and a few of Nikolai's statues. Not to mention a bullet hole in one of the studies for *The Young Queen.* The original, mercifully, was back in the studio, and if these *schweinhunden* didn't burn the house or the storm open up more of the roof—

A green egg-shape soared into the air. A curse followed it, but the grenade was too far ahead of the protest to be recalled. Boll had just time to roll, dragging the dead woman's body over hers as a shield, before the grenade hit and exploded.

Fiery needles drove into her in places she'd been certain were protected. A small axe seemed to gouge the left side of her skull, ending up with its blade piercing her left eye. She knew she shouldn't cry out. For some reason that was easy.

The two terrorists stood up. One of them had a blood-stain spreading down a dangling right arm.

"Why'd you—?" he asked, in a voice that made Boll think of a wounded dog.

"The children as hostages," the other snarled. "If they're still here, she can tell us where."

It was useful to know that somebody among the terrorists was thinking tactically, even if she would never be able to pass the knowledge along to Nieg. It was even more useful to know why she hadn't screamed.

The children.

She fixed a picture of Sophia and Peter in her mind as the two men approached. They weren't alone, but the shadowy figure beside them was hard to identify and maybe it was two people . . .

The mystery wasn't solved by the time the two men were close enough. Boll had the carbine in a firm grip. Now she brought it up and around. Weak as she was, a one-handed grip was still enough at such short range.

Both men died, although one of them took a long time about it. He was still moaning when Ursula Boll died, her last sensation one of frustration that she'd never know who was standing with the children.

Linak'h:

It was ten minutes before Tachin raised anyone. When she did, the reply nearly blasted her ears off her skull and the radio off the lifter's bulkhead.

It turned out to be the convoy commander, a Major Lukkas, grounded some thirty kloms away but relayed through Gold One, courtesy of Elayne Zheng's skilled hands with a console. The major was not happy.

In fact, he was so unhappy that after about two minutes of hearing Tachin try to get in a word, Brian Mahoney took over the radio. He signaled to Tachin that the Ptercha'a were deployed with the Navy team and that the second lifter was returning to camp at Kunkuhn's orders and that if any heads were going to roll over this, he would stick his neck out on the basis of RHIP.

"Major, I don't know or care what the legal aspects of this situation are," Mahoney concluded. "What I'm telling you are the facts.

"The Ptercha'a from the camp are on our side. The camp itself is being adequately defended, or they wouldn't have come to our help. It's impossible to move to the camp without abandoning a Federation facility."

The silence lasted a few more seconds than before. Mahoney pressed his advantage.

"Look. Right now we've got friendlies on either side of

the ridge and the bad guys in the middle. Easy targeting for everybody. We start moving around and we'll have fratricide all over the place."

A still longer silence. Mahoney seemed to take that as assent.

"We can ground our own machines. I don't have authority over the Hunters, but they have two really old and creaky Poshings. I don't know the model, but numbers are 890*LAN* and 213*STO*. Get a visual ID on anything in the air before you shoot it, and you can sort out the bad guys from the good guys."

This time, Mahoney actually waited until it was clear that the major was either agreeing, drawing up court-martial charges, or losing the connection.

"I don't much care which, either," Mahoney said. "Now, flip for who goes to rescue Candy's family?"

Tachin realized she must be gaping and expected Brian to snarl at her. Instead he grinned. He must have worked off a lot of his frustration and bad temper on the major.

"Why do you think I didn't tell him about our vehicles being down? With only two Confraternity lifters available, he'd have made it a direct order for us to stay out. By the time we'd settled that, I'd be up for a court-martial and every terr from here to the Braigh'n would know what we were up to." He pulled out his lucky piece, a blessed Saint Patrick medallion. "Tails, you go."

The medallion came up tails. Mahoney didn't have an easy job picking the rest of the party, because everybody wanted to volunteer.

Linak'h:

Something was terribly wrong. Mother had not come back. Sophia knew that this was the only reason why they were not all of them out in the forest by now. (Or at least all of them who could travel; Mother had not said anything, but it seemed likely that Father was too badly hurt to travel.)

Still, whatever had happened was something that Mother must have known could happen. Otherwise why would she have told them to stay hidden in the shelter if she did not come back? Stay hidden for a whole day—there was a clock in the shelter along with everything else—and then listen for another half-day to make sure there were no bad people—"terrorists," she called them—in the house.

The terrorists must have come while Mother was in the house. She had fought them; Sophia recognized the sound of shooting, even though the shelter had thick walls that kept out most of the sound. The same walls also kept in the sound of Peter crying. He could hardly talk at all now, and if that went on *and* Mother did not come back he would start screaming instead.

The walls might not hide that much noise, if the terrorists were still around. Maybe they weren't. Maybe Mother had killed them all and was upstairs because she needed to take care of Father.

But maybe they had hurt her, too, so that she couldn't move. That thought scared Sophia almost to the point where *she* was ready to scream, but she knew that if she did, Peter would never calm down.

It would be nice if Cousin Candy would come around. She was an even better soldier than Mother, and with her in the house there would be nothing to be afraid of. She would also want to know that Sophia and Peter had done what their parents told them to do.

"Peter, you can't do anything by crying. Mother and Father told us to be quiet."

Maybe Peter took a deep breath before the next sob, maybe he didn't. Sophia said, "Peter. Mother and Father will both be angry with us, if we get in trouble by making a noise."

This time there was almost silence. Sophia prayed (she thought God might look a little like Cousin Candy would when she was an Old Queen instead of a Young one).

"Cousin Candy will have to get us out of trouble if we make noise. She will be angry."

Somehow the threat of Cousin Candy's wrath seemed to work. Or maybe it was the idea that somebody could get them out of this trouble.

Peter snuggled up to his sister the way he did to his mother. Sophia put an arm around his shoulders, the way Mother had done. She wished she could do more. In fact, she wanted Cousin Candy to help them just as much as her brother did, but she couldn't tell him that or he would get scared all over again.

Linak'h:

Just after the rescue mission lifted off, Brigitte Tachin decided that it was improvised to the point of sloppiness and irregular to the point of insubordination. She wondered if Brian was showing off and she was cooperating to make him feel better, or if both of them simply resented Major Lukkas's attitude that Navy people couldn't fight on the ground without three bodyguards and a nanny.

She also decided that the rescue mission, even if ill-judged, was the only alternative to doing nothing while children might be in danger. This improved her spirits considerably, although it did nothing to improve the smell in the lifter's cabin.

The Ptercha'a pilot seemed a complete master of low-and-slow flying. Tachin wondered if all his experience had been gained legally. He not only flew at treetop level, he flew between the trees and would have flown between the branches if the lifter had been small enough. As for speed, on level ground a fit rider on a good bicycle could have kept up with the lifter.

It was Tachin's decision to go straight in. She was leading, and a complete electronic blackdown was in effect until they reached the house. If nobody was there, no problem; if there was a trap, the terrs crewing it would have less time to react.

So they covered the last few hundred meters at regular cruising speed, everybody gripping weapons and nerves. The pilot pulled them to a stop directly over the house, and all doors and hatches popped open. The two Hunters and one human of the first team tossed out their ropes and abseiled down to the gaping hole in the rain-slick roof of the house. Then the lifter sailed off to the west, everyone except the pilot either scanning the ground or frantically winding up the ropes before they tangled in fans or branches.

The lifter grounded less than a klom from the house. Tachin assigned the pilot and one human to security for the lifter and organized the rest into an improvised squad. "Don't even think about anything heroic," she told the security pair. "If any strangers show up, run until you can hide. Do not worry about losing touch with us, either. You cannot possibly run fast enough to stay ahead of us, if *we* run into serious trouble."

That was for the record. Personally, she would rather die than leave the house before she knew what had happened to the children, but she couldn't order anyone else to die for her feelings. She was even coolheaded enough not to take point as the squad approached the house. One of the Ptercha'a did that, a woman who spoke neither Commercial Merishi nor any human language but said enough with hands, ears, tail, and a judiciously pointed rifle.

The caution was wasted. The human abseiler met the squad at the door, with a face that said everything Tachin had been afraid to learn. She gripped the doorjamb for a moment to steady herself. She hoped her legs and stomach would hold up to knowing that they'd been too late even for the kids.

Just for a few more minutes, please, God.

It was both worse and better than she'd expected. Both Nikolai Komarov and Ursula Boll were dead, but so were the four terrorists. From the way the bodies lay, it looked as if Boll had taken all four of them with her, defending her helpless and dying husband.

One of the terrorists was not long dead. A few minutes earlier and he might have been patched up for eventual interrogation. That was the only difference a quicker rescue mission could have made.

Or was it?

"The children!"

"Ehhh—?" several Ptercha'a and humans said together.

"Two children, a girl about nine Standard, a boy a couple of Standard younger. Find them!"

The eight rescuers split into pairs and started a room-by-room search. With heroic self-control, Tachin waited until they had finished searching the house and outbuildings before calling Brian Mahoney.

"No sign of them?"

"Most of their stuff was in their rooms, but they're not in the house."

"And the rain would have washed out any tracks."

"It's slacking off." Visibility was now close to a hundred meters. As she spoke, Tachin was staring into the forest, eyes fixed intently on a clump of measlewort, as if sheer power of concentration could materialize the children.

"They would have left the house a while back, while it was still pouring. Uncle Maurice himself couldn't trail them now."

"We're not going to try. What's the situation back at your end?"

Tachin only half-listened to Mahoney's report of a second terrorist force, armed only with light weapons, coming in from the north to link up with the one on the ridge. "Uncle Maurice" was their private code for telling a cover story over insecure com channels.

Brian didn't think the kids had run off. That left— kidnapping? Possible, and her stomach twisted at the thought of TacAir riding in and hurling flame and thunder on the children as well as the terrorists.

More likely, though, there was a hiding place in or around the house. Almost certainly well concealed, sound-proofed, and accessible from the outside only through the household system computer or one of the personals.

"Brigitte, do you read me?"

"Sorry. I was trying to put myself in Uncle Maurice's place. What would he—?"

"He'd haul his fat arse out of there, and you do the same even if yours isn't fat. The second team of terrs is between the camp and you. If the camp beats them off, they may retreat right past you. Move!"

No way to beg a few extra minutes without breaking security. If the children weren't already hostages, retreating terrs would tear the house apart to make them so. She broke the circuit and turned to her people.

"Anybody got a grenade?" she called. About four people at once held them up. All Ptercha'a models, she noticed.

"Good. Booby-trap the main terminal, grab the personals and bring them along, and haul your tails out of here."

She had expected Mahoney to sound frantic when she called him back from the lifter. Instead he sounded relieved.

"You didn't waste any time, did you?"

"I hope not."

"Good. Our friendly major has justified himself at last. He drew some of the right conclusions and led a CA right on to the ridge top. The camp is safe and counting casualties, and the surviving terrs are retreating. Some of them might still come your way, so keep your heads up."

"Can do."

The sky was lightening now, and the rain had almost stopped. Tachin realized that the thumps and rattles from the northeast were the CA-spawned firefight, not the storm, and that the water in her eyes was sweat instead of rain. She pulled off her helmet and ran her fingers through her hair.

Not as bad as it could have been, so far, and more thanks to Ptercha'a improvisation and self-defense than to anything humans had done. Also, it could still get worse. The children were still missing.

Fourteen

Victoria:

Even awakened before dawn, Lucco DiVries could recognize Colonel Peter Bissell's voice. The voiceprint scan on the com and the three authentication codes were just icing on the cake.

None of them answered the question of what Bissell was doing back on Victoria instead of on Linak'h. Not that DiVries expected the Victorian chief of intelligence to broadcast his movements, but it was reasonable to hope he would not create unnecessary mysteries.

War, however, was not the province of the reasonable. Sophie Bergeron had said that more than a few times. She'd been right, too—if not, why wasn't she still alive and married to Lucco?

This hour of the morning was already depressing enough without such thoughts, DiVries decided.

Bissell's cake quickly turned to sand. Cold, gritty, mineral-laden sand, like the dunes west of DiVries's station. Peter Bissell was using free cryptic even on what was supposed to be a secure circuit. He was describing a situation that anybody who'd survived Victoria's first round of wars could recognize as suspicious if not outright dangerous.

"—nobody invited to the party at the barracks. But nobody showed up either. It looks as if they're still shopping, then planning to rent rooms at the hill town."

"They'll need Hennessey's if they're that many."

"You can arrange to provide hospitality in a few other places, can't you?"

"I can, but should I? The help's spread pretty thin."

"We don't want a big party."

"I don't want my people spread so thin that they can't

handle somebody who drinks too much or we run out of good stuff."

Translated, this meant that unidentified and apparently armed people were gathering outside Fort Bergeron in Mount Houton, to the northeast of DiVries's station. They were also registering on sensor scans of the desert to the south of Mount Houton and its sister city of Kellysburg.

Peter Bissell wanted DiVries to discreetly call up his covert-operations people and keep all these unidentified people under surveillance. Presumably this would go on until they were identified, and if they were ID'ed as hostile, the Victorian Ground Forces would move in.

The problem was that Bissell didn't have a reliable head count, except in Mount Houton, and there it was "platoon-plus," which might be anything up to a hundred people. Also, Bissell wasn't saying anything about weapons.

If everybody cooperated, DiVries could call out maybe eighty people, plus three lifters armed with heavy weapons—enough for one short battle, at least. Not enough to break up into a dozen scout teams, without tempting the bad guys to try cleaning them up—and far too many to lose if the bad guys did yield to temptation.

"I still say we want one big party and not a lot of little ones. I can pilfer-proof the hospitality supplies, no problem."

"What we want may not be what our guests would prefer."

"They'll see reason." DiVries hoped he hadn't crossed the line from advice and dissent to outright disobedience. Facts weren't a problem with free cryptic; subtle shades of attitude were.

"Maybe. Be damned sure about the pilfer-proofing, though."

"The barracks hospitality committee is your people, isn't it?"

"They may need some help."

Meaning that Bissell wasn't sure the caretaker party at Fort Bergeron had the guts or the loyalty to blow up the critical supplies if threatened with capture.

"What I can give them, they'll get." *Now pray that that's enough and that Jump Shock hasn't turned Bissell into a martinet or a micromanager.*

"We want to keep the party under control. But you know the people on both sides better than I do."

"I damned well hope so. Otherwise I'd better stay on the farm and leave the cities alone."

Bissell was already off-circuit. DiVries was calling up a roster of his covert-network people when he felt a warm breath on the back of his neck, then warm arms around his shoulders.

"Hi, 'Reesa."

She kissed the back of his neck. It was a silent thank you for not saying "Sophie," as he'd sometimes done during moments of intimacy or stress. 'Reesa didn't mind sharing Lucco with a ghost most of the time, but she did like him to be able to tell the real woman from the ghost.

He summarized the conversation. 'Reesa nodded approvingly. "I wish Bissell wasn't playing at all. But at least he seems to know the rules."

"He may be trying to get something out of Gist and Parkinson. The last time I heard, he wasn't too happy about the whole Expeditionary Battalion idea. He may think that if he's nice to the local people, they'll be on his side."

"*Mierda*!" 'Ressa said. "What makes him think there is anybody crazy enough to go off to Linak'h and fight a war there?"

"If there are people crazy enough to want another war here—"

"A good argument for keeping all the crazy people at home, where the sane ones can watch them!"

In the next hour, DiVries's network turned out forty armed people with six lifters. Three of them were cargo haulers, and DiVries's orders to them were to evacuate any depots that looked threatened but couldn't be protected. Twenty people had that job; the other twenty were going to Mount Houton.

"I'm not worried much about Fort Bergeron," DiVries said. "What worries me is the local Merishi up there."

"I can't imagine them working with another rebellion."

"Most of the ones who got their claws trimmed in the last war have left. Space Security might have slipped in a dozen of their people since then. Besides, what if the anti-Merishi campaign's about to go beyond wall-scrawlings and calls for boycotts? There's no safe enclave for them up there."

"I'd say there was no sense in the Merishi going back to Mount Houton in the first place."

"Craziness isn't limited by race."

Victoria:

President Gist was less than delighted to hear that Colonel Bissell had alerted all four Intelligence AO's on his own authority. From the look on Alys Parkinson's face, she was ready to remove part of Bissell's skin or even all his authority, but there was no one to take his place, and no good ever came of humiliating a junior officer in public.

The three digested their breakfast and the first reports from all four AO's at the same time. Gist decided the sausages tasted better than the news.

"I wouldn't worry so much if we didn't have that damned Scaleskin cruiser sitting overhead," he said. "If more than a few Merishi get killed, they'll have an excuse for intervention."

"How?" Bissell asked. "They can't do much with ship weapons from orbit, and they don't have any ground fighters around."

"Have you looked at the capacity stats for those 'chartered' Scaleskin merchanters in orbit? Even better, have you or anybody else gone aboard them?"

"I've been too busy—"

"Rescuing your power base in Intelligence," Parkinson finished for the colonel. "Peter, I don't criticize that. We don't doubt your loyalty, so having you firmly in control of Intelligence is a good thing. But there are a few things that haven't been done that should have been. One of them is making sure those transports don't have a couple of cohorts of loyal Pussy mercenaries aboard."

"I'll have to coordinate that with the Ministry of Transport's Inspection Division. While I'm doing that, I can also see about getting the company aboard *Somtow Nosavan* down—"

"No," Gist and Parkinson said together.

"Why?" Bissell asked. He was as close to open defiance as Gist had seen him. Long-deferred tension seemed about ready to escalate to confrontation, and he wasn't going to ask Alys to play peacemaker again.

You were a soldier too, once, in the Late Renaissance. Or so you've said. Time to back it up.

"Up there, the company's aboard a trustworthy ship. Aboard a shuttle, they're a vulnerable target for sabotage or a suicide ramming. Down on the ground, they're just one more company, who could land a thousand kloms from where they're needed.

"The Merishi can't openly fire on Defence Force shuttles without committing an act of war. I doubt if they're ready for that. In a few hours, we should be ready to protect the shuttles against anybody else.

"Right now, I want to protect the local Merishi and Government House first. There aren't enough crazies on Victoria to put through a rebellion if they don't have outside support and we're still alive. But if we're dead and the Merishi are offering to help—a lot of people may be more afraid of chaos than they are of the Scaleskins. Then Victoria winds up with a legal Merishi puppet government."

That image apparently bothered the others even more than it did Gist. He suspected that even the Merishi wouldn't plan to use a coup on Victoria as more than a diversion from Linak'h. Victoria was a bargaining chip that they could offer to give up in return for a free hand on Linak'h.

In such a situation, Gist honestly didn't know what the Federation would do. But he was damned sure that even a few days of Merishi goons roaming the streets would be too many, entirely apart from Alys and him being dead.

"Colonel, you handle the ships and your covert-operations people. Be sure to take a good bodyguard any time you move. Make it clear to all ships in orbit that we have a security threat of indeterminate size and duration. They should give us warning of any maneuvers and search anyone coming up from dirtside.

"Alys, the company aboard *Nosavan* stays put, but you start scaring up escort for the shuttles in case we have to move them. The two companies from Port Harriet come in to Thorntonsburg. One secures an area that includes Government House. The other cordons off the Merishi area and transports into it any Scaleskins who don't want to take chances."

Bissell frowned. "What about other troops besides the VEB?"

Gist's laugh was explosive. "You've been saying since you got back that those handpicked troopers were more useful on Victoria than on Linak'h. No logistic problems, and so forth. Afraid of casualties?"

This time it was Parkinson who glared at the president. "That, Jere, is not necessarily a vice. In fact, I think you owe the colonel an apology."

"Sorry. Didn't mean you were soft. But I think I'm missing something."

"We can argue the softness some other time," Bissell said. "What I'm thinking is that we don't want the Defence Forces guarding the Merishi. We want Special Branch."

Gist had thought Bissell had lost the ability to surprise him. He wasn't sure he enjoyed being proved wrong. "Those bastards! Why?"

"If the troopers are all around the Merishi, it's easy to arrange an incident where they'll look at fault. Then the Merishi can claim the Defence Forces are a menace, and they *can* take out most of our key facilities and a lot of people from orbit. No need to land troops to wreck the Army so thoroughly that their friends can take over without a serious fight.

"But if the Special Branch people do it, we put the disloyal ones in a nice dilemma. If they go along with a lot of Merishi-killing, they'll be the target for retaliation. If they do the job we tell them to, the Merishi will have to arrange the incidents some other way. That may be more than they can do in the time they'll have available."

Gist contemplated the fine hairs on Alys Parkinson's upper lip. They told him neither the secrets of the universe nor even what games Bissell was playing.

The man's reasoning made a brutal kind of sense. On one condition—

"You have, I presume, infiltrated Special Branch, or at least turned a few of the Scaleskin agents?"

Bissell shrugged. "A sensible precaution, wouldn't you say? We didn't want any more trouble like the attack on Franke and Morley, and we couldn't purge the SB's without control of the Ministry of Justice."

"Amen," Gist said. "I don't suppose you could also tell me if you accepted Federation help with the infiltration?"

"Wait for my memoirs, sir."

"If you live to write them. All right, Colonel. Launch!"

Gist's sigh of relief nearly blew Colonel Bissell out the office door. Parkinson put a hand on his wrist.

"Alys, that's likely to send my pulse rate up, not down."

She shifted her hands to the back of his neck. He leaned into her fingers, soothing even with only a few moments to work.

"One thing more we're going to try," he said, after letting out quite a different kind of sigh. "Get me the most secure circuit you have and put me through to Payaral Na'an."

Parkinson actually looked blank for a moment, then dubious. "He may not want to cooperate. We may be putting him in danger by even asking."

"He also doesn't want to lose Simferos Associates' trade monopoly. Or he didn't the last time we talked. And the last time I looked at the records, three of those four ships were Simferos charters and the last one was a subsidiary holding.

"We may learn quite a lot without owing it to Peter Bissell. Even if Na'an plays stoneface, we'll know more than we do now."

Victoria:

Payaral Na'an's private chambers were soundproofed from the outside, echoproofed within, and periodically scanned for eavesdropping devices. Still, he waited for even the memory of Jeremiah Gist's harsh voice to die before he called up a map of Thorntonsburg.

The enclave would do its intended task. The Folk within it would not even suffer much discomfort, save by design, unless they were confined there for rather longer than seemed likely.

(Or desirable. If this crisis was not resolved within a few days, it would likely end in a victory for what Gist called "the bad buys." Na'an preferred to call them "those of limited vision," being a trifle less willing to see evil in his own people.)

But the Special Branch protection gave Na'an a problem. He would lose his secure communications with far too many people if he settled into the enclave. He also could not ask enough of his trained people to stay with him to physically secure him here in the office complex. Nowhere near enough; they would be needed to organize the evacuation of their fellow employees and, when that was done, to offer their services to others of the Folk. Na'an sipped fruit juice while he planned, and finished his third cup before he felt ready to call for the First and Third Watch Leaders. (The Second was out in the suburbs of Thorntonsburg, busy enough for three beings with the work of organizing the Simferos Folk out there *and* preparing to send aid north to Mount Houton. The more of the Folk who were in Na'an's debt, the better for all concerned—and that went far beyond Simferos Associates and its allies.)

"As soon as we know that our people have assigned quarters in this area, they can begin moving," he said. "Everyone should have at least one change of garb and two days' self-preserving food."

The First expressed doubts. Some of the survival supplies showed signs of having been tampered with. Na'an advised taking samples, sending one set up to the cruiser *Gyn-Bahr,* and giving him the other.

He did not mention giving the other to the humans, but both Watch Leaders seemed to guess his intention. They vowed silence, but left with expressions that suggested they expected Space Security guards to spring from the floor and drop from the ceiling.

Na'an watched them go without anger. Five years ago, the idea of keeping secrets from Space Security would have been more alien to him than the rituals of the Hunters' House of Light. Both he and the Folk's chosen defenders had changed in that time.

Victoria:

"All well with the ships?" Gist asked the returning Colonel Bissell. In the corner, Alys Parkinson hissed like a leaking hydraulic line with the effort not to laugh.

"The good news is that they're all willing to go along with not letting anybody aboard unidentified or unreported. The only exception is *Gyn-Bahr.*"

"I didn't expect any different," Gist said.

"None of them are happy about facing a security situation," Bissell said. "The CO of the embarked company was outright unhappy. I told him that leaving *Nosavan* without your permission would be mutiny, and that Captain Marder was empowered to act on behalf of the Victorian Defense Forces in suppressing it or him."

He added hastily, as Gist's frown turned into a glare, "I take full responsibility for that order, Mr. President. I don't think the CO will make serious trouble, anyway. He has a good ground combat record, but this is his first time in space. He won't try butting heads with Captain Marder."

"If he does, I know whose horns will be broken," Parkinson said. "Someone who's been to Hell isn't bothered by a short detour through Purgatory on the way to settling a few debts."

Bissell nodded. "I couldn't obtain any information on cargoes. The Customs Division has developed a habit of not asking Merishi ships for declarations unless they state an intent to land cargo."

"We can deal with Customs later," Gist said. "For now, I have some intelligence on those ships. Three are carrying general cargo—I won't bother with a detailed list—that could be sold at any one of twenty planets around here. Most of it could also be used as relief supplies to a planet suffering from war or natural disaster.

"The fourth ship is a passenger liner—more like an emigrant ship, actually, although the Merishi don't have that exact category. She's empty, and I assume she was sent here to be ready to evacuate Merishi or anyone else who wants off-planet in a hurry."

"Ah—can you tell me anything that might let me judge the reliability of your source, Mr. President?"

"If you've been checking with Customs enough to catch them taking Merishi bribes, you should have come across that bit of data yourself."

Bissell looked bemused. Gist fumed quietly. "Simferos Associates chartered three of them," Bissell finally said. "That suggests who. But it doesn't say much about his reliability."

"No, but my guts say a lot."

"Mr. President, do I have to—?"

"Trust my guts? Yes, unless you want to be hanged in a rope of your own."

From Bissell's look it was clear he didn't think the joke was funny. It didn't help that Parkinson finally lost her battle to stifle laughter. Gist had to clap her on the back to keep her from choking. Bissell watched the whole spectacle with frozen dignity, except for the fingers of his left hand, which kept twisting in and out of his beard until it looked like a hoopnester's crest.

"Yes, Colonel?"

"Permission to—"

The com alarm rang. Gist listened to two messages—the Port Harriet companies had loaded and were about to lift, and several suspicious vehicles had been sighted in Parrville.

Parrville was the roughest quarter of Thorntonsburg, the source of a good deal of trouble during the First Victoria War (that title might be useful within another day or two). The people there weren't all evil or even desperate. But some of them were more easily led than others, and a great many were willing to look the other way if somebody infiltrated agents trying to appeal to the rest.

Also, Parrville offered a secure base within easy striking range—even medium-tube range—of the Merishi enclave, Government House, and the President's House, where they sat now.

A flight of lifters passed overhead, low enough for their whine to penetrate even the insulation of the President's House. A call for screen showed the tails of a dozen civilian lifters, with Merishi faces visible in windows.

It was a race, with half a dozen runners each moving at an angle to the others, collisions almost certain, and Victoria the ribbon for whoever picked themselves up the fastest.

Victoria:

Payaral Na'an spoke the final voice command just loudly enough for the computer's sound pickup to record it. That was the end of the sequence; anybody who tried to retrieve the most vital data without using that command would now wipe the data from the central core *and* detonate the bomb in the console.

Na'an admitted that the last step was unnecessary, even vindictive and a risk to innocent people. It had probably been a risk to him as well, as he was by no means an explosives expert. Just a boy who had played with chemicals and electronics, grown to a man who would probably not live to see a nest-free son of his own. If his marriage had been successful—

The noise of the door opening made him turn slowly, his hands spread and held well away from his sides to show that he was unarmed and submissive. As he turned, he looked at the display of the Watch positions. Only four guards left in the building now, just enough to prevent theft as people evacuated, scheduled to evacuate themselves in—a look at the clock—half a tenth-day.

Which one of them was working with the visitors?

There were three of them, two Folk and a Hunter. No, three in the room. A shadow and soft breathing proved a fourth and suggested that it was human.

Na'an had wondered what it would take to calm him in the face of death. Now he knew. His powers of observation were as acute as ever. He might almost have been in Assimilation Mode. He could even detect the subtle hints that the second of the Folk was Security, probably Space but perhaps Ground Vanguard.

If Space Security has not approached some of our own ground-fighters for an alliance, they are relying entirely on the Hunters. Which makes them foolish and doomed.

Watching doom overtake fools was always entertaining to wise men. Unfortunately, Na'an doubted that it was an entertainment he would be spared to attend.

"Why am I not surprised to see you?" he said to the first Folk. "You have left your post, betraying the people I entrusted to you."

Na'an could not risk turning his head to see if the consoles were free of any signs that the hidden camera was recording this scene. He settled for reading the killers' eyes. None of them seemed to be noticing anything unusual.

The Second Watch Leader's face twisted, eyes half-closed, a muscle jerking in the side of his neck.

"You have betrayed the entire race of Folk!" the second Folk said.

Nobody but a Space Security fanatic could say that without smiling.

The Second Watch Leader's hand came up, a needler in it. Na'an heard the *phut* and felt the half-punch, half-sting of the needles driving into his chest. *Three of them,* he thought.

He felt very calm, because he had calculated that the Second Watch Leader was the most likely traitor and for that reason had trusted Emt Desdai with most of the security precautions. One of the Folk who despised Hunters as the Second did would not think one of them capable of doing a tenth of what Desdai had done. It was like expecting a nestgrubber to recite poetry.

Na'an's calm even survived the numbness spreading from where the needles had gone in. Five-phase, it felt like—one of the standard non-lethal needler loads, probably with a hypnotic added.

Not surprising. The surprise would come later, after his self-administered dosage of kylon produced a lethal allergic reaction. Lethal immediately to their hopes of interrogating him, lethal eventually to him. If one was about to become a corpse, it helped to become an encumbrance, even a menace, to one's killers.

Just as a final precaution, however, Na'an fell sideways when he felt his legs weakening. He had enough control to crack his head hard against the edge of the worktable, and the last sound he heard was an explosive curse from the Second.

Victoria:

"There's been an explosion at the Trade Commission," Alys Parkinson said. Behind her on the screen Gist saw what seemed to be half the officers on her HQ staff hunched over displays or talking with their heads together.

With the Security Company fully deployed around the President's House and all the electronics on-line, they'd decided to set up the main HQ here. Government House could serve as a backup, handling less-critical material unless and until Gist and Parkinson had to withdraw to it.

Meanwhile, it would serve as a protected refuge for the politicos, and by keeping them out of Gist's hair would reduce his chances of having to retreat. He had not reached the point of handing out "They shall not pass" buttons, but the look on his face and Alys's conveyed the message well enough.

"Any sign of attack?"

"I'll ask the AOP's, but we hadn't recorded any heavy weapons within range at the time."

"That doesn't mean—" Gist began. The com alarm prevented him from insulting Alys by telling her how to do her job.

Then the alarm note changed; somebody wanted the ultra-secure circuit.

A dead man—dead Folk, if one wanted to be precise—was calling. Gist watched the replayed scene of Payaral Na'an's death, then the data marching across the screen. He let his terminal's on-line memory record the whole file before he moved a muscle. Then he dumped the file into the same secure storage as Na'an's previous contributions and the material supplied by Franke and Morley before they left for Linak'h.

He called Parkinson back and said that he had reliable information from a secret source that the explosion at the Trade Commission was internal.

"That's not what the cruiser captain says."

"What does the Scaleskin bastard say that has to do with anything?"

"He says that the explosion was an escalation of terrorism against the Folk population of Victoria. The present government seems unable to control it. He is requesting permission to land Ground Security investigative teams to work with our Special Branch people."

"Tell him to bugger off."

"Don't tempt me. Those exact words?"

"As you said, don't tempt me. Put it that we disagree with his estimate of the situation. Our people can handle it. If he was right, we could not guarantee his people's safety and they would be too busy ducking to get any work done."

"I'll dress it up a bit. Oh, the Port Harriet companies have a new ETA, eight minutes earlier than the last one. Tailwinds, I suppose."

"I don't care if they've chartered dragons to tow the lifters!"

Gist looked at his watch. Four hundred reliable troopers would be on the ground in Thorntonsburg in another twenty minutes. But if the bad guys had quick reflexes, they could still send the situation out of control in that time.

Gist switched to a semi-secure outside line. He wasn't

going to be swapping secrets with any politician at Government House, not even everybody's honest broker Senator Father Elijah Brothertongue.

Aboard R.M.S. *Somtow Nosavan,* off Victoria:

"Captain, I continue to protest—"

"Major Bleeker, I've registered enough protests from you to fill a whole file," Joanna Marder said. "May I remind you that I don't have the authority to call up escorted shuttles? I do have the authority to refuse to let you endanger yourself and your men.

"I have it by law, as captain, and I also have it by the request of your superior officers. The terms of our charter oblige me to cooperate with—"

"I can protest those orders," the major expostulated. He repeated that, with variations that included sexual innuendos about his superiors, for a couple of minutes. Marder saw faces behind the major, the company HQ preserving a careful neutrality except for a couple who looked either scared or disgusted.

"I must request you to provide me with communications facilities for a message to Defence Forces HQ," Bleeker concluded.

"I can comply with that request, up to a point," Marder said. She exchanged glances with Charlie Longman. Her lover and chief engineer looked mystified, encouraging, and a little scared himself.

"I have been ordered to keep all secure channels available for messages from the ground," Marder went on. "Your request would have to go in clear."

That was so close to a lie that if he challenged her on it there would be even more trouble. She was gambling on his being too scared to think straight—and on his officers being too loyal to the Republic to straighten him out.

"I—I will reconsider that request. In fact, I withdraw it. Please keep me informed of the tactical situation, though. I am more concerned with my company being out of the fighting than I am with danger on the way down."

And the Baernoi are vegetarian pacifists.

"I understand, Major."

Marder blanked her screen and reached out vaguely to

the left. She half-hoped the hand would return with a glass or even a bottle in it. She told herself she didn't like the taste of liquor anymore; she just wanted a little blunting of her senses and soothing of her nerves.

Instead the hand touched a human form—demonstrably male and just below the waist. Marder snatched her hand back as Charlie Longman laughed.

"The last time you took hold there—"

"Mr. Longman, duty calls. Specifically, it calls you to man Engineering Control. You, Butkus, one tech—so you can maneuver the ship as well as run the internal systems."

"And secure it?" he asked. He spoke so quietly she knew he must have realized what she meant, but somehow he looked less scared. Not surprising—Charlie was a worrier. If he didn't have a chance to worry, he came through in fine style, both in bed and out.

"Right," Marder said. "If we split control of the ship, and the troops know it, the hotheads may cool off."

Longman made what looked like a gesture of aversion.

Marder grinned. "Isn't that the Tusker gesture for warding off impotence? Not that I wish you to suffer from it—"

"You honor me, Captain."

"—but save the prayers and rites for keeping that bloody Merishi cruiser out of our hair."

"Aye-aye, ma'am."

Longman sketched a salute and turned to Boatswain Butkus. Marder adjusted trousers that seemed about to cut her in two at a vital point and switched the screen. *Gyn-Bahr* hadn't maneuvered, but had her shuttle dock been open ten minutes ago?

No. The playback made that sure. Knowing that, Marder was almost sure of something else—the Scaleskins were getting ready to make their move. Not knowing all the details of the ground situation, she couldn't be sure what that move would be, but knowledge of the capabilities of a *Ryn-Gath*-class cruiser led to several scenarios.

Somtow Nosavan could prevent all of them, but as an unarmed ship she had only one method open to her. Marder was confident that with surprise on her side she could use that method. She was equally sure that evacuating the troops would give the Merishi both warning and time to make *Nosavan*'s move futile.

One more sure thing: she would take the helm herself.

The backup command team could handle evasive action but not the fancy maneuvering needed for ramming.

Victoria:

Gist kept one eye on the updating of his private status board while the other watched the screen with Father Brothertongue on it. Finally he was satisfied that everything—mob, heavy weapons, ETA of the reinforcements, *Somtow Nosavan,* Merishi (cruisers, rabble-rousers, assassins, and anything else the Scaleskins were contributing to this witches' brew), Alys's nerves—was either under control or at least no more out of control than it had been ten minutes ago.

"So everybody's coping?" he asked the senator.

"That is one way of putting it. I would say hoping, myself. Hoping that this stops short of bloodshed. Or the shedding of more blood, at least."

"Nobody can hope that more than I. Which is why we're sending Government House a whole company."

"Troops can be a provocation as much as a defense."

Gist took the effort to reply politely. Brothertongue was something of a pacifist but no kind of fool, a rare and valuable combination even when he wasn't on your side.

"That depends on how ready the would-be enemy is to be provoked. We've had too much experience with the damage hotheads can do if they think they've got a free ride."

"That, I must confess, is entirely too true. I once believed it was the Fallen State—"

An alarm cut off Brothertongue's voice.

"Alys?"

She came on-screen, her face like Athena with a hangover. "There's been an unauthorized takeoff from the port. Human shuttle, but we're getting Merishi signals from it."

"Monitor, follow if possible, and warn *Nosavan.*"

He heard a salute in her voice. "Also, that Parrville crowd is starting to move. Three, maybe four columns. No signs of heavy weapons and only light personal armament."

"All right. Have the riot teams deploy to the planned chokepoints. Oh, and the companies—same ETA?"

"Yes."

"Have one drop off two platoons at the Trade Mission building. It's a good defensible OP for watching the crowds, no matter which way they move."

Alys didn't argue, and he didn't dare discuss the real reason for securing the Trade Mission. If the Merishi or their pimps who had to be in the crowd saw troops at the Trade Mission, they'd think the Victorians were searching it for intelligence. Intelligence it would be life or death to deny to the plotters' enemies.

Intelligence that Payaral Na'an had already given his life to collect and transmit to his human allies, who already had it safe and secure as long as *they* lived. The mob would be chasing marshlight. If they went on chasing it until they were too footsore, frustrated, and thirsty to do anything else—diversions had been standard tactics since there were tactics.

Forgive me, friend to all our races, if this diversion causes your body to be mutilated. I will do the Ritual of Shame before your father and anybody else who thinks they have a claim, but—

"Incoming!" somebody screamed over the circuit.

That had to be a visual sighting, because the explosion came only seconds later, with two more right behind it. As the screen went blank, Gist's chair toppled, wall panels popped free, and ceiling insulation cracked and tumbled. Dust swirled in miniature sandstorms across the stretch of floor in front of the President.

Fifteen

Linak'h:

From three thousand meters, Marshal Banfi could see five smoke columns instead of three. He decided that two of the ones he'd spotted on the last low pass were smaller, one was bigger. Neither good nor disastrous.

That phrase seemed to cover the whole situation. Terrorists (more accurately, guerrilla fighters, seeing how long they'd been in the field without being detected) had planned a major strike at the Administration-Federation-Confraternity alliance. Major targets: the refugee camp and Fed supplies—a massacre to put human and Hunter at each other's throats, and massive destruction of Federation supplies to weaken both fighting power and morale.

The attackers' reach had exceeded their grasp. Over a hundred casualties at the refugee camp, half of them fatal, but there should have been ten times that many.

One supply dump totally wrecked, with fuel, power packs, field support equipment, and much more under one of those smoke columns. Six Forces people dead and one TacAir squadron stuck in a fixed base for the duration of the crisis.

One restaurant in Och'zem wrecked, with casualties—eight dead, the last figure Banfi had. But they were from both races, as was the posse out hunting the restaurant-wreckers. Not just both races, but every faction of both. Some of the human refugees might still not embrace a Confrere as a brother; that didn't make them easily led into shooting one on sight.

For every other incident—eleven more, at last count—casualties didn't reach double figures and damage was minor. Everybody's infrastructure was intact, and mutual trust only needed patching.

Banfi had spent the morning at his desk, seeing that the Warband was ready, praising the judicious, cooling the hot-tempered, reassigning one cohort leader outright for short-changing a Confraternity militia unit on medical supplies. Meanwhile, he kept both official and unofficial channels open to Linak'h Command, and in the odd spare second he studied the Confraternity files on the Baernoi.

The Confraternity seemed to have more sources in the Baernoi Territory than everybody else on Linak'h put together, even though Banfi suspected he was getting carefully edited material. He was still human; the Confraternity was still an institution that humans had been willing to see outlawed for several centuries.

"Convoy coming up," the pilot said. She was Warband, Banfi's six bodyguards were half human and half Hunter, and the lifter itself was human-built, with universal controls.

Banfi looked out the window. Another smoke column on the horizon, and five hundred meters below, a big Fed lifter with two gunships and a light attacker riding escort. From the course they were steering, Banfi suspected they were on the way to the refugee camp, now the center of a two-battalion AO.

He hoped it was the load of non-lethals Nieg had said Tanz was sending out. Between the missing children and the miscellaneous civilians still in the area, neither the First/222 nor the Third/218 could really let fly. There was plenty of wilderness out there to hide guerrillas, if the two battalions couldn't find, fix, fight, and finish them before darkness fell.

In the seat behind the Marshal, Colonel Davidson was trying not to fidget. Sergeant Major Kinski wasn't even trying. Kinski had flying in his genes, not just his blood. Two hours of being flown by somebody else always had him ready to bite his nails or throttle his pilot.

Banfi leaned forward and said in True Speech, "All right. Sight-seeing time is over. Lay me down gently on Leader Tanz's flier pad."

If Tanz had any objections to Banfi's appearing in his capacity as Supreme Warband Leader of the Administration, the sooner this came out, the better. If Nieg's message about the sunflower seeds being delivered was correct, the worst dangers had been averted—although the faster 222 Brigade's own net came back up on its own, the better.

Tanz couldn't be a fuser to Banfi or anyone else now. But he could still be a webhead in Banfi's fans, and that would cost time that the Marshal didn't think Linak'h had. Or at least that the reasonable people didn't have—and some reasonable people might go the other way if they saw an easy victory in their grasp. Human and Hunter minds worked exactly the same way in that area.

"Course one-sixty, speed two-ten, altitude constant," the pilot said. "Escort reports they will need fresh power on this landing or the next."

"What—?" Davidson said. Banfi thought first that the colonel didn't trust Tanz to recharge their lifters, then realized he was staring out the window.

In the north, at the very limit of visibility, a glowing cloud hung halfway up the sky. It expanded, dissipated, and stopped glowing as they watched.

Then the alarms on the nudet sensors screamed, and automatic restraints gripped Banfi like an overfriendly K'thressh. The lifter seemed to tilt in three directions at once as the pilot threw it into evasive action and headed for the deck.

Linak'h:

Olga Nalyvkina's day so far had been her career high of "Hurry up and wait."

Up before Father-rise, a quick breakfast (cold cereal, lukewarm eggs, blessedly hot tea), then morning Officers call. Assignment to the ready-alert gunships, back to quarters for personal equipment, then out to the pad. A briefing from the crew chief, then up and in (and thanking God the squadron CO didn't insist on harness tight or canopy down; he'd put in enough cockpit hours to know about chafing and dehydration).

Then waiting, sipping water from one of the baby bottles (not too much, both to save it for emergencies and to avoid having to use the relief gear), checking displays, finding everything nominal seven times in a row, watching the clock creep around toward the end of the two-hour alert shift—

Electronic and visual alarms went off all over the field.

Nalyvkina was already doing the final preflight display scan when her radio shouted at her:

"Ready-alert flight, scramble!"

Her ears were still ringing from the blast when her winger took off on fan and lift combined. She was only ten seconds behind, the minimum interval to avoid fanwash, and the ASI read ninety km/h before she was over the field boundary.

As they climbed past two thousand meters, Nalyvkina saw the thunderheads pushing above the horizon to the north and west. The two gunships swung into a circle, waiting for orders that she hoped would *not* include a course straight into that weather front. She'd had a lifter pilot's license since she was seventeen and five hundred hours in gunship-type machines as well, but she'd never taken a combat-loaded gunship into that kind of weather and would be happy not to start now.

"You are Cheetah Flight," the radio said. "Course oh-two-five, maximum cruise."

Another glance at the displays, the terrain map in particular. That suggested a rendezvous with the 218 Brigade convoy on its way north to take over security at the refugee camp. Which cretin had sent it out without organic air-to-ground assets?

Probably the same one who will hang you up by your own briefs if you don't pull their nuts out of the fire.

"Cheetah Two," the radio said, in Second Lieutenant Bihrimati's voice. "I read a go order."

"That is a roger." Nalyvkina cut power to let Bihrimati close to the normal hundred-meter cruise interval, then gave him a visual thumbs-up. Fans whined and the two gunships raced north.

That was the last thing they did quickly during the whole morning. They didn't have to fly through the thunderstorm; the convoy had swung well to the west to avoid it and grounded. They also weren't alone. Apart from the company-plus of miscellaneous lifters scattered everywhere, two light attackers and a heavy showed up. Both must have pushed Mach limits most of the way from wherever they'd started, and the lights at least seemed a bit skimped on firepower.

Then the weather rolled over them, and Cheetah Flight had to ground in the rain-drenched security perimeter of the rear half of the convoy. Nobody seemed to have fresh power packs or quick-charge gear, so Nalyvkina ordered a shutdown.

"Is that wise?" Bihrimati asked.

"Yes," Nalyvkina said.

"We lose time getting out—"

"We lose too much power, we won't get out at all, except as passengers. The chain of command will be unhappy, all the way up to the taxpayers."

"Yes, ma'am."

What hadn't been wise, Nalyvkina realized now, was accepting element leadership this soon after joining the squadron. She knew pure field-and-fan work much better than most of her rank and age. She hadn't learned as much about the nuances of combat flying or weapons delivery. She also couldn't easily silence those who thought the step-up was a favor to Banfi.

That weather didn't break for more than an hour, while the Cheetah Flight pilots took turns monitoring the radio and going outside in the brief intervals between rain bursts to survey the ground and use a convenient tree for nature's calls. From the radio and a couple of visitors, they pieced together a working sketch of the tactical situation. Nalyvkina was relieved to see Bihrimati unprotesting about the strict Rules of Engagement in force. No amount of vengeance was worth having children's lives on their conscience.

Then the clouds and everybody's spirits lifted together. Six more gunships came in, with enough pilots senior to Nalyvkina to relieve her from sitting on Bihrimati or dealing with Major Lukkas (if the major was still OTC; reinforcements seemed to be piling in to the area like rush hour on the Yeltsinsk Metro).

Cheetah Flight acquired two of the newcomers; they formed the ground reserve while Nalyvkina and her winger grabbed a quick bite and took off again. Another hour of orbiting, impeller-charging the power pack as they circled, keeping a 360-degree eyeball watch, more to avoid midairs than to find targets. (At one point she counted thirteen different lifters from 218 Brigade in the air at once; visibility still restricted her view into the 222 AO, but radar showed a bug-swarm that must be the same thing happening to the northwest.)

"Cheetah and Treetiger flights, reload alert. We have groceries and dry clothes at LZ Crimson. Treetiger Flight first, beginning at eleven-thirty-five."

That meant the load of non-lethals was in and ready to be loaded on the gunships' weapons racks. Nalyvkina let out a Tartar war cry. Now they could go hunting seriously.

"Now" was slow to come; Nalyvkina's element ended up at the tail of the line. They'd just swung into the approach pattern when the radio blatted again. For the first time this morning, a scrambled radio voice sounded upset.

"Urgent, urgent, urgent. Large formation bogies crossing the Braigh'n Delta, bearing oh-four-five—"

Nalyvkina wanted a repetition of the speed, altitude, and estimated numbers. She distrusted AD sensors somewhat and orbital sensors a good deal more, and the figures made the bogies sound like the vanguard of an invasion from the Merishi Territory.

But nobody on the line was being sympathetic. All vehicles armed for air-to-air combat were to close on the bogies, identify, and if hostile engage and repel or destroy.

Nalyvkina realized, a moment before she heard Bihrimati's own war yell, that Cheetahs One and Two and the heavy attacker were the whole air-to-air force currently available.

"Cheetah One to Cousin Three. Want us to air-dock?"

"Affirmative."

The attacker dropped to five thousand meters to let the two gunships hook on where the air was thick enough that they could maneuver freely. Then they pressurized their cockpits, folded their fans, and settled down for a supersonic ride north to the Braigh'n Delta.

They were over the westernmost of the six channels in the Delta just after 1200. The weather front in the south hadn't reached up here, but another squatted over most of the Delta and nearly the whole border between the Federation and Merishi territories. As they undocked and started dropping from fifteen thousand meters, Nalyvkina looked for the southern edge of the burn from the Great Fire, but it was lost in the weather.

In plain sight was a large formation of mixed Ptercha'a and Merishi lifters, mostly civilian models in civilian markings but with a few Coordination Warband designs ambling along with the rest. It was hard to tell how many of each, never mind what they were.

It was not so hard to tell that they were on the wrong side of the border. If her map display wasn't enough, all Nalyvkina had to do was listen to Cousin Three's translated warning.

"Warning, warning, warning. You have crossed the border into the Administration's Territory without authorization or identification. Please show your authorization or identify yourself.

"If you do not, you will be required to land and submit to examination. If you refuse the order to land, we will be obliged to treat you as hostile and fire on you, if necessary with lethal force."

This was repeated in Commercial Merishi, High Merishi, and True Speech. Nalyvkina could follow the first, ignored the second, and struggled to piece a few words out of the third. She had been learning a fair amount of True Speech with Malcolm, although much of it more useful for reading *The Book of the Magic Mat* than in tactical situations.

The gaggle started to circle, its formation even looser than before. Nalyvkina tried to count again and got up to thirty-five before sunlight glinting off canopies warned her that some of the lifters were diving—toward the border.

The Feds were already weapons-free, but in this situation first shot went to the senior officer, Cousin Three. *Too bad we didn't get air-to-air non-lethals, as well as air-to-ground.* Chopping a lifterload of refugees like the people who'd attacked the *Old South* out of the sky would be almost as bad as killing the Komarov-Boll children.

A laser stabbed from the belly of Cousin Three. Nalyvkina recognized a precise, almost surgical stroke of minimal force, intended to hit and take out a fan or, at worst, fry electronics without more than singeing fur.

That took luck, and Cousin Three didn't have it. The target lifter spewed smoke from every opening, then the rear door blew out in a gush of flame. Smoking figures dropped from the flame, beginning a three-thousand-meter fall to the Braigh'n's waters below.

The circle fragmented almost explosively, thirty-odd lifters moving in as many different directions and at as many different speeds, all taking evasive action as they moved.

No easy targets for a disabling shot. The sons of bitches weren't going to be any easy target for any kind of shot!

Curse you! Identify yourselves. Are you looking for a martyr's—?

Four of the Warband lifters whipped into turns that shouted high power and light loads. Reflexively, Nalyvkina called for a sight picture on the nearest one.

She'd just had it when fire stabbed upward from the bottom of the formation. Her helmet visor polarized automatically, let her see the trace of superheated air leading up from the island to Cousin Three and into the attacker's belly.

Nalyvkina barely had time to crank her gunship into a tumbling half turn, half spin that somehow got it pointing the other way, when the sky behind her turned to fire.

Linak'h:

The years had told on Marshal Banfi. It was minutes after the lifter touched down on Tanz's pad before his joints and teeth stopped rattling. (Although his teeth might not be the fault of the low-altitude dash to the Zone so much as the seconds when it seemed their IFF wasn't working and the AD weaponry was going to blow them out of the sky.)

He walked to Tanz's office, with Kinski ahead, Davidson behind, and both of them looking in every direction at once. If he really needed bodyguards in Linak'h Command's ground HQ, the situation was even more out of control than he had thought.

Still, his escort's alertness let Banfi make his own survey of the terrain, and he found himself liking what he saw of Tanz's staff. Nobody looked panicky, nobody was shouting, and while nobody was loitering, few were running and those mostly toward bathrooms (where Nature could force the bravest and coolest to throw dignity away). Banfi saw pale faces, hunched shoulders, tousled hair, and rumpled or incomplete uniforms, but he'd never been fussy about regulation military appearance (it would have been the black hole calling the neutron star dense), only about useful military results.

So far, Tanz seemed to be getting them. This made Banfi's self-assigned mission all at once seem less of a priority. No, make that—only as much of a priority as it needed to be to solve one particular problem. Otherwise, Banfi was prepared to temper his wind to the shorn lambs among Linak'h Command.

Linak'h:

Olga Nalyvkina might have been upside down and inside out as well as turned around. For a second at least she was completely disoriented, all visual and electronic cues swamped and nothing to orient her but an inner ear pushed to its limit.

Survival reflexes built into nerves and limbs by two thousand cockpit hours took over. Data projection switched from the windshield to the inside of her helmet visor. Automatic cockpit polarization came up, to cut the outside glare to the point where she could read the projected data.

Interpreting it, she learned that she was upright, in level flight, with somebody's radar locked on her. The projected data was limited, but enough for evasive action, and her hands and feet knew the controls of their own will. (*Now we'll see if those spatial-orientation scores meant more than an ability to find the soap when I drop it.*)

Bank, dive, and turn, using all three axes of motion in a fast random sequence, while jamming as hard as she could with the limited ECM suite of a gunship. (Cousin Three could have done more, but Cousin Three was radioactive particles; the particles were probably doing more jamming of radar and other electromagnetic sensors than the ECM suite.

The missile-warning indicators went dark and silent. Then the canopy depolarized and the data display shifted back to the windshield. Nalyvkina saw that she was inverted, two thousand meters up, and diving fast.

She stayed in the dive long enough to orient herself and find Bihrimati. He was doing similarly extravagant gyrations about three kloms away, in the middle of a furball of lifters. Some of them seemed to be using lasers or light guns, but not hitting; Nalyvkina's quick glance showed her no externally mounted missiles.

She decided that Bihrimati would never have to buy a drink again anytime the two of them were in a bar together.

His evasive action had probably saved her, and also put the other side at a disadvantage. They'd been so eager to get a shot at him that they'd crowded into a formation where they risked midairs and completely blocked their ground-based friends from taking a shot at Bihrimati.

The big laser might even now be locking on her; however, Nalyvkina decided to stay in the dive until she could level out at ripple-top height. If they thought she was disabled, they might waste time trying to get a shot at her winger.

They might even hit one of their own people. Better yet, they could give her a position on their weapon. Lasers weren't always line-of-sight (a lot of them did it with mirrors, and you did them in with smoke or scatterdust), but at the base of that beam there had to be something the other side was going to miss.

Linak'h:

"Marshal Banfi," Kinski thundered, in a voice probably heard in Och'zem.

"Come in, come in, Marshal," Tanz's chief of staff, Colonel Sophie Blum, replied in a more moderate tone. Banfi pinned Kinski with a choice Italian phrase about Rome and the Caesars being long dead and far away, then led his group into Tanz's office.

Banfi mentally compared Tanz with his staff. He was pale by nature, but his shoulders and the rest of his torso were too solid to hunch. His hair was also too short to rumple, and he wore battledress instead of uniform, neither ostentatiously neat nor ostentatiously dirty, without a helmet but with a carbine slung over the back of his chair.

He rose and saluted.

"Good morning, Marshal and Supreme Warband Leader. Welcome to the madhouse. Sophie, when is Admiral Longman supposed to be calling for her update?"

"In about ten minutes. It's ready, so I can give the Marshal a display for himself. Or has the Warband Liaison team been keeping you up to date?"

Banfi shook his head politely. Blum apparently knew that he liked being approached directly, and he'd been on the move for the past hour, with limited secure communications.

"Not as up to date as your report would make me," Banfi said. Blum directed him to a screen and handed him a hard-copy supplement, then left him in peace while she directed three agitated calls elsewhere without raising her voice and took an update from the Assistant Chief of Staff for Tactical Air.

Two points struck Banfi. One was that his original mission here began to look like a fool's errand, one that could end in his having to admit the folly.

He had reached an understanding with Rubirosa and Longman before he'd come to Tanz. Anything else would have been bluffing against a man who didn't bluff easily, whatever his other limitations, but Banfi was now at the mercy of the tact of the Governor-General and the commanding admiral of the Linak'h Task Force, as well as Colonel Nieg's cowboy instincts.

The other point was that if the Coordination or their masters were choosing this moment and method of beginning the war, they were doing a remarkably sloppy job. Not hopelessly so—if the planned massacre at the refugee camp had come off as planned, Ptercha'a and human might indeed be at each other's throats.

But using the terrorists (apparently the hard core still under Merishi control, with recruits from the refugees upcountry) had been a mistake. Two separate bands commanded and moving independently were supposed to rendezvous at the camp and eradicate it. Instead, one arrived too soon, with a chip on its shoulder against the Federation. The people used on what they thought was the Federation vanguard most of the heavy weapons that could have turned the camp into a slaughterpen.

By the time the infantry-heavy second column arrived, the camp was alert, the noncombatants as safe as possible, and the camp's armed defenders fighting back. (So well armed and organized that Banfi saw the Confraternity's hand and possibly Nieg's as well. He would forgive both much if this was true.) Without heavy weapons to either break into the camp or fend off the Federation reinforcements, both columns could only flee when those reinforcements arrived.

They probably weren't going to stop running for a while,

either. The only question remaining was, What prisoners were they carrying with them?

"Any outcome on the air fight over the Delta yet?" Banfi asked when he'd finished.

Tanz was on-screen to someone; Blum shook her head. "We expect Hufen to claim navigational error and unprovoked firing on our part. We may let them get away with some of it if we can't get air-to-air non-lethals into the area fast enough to ground those lifters. Coordination Warband machinery that far into Merishi territory doesn't smell right to me, though. I'd like to find out who's in those lifters and what they were supposed to do if they landed safely."

Banfi was about to raise the question to using Confraternity access to Baernoi intelligence data on this question, when the emergency alarm on Tanz's personal screen began wailing. The general cut his caller off and switched to the ultra-secure channel.

Except that the caller wasn't Admiral Longman. It was Brigadier General Kharg.

Linak'h:

Anyone who had learned to fly at sixteen Standard inevitably soaked up a good deal of the history of aviation, all the way back to Montgolfier, Wright, and Armstrong. Olga Nalyvkina remembered spending nearly a month's evenings reading up on twentieth-century air combat, and one passage in particular.

> It's worth noting that modern
> air-to-air combat among fan-propelled
> vehicles would make a World War I
> aviator feel quite at home. The
> technology dictates some differences,
> particularly in weapons, but speeds,
> altitudes, and the general confusion
> might be familiar to Baron von
> Richtofen.

Baron von Richtofen, however, never had to maneuver his—what had he flown, a Fugger Threeplane?—anyway, he had never had to maneuver it with several tons of external stores. The lift-field did wonders for their weight but nothing for their mass or inertia. Also, one technological difference was not trivial. Bullets did not travel at light speed. Laser beams did.

Bihrimati was not going to be a good target for the laser as long as he was in the middle of the furball. Nalyvkina would be a fine one as she maneuvered to get a sensor picture of the target area that she could send to her pair of racked Assegais. Unfortunately, she might not survive the laser's opening up long enough to launch the missiles.

She made a hard turn to the right, heading farther out into Braigh'n Bay, noting that Baernoi AD radars or maybe regular ATC ones were locking on her. Nothing with a Ptercha'a signature, though—but what if the laser was operating off a Merishi radar? Not just Merishi-supplied, but an actual Merishi ATC radar?

She switched her ECM pod to scan that range of frequencies, holding her nose toward the laser's general area and wishing for a satellite relay. Of course, wishing never did any good, and a relay from a satellite that hadn't spotted the laser flash was just as useless, but she felt so incredibly naked up here—

"Horrido!"

The laser was using a Merishi Type 112 (at least that was what Fed manuals called it). Nalyvkina's hands and feet worked independently of a mind absorbing display data and turning it into a tactical solution. The gunship swung as hard left as it had right; Nalyvkina wanted to fire her Assegais from behind the furball, which would shield her from the laser but not the laser from her—

The laser seared the sky again. Something unidentified exploded; still more unidentifiable fragments smoked toward the water. The warble in Nalyvkina's ears told her that the Assegais had their own solution. Her eyes told her that more friendlies had joined the fight.

No maneuvering now. From behind the furball she'd have too many friendlies between her and the target, not to mention that a randomly selected Coordination lifter wasn't worth even one Assegai. Her thumb caressed the firing button built into the control stick.

The gunship leaped as a ton of missile dropped free. Solid-fuel rockets blazed more brightly than any laser. Nalyvkina's helmet polarized again, shutting out not only the glare but most of her view of the missiles' course. They were on fire-and-forget, anyway, stuck with making their own decisions about homing modes and targets. Theoretically, Nalyvkina didn't even need to be alive when they hit.

Practically, she objected to being dead and intended to avoid that condition as long as possible. She began maneuvering radically, opening the distance from the furball in case somebody got too excited and used a fuser.

They were certainly using almost everything else. She saw laser flashes, heard the static of microwave and other beamed-energy weapons, and saw streams of tracer from randomly wielded guns. No missiles—in this kind of close, confused fight they were about as useful as bayonets.

At least she and Bihrimati weren't alone anymore. She might even live to find out who the Devil was in those Coordination and Merishi lifters. She'd bet ten years' worth of vodka that it wasn't civilians!

Linak'h:

Marshal Banfi stepped back and aside from the screen's view. He would have jumped if he'd been limber enough, and gut his dignity! Linak'h Command didn't have enough senior officers to survive losing both Kharg and Tanz.

Then he saw that Tanz had the screen one-wayed; he could see but not be seen. Tanz put a finger to his lips and pointed at a chair in the corner. Banfi hadn't moved stealthily since his patrol-leading days.

"Good morning, Soliman," Tanz said. "How is the search of the camp area going?"

"My people haven't found anything. Ask Edelstein. I've been busy putting reinforcements into the Delta fight." Kharg's heavy features seemed to solidify further. "It might have helped if someone hadn't sabotaged a good part of my HQ computing capacity. My personal machine is totally locked down. Either negligence or a virus put a lock on some of the tactical hardware too."

Banfi nearly jumped out of the chair he'd just taken. The target had been strictly Kharg's personal files; anything else had been unauthorized. In fact, anything else *was* sabotage, even if accidental.

The Marshal decided that he would stand by Nieg, even if Nieg's chosen people had stepped on their equipment. However, there were going to be serious negotiations between him and the colonel if that was the case.

Meanwhile, Kharg seemed to have redundant hardware or good guessers among his staff; his update on the air battle gave Banfi a good deal that he hadn't learned. One thing he would have gladly not learned even now: Olga Nalyvkina was in the middle of the fight, if she was still alive.

"Keep on top of the fight," Tanz said when Kharg was done. "I'll go to Liddell or even up to Longman to get the Navy down in force if they aren't already on their way."

"What about my HQ? We're on Security Red One Alert already. It is not helping our tactical capabilities."

Tanz's hesitation was barely perceptible to Banfi, who was alert for it. The Marshal doubted that Kharg had noticed anything.

"You have an Administration Warband liaison team at your HQ, don't you?"

"Yes."

"With full tactical communications?"

"I hadn't discussed that with them—"

"Ah, General—they are liaison from our de facto allies. There are regulations about cooperating with them, which I would prefer not to learn you have violated."

If Tanz had turned into a purple-furred grumbler, Kharg could not have looked more surprised. He controlled his face quickly, however, and his voice was steady as he replied.

"You recognize that the—they may be the saboteurs?"

"We don't know that sabotage has taken place," Tanz said smoothly, at the same time gesturing behind his back to Banfi. The hand signal was explicit: *I want the name of Nieg's man in Kharg's HQ.*

Banfi scribbled a name on his notepad, then held it up.

"Consult with Major Silbermann and give her a free hand," Tanz said. "We'll also courier you out new hardware so you can reload the data and operate while Silbermann is investigating. You shouldn't have to depend on the Ptercha'a for more than an hour or two." Kharg's face spoke eloquently if silently about his dislike of relying on Pussies for even one or two minutes.

"One suggestion," Tanz concluded. "I suggest that you send a ground force to the gulf coast as soon as possible. Those mystery lifters may decide to ground and let anybody suspicious aboard E & E. The sooner we have people in place to discourage that, the better."

"I have A & C of my Fourth ready to lift out already," Kharg said. "If we're going to use the Warbanders, I want their liaison group to send a team with my people."

Banfi read faces again and saw that Kharg and Tanz agreed on one thing: the Administration Warband was going to have to put itself on the firing line against fellow Hunters before they'd trust it completely. Banfi realized that this surprised and offended him, and also knew it shouldn't have done either. Loyalties in the Administration and its Warband were neither simple nor undivided.

"The liaison group is at your disposal," Tanz said. "For a commitment of Warband combat troops, I would have to go through the Warband seniors. I would hope to settle the matter without bothering Marshal Banfi."

Banfi looked at Tanz with new respect, at least for the man's ability to keep a straight face. Then he was looking at a blank screen, as Kharg went about his business, and after that at Tanz swiveling around in his chair and fixing his eyes on Banfi's left eyebrow.

"Now that we have a few minutes free of General Kharg, may I ask a question?"

"As many as you please."

"I am not sure it is wise to give me such an open account, as I am more than curious about many matters. But I will start with one question.

"Is there any reason why I should not have you placed under arrest?"

Linak'h:

Olga Nalyvkina's world was hazy from high-G maneuvering and a polarized helmet faceplate. She could barely find the displays, let alone read them. Basic data projected on her faceplate reached a brain that only her G-suit kept from being alternately starved and overloaded with blood.

Somewhere in the dimness and uproar she heard a cacophony of human voices. Seconds after that, she found herself flying straight and level, if inverted. No pilot worth her wings let inverted flight addle vision; she did a thorough eyeball check of everything she could see, starting with damage-indicator displays.

Her gunship was intact. From the smoke clouds that she saw, a number of other people's machines were not. Neither was her target.

At least a scan for the relevant frequencies turned up nothing, and a cloud of smoke was drifting away from a patch of delta close to where she'd aimed. If the laser wasn't down, maybe it had lost its radar or the crew had lost their nerve.

Time for a closer look later, if anybody had been watching. The furball had broken up and the other side's lifters were scattering in all directions. Some of them were already close to the shoreline. Others were heading out across the Gulf. Nalyvkina looked at her power readings, then up toward the zenith, searching for heavy attackers to give her a jolt if she needed one. At the same time she listened for orders.

Half her power left. Zero heavies in sight, zero orders on the air. No sign of Bihrimati, and standing orders were *deadly* on the subject of going off solo, even to trail, let alone attack.

A light attacker bobbed up from below and behind. Nalyvkina added more sweat to her already soggy flight suit when she realized that the friendly had been in her six. Tail-warning suite out or just her own head up and locked?

"Gunship Nine-oh-three, this is Diadem Three. Form on me. I'd like to trail those characters back to their own coast and see what they do."

An order at last, from somebody who knew what he wanted to do even if he wasn't authorized to do it. Also *to* somebody who didn't care that much about authorizations.

Hope this won't embarrass Malcolm.

"That is a roger, Diadem Three, But I may need to recharge if we get into another brawl."

"Can't help you there, Cheetah. But we're fat on power and fuel. We can give cover if you set down."

For the first time Nalyvkina realized that her new winger was a two-seater, with the various bumps and projections of an EW machine. She laughed. The other crew must have been just as itchy to move in on the Merishi coast, to listen and scan instead of just eyeballing, and just as glad to find somebody to make it legal or at least to share the court-martial.

"Give me a heading, Three."

"How about oh-seven-oh true?"

"On the way."

She did not hear Diadem Three reporting the new mission to Higher Authority.

Linak'h:

"I can give you at least two reasons for not arresting me," Marshal Banfi said.

"Good relations with the Hunters is one," Tanz said, frowning. "I presume the other is the confidence of Admiral Longman and other senior officers of Linak'h Command. I can't think of any others offhand."

"You don't need to treat me like a fool," Banfi snapped.

"Oh? You've done the same to me. Your baton may give you the right, but does your baton make it expedient?"

"It would have been more than expedient to keep you in the dark, if your loyalty had been in question."

Tanz took that bodycheck with nothing more than raised eyebrows. They were nearly invisible, but managed to be expressive.

"Is my loyalty now genuinely unquestioned? Or are you merely withdrawing your questions about it to avoid a high-level brawl?"

"The worst I will now believe of you is that you once thought ignoring Kharg would make your way to three stars easier. I think you have now realized that they have to be earned the hard way."

Tanz's laugh held no humor. It reminded Banfi of the cry of one of the Gray People, calling up the pack to the hunt. "I doubt that the hardest course of action would have earned me any stars at all. Arresting Marshals has been done, but it never helps the career of the arresting officer."

Tanz stood up. Banfi also rose. He'd be damned if he was going to give Tanz a shred of dominance, and fortunately he had a couple of cems or so on the major general.

"Marshal, I would like to bury the past and plan for the future," Tanz said. "Would the term 'bargain' offend you?"

"Officially, it can't exist. Unofficially, it can stay between us. Even if I don't agree, I will keep silent."

"Good." Tanz's frown deepened. "I will discreetly investigate Kharg's withdrawing security from the refugee camp before 218 Brigade took over. I don't recall precisely the text of my orders, but they may have been ambiguous enough to lead to an honest misunderstanding.

"I also intend to investigate the delay in getting air reinforcements to the Gulf. We may have suffered unnecessary casualties and lost priceless intelligence about the Coordination's intentions because of that delay."

Tanz clasped his hands behind his back. He did not look particularly graceful in the position, but Banfi knew the look of a man who had to do something with his hands to keep them from shaking. Confrontations with Marshals were not in most officers' list of duties.

"If Kharg has been culpably negligent or had any suspicious contacts, I will relieve that *arschlocker* from command at once. I suggest putting General Langston in his place."

"I have no problem with that."

"Good. In return, I want Colonel Nieg on a very tight rein. Ideally, I want him out of the circuit completely and that damned alternative intelligence operation of his closed down."

"That might cost us our chance to prove or disprove Kharg's loyalty. It would also leave Nieg's people in 222 Brigade at Kharg's mercy."

"Be serious, Marshal. He's hardly going to frag them."

"With the opportunities combat offers, are you sure of that? Particularly if he's connected with the no-emigration situation? He could face twenty years of corrective detention at least. Add letting the refugee camp hang in the wind, and it could be a firing squad.

"I don't say that he *has* these reasons. I merely wonder if we can risk loyal officers on our faith in Kharg's innocence."

"Loyal to whom? Besides Colonel Nieg, that is?" Tanz's voice hardened. "Or are you going to pretend that Nieg was not deliberately slow in telling us about the Confraternity coup because he feared our intervention against it? If we are going to discuss acts of questionable legality and the penalties for them, Colonel Nieg's name may come up."

Banfi found no answer. Tanz sat down again. "I admit

that both Nieg and his people are valuable. However, I would still prefer that Nieg turn over the command of the group to Commander Franke and Major Morley. If they're fit for duty, that is."

Banfi nearly choked. He caught his breath and laughed. "They have been back on duty for ten days, and doing very much what you suggested. This has freed Nieg for covert fieldwork."

"I suppose we should be thankful he didn't try to assassinate Kharg," Tanz said. "In that case, Longman and I can give Franke a local fourth stripe and make it official. Or are there problems with that?"

"Only that Nieg ought to remain the contact person for sources he developed personally. They might not trust anybody else, let alone somebody with Kishi Institute connections."

"That is one of the reasons I trust Franke more than I do Nieg," Tanz said. "Those connections may make him more cautious about cowboy tactics or conduct that borders on disloyalty."

Banfi decided that Tanz had conceded the major point. The minor point was that many of Nieg's personal contacts were Hunter or local civilians, and for those he would report either to Banfi as Warband Leader or to Marcus Langston as a Civil Action committee member and colonel of militia.

"If you are satisfied," the Marshal said, "then I am. Shall we see about getting General Kharg's new computers in the air and his old ones investigated?"

"As soon as I have an update on what the Navy is doing about the Gulf situation, yes." Tanz didn't bother with the intercom, only raised his voice and shouted.

"Sophie! Coffee, chocolate, tea, and a circuit to *Roma*!"

Linak'h:

Maximum speed for Nalyvkina's gunship was cruising speed for the EW attacker; it would also drain her slower craft's power before they reached the coast. So Nalyvkina plodded toward the eastern shore of the Gulf at a fast cruise while her companion zigzagged back and forth in front of her, keeping an all-around listening watch.

They also stayed low, two hundred meters or less. It would have been even less, except that the warm air pushed south over the Gulf by the weather front was reacting as usual with the colder sea water. The bottom of the Gulf dropped off sharply just south of their course, and deepwater currents kept the temperature down. Putting warm air over cold water could only bring fog.

To look on the bright side (if one could find it below five hundred meters), the fog made visual detection hard. Both Federation vehicles had good passive detection; they could stay back out of even Ptercha'a eyeball range and still track their targets. To look on the other side, poor visibility meant greater danger of surprise and the need to use detectable communications with any friendly forces in range.

Nalyvkina was beginning to feel that she and her winger had flown over the line that separated "taking an opportunity presented by the tactical situation" from "going off on a damfool hunt for medals."

Seventy kloms offshore, a surface contact joined the blurred formation of fleeing lifters. From the size, Nalyvkina suspected it was a local merchant vessel, and she thought that operating it in what was virtually a war zone made it a shipwreck waiting to happen.

What happened instead was a momentary blurring of the surface contact, as the airborne lifters passed over it. Then the surface contact steadied again—but wasn't the airborne one just a little larger? A little larger, and now with a sort of tail?

As if something had taken off from that ship and joined the lifters as they passed over.

Nalyvkina had just opened the circuit to Diadem Three when a yellow glare erupted out of the fog below. A missile soared out of the grayness and homed in on Three's exhaust.

Nalyvkina dove for the water, her ECM at maximum. The second missile didn't switch from heat-seeking to radar-homing modes in time. It shot up as she shot down, flipped over, and tumbled out of sight.

Now the glare was orange, as the missile's warhead erupted just behind Diadem Three. Their radio squalled.

"Data dump, data dump. Open all circuits, Cheetah Two. We need to give you—"

She had her circuits and computer ready before they'd repeated the message a third time. She wondered briefly why they didn't squirt the data upstairs, then realized that any Feds farther away might be jammed.

As a precaution, she linked the memory in her suit to the computer. By regulations the link was supposed to be there at all times, but the wiring restricted movement on long flights.

Nalyvkina had just time to know that she had Diadem Three's data both in her computer and in her suit memory when glare swelled around her again. Orange as Diadem Three's fuel and power went up, yellow as a missile homed on her, and more orange as it exploded below her left wing.

The gunship had no fuel to explode, and the fragments didn't hit and explode the power pack. But they wrecked two of the three fans and most of the avionics and sensors. One fragment nudged Nalyvkina in the thigh; another gouged the top of her helmet, hard enough to slam her head against the canopy.

When the moment's blackout ended, she found herself just high enough above the water to pull out. She was afraid of pulling out so hard that she would shoot up onto radar screens again, but skill or luck leveled her off barely twenty meters above the gray waves.

Luck, she realized, as she studied the remaining displays. Not necessarily good luck, either. The lift generator must have been damaged; it was fluctuating and pulsing, and sometimes dropping to 80 percent power, With only one fan and a damaged wing, her gunship could no longer stay up aerodynamically.

She reminded herself that land had to be less than sixty kloms away. Not far if she didn't have to swim. Then she realized that maybe she would be better off swimming— until hypothermia took her, at any rate. The nearest land was the Merishi Territory.

She would be surprised if the Merishi didn't know enough about her to realize what a valuable prisoner she would be. She also doubted that they would have any problem making her disappear once they had wrung her dry, if her presence in their hands became an embarrassment.

At least it would help to get out of this area. Whoever had launched the missile would be coming around to look for results. If they found only floating wreckage they might not look farther.

That hit in the thigh began to feel like more than a nudge, and her wrenched neck was hurting. *Nothing to put me into shock, please God.*

Linak'h:

Several calls over the most-secure channels General Tanz could find failed to turn up Colonel Nieg. Neither Banfi nor Tanz was pleased.

Both also realized that putting out the equivalent of a police alert for Nieg would be counterproductive. If he wanted to carry his cowboy act to the ultimate extreme, it would simply be warning him to go underground until the war and his job (as he interpreted it) were done.

Banfi had sometimes chided himself that his backing Nieg was trying to achieve authority without responsibility. Now he began to suspect that he had in fact achieved responsibility without authority.

"I'm sure Captain Franke will appreciate that," Tanz said, when Banfi shared this insight. "Right now, however, you have a Warband to organize for war and I have one air-intelligence and one search-and-clear operation to run, or at least watch over. Would it be unreasonable to ask that we trade philosophical observations some other time?"

Short of physically manhandling Banfi out of his office, Tanz could hardly have made the dismissal more complete or less friendly. Banfi was prepared to take it as he suspected it was intended: a warning that good relations between the two senior ground commanders on Linak'h would depend on his carefully keeping their bargain.

His mood of tolerance vanished the moment he stepped outside and confronted his staff. Hunters had surrounded Colonel Davidson and were rocking back and forth in a form of the mourning ritual. Sergeant Major Kinski stood to one side, his eyes aimed at the office door. He blinked as he saw Banfi come out, seemed surprised that the Marshal had all his limbs intact, then stepped forward.

"Message just in, Marshal. We lost two more aircraft over the Gulf. They were running an improvised EW recon of the Merishi coast and—"

"Olga was one of them." He could not have said, "Lieutenant Nalyvkina."

"Yes, sir. She's listed as MIA, but—"

"Sergeant Major, we're going back to Warband HQ. Call ahead, and see if there are any communications from Colonel Nieg. Malcolm . . ."

Banfi's voice trailed off. The Hunters saved him from standing there mute. They opened their circle and let Banfi step inside it, so close to Davidson that the men could have embraced. Then the swaying started again, and one Hunter began a soft keen.

Sixteen

Victoria:

On President Gist's screen, Senator Brothertongue's face was his bland politician's mask. Personally Gist would have preferred old comrades' frankness or even the clergyman's spiritual exaltation. But Gist didn't have Brothertongue's job of keeping the politicos who were already at Government House from panicking and the ones who weren't there from starting a perilous and pointless journey to get there.

"What should we do if any of the Merishi claim refuge here?" Brothertongue concluded. The mask had slipped a bit, Gist noted.

"Are you set up to scan or search Merishi?" Gist asked. Alys probably knew; she was also on another circuit with the VEB CO and not disturbable short of an imminent supernova.

"Not that I know. I can ask our security chief."

"What department?"

"Special Branch."

Gist kept his face straight and his voice level; the line was only semi-secure. But this was not good. Special Branch traitors might not risk Scaleskin lives to create an incident. A human Senator or Delegate (even more likely, one of their staff) was expendable.

"How many people does he have?"

"Fourteen or so."

Gist made two decisions and announced the first one to Brothertongue. "No Merishi at Government House, unless it's a medical emergency that can't wait for the enclave. They have doctors and medicine as well as security there."

"The Merishi seem to have planned well," Brothertongue said. "In their situation I would have done the same."

Gist nearly blanked the screen on the spot. That accusation sliced too close to the bone: either Gist was prejudiced against the Merishi or he was at least unwilling to control allies who were.

"It's the classic dilemma of a democracy," Gist said. "How much of what you value can you sacrifice in fighting people who don't value it at all, without turning into them?"

Brothertongue's face said that old phrases from middleschool history courses wouldn't do as a permanent answer, but that he understood the need for waiting. His mouth uttered polite phrases, then he blanked off.

Gist briefly prayed that Bissell's and Feddie counteragents in Special Branch would be both effective and discreet. Then he asked for Alys and to his surprise got her. He even got her to order MP's and a Merishi-qualified medic straight to the roof of Government House, without argument or request for an explanation.

That used up the morning's quota of miracles. The next message Gist received was that the Merishi cruiser's captain was repeating his request to be allowed to provide security for Folk in "threatened areas." The tone of the message was more peremptory than before; Gist hoped the translation program was malfunctioning.

That hope disappeared about the time the first lifters of the VEB reached Government House. Peter Bissell brought the bad news himself.

"Space Scan report, Mr. President," the colonel said. "They have an energy-signature reading from *Gyn-Bahr*. She appears to be preparing to get under way."

Aboard R.M.S. *Somtow Nosavan*, off Victoria:

Somtow Nosavan's command and control people were now properly split into two independent teams at the two most widely separated stations. This left the ship much less vulnerable to internal uproars or even external attack; it also left Joanna Marder feeling painfully naked.

It was an endurable pain, like a cracked tooth rather than a belly wound, and there was no comparison to what Marder had endured as a terrorists' prisoner. It still forced her to make a real effort to look calm, probably a wasted effort considering the lack of cooperation from her sweat glands.

Scanning the displays looked right, at least, even if it didn't help improve her spirits. *Gyn-Bahr* was under way now, at about one-third power, all her navaids doing what they were supposed to when a ship was maneuvering in a medium-altitude, moderately crowded orbit. If one didn't know about those messages that the cruiser was blasting to the ground, one might even think the display of riding lights was rather pretty.

Certain displays flickered. Marder stared hard at them, as if she could intimidate them into a more agreeable reading.

"Secondary—" she almost said "—Battle Command," as if *Nosavan* were an Alliance warship. "Bridge to Secondary. Check the readings on *Gyn-Bahr*."

Longman's voice was steady as he read them off. *Not a malfunction, then. The Scaleskins have cut power.*

Using hand input rather than voice command, Marder asked for a projection of the cruiser's trajectory. She was not surprised when it turned out to pass directly over Thorntonsburg in about ten minutes.

Nosavan's window of opportunity was now more like a viewslit than a window. Also, her ship's maneuvers were going to have to be much less ambiguous. Marder doubted that the cruiser's sensor teams were going to be proportionately less alert.

It was just possible that the Merishi cruiser had no hostile intent. Marder didn't know the ground strength of the Scaleskins' allies. She also couldn't take the time or risk the leaks involved in communicating with the ground.

Besides, even if the attempted coup was a wild gamble by a handful of hotheads, they might get lucky. They also might have fusers.

No, assume *Gyn-Bahr* was hostile and proceed from there. Next assumption: the Merishi would open fire when directly over Thorntonsburg, and from low altitude. This was surgical fire support, no job for missiles. The shorter the range and the less atmosphere to punch through, the better for lasers.

Check readings again. *Gyn-Bahr* didn't have her shield up, but the best reason for the power cut was being free to raise it at any moment. The same laws of physics bound

Merishi and human: a ship could not run her drive and maintain her shield at the same time.

Corollary of this: *Nosavan* would be under power and therefore unshielded. That didn't matter if she got in close enough. At the very least she would interfere with the cruiser's sensors and field of fire, possibly force her to maneuver enough to spoil her aim. Closer still, *Nosavan* herself might not be a safe target—if she was hit and shed major fragments, *Gyn-Bahr* would have to either raise her shields and cut power or evade unshielded by radical maneuvering.

Then the two ships might get into a shield-flicker contest, which could go on for hours until somebody made a mistake. That would almost certainly be *Nosavan;* the cruiser would have more shifts of better-trained people for her maneuvering and weapons boards.

But forcing the contest itself would be a victory. The outcome on the ground might be decided within a couple of hours. At worst, the various sides might end up so mixed that nobody in orbit could tell friend from foe.

"All stations report for getting underway," Marder said. The eight calls came in crisply, even though she could hear the tension in some voices.

For damned sure they can hear the tension in mine.

"R.M.S. *Somtow Nosavan,* getting under way for security reasons at—" she looked at the clock "—oh-eight-two-one." The log recorded the message; Communications relayed it to Space Scan. Marder switched to the intercom.

"This is Captain Marder. We are getting under way because of the ground situation. It may spill up into orbit, and I'd rather not be a sitting target. We won't go far, so everybody sit tight. Oh, and strap in. We may be facing internal-gravity surges."

That was perfectly true. In a merchant ship of *Nosavan*'s age and condition, switching from shield to drive and back could affect the internal gravity. Marder wasn't planning to use more than the five G's that anyone sitting down could take easily.

What would happen when the two ships closed to knife-fighting range was another matter. At least the people pods had been reinforced and upgraded since the voyage to Peregrine; they now had military-grade life support, armor, and internal compartmentation with independent fits of survival gear.

If the soldiers' training held good and they kept their heads through the coming dogfight, they had as good a chance of surviving as anybody aboard *Nosavan*. Better than Marder's chances of remaining *persona grata* on Victoria, anyway.

She scanned the displays. The Merishi cruiser was sailing along on the projected trajectory, for the moment fat, dumb, and happy. No sensor lock on *Nosavan,* either.

Then the radar alarm made peremptory noises. The words formed in Marder's mind at the same time as she heard them from the navigator.

"Captain, two of the Merishi merchanters are also getting under way."

Victoria:

Sebastian Gullking had been a sergeant since two days after he helped rescue Herman Franke and Lucretia Morley from assassination. He'd been a platoon sergeant a few days after that. Just two days ago he'd become a platoon leader when the lieutenant came down with mite sinusitis.

Gullking thought now that this might have been a diplomatic illness, to get the man out of a dangerous conflict of loyalties. It hadn't bothered him at the time; any sergeant trained by Top Zimmer could take over a platoon.

Nothing about the situation on Victoria had really bothered Gullking until ten minutes before, when his platoon was suddenly transferred to security duty at Government House. Not on the perimeter around it, but right up on the top three floors out of the fourteen, where the politicians would be so close you could smell what they'd had for breakfast.

The lifters swung into a tight circle and landed on the roof pad. Gullking led his twenty-six people out, put four squads on duty, and broke the short fifth squad down for bearers to unload the supplies and ammunition.

The Special Branch people already on duty watched the new arrivals with an absolute lack of any definable feeling. After trying to stare them into some response, Gullking pulled out a hard-copy map of the building and alternately studied it and the sky over Thorntonsburg.

The building offered the usual combination of routes from the street up to the upper floors, where the serious trouble would come if anyone was willing to bring it. The sky offered the spectacle of formations of lifters thrashing back and forth in a brisk morning breeze. From this distance it was impossible to tell which were carrying humans and which Merishi.

Gullking was relieved to find a few more people on his side, when two more military lifters landed and disgorged two squads of MP's and a team of medics. Common training under Zimmer let Gullking and the MP sergeant avoid arguments over seniority and present a common front to the Special Branch people.

"I don't know about turning this place into a Merishi hospital," the SB detective said, after the chief medic explained the situation. "I thought they were all in the enclave with their own healers."

Orders were orders, however, and the detective seemed a good deal more cheerful after talking with one of his superiors. Also, to Gullking, he seemed a little more tense, and the sergeant decided not to dismiss that as his imagination.

He called the medic and the MP leader over and they studied the building layout. The MP leader seemed to have the same healthy streak of paranoia as Gullking did. The medic was too glad to have others taking charge of the shooting side of the business to argue. They quickly worked out deployments.

One squad each of MP's and Army on the pad. One squad each divided up into roving two-person teams running all the way down to the seventh floor. One of Gullking's squads tight around the medics' facility on the twelfth floor—originally a small gymnasium for health-conscious government functionaries. Another (under the most trusted corporal) watching the elevator and stairs at the security lobby on the eighth floor. The squad that had been hauling supplies to stay with Gullking, going where he went and acting as messengers, reserves, and so on.

"You getting bad feelings, Corp—unh, Sarge?" the elevator-watcher squad leader asked.

You didn't lie to Mitzi Ionides. "Had 'em for days,"

Gullking replied. "Just as happy if I'm wrong, you understand, but why take chances?"

A gust of wind drowned her reply. She'd have repeated it, but Gullking saw two more Special Branch people step out of the elevator and shook his head. Instead he punched her lightly on the shoulder.

"If you have to kick, kick hard."

"They'll need surgery to get my boot out of their tonsils," Mitzi said. "Third Squad, mount up!"

The five soldiers had just disappeared when a line of lifters slid into view, approaching Government House on a widely curving course that would take it clear of Parrville. Six of the seven lifters sailed on past, toward the Merishi enclave.

The seventh broke off from the tail of the line, reversed its fans, and let the wind carry it down toward the Government House pad. At the same time, lights blinked from the cockpit.

"They're declaring a medical emergency," the SB man said.

Behind his back, Gullking crossed his fingers. Then he crossed himself and murmured a very old incantation. Luck, God, and the spirits of his aboriginal ancestors were now all propitiated. The rest he'd have to handle himself.

Aboard R.M.S. *Somtow Nosavan*, off Victoria:

By now Charles Longman had memorized the layout of a Merishi *Ryn-Gath*-class heavy cruiser. Having it on his personal screen was just giving him something to look at besides the overhead, while Boatswain Butkus monitored the displays and they and the junior navigator waited for Jo Marder's plans to bear fruit.

It was easy to keep the doubts out of his mind now. Not the fear—Longman knew he'd always be on the verge of needing to change his pants in a situation like this. But he and Jo had gone over every practical and ethical problem several times, in bed and out (their personal variation of the old Persian adage about discussing things first sober, then drunk).

They'd come up with only one conclusion: if the Merishi

showed signs of being ready to bombard Victoria in support of a dirtside coup, they had to be stopped at all costs.

"The merchanters are dancing all around the cruiser," Butkus muttered. "Damned if I'd like to be in the cruiser CO's sandals now. Those two Helpful Harrys are going to muck his field of fire unless he uses missiles."

"Too slow and too chancy," Longman replied. "He'll use lasers the minute he has an excuse."

Butkus grunted and nodded. The boatswain was merchanter first and last, but nobody spent so many years in spacing without learning the basics of ship-to-ship combat.

One of the merchanters had practically matched velocities and course with the cruiser. From the sensor readings, she was refining the match by remaining under power. Of course, she didn't have anything to fear from either Merishi or Victorian.

The other merchanter was accelerating steadily, pulling ahead of the other two ships although maintaining the same course. Longman ran an extrapolation of her trajectory. It took her through the same patch of space as the cruiser would need for a clear shot at Thorntonsburg, anywhere from forty to sixty seconds before the warship.

That was just peculiar enough to be worth passing on to the Bridge. Jo gave a tight-voiced acknowledgment and went offscreen. A view of the Merishi ships replaced her.

Longman enhanced the images. The lead merchanter was opening the gap; apparently the warship captain didn't suspect anything or didn't want to offend Simferos Associates.

He also noticed that the merchanter out in front had external cargo pods mounted on her hull, two bands of six each amidships. His nerves eased. That was one ship that wasn't going to play any fancy tricks. Not when that much valuable cargo was out in the open, vulnerable to everything from heavy lasers to thrown welding torches.

Victoria:

Sergeant Gullking had obeyed orders to divert his platoon to Government House without asking questions. There was no secure channel for arguing various scenarios. He also didn't want to expose anybody to a conflict of loyalties.

In his own mind, he was satisfied that his superiors expected an effort to infiltrate Government House with a fake medical emergency. But the Merishi lifter unloaded two Folk who looked about as sick as anybody could without actually needing a stretcher.

Two medics and a Special Branch spoke Commercial Merishi, and one of the lifter crew spoke Anglic. The discussion left Gullking with the vague impression that the sick Merishi had been traveling for hours and needed rest as much as anything else. Also an injection of something that apparently the lifter convoy didn't have in its medpack.

The medic did. She started unpacking and laying out boxed injectors while the other Merishi carried the two patients inside, out of the wind. Gullking followed, stopping near the medic.

"Watch your medicines, Doc."

"I packed them myself this morning."

"I'm sure you did. There's such things as switches, though."

The medic's eyes widened briefly, and she nodded. No sand between her ears. Gullking moved on to the Merishi who spoke Anglic.

"I am Sergeant Gullking, working with Special Branch to provide security for Government House. Our Healer is qualified to give your comrades what they need. It would still help if you could fly to the enclave and bring back a fully qualified Healthwatcher."

For all the response he got, Gullking might have spoken in a tribal dialect of True Speech. "Be that way," he muttered under his breath, then surveyed the scene.

The other lifters of the VEB were now mostly down and unloading; a nice little cordon of troops showed in the streets and nearby rooftops were already sprouting snipers. Government House might not be *the* target for that half-arsed Parrville mob, but it was one that had to be defended. The politicos could piss and moan just as loud as the Scaleskins, and they had votes in Parliament besides.

The Special Branch people were trying to watch a complete circle, which was their job. It wasn't their job to be so busy looking outward that they didn't notice a Merishi edging toward the medic.

Gullking signaled to the other squads, then stepped into the path of the Merishi. "Please do not interfere with our Healer," he said, hoping the other understood Anglic.

The Merishi kept right on coming, until he (at least Gullking thought the pushy one was male) and the sergeant were chest to chest. Gullking waited until the other troopers were in position, then signaled them forward. They gathered around the medic and escorted her toward the door, while Gullking stepped back.

Unarmed combat with a Scaleskin wasn't quite as risky for a human as it was with a Hunter. If this one felt like a fight, Gullking was ready.

He was also doing mental arithmetic. When the sum came up right, he keyed in his com gear.

"First MP's secure the elevator. Second MP's, surround the two Merishi patients. Don't let anyone get within five meters of them except our medic or one of their Healthwatchers."

He'd deliberately spoken loud enough for the Special Branch people to hear, and he got the reaction he'd expected. One of them started subvocalizing. Gullking didn't rely only on the com; he shouted loud enough to be heard over the wind and through the door:

"That includes Special Branch people. MP's, move it! Army on the rooftop, secure the door!"

The Merishi facing Gullking stepped forward. One behind him turned, took one step toward the lifter, then leaped for the rear door.

An MP went to his knees, popping a stunner carbine to his shoulder and firing in a single flow of movement. Three rounds went off, taking the Merishi in midair. They held a universal soother (*well, maybe it wouldn't work on K'thressh*), and the Merishi went down.

Gullking's peripheral vision showed Special Branch people going for weapons and troopers doing the same. He gambled that his back was safe and his reflexes up to the job, and kicked the Merishi in front of him in the groin.

The kick caught the other shifting his feet into combat stance. His riposte was fast, but Gullking was able to ride it. He was also able to chop the Merishi hard in the side of the neck, then throw him with an armhold. The second Merishi came down on top of the one hit by the MP.

Gullking threw himself on top of both Merishi, as a third thrust head and weapon out of the cockpit window. The sergeant stared at the weapon's muzzle and his own death for two heartbeats. At the third, the Merishi sagged forward, the weapon clattering to the pad.

Gullking started as a pulser shattered cockpit windows on the other side of the lifter. Then he dove half under the lifter's skirt as Special Branch people briefly opened fire, before a single heavier burst from the troopers and the MP's beat them down.

Gullking hoped his people had used non-lethals but didn't particularly care. He pushed himself up, conscious that he had spent half the firefight hiding behind a couple of knocked-out Merishi. Then his heart nearly stopped as a Merishi (female, and big) climbed out of the lifter and picked up the fallen weapon.

His next near-reflex was to shoot her. But she was holding the weapon—the Merishi equivalent of a snub carbine—by the muzzle and making peaceful gestures with her free hand. Then she pointed at the Merishi Gullking had knocked out and patted the pockets of her own padded jacket.

"Translator!" Gullking shouted, and knelt to search the fallen Merishi's pockets. When he turned up a red plastic folio with half a dozen thin tubes in it, the big Merishi woman smiled, or at least displayed an impressive array of teeth.

Before the sergeant could even use sign language to ask about what he'd found, two shots sounded from inside the reception room. A Special Branch officer staggered out the door, a hand clasped over an exit wound in his chest. He fell, twitched a couple of times, and lay still as the wind rippled the pool of blood flowing from both mouth and chest.

The medic came out, looked down at the dead policeman, then at Gullking. "What the Hades is going on?" she said. "And what is that you're holding?"

"Ask him," Gullking said, pointing down at the fallen Merishi. "Or her," pointing at the big Merishi woman. "Do that, then tell me," he concluded.

"Check your elevator squad while I'm doing that," the medic said. "I heard shooting from down below."

The shooting turned out to have been both troopers and MP's in a firefight with a team of well-armed civilians who had come up the emergency stairs. The defenders had lost one, killed four, and taken two wounded prisoners. They suspected there were more below, but had booby-trapped one flight of stairs, grenade-sealed the door to the other, and locked the lobby doors to both main and freight elevators.

"Well done," Gullking said. They weren't finished yet, and it would take two platoons with lifter support to clear Government House as thoroughly as it had to be. But for now, any plans that depended on having Government House in the hands of Merishi puppets had been thoroughly blown away.

Gullking hoped nobody would notice that he'd spent half his first fight as a platoon leader crouching behind a couple of knocked-out Merishi and ended it being reminded of his duties by a medic!

Aboard R.M.S. *Somtow Nosavan*, off Victoria:

Joanna Marder wouldn't have trusted Charlie's jury-rigged tactical programming for a serious engagement. But then, she wouldn't have trusted *Somtow Nosavan*, rugged but ponderous, for one either.

The one shot they would get did not constitute a serious engagement. She had to believe that it would constitute enough of a delay to ruin any Merishi plans that depended on split-second (or at least split-minute) timing.

The Emergency channels came ear-piercingly to life with a Merishi distress call. Marder gritted her teeth, turned down the volume, and scanned the displays.

Out ahead of *Gyn-Bahr*, the Merishi merchanter with the belt of cargo pods was suddenly decelerating. A quick glance told Marder that the merchanter was nearly at the best point for the cruiser to aim at Thorntonsburg.

Then the Emergency screams and wails turned to computer-translated words. Even through the computer, Marder caught a hint of panic.

"Warning! Warning! All ships in our area. We have a potential explosion in one of our external pods. We may have to jettison. Warning! Warning!"

Before the voice was halfway through the second repetition, Marder had run up the magnification. So she saw clearly two of the cargo pods break free of the ship, as explosive bolts cut them and their racks free of the merchanter's hull. She saw them drift back, directly toward the Merishi cruiser.

Gyn-Bahr stayed on her unpowered trajectory, shield up. A captain with head up and locked, or one who would abandon his mission only when his ship disintegrated under him? Certainly one whose maneuvering room was constrained; he had *Nosavan* behind him, the pods ahead, and the other merchanter off to port.

Fire blossomed in vacuum, an orange sphere thrusting out gold and silver points, like a spine-sponge. But each spine was a piece of debris, perhaps with mass and velocity enough to gouge or pierce a ship's hull.

The cruiser could ride through the debris and take the hits on her shield. But in the debris-strewn area of space, there would be no easy firing solutions and no precision laser work, not for many minutes. Minutes the cruiser couldn't possibly have.

Marder's thoughts must have kept even with those of the cruiser captain. The displays registered the cruiser's shield going down and power up. Marder punched in the OVER-RIDE for the anti-collision module of the guidance program, and in nearly the same motion opened her ship's drive.

"All hands, prepare for collision!" she shouted. The collision alarm hooted, as she activated *Nosavan's* own Emergency warning and the not-under-control signals.

Play it out to the end. Every second's confusion for them is a victory for us.

She had just time to complete the thought before *Nosavan* passed the critical distance. The cruiser now could only maneuver, not raise her shield. The shield would intersect *Nosavan;* the resulting explosion would be fatal to both ships.

Or at least to the cruiser's fighting ability. We only need a capability-kill, not a hard one.

Then the two ships came together. Kinetic energy is mass multiplied by velocity—relative velocity, which was only a few hundred km/h compared to the 9 km/s absolute orbital velocity of the two ships. As it was the velocity of an object weighing something like sixty thousand tons, it was enough.

Everybody aboard the two ships who wasn't strapped in went flying. Every piece of equipment that wasn't shock-mounted was jarred from case top to base plug. New equip-

ment suddenly needed maintenance. Equipment needing
maintenance flashed red lights (aboard *Nosavan*) or silver
ones (aboard the cruiser).

Lines for liquids and gasses, power and hoisting, broke.
Some of them whipped loose ends around like furious
serpents. By the grace of those Higher Powers who watch
over spacefarers, none of the serpents inflicted lethal
damage.

Aboard *Nosavan,* the soldier-loaded people pods strained
at their reinforced mountings but didn't break loose.
Aboard *Gyn-Bahr,* a missile being readied as a backup to
the lasers did break loose. It smashed into a bulkhead
loaded with shorting electrical circuits, hard enough to
break the casing of the propellant module.

Solid chemical propellant spewed onto electrical fires. It
didn't explode, but it burned with vast clouds of toxic
smoke. The cruiser's Weapons team were good; they
masked and evacuated without fatal casualties, then applied
standard damage-control techniques for a shipboard fire—
i.e., venting the compartment to space.

The heat and pressure made the venting more violent
than usual. Everything loose went with the heated air and
toxic smoke, including a couple of vital components of the
main lasers' power system. The cruiser captain found himself suddenly lacking the ability to deliver precise laser fire
on any target more than five kilometers away. The captain
cursed, he danced on the deck, he ordered a maximum
damage-control effort. His crew obeyed. He did not think
of firing on *Somtow Nosavan* until the human merchanter
was out of range.

At least he had enough detectors left to see that the
other ship was leaking air and debris and that a good
part of her outer shell was crushed in. The humans would
pay the price for their intervention without his doing
anything.

Aboard *Nosavan,* Marder sat in her sweat-drenched ship-
suit and watched the pod-dumping Merishi ship open a
shuttle bay. No, not a bay hatch, a main hold one. A shuttle
larger than a heavy attacker drifted out, followed by a couple of smaller ones.

Then the Emergency frequency came to life again. The
voice was live now, speaking accented Anglic and High
Merishi.

"*Yagro's Star* to *Gyn-Bahr* and *Somtow Nosavan*. We have successful jettison of pod. Please to inform if help needing. Can provide."

Marder didn't catch the fine nuances of the cruiser's reply, if any. She understood enough High Merishi to recognize an emphatic negative when she heard one.

"*Somtow Nosavan* to *Yagro's Star*. We have sufficient damage aboard to make assistance desirable. If you can spare a few hands—"

"*Somtow Nosavan*, we send a shuttle at once. Is your dock of shuttles functioning?"

Marder nodded to Life Support. She cut off the line rigged to vent air and water through the dock, simulating major damage.

"We had a life-support leak in that area, but it is under control now." Then she signaled to Communications, to transmit an updated data set on *Nosavan*. Her ship was a Gollancz & Harvey Standard Four, one of the designs theoretically adaptable to all three major spacefaring species, but she'd been in service a long time and very little of it Merishi-crewed.

"Engineering to Bridge. Repeat that last message to the Scaleskins."

Chief Engineers did not give orders to Captains, even when they were bedmates. Marder started to snarl her reply, then realized that Charlies must be right on the edge.

She repeated the message, then added, "Engineering, do you have any problems you haven't mentioned?"

"Ah—not really."

Other than not having the foggiest idea what's going on. Marder recognized the tone, managed not to laugh, then realized that Charlie might not be the only one in a fog. She switched on the intercom.

"All hands. This is the Captain. We are taking aboard some Merishi merchanter hands to help with damage control. This will be a temporary measure, until we can get human help from dirtside. We will also be able to compare notes on this incident. There will certainly be a Board investigation, don't forget."

There would be, and with no guaranteed results. Diplomacy had pressured Boards to throw captains off homeworlds or even out of space before now. But one thing that was not going to happen, with Merishi aboard *Nosavan:* the cruiser's opening fire.

Victoria:

The fast work at Government House and in orbit ended the attempted coup, before U.F.S. *Lysander* appeared to keep an eye on the Merishi and embarrass Gist with an offer of Federation support.

Unembarrassed, he requested and received a State of Emergency from Parliament. The only immediate edict suspended the operations of Special Branch, pending that overdue purge. In the longer term, everyone understood that the gloves were off.

This was good news to many. "The buggers are dead but they won't lie down" was the epitaph on the rebels, and few on Victoria had much enthusiasm for being Merishi pawns.

Lysander rode off Victoria, with *Gyn-Bahr* always in her sensor envelope, for several days. *Somtow Nosavan* proved past repairing for an interstellar flight, at least in time to carry the VEB to Linak'h.

Disappointment did not last long. Peter Bissell had won a qualified victory: the troops of the VEB would stay on Victoria. So would he. However, there would still be a VEB; Alys Parkinson drafted an order enlisting the whole Civil Action Group on Linak'h in the Planetary Republic of Victoria's Territorial Militia.

They would need some intelligence help, however. *Somtow Nosavan*'s senior officers would provide it, along with the newly commissioned Lieutenant Gullking and the long-lost Ezzaryi-ahd, who had been too late to save Payaral Na'an but had certainly pulled her weight at Government House.

The intelligence mission would ride aboard one of the Simferos Associates merchanters, and all four would travel to Linak'h in a convoy escorted by *Lysander*. If the captain of *Gyn-Bahr* took time off from repairing his ship to protest this relationship of Folk and human, nobody noticed.

The mission would also carry a letter from Lucco DiVries to Karl Pocher. DiVries had found the rebel bands near Fort Bergeron, all right—completely demoralized by the defeat in Thorntonsburg and surrounded by armed Ptercha'a sent by the Mount Houton Merishi.

The immediate danger seemed to be over, DiVries wrote. But Victoria might not find peace until *everybody* gave up their private armies. Did Karl have any bright ideas, now that he was a captain in the Militia and legally entitled to have them?

Seventeen

Linak'h:

Candice Shores was not a happy warrior as she flew toward her father's house. The knowledge of his death and the missing children echoed softly in her mind. It would echo deafeningly if she let it.

She had not in fact been a happy warrior even before the news reached her. The terrs hadn't moved in her battalion AO (the suspicious persons turned out to be a Militia training patrol, authorized all the way up to Marcus Langston), but her A and B companies were snatched away as reinforcements for areas where things weren't so comfortable.

A Company vanished into the maw of 218 Brigade, and B Company was unconscionably slow at mounting up and moving out. She also couldn't do much about either. She owed Edelstein too much, and she couldn't take heads in her own battalion at this stage of the crisis.

(Never mind the Coordination's sending some of their reservists back to work; their quick-recall system was nearly as effective as that of a well-run Federation planet, if not up to Bar Kochba's. They might be on the edge of peace rather than war, but it was a sharp edge either way.)

Her AO also included a project where the Victoria Civil Action Group had nearly half its people. At mid-afternoon she flew over to check their security. By then more thunderstorms had moved in; she flew and landed in a pouring rain that had Warrant Officer Konishi openly skeptical about letting her take the controls.

She got them there and down, but she was sweating and shaking when she climbed out. The Vics had all vanished into improvised shelter, except for a few standing security with old but clean weapons and even older but not so clean field clothing.

She remembered that the Victorians' major virtues were courage, endurance, and pride, not sophisticated training or weapons. She also remembered that the terrs had inflicted casualties on more-sophisticated security arrangements and that a massacre of Victorians would make political waves all the way back to Charlemagne, apart from possibly killing people she knew and mostly liked.

She was in the middle of sketching on her notepad a revised security arrangement for the Group area when Colonel Nieg materialized behind Karl Pocher. The colonel looked so parade-neat in spite of the rain that Shores wondered if the long-sought personal shield had at last been perfected and Nieg given the job of field-testing it.

He let her finish the sketch before he took her aside and broke the news. After that he answered her questions about what else he'd been doing besides letting her father die—at least she remembered asking such questions, although what they were and how Nieg answered flew right out of her mind.

"Thank you," she remembered saying.

"Ah—Candy—"

She wanted to say, "That's 'Colonel Shores.' " Like slapping him in the face, it would accomplish nothing except relieving her feelings.

Find a better way for that, Candy.

The voice in her mind sounded curiously like Marshal Banfi's, instead of (as more usual) her mother's.

"What else is there? I've got a battalion to run."

"Candy, the children are missing."

She controlled her face and jaw by a miracle. The miracle didn't help her voice. "Who took them?" she croaked.

"We don't know. Maybe nobody. Maybe the terrs. Our people in the area have strict ROE's to protect the children. But that underground shelter—"

"Your excuse for not guarding the place night and day?"

From his face, she might as well have slapped him. She decided that his conscience would do worse than she dared, and shook her head. Her thoughts seemed to come slowly. Had the rain crept into her brain through her ears and clogged her synapses?

"Yes. We had it equipped so that the children could hide

in it unaided. They may be in there now, afraid to come out. We can't get in without their cooperation, because your stepmother changed the access codes, then wiped all records of them.

"You might be able to talk them out. If we—"

She held up a hand that didn't shake. "Me?"

"You. Candy, it is entirely possible that you are the only human being left in the Universe that those kids will trust."

To her, it seemed entirely possible that Nieg had gone out of his mind. Possible, but not certain. Which made it possible (but not certain) that he knew what he was talking about. She'd taken his advice about how to handle the kids and Ursula before this, and it usually worked.

He was certainly right that he knew more about the workings of the civilian family than she did. She'd gone almost straight from her own peculiar household into the equally peculiar, if more functional, family of the Forces, and never established any relationship that lasted or was expected to last more than half a year.

Not until she met Nieg, at any rate.

She put that thought firmly aside and pulled her gear and guards together. Esteva and three hand-picked troopers followed her out to Nieg's lifter and didn't wait for anybody's invitation before they climbed in.

She shook off Nieg's hand, but didn't object when Konishi slipped into the pilot's chair and seated Nieg in the copilot's. She was also glad of the rain; nobody could tell what she was blinking out of her eyes as the lifter took off.

Aboard U.F.S. *Shenandoah,* off Linak'h:

Shenandoah swam up toward geostationary orbit and the rendezvous with *Roma* and *Intrepid* with all sensors on maximum power and all com channels open for messages or EI.

That might include intercepts from friendly forces, Rose Liddell realized. Linak'h Command's arrangements for keeping the Navy informed of what was happening on the ground seemed to have broken down. Busyness would be an adequate explanation as long as nothing went wrong; there would never be an excuse.

Liddell knew that some of her short temper was frustration. The Navy couldn't do much against even this half-arsed terrorist uprising except provide EI and surveillance, and help move people and supplies as necessary. Not that she really *missed* fighting off a kamikaze-style attack on the Low Squadron—

When things are slow, thank the Gods of War, she remembered from a long-ago War College course. *Use the time to sleep, or if you're rested up, think ahead. A mind that's ahead of the enemy is worth a hundred kilotons of response afterward.*

She leaned back in her chair (tinkered back to and beyond its original ergonomic level—now she could do everything short of take a bath in it) and free-associated. In five minutes she had two signals going out.

One to Captain Moneghan: he was to maintain a real-time surveillance of the Administration coast of the Braigh'n Gulf, periodically updating both Command HQ and *Shen.* Stay out of either Coordination or Merishi airspace.

The weather over the Gulf was deteriorating; some of those Coordination and Merishi lifters might be able to ground on the Administration side of the Gulf. Some might have to, even if that wasn't their intention, and Liddell wasn't betting a bale of polishing rags on that. "Civilian movements," "navigational errors," and "overreaction by ground bases" were nice diplomatic phrases or, less elegantly, lies.

Liddell was damned sure that the Coordination and/or Merishi were trying to sneak ground troops into lightly held Administration territory. They could reinforce the terrs, provide a secure LZ for reinforcements if war broke out, or carry out raids and sabotage on their own.

That thought led to the second message. Every ship in the Low Squadron should inventory spares and supplies that might be transferred to the attackers. *Intrepid* would be Longman's left hook against the Coordination cruisers and any Merishi backup for them; not much help there. As for the ground bases, a ground-based attacker was vulnerable to two kinds of attack: sabotage and fusers.

Longman had delivered a blistering warning about the kind of retaliation any use of fusers would draw. It should impress the sensible, but any opponent had to have its share of fools. Three-dimensional warfare also had few places where a determined opponent couldn't infiltrate a squad of Ranger types, willing to trade their lives for a heavy attacker or a brigade HQ.

When Moneghan and the squadron acknowledged the messages, Liddell tilted her chair back and kicked off her shoes. She'd need them back on for the conference with Longman, but that was an hour away; meanwhile, bare feet gave both comfort and the right image. The Old Lady, they would say, was as calm as a hibernating brown browser.

Linak'h:

In the after-rain haze, her father's house looked almost normal to Candice Shores. At least it did until the lifter flared for landing and she counted the other troop carriers around it, not to mention the gaping hole in the roof.

"Where—?"

"The bodies?" Nieg said, before she could finish. She wanted to hug, hit, and curse the man. "They're at the camp. We've set up a temporary morgue for all the casualties. Healer Kunkuhn and one of our medics—"

There was more, but she didn't hear it. She had discovered that it was easier to keep control if she focused completely on the children and didn't think about their dead parents.

At least two reliable people were in the circuit, Kunkuhn and Nieg (well, mostly reliable). Brigitte Tachin met her at the door of the house, and immediately became a third.

Shores found it easier than she'd expected to listen to Tachin's story of the gap in security and all that followed. After checking the house for the living, friend or foe, the Navy people had withdrawn into the forest and stayed there for two hours, so well hidden that the fleeing terrorists never spotted them.

"In fact, we had to signal the troops when they came. It was that which made me suspect the children might be hiding. So when this *espece de chameau* wanted to flood the tunnels with gas—"

"What?" Shores and Nieg said together. A sergeant with Combat Engineer insignia and 218 Brigade patches cringed. Then he backed away three steps. He would have taken a fourth, except that he was up against the wall, with Shores staring him down from a distance of about four centimeters.

"I don't think gas would be wise, because of the concentration factor," Nieg said in a level voice. Shores realized that he was trying to calm himself as much as her. In principle, he would not object to helping her dismember this Federation's bad bargain.

"We could try—no, I don't suppose those tunnels are in shape to stand blasting."

"No, they are not," Shores said. Nieg nodded in confirmation.

"All right, sir, ma'am," the sergeant said. "But we can't spend all day—"

"We can spend as long as we need either to get the children out or to confirm that they're not in the tunnels," Nieg said. "Sergeant, what we need is a borer and a snake with a microphone on the end."

Shores shook her head. "A miniature holoprojector," she said. "Voices can be faked."

"So can images," Nieg said. "And will the children know this?"

"Sophie will," Shores said, after a moment. "Remember, they're my father's kids. He worked in the visual media. They'll be visually oriented." *Which might make no difference in the end, but right now we are just at the beginning.*

"Very well," Nieg said. "Sergeant, you take a lifter, my authority, and get everything we need."

"Sir—"

"Load and lift ten minutes ago, and be back before you left." Nieg was a head shorter than the sergeant and might be taking a hard line out of guilt. The message that this was the sergeant's last chance to redeem himself got through. He was out the door before Shores could turn around to thank Nieg.

The colonel waved the thanks aside. "We also need a few more people for security and searching the tunnels," he said. "Lieutenant Tachin—?"

"Our Navy team is spread pretty thin," she said. "But anybody we can spare . . ."

"Fine. Colonel Shores"—she blinked at the formality but thanked him with her eyes—"take a couple of people for security and go downcellar. The rear left corner of the second room you come to, behind the processor, is where we start. Talk loudly; maybe they're close enough to hear you.

"I'm going to make one last try at cracking Ursula Boll's code. Demons roast those half-witted thugs for ten eternities! Intelligence lost a really fine officer when Ursula Boll died."

Shores rolled her eyes at the ceiling. This was one of those times when she wanted to pick up Nieg and throw him hard at the nearest wall, aimed so the point on his head would drive twenty cems into the wall and he would stick there, quivering like an arrow in a target as a warning to the tactless.

Tachin threw her a sympathetic look and unslung her carbine. "I'm one," she said. "Find another, and we can go down."

"Sophie?"

Sophia Komarova-Boll recognized her name. It was the first word she could understand that Peter had said for quite a while. She hoped this was only because he was scared. She was, too, alone here in the darkness.

She also went on climbing. Finally she came to the top of the pile of crates. She'd discovered them only after they'd been in the tunnels for some time, and didn't know what was in them. They were about the same size and shape as the ones she'd seen when they were packing up to leave the old house in the forest.

"Ssssh, Peter," she whispered. "I'm trying to listen."

She was trying very hard, but she couldn't hear anything for what seemed like another long time. Then she heard faint footsteps that sounded like the feet were in boots or heavy shoes. She heard more faint voices, some of them men's, some of them women's.

One of the voices made her stiffen and bite her hand so that she wouldn't cry out. It sounded so much like Candy Shores's voice. If she was here, it was safe for them to come out.

But it was only a voice that might be Candy's. Sophie knew she might be hearing things, or hoping so much that she didn't hear what was really there but what she wanted to hear. She'd heard stories of that from both her father and mother.

She would wait, although it was going to be very boring

to wait with nothing to do, and besides it was cold in here. She wondered if the crates had any warm clothing in them, then knew it didn't matter. She and Peter didn't have any tools, and opening the crates would make noise that people upstairs might here.

She and Peter would have to be quiet, until somebody they could really trust came along.

Aboard U.F.S. *Shenandoah,* off Linak'h:

Even with tight beam and scramble, this was a conference that couldn't be allowed to leak. The three flag officers also couldn't leave their ships. Thus the compromise: the three flagships practically within light-cannon range. If the ACC had possessed a porthole, Commodore Liddell could have looked out it and read the serial numbers on *Roma*'s hull.

Instead she was looking at four displays on two different screens. The smaller communications screen showed Admirals Longman and Uehara. The larger tactical one was also split, between a simulation of the situation dirtside and a real-time display of the Linak'h Task Force's current formation.

Liddell was giving most of her attention to the two senior officers. *Shen* could hardly influence events dirtside from out here in geostationary orbit, and the formation was a standard one that guarded against most contingencies. In an emergency, each capital ship could pick up its escorts and buses (four apiece from *Shen* and *Roma,* two plus an attacker flight from *Intrepid*) and rapidly maneuver into clear space, while keeping weapons arcs open.

"Any plan to abandon Linak'h in the face of a Coordination attack seems to be officially dead," Longman was saying. "Our authorization now includes all appropriate measures against the Coordination that may be required to protect Federation Forces and citizens or prevent the invasion of the territory of the Administration. We are not allowed to operate against the citizens, territory, or ships of the Governance unless they become directly engaged in presenting either of the above threats.

"We are also authorized to consider this a War Warning. I intend to so consider it. Do either of you have any comments on that?"

That was a less hypocritical word than "objections," which Liddell doubted that the Golden Vanity would entertain for more than a nanosecond. Since the commodore had none, the tact was wasted—but the display of it was a good sign.

"Good. This Task Force is now in a War Warning condition. Please adopt Alert levels appropriate to the situation. I don't think I need to warn you not to overdo Alerts One and Two."

Liddell would have expected Longman to need that warning herself. Once again the Golden Vanity was demonstrating that while she might still have horns and fangs, she had learned something in the last few years about the best use for them.

"I have drafted a message to the Coordination. With your concurrence, I will submit it to the Governor-General for transmission, either directly or through the consul, if we haven't closed down the office."

Longman's face gave way to a slowly scrolling message. It was a succinct warning to the Coordination against allowing its territory to be used as a refuge or base for further terrorist actions. It also warned that any use of fusion weapons against the Federation or its allies would be considered a first use by the Coordination, and the relevant policies governing Federation retaliation would apply thereafter.

This might be holding the Coordination responsible for acts it did not approve and could not prevent. It might also deter them from attempting fuser terrorism to degrade Federation or Administration capabilities without taking any responsibility for it.

With nerves drawn this tight, the Coordination not only had to be innocent, it had to look innocent.

"Do we have any intelligence updates on the Administration's arsenal?" Uehara asked. "Even if the Coordination or the Governance haven't supplied them, the terrs might have fusers stolen during the putsch."

"I've queried Banfi on that," Longman said. "So far I don't have a reply."

There seemed to be no useful comments on that. Longman continued. "We will adopt Standard Eight deployment, effective as soon as this conference is over. Those four Coordination cruisers have been joined by one very large shuttle or interplanetary vessel, but otherwise have taken no observed unusual or threatening action."

Problem: they can make their move without giving us any warning, if they're good enough at low-altitude work.

The Coordination's cruisers were in an orbit that kept them entirely out of Federation or Alliance restricted space. Orbits, however, could be shifted in minutes and attacks launched while shifting or immediately afterward.

Further problem: how precise do they want to be, if they want to start shooting at all?

Speed usually cost precision, and reducing precision raised collateral damage—which, translated from jargon, meant dead civilians, the corner shop in flames and the doctor's office in ruins, and the inherently nasty business of war made even nastier. Left a free choice, Liddell doubted that the Coordination would risk a wholesale slaughter of Hunters—but they'd winked at the terrorists. And did they have free choice?

Liddell returned her attention to the screens for all the remaining two minutes of the conference. Then she relaxed. *Shenandoah* was already on station, her escorts and buses in proper formation around her, and free of any duties except to watch the planet while the other two squadrons were maneuvering and therefore less free to go into action.

Once all three squadrons were on station in geostationary orbits, the potential war zone would be covered, one squadron usually hidden against the sun, and all approaches to the planet under continuous sensor scans. If the scans did detect hostiles, there'd be plenty of room for fire and maneuver by all three squadrons without mutual interference.

After weeks of hard work at low altitudes, Liddell felt almost buoyant at riding high and free of responsibilities. She had to check the displays to be sure that no one had adjusted the internal gravity while she wasn't looking.

It wasn't the way she had expected to feel upon learning that war might be only hours away. But then, for anybody who'd survived the hardscrabble improvisations on Victoria, Linak'h Command was positively going to war luxury-class.

Linak'h:

To Candice Shores, it seemed that the engineer sergeant must have had to send up to orbit or even out-system for the equipment he'd promised. She kept looking at her watch, certain each time that hours had passed, yet discovering that it had only been five minutes.

Meanwhile, she was sitting in front of what Nieg said was the hidden entrance to the tunnels, trying to shout reassuringly. She wasn't sure of how far back into the tunnels the children were, the tunnels' acoustics, or much else about the refuge that might have become a trap.

She was glad that Nieg had stayed upstairs, even if cracking the access code might be more excuse than possibility. She couldn't give him any reassurance or forgiveness that he'd believe, and being suspected of lying would kill their future. Right now it had only been triaged into the Class Two Wounded (severe but repairable).

Trying to get a response from whoever was beyond the basement wall kept her from worrying too much about Nieg or her battalion. Unintentionally, Brigitte Tachin did the rest.

At first Shores thought that Tachin was seeking reassurance for herself, about whether the Navy ground team had done the right things. Shores doubted that she had all the facts to be a good judge, even if she was a ground-pounder, and the Navy team couldn't have done the one thing that really mattered anyway—preventing the murders and the missing children in the first place.

"I know that," Tachin said, when Shores finally let it slip. "Brian doesn't."

"Brian?" At the moment this seemed to be the name of someone from the remote past of a nonhuman species. One of the Great Khudr's staff officers—

"Candy, did you think *I* was torturing myself?" An upraised hand kept Shores silent. "It's for Brian."

This time the name was associated with the right person. "Why? Or rather, if it's for Brian, why can't I say it myself?"

"Because you have other things on your mind. I was not even sure I should mention this at all."

"Hey, what are friends for?"

"*Merci mille fois.* Also there is no way you could talk to Brian soon enough that would not make him suspicious."

All that kept Shores from loudly wishing Brian Mahoney and all his complexes in Hades was Nieg's arrival, leading the engineering team with the sergeant and three new tech ratings. The sergeant was carrying more than his share of the gear.

On Nieg's instructions, the borer hissed and whined into action. A hole appeared in minutes; the snake was already powered up, with only the projector to be locked in place at the head. Then the sergeant squatted beside the control box and signaled to Shores.

"Colonel, if you can stand right here, where the circle of light is—a little to the right—fine." Mysterious lights flashed; still more mysterious noises came from the controls. The sergeant looked and listened, then nodded.

"All right. We are getting a projection, about twenty feet inside, and two-thirds life-size."

"How far can they see it?" Nieg asked.

"Depends on the light level inside," the sergeant said. "If it's completely dark, you can see that *something's* happening three hundred meters away."

If the children were three hundred meters inside the tunnels, it was hard to imagine that they'd have a clear sight line to the image. The audio couldn't substitute completely, either—it could distort her voice, frighten the children, or even bring down unstable portions of the tunnels.

Shores took a deep breath, let it out—

"Sophia, Peter. If you can see a light, come closer to it. This is a projection of me, because I can't get in unless you open the door you closed behind you. If I can't get in, I can't help you—"

Sophia saw a light. She put a hand on Peter's shoulder. Gently, so that she wouldn't startle him into making a sound. They had to be quiet, because that light had to mean that somebody had opened the door—

"Sophia, Peter. If you can see a light, come closer to it—"

Sophia got down on her stomach on the floor and started

crawling toward the light, while the voice went on. She'd heard that was what soldiers did when they wanted to learn what was going on without being seen or heard.

" 'At's Candy," Peter said behind her.

Sophia started and banged her head on the edge of a crate. It hurt so much that she wanted to cry, and she thought it was bleeding. She turned and shook her head at Peter, then realized that he couldn't see her in the darkness, even if the light was making it not quite as dark as it had been.

"Sssh," she hissed, hoping that he could hear her and that the others couldn't.

She knew he'd heard her, but that just made matters worse. "Candy's here!" he said, firmly and clearly. "We have to tell her."

Then before Sophia could move or speak her brother ran from his hiding place, toward the light. She jumped up and ran after him, hoping that he would trip, knowing that if she didn't she had to be with him when he reached the light. He was her brother, after all, even if sometimes she wished she didn't have one.

Peter didn't trip, but Sophia's longer legs let her catch up with him as he reached the open space by the door. Nobody was there. At least nobody real. The image was Candy Shores's, but anybody could tape an image of her and project it. Both of Sophia's parents had told her about that sort of thing when they were telling the children how to use the hiding place.

The image went out, but the light didn't. Then the voice came again.

"Sophia? Peter? Is that you? Are you all right?"

"Candy!" Peter screamed. The rest was the gobbling like a sick animal that didn't have any words and didn't make any sense, until he ran out of breath.

They could have recorded Candy's voice, too. But could they have done it so she sounded like she was hearing them and answering them? Sophia didn't know.

She did know that Peter couldn't open the door by himself. If they were going to open it, she had to do it. If she didn't do it and he was sure that Candy was out there, ready to help him, the two of them were going to fight.

"If you ever use the tunnels, you have to be a team, like

the Rangers," her mother had said. And Peter did seem very sure that it was really Candy, although she didn't know how or why.

Sophia stepped forward. "Peter, push that button by the lock," she said. It took him three tries to get the right button, but he finally did. The green light came on over Sophia's side of the door, and a plate opened in the wall. A switch wiggled, then swung down.

She pushed it up as she'd been taught, and somewhere a motor whined. Then the door slid into the wall. Beyond it was a short tunnel, not much longer than Sophia was tall, and another door that was already quivering. On either side of the short tunnel were more crates.

Then the second door opened, and Candy Shores ran through it, to kneel in front of Sophia. Peter ran into her arms, she reached out and pulled Sophia close, and they were all crying. Sophia thought she saw Colonel Nieg standing beside Candy, but right now she didn't really care about anybody but Candy.

She was here. Somebody they could trust was here. Now they would know about Papa and Mama, and even if it was bad news they had another good person with them.

Linak'h:

Fomin zar Yayn received his war warning from Muhrinnmat-Vao in his leader's post in a cave near the Braigh'n. It was made very clear to him that he was expected to stay in that cave for the war.

"The Tribal frytinzi may be needed on the firing line. You are not."

Zar Yayn thought of challenging the senior with a question: if they feared a Confraternity sympathizer's becoming a hero, why had they given him so many warriors in the first place?

He also thought that would be a bad ending to his friendship with Muhrinnmat-Vao, one of those he could hardly be sure of ever seeing again. So he merely gave his own variation of an ancient ritual phrase.

"In mind and body, I will be where my duty calls me, ready for what the Fates may send, and loyal to both my Seniors and my Band."

Muhrinnmat-Vao looked less out of temper after that, and they blanked screens with good wishes in both directions. Zar Yayn switched the screen to LETTER mode and began dictating.

It would not have taken him as long if he had not been trying to say something that he had not said to his wife or his wife's son on his last brief leave. Finally he decided that the inspiration to say anything better was going to elude him for longer than he could allow.

My dear ones,

I write this to be read after my death. There is precious little pleasure in the thought of even the most worthy death, as it will take me away from you.

But I also know that Fate rules all. Even more on the battlefield than elsewhere, one can but do one's best and hope that is sufficient.

If I must leave you, I do it knowing that I leave behind two who will mourn but live on when the mourning is done. I also know that the child to come has good blood on both sides, and will be in the best of hands during all the years he or she may need them.

That last took a trifle of diplomacy; zar Yayn was not entirely sure about his wife's kin. Hunter inheritance laws offered too many opportunities for the disputatious, and no one could say what spirit might prevail among those kin when the war was done.

Everyone's problems will be of course much simpler if I survive the coming war. I wish to; I wish that all under me do likewise; I even wish that our foe yield readily. (Equal displays of courage often end in equal slaughter.)

But the cosmos is not made to please those who wish the simple life. That you know this too is one reason I have loved you both; teach it to the child and my spirit will rest easily.

With the touch of caring,

Fomin zar Yayn

Eighteen

Linak'h:

Candice Shores's flight of lifters had crossed the tip of the southernmost tongue of the Great Fire ten minutes ago. Now that the Yellow Father had come out, the tall trees cast long shadows across the hillsides and cleared fields.

In those shadows, the farmhouses mostly lay abandoned or defended themselves by looking that way. Few had lifters parked outside. Cruising by a thousand meters up, Shores couldn't tell if the lifters were civilian, Administration, Federation, Confraternity militia, or terrorist.

At least nobody had shot at them yet, as they made their long dogleg inland to approach the Federation Zone well clear of the Braigh'n Gulf. Nor did Shores think anyone was likely to. There were too many units of everybody's forces on the move to make "shoot and scoot" feasible, entirely apart from all the armed civilians who hardly sympathized with the terrorists.

"Son of a—!" Konishi snarled. "Go back to driving the she-ox who bore you!" The command lifter tilted as he wrenched it to the right, away from three civilian lifters escorted by a gunship sailing out of nowhere on the left and vanishing toward the distant line of the Wambaku Hills.

Those were the first words the pilot had spoken since they had left the Komarov house. Silence from both friends and enemies was something Shores appreciated right now.

As the lifter took off, the children's tears finally came. By the time she'd consoled them into a troubled sleep, one on each side of her, Shores had nearly exhausted her own self-control.

She didn't care if Nieg saw her cry. In fact, right now, she didn't think she'd care if he decided to leave the lifter without its landing or his wearing a parachute. She also knew that her formless anger at him for not sparing her the job of identifying her father's body was unjust. Too many faceless bureaucrats would question an identification by Healer Kunkuhn, a Confraternity Hunter and militia leader as well as Healer.

"I assume we are returning to the Zone," Nieg said. "May I ask what you intend to do there?"

"You may ask."

He looked away from the stone in her face and the alloy blade lurking in her voice. That bought her time to organize her thoughts. Crying wouldn't have bothered Nieg; her not having a plan for the children might have looked suspicious. She refused to lose either the children or her battalion to anybody's suspicions.

"I think they have a firm claim to quarters in the Family Care Center. They can get a thorough medical exam, a private room—"

"Are you sure?"

"Liew, you know the situation in the Zone better than I do. But you owe me—you owe the children—that much. I expect you to find them a room, a doctor, and a speech therapist for Peter if there's one left on-planet."

"You're remarkably willing to be bribed all at once."

"Who said anything about bribes? I consider this paying a debt."

"And afterward?"

"Are Herman Franke and Lu Morley still on light duty? I thought they might be able to give the children some personal attention."

"Lu Morley has all the nurturing instincts of a Farsi Blue Death."

"I disagree, and you didn't answer my question."

"They'll be a high-priority target for any terrorists still roaming around."

"That's still not an answer."

Nieg sighed and rested a hand on her knee. Under other circumstances, Shores would have felt like apologizing.

"All right. Neither the pilot, the children, nor you is really cleared for this, but—"

He summarized his role in the day's events, not only the terrorist attacks but also high-level intrigues that hadn't even reached the beervine network yet. Shores didn't know whether continuity in command outweighed the risks of leaving Kharg in command of 222 Brigade. She also didn't ask what his files had revealed; not even God had clearance for that.

She certainly wasn't surprised at Nieg's conclusion. "Right now, it is generally felt that the less I am seen around either HQ, the better. So I am going into the field with the Rangers covert-operations teams. The Special Intelligence Group will become part of Linak'h Command HQ, with Franke and Morley in charge. I don't suppose we could borrow back Sergeant Esteva?"

"Not a chance in Hades!"

This time he squeezed her hand. Shores thought Sophia was awake enough to notice the gesture, and she could almost imagine she saw the girl smile.

Linak'h:

As a Ship Commander First Class, Brokeh su-Irzim was really too senior to be doing the work of an inventory clerk. However, supplies and Hunters of all sorts and conditions were flowing through the Inquiry base and on into the field. Every hand was needed, whether it had three digits or four, and many Hunters liked to see their seniors getting their hands dirty.

Besides, su-Irzim had never been given to settling back with beer and women before the battle. Afterward, perhaps, but never before.

It was a woman, Lyka ihr Zeyem, who brought su-Irzim the message from Rahbad Sarlin and Behdan Zeg. She found him in the underground warehouse, surrounded by Hunters who were carting away substandard components and recrating those that passed the random inspection.

Radio listeners had heard a faint Federation rescue beeper. They were attempting to get a more accurate fix, but at the present time they could say only that it was close to the shore and in the People's Territory.

Because the signal was so faint, this might take a while. However, Federation rescue forces might have picked it up, from the air if not from orbit. They might be operating close to the People's borders, seeking their strayed one. The risk of the Hunter Militia's being detected therefore had to be balanced against the speed of moving them into the area by lifter.

Sighing could not do justice to this situation. Su-Irzim knew that he was being asked for advice. Perhaps even for orders that would let the two field commanders blame him for any disasters that might come?

No, that was not the way they waged war, not even Behdan Zeg (At least not since Zeg had discovered that his call in life was to lead Hunters to battle). "The field gives courage, the couch gives suspicion" was a much-quoted saying that still held a seed of truth.

"Tell them that the best outcome would be for the Federation to recover their man without any penetration of our Territory that we have to notice. They should do what they think best to bring this about.

"The next best outcome will be for us to recover the pilot and have the honor of rescuing her. If he has valuable Inquiry material, we may be able to learn some of it in return. If he is held by our Hunter militia, the Governor can honestly deny that he is holding any Federation prisoners."

Ihr Zeyem smiled. "As you command. Oh, Kalidessouf threatens a formal petition to the Khudr if he is not allowed to go into the field when the last load of supplies is sent out." She smiled. "I can speak to his being healthy."

"Battles are not won on couches. I will threaten him with a formal execution for mutiny, desertion, and theft it he goes. Anything more?"

"*Perfumed Wind* has the last load nearly aboard the shuttle. It will be undocking in a tenth watch. There is more shuttle activity around two of the Coordination cruisers than usual, so our shuttle may have to—"

"How does she know that?"

"Ah—?"

"Did she probe or listen? If she probed—"

"If you will recall, Commander, *Perfumed Wind*'s orbit brings her close enough to the Coordination cruisers for visual observation, using the Guidance telescope."

Su-Irzim had not recalled that; he felt the blood rushing to his face. "Now I do. Do me the honor of forgetting that I said this."

"I shall, Commander. We are all tired."

Linak'h:

"How is Peter, Doctor?" Candice Shores asked.

Major Feinberg shrugged. "Well enough to be asleep. I gave both of them a light tranquilizer with their dinner. They ate about as much as one could expect under the circumstances and kept it down."

"You aren't answering my question, Doctor." Shores tried to keep her voice level. She wanted Feinberg thinking medical down-check even less than she wanted it from Nieg. She also wanted answers about the children more than she wanted any answers Nieg could give.

"The diagnostic scans have eliminated any risk of brain damage causing the speech problems." Feinberg said. She frowned. "Otherwise, I didn't see any reason not to let the children get a good night's sleep before we started running tests on them."

Whatever Feinberg saw on Shores's face made her put on her best doctor-knows-best manner. "Colonel, there's as little chance as we can measure of serious injury. Everything else, Peter's speech and all, is a matter for long-term therapy. Part of the therapy will have to be you being calm and optimistic."

"I know that will be hard, under the circumstances. If I have any ideas about how you can help the children and still grieve normally, I'll pass them on to you." Feinberg gave Shores a thin smile. "Or I can pass you on to Colonel Nardesian—"

Feinberg took a step backward as Shores's face made her realize her joke was over the line. Shores flexed the fingers of the hands that had turned into a flat blade ready to chop, and squeezed out a smile in return.

"At least let me see them. I won't wake them for goodbyes if they're still asleep."

"I can do that much. Oh, I almost forgot. Our own speech therapist is fully booked, but I understand there's a qualified civilian one. I believe something is being done, to get her a Forces permit and a security clearance."

Shores blinked eyes that seemed to have spent all day staring unprotected into a duststorm and rested one hand on the back of the nearest chair. When she found she needed to use the other hand as well, she realized just how close to the edge she was.

"If you don't mind a sleeping bag, I can make up a bed for you on the floor of the children's room."

"I thought I was supposed to—ah, detach myself—from them?"

"I said no such thing, and you're too tired to think. Also to do your battalion any good, if you return to it in your present condition."

"It's a two-hour flight. I was thinking about a nap on the way."

"You need more than a nap. I won't insist on a tranquilizer, but—"

Shores held up a hand. "Just the sleeping bag, to start with. If the children wake up, I want to be able to wake up too. Otherwise, what the bloody good am I going to be to them?"

Feinberg seemed to have several answers to that question and the sense to give none of them.

"Look for Room Three-Four-Two. I'll warn the ward nurse and send up the sleeping bag."

Linak'h:

Emt Desdai had wondered sometimes if his social skills and Seenkiranda's were equal to all the occasions they might face in the service of Isha Maiyotz.

Tonight he expected the answer. They were on their way to visit a Supreme War Leader who was also a Marshal of the Federation. Such an experience they had never had; such an experience Desdai, at least, had never anticipated.

Fortunately the flight from Administration House to Banfi's Warband House wasn't long enough to allow much brooding. Desdai's tension had just begun to ebb when they landed, and the first thing he saw out the window was a pad entirely ringed by Legion One-Five Warriors.

He wanted to tumble out onto the pad and made every gesture of conceding dominance, both civilized and Tribal. Instead he let Seenkiranda take his arm; he was not sure who was giving strength to whom.

Their combined strength took them through the successive arches of the entryway, past the potted plants in the lobby (somewhat in need of watering, Desdai thought), and into an elevator so filled with more armed Hunters that there was barely room for the messengers. It let them out on the fifth level, and successively higher-ranking leaders inspected their authorizations, scanned their eyes and chips, and passed them on to the next. It seemed half a day, but it was less than a tenth of that, before they were facing Marshal Banfi.

The Marshal knew the Hunter etiquette of greeting and went through it with as much grace as any human could. This eased Desdai's nerves enough to let him realize that Banfi spoke True Speech with a slight Nilyan accent.

"But I beg that my hospitality may wait upon your business," Banfi concluded. "If you will not speak dishonor of my house—"

"It is not in you or your house to show dishonor," Desdai said, more smoothly than he'd dared expect from his dry lips.

That concluded the etiquette. Banfi placed both hands flat on his desk. "Sit down, Confreres. I understand you have important material for me. Isha Maiyotz was rather oblique about its nature, so perhaps you can give me a summary if it is extensive."

"It is," Desdai said. "It is complete material on all the Confraternity's refuges, tunnels, and supply depots."

Banfi's eyebrows had more hair than his head. Now every one of those white hairs stiffened like those of a Hunter's tail on the verge of battle. "A large gift, and none too soon."

He stared at the two Hunters. The eyes gave more dominance than his height, which was only a trifle above that of most Hunters. "Would I be right, in assuming that Boronisskahane was the cause of the delay in assembling this data? Or at least in sending it to me?"

Desdai started to speak. Seenkiranda's words came first.

"A large question, Senior, and one we will gladly answer if you answer one of ours."

Desdai's whiskers rose as Banfi's eyes narrowed. Then the man nodded. "If I know, I will tell."

"Have you taken command of the Federation Warband as well as of the Administration?"

"I am tempted to ask why you wonder, but the answer should be obvious to a child. Rumors?" Seenkiranda nodded.

"Certain Hunters will learn about letting their tongues wag, and from one much harsher on such matters than even I," Banfi said. "But the truth is no. I lead only the Administration's Warband, although as both a Marshal and an allied senior, I have the right to make myself heard with both Longman and Tanz."

A woman with Confraternity badges and the rank markings of a Band Leader pushed in a cart of covered plates and insulated jugs and bottles. "When I heard you were coming, I knew you would be here through your dinner hour and mine alike," Banfi said. "I think the food has the vices of both Hunter and human cooking and the virtues of neither, but offer your opinion freely."

When the covers came off the plates, Desdai realized that he was too hungry to be a very good judge of cooking. Meanwhile, Banfi was doing a quick scan of the data. When he'd finished, he looked at the two Hunters over the rim of a silver goblet engraved with Myu'un rune-scrolls.

"It does not say which of your resources are still under Confraternity control, you know. Was this not considered important, or is it something on which you have no knowledge?"

Desdai and Seenkiranda exchanged looks; Banfi laughed. "I am not one to kill the messengers of incomplete news. I merely wondered if anyone had thought of the trouble it might cause, if terrorists had seized tunnels and set booby traps or ambushes."

"We did not know this," Desdai said. "I presume that Senior Maiyotz did. She chose not to tell us. Her most likely reason was to avoid shaming Boronisskahane, who is probably even more reluctant to admit this ignorance. Either that, or he thinks that the Confraternity—"

"Boronisskahane would not admit that his pubic hair was white if you presented him with a spectrographic reading and three sworn avowals from sexual partners," Banfi said. He used the coarsest words for several of the relevant terms. Seenkiranda laughed out loud.

More gently, Banfi went on. "He also has a lifetime of distrusting humans to put out of his mind, and for that he has had—what, the sixth part of a Linak'h year? No doubt he will do better with time. Meanwhile, we have much that is useful and the Confraternity has my thanks.

"I also note there is no list of people allowed access to this—"

The screen on Banfi's desk lit up in swirling colors, and electronic whistlings and whinings warned of an urgent message.

"Senior Mountain," Banfi replied, giving his codename.

"Spacewatch Senior," replied the voice out of the colors. "We have Condition Silver. The Coordination cruisers have sharply lowered their altitude. They are off our radar screens. We have requested scans from the Federation—"

"I will make a second request in person. Continue a real-time transmission—"

The screen flared until Desdai had to close his eyes, then it went dark. So did other displays. Some of them came back on, others remained dead.

Banfi seemed to fly out of his seat and vault his desk with the ease of a Hunter, so fast did he move to the nearest active display.

"Senior Mountain to all Warband units. Senior Mountain to all Warband units. Condition Gold. Condition Gold. We are at war. The Coordination has attacked the satellite network. We must expect air and ground as well as space attacks at any moment."

The message had been recorded as he spoke it. Now he ordered, "Continuous playback."

The message was going out for the fifth time when a sonic boom rattled the building. The window cracked, one of the jugs toppled off the cart and spilled something brown and steaming-hot across the rug, and more displays either went dark or went random.

Yellow light blazed through the window, and another sonic boom slapped the building even harder. This time the window shattered. Before he joined Banfi and Seenkiranda on the floor, Emt Desdai saw a missile thundering into the ruddy Fatherset sky and Seenkiranda holding one side of her face where the blood ran down between her fingers.

Linak'h:

Candice Shores woke up to see the ceiling of the hospital room vibrating. She'd seen it doing the same thing when she fell asleep, but that had been a hallucination from sheer exhaustion. Now she'd had at least a couple of hours' sleep. The ceiling must be really moving.

Before she could consider possible explanations for this, she heard a high-pitched cry from Sophia. The girl was awake and the tranquilizer seemed to have worn off. Shores hopped over to Sophia's bed, carrying her boots (the only thing she'd taken off) in one hand.

She'd just hugged the girl back into something like calm when either a sonic boom or an explosion rattled everything that was even slightly loose. Peter woke up this time, staring wildly around him; Shores reached to include him in the embrace.

Then the speaker system added to the din.

"Attention, attention! Alert Red One. Alert Red One. We are under air and space attack. All hospital personnel report to your emergency stations. All nonhospital personnel assemble at the main entrance for transportation back to your units."

Shores knew her way around the hospital just enough to be useful for moving the children down to the shelter. It helped that they were both ambulatory and that they hadn't unpacked anything from their bags except pajamas and a stuffed animal apiece.

She had them out in the hall on the way to the elevator by the time the speaker system started calling individual people. Halfway down the hall they passed the nurses' station. No one was monitoring the displays now, but Nightingale Khan was standing by the counter, dispensing orders, advice, and emergency life-support packs. To Shores's adrenaline-enhanced vision, he seemed to have as many arms as a Hindu god.

"Hey, where do you go with those—?" he called when he saw Shores.

"To the shelter."

"You go back to your unit. Didn't you hear the—?"

Suddenly Nightingale Khan found himself with only two arms, and one of those was jammed behind his back as Shores slammed him against the counter. He tried to raise the other, but the spectacle of Shores's face glaring into his at nose-to-nose distance seemed to paralyze both his muscles and his vocal cords.

"I know I have to get back to my battalion," she said in a tone she would have used to a dog who had pissed on her dress uniform. "I will obey that order. But I will take the children down to the shelter first. They will not see me running off and leaving them before then."

The nurse was still standing, more like a temple column than a temple image, when the elevator door closed behind Shores, the children, and what seemed like forty people and half a dozen gurneys and equipment robots.

The hospital shelter was part of the Zone's underground complex, fifty meters into bedrock. Both signs and live orderlies were directing traffic by the time Shores arrived. One look at the children—or maybe at her expression—got the children their own private orderly, who led them down a corridor marked CHILDREN'S QUARTERS, among other things.

Then they stopped, so suddenly that the orderly leading them nearly ran into a wall. They turned.

"Candy?" It was Peter who spoke. Sophia was staring. Both looked as if they wanted to cry and beg her to stay but thought they were too big for that.

If anybody is going to cry now, it's me.

She knelt and threw her arms around them. "Remember, I'm a soldier." She managed not to add, "Like your mother." "The people who fought your parents are now trying to fight everybody. That means it's my job to go out and fight them until they stop it. Other people have the job of taking care of you until I come back."

Sophia nodded. "But you will take care of us when you do come back." She didn't put it as a question.

"Yes."

Linak'h:

The first sonic booms Olga Nalyvkina had heard were either small vehicles close by or large ones far off. Then she saw the laser and missile traces when they crossed a patch of clear sky. One blaze against the stars had to be a ship or satellite dying.

She was quite satisfied that the war had started by the time she heard light attackers low overhead. At least war seemed more plausible than simultaneous live-fire exercises by Federation, Administration, Baernoi, Merishi, and Coordination.

The northbound attackers—she counted five flights in twenty minutes, all of them low and doing just under Mach One—confirmed the rumors that the Coordination was basing air assets on its shore of the Braigh'n Gulf. Added to the probability of other formations based in the Merishi Territory, this meant a much more hotly contested air campaign than anyone had expected.

A campaign which she might have to sit out on the ground, if E & E'ing gave her any time to sit. Survival training kept her from swearing out loud, but her thoughts about the Furball who had shot her down were not complimentary.

At least if a crash landing and a six-klom swim to shore hadn't killed her, nothing tonight offered was likely to finish the job. She had lost some survival gear, including two of her three radios and her pistol, but she had one radio left and no more hypothermia than she could cure by burying herself in a pile of dead leaves while the radio beeped plaintively.

Nobody from SAR had beeped back, unfortunately, and an hour ago she'd turned off the beacon. It was going to stay off for a while, too. SAR was not going to move into hostile or neutral airspace without some sort of escort, which nobody was likely to provide until Linak'h Command had weathered the initial attack.

On the other hand, whoever watched where she was (she suspected Baernoi ground) undoubtedly had EI posts and ground and air assets to move in on anyone who broadcast their presence. Silent and invisible was the way now—and gather as much intelligence as she could, besides hanging on to that suit memory store with the data from Diadem Three.

Right now she was too close to the shore for anything except easy access for the Fed SAR people who wouldn't be coming. Any fool could spot her in this waste of scrub, sand, and salt marsh. A few kloms inland lay cover, concealment, and fresh water, which she badly needed, both internally and to get the salt and muck off her skin.

The sky clouded over completely before she reached the treeline. Under the trees it was too dark to navigate, so she chose more open ground, moving in short rushes from cover to cover. It was quieter than pushing through an invisible labyrinth of trees and undergrowth, but she still found vines to trip her, rotten logs to collapse jarringly, and thorn bushes to scratch exposed skin and scar her survival suit.

She estimated that she had covered three kloms when she found a stream flowing between two mossy rocks into a pool. She lay behind the rocks, studying the ground, for a few minutes. It seemed longer, as the salt and muck that had crept in everywhere were beginning to itch more every time she shifted. Something like nettles in the swamp, maybe.

Finally she took off her boots, peeled off her outer suit, and crept down to the water in the underlayer, canteen in hand. She filled the canteen, added a purifier (this was a low-population planet, but even on a totally virgin one there could always be something dead just out of sight upstream), and shook it thoroughly.

A canteenful of water seemed to double the number of functional brain cells and make the itching even more unendurable. She stripped off the underlayer, then realized that her underwear was also soaked. It felt, in fact, like a couple of viper slugs curled around her chest and waist.

Off with them, then. She waded naked into the water, rather wishing that Malcolm was here to be an appreciative audience.

She was waist-deep in the pool when she realized that she did have an audience. Appreciative or not, four Ptercha'a (she saw eight eyes, at least) were watching her from under bushes on the far side of the pool. Either they had been concealing themselves while she did her business or they had slipped into place so silently that she hadn't heard them over the noise of running water. Either was possible, for woods-raised Ptercha'a.

She did not try to cover herself, or even stop scrubbing as best she could with bare hands and a few leaves posing as a sponge. If they'd wanted her dead, they would have shot her on the spot.

As it was, she had now moved from the Federation's first MIA of the war to (probably) the first POW. For her own self-respect if nothing else, she was going to arrive at the camp as clean as she could get.

Nalyvkina went on scrubbing until finally two of the Ptercha'a moved along the bank, jumped over the stream at the outlet of the pool, and squatted by the lieutenant's clothing and gear. One of them made a gesture, the other raised what looked like a Merishi-issue carbine.

Linak'h:

Candice Shores reached the hospital entrance just as the last bus for the airfield pulled away. Nobody was flying until further notice, and, for reasons that escaped her, nobody returning to a unit outside the Zone was being allowed to walk, even to the nearest pad.

Another solution presented itself, though. Not quite under guard but not quite free to leave were half a dozen Ptercha'a couriers, messengers, delivery people, or whatever. Most of them were sitting by their three-wheelers or cycles. One cycle had a sidecar.

Shores walked over to them, past MP's who seemed unwilling to confront a light colonel without good reason. "I need a ride back to the airfield," she said in True Speech. "Is anyone here able to take me?"

"How much?" several Ptercha'a asked at once.

"For your courage?" she asked, deliberately using an insulting intonation.

"No, for the machine," one said. "Also for our kin, if we do not come back."

Shores pulled out a credit slip, transferred five hundred stellars to it from her belt unit, and handed it to the first Ptercha'a who stepped forward. "If you do not come back, probably neither will I. This is yours regardless."

The volunteer turned out to be the owner of the cycle and sidecar. He was also kinless and supremely confident, from the way he drove. They seldom dropped below 70 km/h in zones posted for 20. Shores ended the ride ten minutes faster than she'd expected and glad the driver was on her side, or the Coordination would have had at least one candidate for a kamikaze attack.

An MP lieutenant loomed out of the shadows by the field gate. "Ma'am, did that—ah, did he know who you were?"

"Somebody in a hurry with money to make it worth his while. I'm here and he's gone, anyway." Using rank and command voice wasn't as emotionally satisfying as assaulting a bigot, but MP's were off-limits even for lieutenant colonels, if they wanted to get back to their units in a hurry.

Before the conversation could go any farther, a HQ major that Shores recognized joined them. She'd barely opened her mouth when the grandfather of all sonic booms knocked out windows, sprang doors, stripped leaves and branches off trees, and flattened all three officers and the security detail.

Shores clung to the ground as tightly as she'd ever clung to Nieg until both ground and air stopped shaking. The HQ major was staring up at the sky, eyes so wide and blank that Shores thought she'd been concussed.

"Son of a samurai!" the major said. Her voice grated like a rusty machine tool. "That was a spaceship!"

"So?"

"The Coordination cruisers dropped orbit, then crossed the border at low altitude. They took out the Admin's AD network and air and some of ours, while another Coord attack came up from the south. The last I heard, they've got ground forces coming across the border to the north and more along the Braigh'n."

Extrapolating from that brief sketch did nothing to improve Shores's mood. The Coordination cruisers were invulnerable to conventional AD weapons, and neither ground forces nor *Shen* could use shipkilling fusers at low altitude over their own troops. The cruisers might stay over the Administration, expending themselves if necessary, until the allied defenders had lost most of their air mobility.

If they lost that, they might lose the war. But win or lose, Shores was going to fight it at the head of her battalion.

Golden fire blazed in the clouds. Something large plunged out of them, shedding molten bits as it fell, trailing more fire until it ended in a final flare beyond the rooftops.

"Hope that was one of theirs," the major said, tapping her front teeth with the muzzle of her carbine. Shores hoped she had the weapon safed.

"How do I—?"

"Over there at Receiving. Get yourself a chute and helmet. You are—no, I forget, you're LI. You'll have to jump in, if you don't get in a fight with—"

"Jump from what?"

"We've got a couple of heavy attackers coming in. They'll make one pass, pick up high-priority passengers like you, and drop them on the way north. Once they've dumped you, they'll hit the Coord ground-pounders or run interference for a strike on the cruisers."

If the cruisers hung over the Administration until they ran out of ammunition or were blasted out of the sky, the attackers might have a problem executing any mission at all. Shores told herself that she was a decorated combat veteran, a Light Infantryman, a field-grade officer, and a battalion commander.

None of these composed a mantra effective against the idea of being turned into vapor or worse, a charred and dying *thing* in half-melted wreckage, in an air-space battle.

So just load yourself aboard, nerves and all.

The chute was Federation issue, with tell-tales to prove it had been packed, or at least that the tell-tales said so. Shores was strapping it on when somebody stuck their head into Receiving and shouted, "Passengers for the Linak'h Brigade, front and center!"

Shores joined the rush outside, as the darkened attacker flared to a stop over a pad fifty meters away. The field was blacked out now, but fires in Och'zem and the Zone gave enough light to see the flexible ladder unrolling from the escape hatch.

Shores was the fifth in. It seemed that she'd barely found a place to sit before the last passenger boarded. Then the hatch clanged shut and the lights dimmed as the pilot stepped up drive power. For a moment Shores thought the internal gravity fluctuated.

Or be turned into a reddish paste on a twisted bulkhead by a G-surge.

"Hang on," a disembodied voice said, and the lights came back up. Even through the thick hull Shores heard the scream of rushing air, as the attacker raced away into the night and the fire.

Nineteen

Aboard U.F.S. *Shenandoah*, off Linak'h:

Commodore Liddell's watch said it was two minutes since she'd last studied the battle board. She couldn't really say how long it had seemed.

She swiveled her chair and saw the same mixture of hard data, extrapolations, and pure guesses as last time. Friendly communications security and hostile jamming were playing Hades with electronic data transmission, and from a geostationary orbit even enhanced visuals had their limitations.

Satellites on both sides were still going down fast, which wasn't helping communications. *Roma* and *Intrepid* were presumably waiting on the other side of the planet for *Shen* to make her move or the Coordination cruisers to make their next one.

At least *Shen*'s wait was almost over.

"Flag to Captain. How are we coming with the attackers?" All eight aboard had been fast-cycled out into space. Under blackdown conditions it was hard to keep track of them after that.

"In formation, Commodore. Also three of our cruisers. One of the scouts wanted to substitute for the fourth cruiser. I took the liberty of refusing her captain's request."

"Good."

Through Pavel Bogdanov's measured tones, Liddell understood that the scout was *Powell*. Her CO seemed to think he was under a cloud over his caution during the rescue of *Somtow Nosavan* when she reached Linak'h with her load of refugees from Peregrine. He might be overeager, endangering not only his crew but also a ship whose versatility made her invaluable right now.

"We can manage with three or pick up one on the way.

Your fine Baptist shiphandling is going to be worth more than any number of escorts."

"Flattery will not cause the Coordination to lose its skill."

"No, more's the pity."

Liddell would have given a year's pay to know if the Coordination cruisers were entirely Ptercha'a-crewed or if Merishi Space Security had key posts aboard. If the shiphandling and tactics they'd displayed so far were all Hunter, it would finally prove that yes, they were good in space.

The main display showed the planned coordinates for reaching their low-level cruise altitude, superimposed on a magnified view of the relevant hemisphere. As Liddell watched, another satellite winked out. A burst of static turned briefly into the "War Zone Warning" that Longman was broadcasting on all the standard frequencies and a few others, in case the Coordination was going to push the boundaries of space-warfare law.

Time to move it, Rosie.

"On my count, Pavel—five, four, three, two, one, execute!"

Shenandoah cartwheeled ponderously in space, in the middle of the globe formed by her eleven escorts. Then twelve drives thrust the whole formation forward and down, toward Linak'h.

Linak'h:

So far off that even Rahbad Sarlin's field-seasoned ears could not tell the direction, a lifter whined. Probably one of the supply runs returning home; stopping such air movements would have raised more suspicion than it soothed.

At the rate sensor and communications nets on both sides were going down, before long neither would be up to detecting anything that neutrals might do. Satellites were rapidly turning into orbital debris, while land stations were facing jamming, interception, or outright destruction.

So far the Federation and Administration had lost more than their enemies. The Coordination's cruisers had dumped external pods as they entered atmosphere. Some of those "pods" turned out to be shuttles loaded with either attackers or ground-fighter carriers. Others had been shrouded clusters of scores of cheap but high-performance missiles.

The crewed air vehicles sought their targets or landing zones while the combined defensive systems fought the missiles. Most of the crewed vehicles got through; so did some of the missiles. Then the Coordination's cruisers came racing in through saturated and degraded defenses, to squat less than a tenth-march above the ground and pick off unhit targets with the precision of snipers.

At least that was how Sarlin would have reported the first tenth watch of the Linak'h War, based on data received from *Perfumed Wind* and relayed through the Inquirers' command center by Brokeh su-Irzim and Zhapso su-Lal. He suspected that this account had large gaps but doubted that any of the combatants knew even this much.

So far, nobody was jamming *Perfumed Wind*. It was at Commander ihr Sular's discretion what to do if anyone did so; she could blackdown, continue transmitting, maneuver evasively, or any combination of these. (Sarlin doubted that she could handle herself in a space battle, but she was certain that she would obey no groundling's orders to keep out of one.)

The distant lifter was now out of hearing. Only night sounds and the far-away and intermittent battle noises disturbed the forest. It was hard to imagine that more than three thousand ground-fighters were camped within two tenth marches of Sarlin's underground post. Or it would have been hard to imagine, before he learned how silent even moderately trained Ptercha'a could be.

Some were better trained than that; the Wild Continent levies stood out. Sarlin wondered just how strictly the ban on the Confraternity had been enforced over there. The Hunters who had come across, a few score on each ship or airliner, seemed to be near-kin to organized ground-fighter fours and sixteens. Warband veterans or experienced woodsrunners held key commanders' posts, and all they needed to make them fully effective was better weapons and the time to train with them.

The weapons had been given. The time had been denied.

A Hunter (Sarlin named them so even in his mind) appeared, followed by Behdan Zeg and a guard of four more warriors. Zeg dismissed his guard with a glance and sat down by Sarlin's console, uninvited and unwashed as usual. This had somehow lost its power to anger Sarlin. Now he accepted his half-brother's gracelessness as he accepted wet skin when he marched in the rain.

"We have Hunters in Merishi pay on our land," Zeg said. He thumbed the display to life, then tapped a map into sight.

Sarlin frowned. "How reliable is the location?"

"That frequency is Merishi, which neither side is yet jamming, and there have been no sunbomb-pulses to deafen all alike."

"Not yet."

"All the more reason for haste, then."

"What are we hastening to?" Sarlin suspected that he knew and was only asking to delay the moment of certainty. He hoped his half-brother would not be angered.

"Any child can see it. Merishi patrols along our coast may have many purposes. The Federation will not thank us for allowing any of them. The Governor will praise us for driving them off."

"Even if it offends the Merishi?"

"The Governor holds land sacred. Also, the Merishi Hunters may have taken Federation prisoners. That beeper may have been a Federation pilot who made it to shore from the day's air battle. If we earn the Federation's goodwill by rescuing these people, the Governor will be even happier."

Sarlin could not say the same for himself. There was something about the way Zeg said "Federation's goodwill . . ."

"Mother's son, do you think to hold any prisoners we gain as hostages?"

"Who used such an obscenity? Not I!"

"I know the Federation calls it an obscenity. What of you?"

"Let us first have a prisoner, before we argue what to do with it." Zeg adjusted the display. "One Hunter band has called for a lifter to pick up a prisoner *here*."

Sarlin let his frown deepen to hide the racing of heart and lungs. The Merishi hirelings were wandering about within a tenth march of a band of Zeg's trained Hunters. A road covered most of the way, and the band had at least one sixteen mounted on roadriders.

"Send them, and do not worry about what su-Irzim says?" Zeg asked. He had the rare grace not to look triumphant.

"My face makes easy reading as I grow older," Sarlin grumbled. "But you do our Inquirer an injustice, I think."

"Perhaps. Who goes to the band and with the riders? People should be present, I think, even if hidden."

"Can I stop you from going, mother's son?"

"Only by suggesting another."

"Solidessouf."

"Only if he goes with some who survived the Great Fire with us. They will speak for him."

"We have some to send. Also, it has been said of Solidessouf that his tongue is clumsy but his soul is graceful."

"You are learning True Speech well."

Sarlin almost laughed. "I heard *you* speak of Solidessouf, mother's son. Is it true?"

Zeg looked almost contemplative. "It is, to my knowledge. It is also true that once you did not listen to such, what I spoke it."

"You did not speak. You shouted it in my ears, so that they rang for days afterward. Now you speak like—like one who knows what he wants to say."

Zeg said nothing; both sensed that the other preferred a wordless farewell. But Sarlin knew as Zeg climbed the stairs out of sight that it was all they now needed.

Aboard U.F.S. *Shenandoah*, off Linak'h:

The battle cruiser and her globe of lighter escorts plunged toward Linak'h. Evasive action meant course changes at randomized intervals measured in seconds. Their speed would have meant Liddell's relief from command and confinement to quarters as dangerously deviant if she had ordered it under normal circumstances.

War being abnormal, nobody said anything. The ACC was not as quiet as a tomb; the dead neither breathe, sweat, nor change color. Liddell saw that Lomo Fitzroy had turned a pale green, and she remembered that this was his first combat experience. Other people also seemed to be turning colors that could not be accounted for entirely by the battle lighting and the glow of dozens of hyperactive displays. The tactical problem had not altered since she gave the EXE-CUTE order to Pavel Bogdanov and the escorts. So the solution had not changed either.

It was an unorthodox but not unheard-of problem. Basically, it was a combination of the enemy's heavy ships and lifters at low altitude over friendly territory that could only be defeated by introducing another heavy ship, also over friendly territory, also at low altitude. After that it didn't make a great deal of difference what the enemy did, other than destroying the intruder.

If the Coordination cruisers engaged, *Shenandoah* would use her beam weapons at close range. If they fled, *Roma* and Moneghan's cruisers could engage them more freely as they climbed. Meanwhile, the enemy's lifters and attackers would face the same dilemma in regard to *Shenandoah*'s escorts.

The surprise lay in the Coordination's presenting these problems in the first place. Liddell realized that at some level, probably a subconscious one certainly able to affect decision-making, everybody had made the same mistake.

They'd assumed that the Merishi and the Hunters wouldn't use such a drastic opening to the war. They (and in this Liddell included herself) hadn't adequately considered that neither opponent could afford to lose once they'd started the war, so why not gamble on gaining such a large advantage at the outset that political factors might keep the Federation from fighting its way back to victory?

If the Linak'h Task Force didn't carry off this countermove effectively, the Federation still might not lose. But fighting a way back would be a long, grim process, with unknown political consequences, and the commanders responsible would have short careers and long casualty lists on their consciences.

Liddell left monitoring the formation to others. She had eyes for only one display, satellite status. The satellites on both sides were still going down, about one every two minutes on the average. Or at least going inactive; with the jamming it was hard to tell if a satellite had been destroyed, jammed, or ordered to blackdown, and if it was blacked down it was hard to tell whether it was maneuvering to a safer position or just intended to be overlooked where it was.

Sensor networks and electronic C-cubed, Liddell knew,

were absolutely indispensable to arranging the start of a war. Once the shooting (even more important, the jamming) started, they declined to moderately useful, until one side or the other gained superiority in the war of the wavelengths.

The last enemy satellite that could watch *Shenandoah*'s, maneuvers went down just thirty seconds before the battle cruiser went ballistic. Riding inside her shield, plummeting like a giant meteorite, *Shenandoah* slammed into Linak'h's atmosphere.

The heat and electromagnetic pulse blasted away from the shield effectively jammed any effort to track the escort. They entered the atmosphere under control, at more sedate speeds, and leveled out at the battle cruiser's planned cruising altitude.

That was to be five thousand meters; it turned out to be five hundred lower. No difference in maximum speed; thermal effects limited *Shenandoah* to the local Mach Five in atmosphere, in spite of her heavy hull. Any more, and her sensor suite would not recover from the baking in time.

At 6,000 km/h, *Shenandoah* raced over the ocean, toward the Braigh'n Gulf and the Administration's beleaguered defenders. Above her the escort rode high and wide. Everybody was jamming as hard as they could. From almost any direction they would be an unrecognizable target for most sensors, too fast for most missiles, and too low in the moisture-laden ocean air to be good laser targets except at close range.

Liddell saw that most faces had resumed their normal color. The final run-in onto a target often did that. One was committed, for better or worse, and whatever lay ahead, the suspense was over.

The distance to the targets ahead shrank by the second. Behind them, the hypersonic shock wave generated minor tsunamis, rolling toward the mainland.

High above, the displays showed two large objects that might have been ships, squadrons, clumps of debris, or electronic glitches moving into a position above the Administration. Liddell crossed mental fingers that they were *Roma* and *Intrepid*.

Aboard heavy attacker Gold One, Linak'h:

As she wriggled to find a comfortable position inside her seat harness, Elayne Zheng was angry and impatient, but not surprised.

It had been pleasant, to dream of having more control over the battle than most of the generals, as EWO of the senior attacker and designated senior EWO of the mobile AD. But it could never have been more than a dream, unless the enemy knew nothing about jamming.

So Zheng wriggled and stared at displays that only intermittently told her anything worth knowing. She also studied a display linked to a ground observation post in the hills ten kloms to the east. Using passive sensors and the high ground, a Militia platoon was developing a rough plot of the four Coordination cruisers. They even had data on smaller and closer enemy craft, and were tight-beaming it all to Gold One.

With a tight beam, low power, short range, and the shield of the hills, it was just possible that the enemy might not pick up the platoon's work. Zheng's job was now to survive the embarrassment of being reduced to a transmitting station for ground-pounders' recon work.

"Anything new, Elayne?" The pilot's voice was flat, but she thought with concentration, not fear. Shauli had put up his third stripe on the last promotion list; either that or combat settled his nerves somewhat and improve his manners. *Reasonable stuff there,* Zheng thought, *under an exterior that had made it hard to recognize.*

"Nothing I'm sure of. A couple of signals that might be somebody on the ground close to our friends. Damned if I can tell for sure where, or which side."

It could be either. The enemy's ground-pounders were coming down all over the place, in what seemed to be everything from sniper teams up to half-cohort task forces. The few times she'd had an unjammed view of the cruisers moving, she'd seen the signs of lifters dropping out of formation and off the screens. Otherwise it seemed as if the bad guys were staying close to their big sisters.

It made sense. Ground AD weaponry that could kill troop lifters, gunships, and so forth was shorter-ranged than the big ship-mounted beamers. Detected (as they would be if they shot), they died. Longer-range AD missiles with the speed and fuser heads needed to kill the cruisers were too few to be wasted on troop carriers or even air support.

They were always too few, but tonight they were even fewer. In one area where Zheng had hard data from intercepted signals, the two main AD-missile dumps had both gone up early. One died under the strikes of cruder but more numerous missiles that also got there first. The other was lasered out of existence by one of the cruisers, going up with a fireworks display that hinted that one or more fusers had detonated.

Zheng hoped nobody would think this a first-use and send heavy stuff back the other way. She also hoped there'd been no casualties. Correction: one person she hoped was dead was whoever had given the order to concentrate the AD fuser-heads. That son of a slime wriggler had killed as many Feds as the Pussies, keeping the missiles out of the reach of terrorists but also out of reach of potential targets until it was too late.

She knew that some of the mobile AD companies would be trying to get into firing position on the ships. But they'd have to run the gauntlet of the bad guys' TacAir, ground units (the Coordination had some like Rangers, specially tasked to hit C-cubed, AD, and CP's), and jamming. Not to mention lasers from the cruisers, following the missile trails back to the launch points. (The launch vehicles would be long gone, but whoever wandered into the area in the meantime would be just as thoroughly dead.)

The alarm sounded for an incoming message. Zheng sat up in spite of the harness, as *Roma*'s authentication code popped on one screen.

The flagship had the sensor suite of a dozen satellites; she could come as close as anybody could to punching through the jamming. Doing so, however, would warn the Coordination cruisers. They couldn't do an active sky-scan without losing much of the concealment of low altitude, so probably they hadn't detected *Roma,* riding high overhead and building a picture of the enemy's positions.

The four cruisers and their companions showed up plainly now. So did something that might have been a ship, might have been an electronic ghost, on the far southeastern edge of the screen. (*Roma*'s transmission was reducing an area five hundred kloms on a side to fit on a screen Zheng could span with her arms.)

No ghost; it was moving too fast. Zheng gripped the arms of her seat in order to keep from clenching her fists or pounding on anything. (The furniture and electronics would survive; she needed both hands in working condition.)

"*Shen*'s on her way in," Zheng said. "Commander—when she hits, what about our closing our ground friends? Even if they don't have any bad guys coming in, maybe they can home us in on a few targets?"

"Our orders are to support the counterattack," Shauli said. He sounded decently frustrated at those orders, too.

"*Shen*'s going to be low, the satellites are down, and we can't ask *Roma* to relay everything. If we're over the OP, we'll be out from behind the hills. Line of sight to *Shen* and anybody else worth talking to."

She put the relevant map on the pilot's tactical display and heard him grunt. It might have been assent. Zheng decided to take it that way. She was too busy to ask again, watching the screen, praying for the oncoming blur that was *Shen* to move faster and for the Coordination cruisers not to move at all.

Aboard U.F.S. *Shenandoah*:

Shenandoah and some of her escorts slowed to Mach Two as they stormed up the Braigh'n Gulf. The rest of the escorts climbed to ten thousand meters and held at Mach Four. They would be clearly visible. They would even be identifiable, as no serious threat to the cruisers as long as they used low altitude and Federation territory as shields against missiles.

Without too many miracles, they might even absorb the cruiser's attention for long enough to let *Shenandoah* close to decisive range.

Liddell had two worries as *Shenandoah* held her course toward the Administration coast. One was weather—visibility over the Gulf was somewhere between poor and negligible. The standard remedy for poor visibility was active sensors—but the closer to the enemy, the more likely these would betray *Shenandoah* prematurely.

The other was friendlies and neutrals, both airborne and

on the sea. Even at Mach Two, *Shenandoah*'s shock wave could disintegrate gunships and troop lifters, knock heavy attackers out of control, and capsize seaborne craft.

The high squadron would be scanning actively, and from their extra altitude they should be able to spot and clear away anything in the path of the low-fliers. Anybody at sea level, lost in the wave-clutter, was just out of luck, but Liddell recalled that neither Ptercha's nor Merishi did much offshore fishing. Any "fishing boats" out landing raiding parties or resupplying midget submarines were not going to be the objects of Rose Liddell's sympathy tonight.

Four minutes to landfall. *Roma* was transmitting now, showing the cruisers still at their stately dance over Administration targets.

Either very confident, very stupid, or very loyal to their mission.

It had occurred to Liddell that the cruiser's mission might be less strategic warfare than topcover for massive infiltration of ground troops and light TacAir. With that kind of armed support, the anti-Confraternity elements in the Administration might suddenly decide that the election results weren't binding—

Two minutes. The coast crept onto the main tactical display, relayed from one of the heavy attackers of the high flight. Liddell noted a course change needed in about another thirty seconds, or they'd boom-bomb Och'zem in fine style. An aerial parade of the city's rescuers could be a fine morale booster, if it didn't shake down half the city in the process.

Bogdanov made the course change as Liddell prepared to order it, with a good ten seconds to spare.

Maybe he does *steer by telepathy.*

Shen settled onto her new course. The tactical display showed the high flight going off at a slight angle, to head farther north before they turned. They would come in closer to the center of the rough diamond that the cruisers now formed.

Liddell's eyes shifted to the weapons display board. Again, it was as if her mind had reached out and touched Commander Zhubova's. Everything was clear and green— power links to the lasers and beamers, ready missiles in the launchers, chaff, decoys, and all the other countermeasures, even com links to the buses riding in *Shenandoah*'s wake.

(The buses were bobbing fiercely in the turbulent air; even with only light internal loads they were at their limits for in-atmosphere work. They'd need time to stabilize after they took independent courses, so they were the second- or even third-strike load.)

From starside almost to dirtside in twenty minutes.

Liddell looked at the altitude display. *Shen* could cross the last distance to self-immolation on Linak'h's surface in something like twenty seconds if anything went seriously wrong.

She said a brief prayer that if anyone's failure brought that about, it would be hers.

Let my people go with clean consciences, if nothing more.

"Flag to Captain and Weapons. Prepare to target and engage Cruiser Three. Time at your discretion."

"Aye-aye," she thought she heard, from both Bogdanov and Zhubova.

Was one of the cruisers moving now? Or was *Shen*'s being over the land now interfering with transmissions from *Roma* or the high flight?

Questions, questions, and no time for answers. Cruiser Three would be in range or maneuvering out of it in another four minutes.

Linak'h :

Supreme Warband Leader Banfi (he thought of himself by his Hunter rank more often than he did by his Federation one) watched the picture of the Federation counterstrike build on his displays. They were not quite as sophisticated as he would have had as Federation CG, not to mention that the data being fed into them was much less complete.

However, he saw nothing to alter the conclusion he'd based on the events of the last half-hour. The Warband had essentially two jobs. Preserve what remained of their TacAir (by dispersing vehicles and supplies and policing up wounded and salvageable equipment from the bases hit on the first strike) and engage enemy ground units wherever feasible (to keep them from getting organized into larger units capable of overrunning major positions and formations if they had heavy-weapons support).

Both jobs were going to have to be done at the Band or

cohort level. At this stage of the war, Banfi was mainly ornamental. So he was tidying his desk when his guards announced Emt Desdai.

"Greetings, Supreme Leader," Desdai said, giving both Hunter and human military courtesies, and doing both gracefully. "I bear news."

That was one point of Hunter military etiquette Banfi did not like much. Supreme War Leaders were not allowed to sit in at the communications center and get a real-time flow of data. This restriction was supposed to date from the time when tribal chiefs were kept heavily guarded and away from the fighting, unless they challenged an opposing chief to settle the dispute one on one.

With modern technology this strategy reduced micromanaging, increased frustration and delay, and gave messengers a good deal of power. It also made no sense when the Supreme War Leader would be fifty meters below ground in either office or communications center!

Banfi reached for the message form, unfolded it, then swore. Desdai did not flinch, but he looked as if he expected to suffer the traditional fate of the bearers of bad news.

"Great Warband Leader Tanz is dead," Banfi said.

"Peace and kindly Fates to his spirit," Desdai said.

Banfi nodded absently. The message gave few details; apparently Tanz had been airborne when the Coordination strike came in. Instead of grounding immediately, he tried to make it back to the Zone. An airbursting warhead forced the command lifter down near a deployed gunship flight. That also had been targeted; more missiles destroyed or grounded everything that could take the air.

Then an air-landed force of Coordination—what was their Ranger-equivalent?—something that translated literally as "Vanguard Warriors"—popped up out of nowhere. Banfi suspected infiltration, in cooperation with the terrorists or anti-Confraternity locals. Tanz led his bodyguards in a counterattack to give the TacAir people time to find their ground legs, not to mention their weapons. He succeeded, at the price of his own life.

Banfi wondered briefly if Tanz had been specially targeted, with some help from security leaks. He also wondered, more briefly, if Tanz had been trying to get himself killed.

He decided to give Tanz the benefit of the doubt. Only a fool would try to "restore his honor" at the price of chaos in the command structure of the troops he led, and Tanz hadn't been a fool.

Get the news upstairs, and also to Edelstein, who's the next senior. And then . . . ?

Banfi understood the sensations of being taken up to a high place and offered all the kingdoms of the earth. But he had already refused to take the crown once today, when there would have been a few hours to settle the new command arrangements before the shooting started.

Now the shooting had begun. Banfi would sooner, rather than later, cease to be ornamental. Edelstein was probably already busier than a K'thressh at an orgy. Who was—?

"Shall I inform Senior Maiyotz that you are assuming leadership of the—?" Desdai began.

For many years, Banfi's glare had sent the same message to both human and Hunter. Desdai took two steps backward and bowed deeply. If he had been Tribal, he might have prostrated himself.

"No need to inform Senior Maiyotz of anything yet," Banfi said. "But you can inform me if Colonel Langston is in the complex."

"Marcus Langston, the Civil Action leader?"

"Yes."

"I must go and—"

"Then go quickly. If you find him, say that I request his presence in my office immediately. If you do not find him, tell me, that I may send an urgent message."

Aboard U.F.S. *Shenandoah*:

The first exchange of fire was between Cruiser Three and one of the high flight. It happened too quickly for Liddell to tell which escort it was. She saw only the flare on the display as the enemy laser gouged steel and ceramics, then another flare and a string of numbers as the Federation ship replied with both laser and a missile salvo.

Liddell couldn't tell if the laser hit, but Cruiser Three clearly detected the launch. She also couldn't be sure if the missiles had fuser or conventional warheads.

The reply to the missiles came from Cruiser Four. Lasers

and Mach Ten countermissiles burned the sky toward the Federation launch.

Suddenly the space between *Shenandoah* and Cruiser Three was too crowded for a clear laser shot. But the same was not true for Cruiser Four, even if the range was extreme.

This time Liddell had the pleasure of giving the order before Bogdanov and Zhubova could act. They must have had the order in their minds, though; *Shen*'s lasers ripped across the sky into Cruiser Four seconds after Liddell finished speaking.

It was extreme range even for *Shen*'s main lasers, in moist, low-altitude air. The density and humidity soaked up a good deal of laser power. They didn't soak up enough.

"Burn-through!" more voices than Liddell could count said. At least they didn't shout.

Cruiser Four leaped for the sky. Shield signature showed. She must be planning on letting acceleration carry her out of the atmosphere into orbit.

The countermissiles encountered the Federation launch, and mutual destruction blazed across screens. The blaze swamped targeting sensors aboard *Shenandoah*, but the high flight had a clearer view. *Shenandoah* had also climbed, so that now high and low flights were a single unit for acquisition and launch data. What one ship knew, all knew.

On data from the high flight, *Shen*'s two buses swung wide and launched. Their own sensors and computers guided one around the debris from the missile duel; the second plunged straight through it.

Cruiser Three acquired the first bus as it reached launching position. Lasers flared; missile propellant flared more brightly. None of the warheads detonated, but the first bus rained down from the sky, incandescent debris to scorch friend and foe alike.

The second bus closed at Mach Eight. Zhubova overrode its onboard computer on launch time and let it keep closing. Then she decelerated it radically, dumping chaff and decoys as well as its entire load of missiles—now targeted at the high, visible, slow target of Cruiser Four.

Cruiser Four had just dropped her shield when the missiles acquired her. Her sensors or lasers must have taken damage; all she did was raise the shield again, which slowed her further. She was an easy target for lasers from *Shenandoah*, now many kloms closer, and for two of the light cruisers.

Cruiser Four's shield died slowly, but fast enough for her enemies. Some of the missiles detonated against the shield. Others flew into laser beams and died from friendly fire. Five were still closing when the shield vanished. Four of them were too close to let the cruiser outmaneuver them even with her drive on.

These were conventional warheads, but ship-launched missiles could punch .01-kiloton yields into an enemy's hull. Two of the missiles had shaped-charged warheads; one of these struck a spot already weakened by the laser.

Systems died, taking damage-control crews with them. Cascading devastation raced through Cruiser Four. Thirty kilometers above Linak'h, her power plant died, turning her stern into a ball of fire. Trailing flame and gas, debris and bodies, the rest of the cruiser started her final dive.

By this time *Shenandoah* and Cruiser Three were passing each other so close that Liddell expected to hear someone counting micrometeorite-impact scars on the other's hull. She also expected laser strikes from all three enemy cruisers and anything else they had in the air that could shoot.

The lasers didn't come. A moment later Liddell saw why. Beyond *Shen* a formation of low-altitude craft was sweeping across the Braigh'n; anything that might hit *Shen* might hit friendlies.

The high flight plunged like raptors on the lifters. Liddell saw sparks as hits ate at the formation. She also saw a Federation attacker die in a globe of flame.

And then she saw the three surviving Coordination cruisers leap skyward, accelerating at a pace that must have boom-bombed half the Administration. They soared away from Linak'h, spilling decoys and missiles like a gardener sprinkling grass seed.

Liddell blinked sweat out of her eyes in time to see the drives of both *Roma* and *Intrepid* go on. Their escorts, too—a heavy cruiser and three lights—and *Intrepid* had twelve attackers aboard.

She did not really need the signal from *Roma* to know what to do next:

FLAG ONE TO FLAG THREE. WILL CLOSELY PURSUE HOSTILES IN EXPECTATION OF THEIR LEADING US TO QUEEN BEE. RESUME NORMAL ALTITUDE AND SUPPORT TACTICAL OPERATIONS OF GROUND FORCES AGAINST INVASION. WELL DONE AND GOOD HUNTING.

Linak'h:

Candice Shores still hadn't found a mantra to banish nervousness by the time the attacker reached the drop zone. At least she knew why.

She was facing combat for the first time as a battalion commander, running a unit too big for hands-on fixes if something went wrong. In a company you could go down into the dirt with the platoons or even the squads if you had to. In a battalion you had to hope you had trained your staff and company commanders well enough to delegate that job to them at least 90 percent of the time. If you focused on one company when two or three were engaged, you were doing somebody else's job, not yours.

Also, she was facing combat for the first time as somebody who would be missed. Missed as she would not have been by her mother (her father was another matter, but he had gone on before) or by Nieg (who would have mourned her as a professional mourning a gifted comrade). Missed by two children whose last hope of seeing any stability in a universe run mad could die with her.

So don't die, Candy.

It wasn't the first time the mind-voice had spoken like her father. This time it was so real that she replied, without looking around.

I'm a soldier, Father.

Yes, and a good soldier. That means you aren't careless about anything, including your own life.

She wondered how her father had suddenly become a military philosopher. Probably by associating with Ursula Boll.

The jump light came on, and Shores looked around the compartment as she inspected her opposite. Four people were jumping into this zone besides herself, one of them the senior SFO for her battalion. Two others she didn't recognize, and the last, facing her, was the Victorian Civil Action Group Team Leader Karl Pocher.

Correction, Victoria Expeditionary Battalion Captain *Karl Pocher.*

"You know, this is the first time I've ever jumped," Pocher said.

"Have you told anybody else?"

"Not that I recall. They told me the attackers weren't going to be landing and nothing else was going out for a few days."

"Think you're indispensable?"

Pocher glared his reply.

"Sorry." *Let she who is without sin among you ...*

"Heads up, jumpers." the intercom said. "We are one minute to the zone. Drop altitude eight hundred meters, drop speed three hundred km/h. The smoking lamp is out."

"Trying for the comedy-'cast circuit," Pocher muttered.

The jump light turned from red to amber at minus twenty seconds. At ten seconds the hatch opened, and night air boomed into the compartment. At five seconds the attacker banked sharply into a turn, slowing as it did.

"Go, go, go!"

Shores was the first out. She got a good chute, even doing the whole job manually. As her canopy deployed she heard the *crack* of others doing the same and counted. One, two, three—

The silent sky turned thunderous as the attacker accelerated to avoid making a low-speed, low-altitude target of itself. The shock wave made Shores swing wildly but didn't collapse her chute.

Someone else wasn't so lucky, or had a streamer. A scream shrilled, fading away into the darkness and ending in a silence that could have only one meaning.

Then fire began high up but fell rapidly. Well off to the southwest (if her compass still read true), a big ship was dying. Shores forced herself to look away; she couldn't afford to destroy her night vision trying to identify it.

The light died briefly, then flared again, then died for the last time. Shores risked a brief glance. A hillside was aflame, but the flames lit up no spreading cloud such as you got from a major power-plant explosion. They seldom reached more than a kiloton or two in atmosphere, anyway.

This analysis took her all the way down to the ground,

and the first thing she knew about her landing was getting out of her chute. She had done everything else on pure automatic, and by some miracle hadn't spattered the brains she wasn't using over rocks and trees.

The question that she'd been trying to keep at arm's length stormed into her mind: *Was that* Shenandoah?

Her stomach made a mutinous assembly and her knees quivered. She didn't vomit or collapse; she didn't even pray. She had time to find a tree and lean against it, then a voice called from the darkness.

"Willow?"

Recognizing Juan Esteva's voice finished off her knees. She sat down before she gave the countersign:

"Galleon."

Footsteps now, instead of voices. Good but not perfect noise discipline. Then Esteva materialized out of the darkness, like a vampire turning from bat to human. She would gladly have offered her neck if he'd wanted it, just to end being alone.

Instead he stood back while Jan Sklarinsky came up on the other side of the tree. By then Shores could get her legs under her and stand without tottering or leaning on tree or human.

"How many others?" Sklarinsky asked.

Shores held up four fingers. "I think one had a bad chute. How's the battalion?"

"C, D, and weapons deployed. Standard formation, except that we've laid out a few decoy launchers. Also, any of the remote sensors that aren't being watched are booby-trapped. A and B will be back as soon as it's safe to lift them."

"Sounds good enough for now."

SOP in this case was to move everybody, dispersing enough to avoid offering a target-rich environment while concentrating enough to avoid losing people to small-unit attacks or ambushes. The balance point was hard to find and depended a lot on training levels, terrain, weather, and whether the enemy's main strength was heavy weapons or rifle units.

No way to answer that now. So just report in, ask for an update, and don't joggle anyone's elbow until you're back in the picture.

"Ah—Colonel?" Juan was trying to look at the sky and the ground at the same time.

"Yes."

"Sorry about your father."

"Thanks." She groped for something else. "Don't think we have a special score to settle because of that, please."

Sklarinsky jerked her head. " 'Vengeance is mine, saith the Lord.' But if He needs any help—"

"Let's find the others first, all right?"

Aboard U.F.S. *Shenandoah*:

Shenandoah practically strolled back into orbit, compared to her furious rush down from it. Liddell kept the squadron dispersed enough to be a difficult target and close enough for mutual ECM support to make it an impossible one.

At least for any weapons the Coordination is supposed to have left.

They began by staying in Administration airspace. As they climbed, they drifted out over the ocean, with the whole Administration under surveillance. They finally reached an altitude where all four Territories and most of the Coordination lay below.

Liddell ordered a continuous all-modes surveillance of what lay below, along with a continuous comparison with the existing strategic-target data. Liddell had neither authority, intention, nor reason for initiating strategic strikes on the Coordination, even with conventional weapons. But with the satellite net down and some of the strategic targets mobile, data might be hours old when ten minutes was enough to make it useless.

So from *Shenandoah* and the eight ships (four cruisers, four attackers) with her, the combined sensors of a score of satellites probed the Coordination. For over an hour the squadron played games with the enemy's AD system, forcing radars to shut down at random intervals by painting them as if for a missile launch.

Liddell finally called an end to that game, to avoid panicking the Coordination into a premptive nonconventional strike with whatever such weapons they might have left. The Coordination had proved they were dangerous even when not desperate; no reason to push them to the last step.

What to do if the Coordination did jump was a delicate problem. Liddell was SOPS, but Longman was not technically out of the chain of command simply by being out of range of secure communication. The time factor would dictate what Liddell and Longman could say to each other over a decision to launch fusers, more with each light-second that Longman's ships opened the distance to Linak'h.

Like any sane officer, Liddell prayed that the war would stay below the fuser threshhold. She also prayed that her superiors would show good sense if the Coordination did not.

Strategic warfare with conventional warheads used up a great many missiles, irreplaceable until a resupply that might be weeks away. Linak'h was at the wrong end of a long supply line that might not be immune to enemy interruption even if Longman took out the last three cruisers in the next few hours.

People who believed in war against an enemy's will loved conventional strategic strikes. People who believed that if an enemy's power vanished the will would depart along with it preferred whatever did the most damage in the least amount of time with the fewest expenditures of your own resources (people and weapons alike) and the least damage to your opponent's civilians.

That could be anything from daggers to fifty-megaton fusers, although *Shenandoah* was better equipped to deliver the second than the first. Liddell hoped sufficient daggerwielders were already moving into place; she had bought them time they had damned well better put to use!

Liddell called for each ship to close *Shenandoah* and exchange tight-beams about ammunition, damage, and casualties. She would do the same with Moneghan's ships as they rotated up from supporting the Army.

Meanwhile, the lights were going out all over the Coordination, as cities, towns, and villages down to the smallest crossroads hamlet blacked out. Liddell watched the scene with weary sympathy.

Modern war featured sensors that could detect a town by the heat pulse of the local tavern. Blackouts caused more friendly casualties than they prevented. Their only virtue was reminding your people that they should take the war seriously.

Linak'h:

Olga Nalyvkina couldn't fault the way her captors (that had begun to seem a more accurate word than "hosts") had treated her. She'd been allowed to dress, left unbound and undrugged, and hurried along at a pace she could maintain at the cost of only a little sweat and a few pangs in strained muscles.

For Ptercha'a, that was practically a stroll. She concluded that the Ptercha'a were either in friendly territory, on their way to a safe area close by, or very badly trained. Since she recognized the True Speech words for "humans" and "lifters" in the conversations around her, she began to suspect it was the second possibility.

That was also the worst, in the not-too-long run. Humans operating lifters on this side of the Gulf were either Federation SAR (which she'd believe when she saw it) or the traitors and terrorists working for the Merishi. There would be no limits on their interrogation of her, the moment they found out who she was and what she might know.

Malcolm Davidson, the lieutenant realized, had been speaking both as lover and as fellow professional in advising her against flying combat. In both guises he'd been making more sense than she was willing to admit at the time, and now it was most likely too late to apologize for even the few sharp exchanges that still preyed on her conscience.

At least she wouldn't have to have any betrayals on it. She'd taken the advice of her E & E instructor, to decide as soon as possible what your limits were and how to keep your captors from pushing beyond them, then stick to that decision. "Wasting the calm before the electrodes is damned stupid" were his concluding words.

She'd decided what her limit was: none. Or at least she wasn't going to allow for any. Not when her chances of escape would also be none, once somebody realized who she was. She was pretty sure that she could either escape from these Ptercha'a or force them to kill her. Realistically, escape would only delay death, but if the Federation regained air superiority SAR operations might resume—

And K'thressh might start learning the bagpipes.

She was remembering warnings about unrealistic hopes being hard on morale, when the column halted. Several Ptercha'a in civilian clothes were standing in the road. Ptercha'a night vision apparently was making out details that no human eye could see, that made them appear friendly or at least neutral.

Nalyvkina measured the distance to a stand of dwarf leatherroot. If she could get inside that, she might at least be able to make a respectable last stand. Now if she could just manage to grab a weapon—one of those loosely held carbines with a single magazine would be better than nothing, and a pilot's reflexes were closer to a Ptercha'a's than most humans' reflexes were—

A squall of alarm as somebody saw something unexpected and unwelcome. Carbine muzzles pointed in all directions. Nalyvkina froze, trying not to blink or breathe. Motion might get her down on the ground. It would also attract attention. Her guts told her that more weapons than she could see were aiming into the darkness.

One of them opened fire—a Ptercha'a SSW by the sound. Half the Ptercha'a in front of Nalyvkina went down, some of them screaming, others gruesomely silent. Nalvykina hit the ground as the SSW scythed the air above her and the bodies of Ptercha'a to either side and behind her.

Then more figures leaped from the darkness, carbines and one SSW held at the hip. A larger figure plunged straight through the leatherroot patch as if it was spiderweb, bent over the lieutenant, and snatched her up under one arm. A guttural command, and the new captor was running back around the leatherroot, drawing the newcomers in his wake like a magnet drawing iron filings.

Nalyvkina twisted her neck to look behind and caught a glimpse of a trail littered with dead and dying Ptercha'a. Live Ptercha'a were running behind her captor, a dozen of them at least; she saw carbines, two SSW's, and at least one infantry launcher slung across somebody's back.

She also saw that the hand of the arm holding her was smooth-skinned except where stiff dark hair covered it. No sign of scales, no web between the fingers—and there were only two fingers and a thumb, with the thumb nearly as thick as her wrist and the nail elaborately carved under the dirt.

Baernoi. Wherever she had been, she was now being carried off by one of the Tuskers, with a dozen Ptercha'a apparently willing to kill their own folk at his command. This was something that it would be logical to dismiss as a hallucination. It would also be logical to accept it, but as a prelude to even worse captivity and more brutal treatment. Which made it all the more important to provoke the final battle; if she could just get her head around enough to bite that revealing hand—

"Arrcckkkh!"

The Baernoi did not drop her as her teeth sank into his hide. Not very far; Baernoi *did* have thick skins. She penetrated far enough to cause pain, judging from his yell. But instead of dropping her, he reached around with his free hand, clamped it over her mouth, then shifted the grip of the hand she'd bitten to her belt. All this, she noted, without missing a step.

Baernoi strength had never been so real to her. If all else failed, she supposed she could provoke him into punching her hard. He could undoubtedly break her neck or crush her windpipe without using his full strength.

How long they ran, Nalyvkina never knew. She remembered hearing distant sonic booms and once seeing a laser flare in a patch of open sky, unblocked by either trees or clouds. The trees began to thin out, and her new captors ran faster still. It seemed that their feet hardly touched the ground, and she saw that they were all running unshod over terrain that would have reduced her feet to bloody ruins in minutes.

Maybe this was a hallucination after all. Maybe everything since she had struggled free of her sinking gunship was a dream, and she would wake up just in time to die of hypothermia in the gray, chill, fog-shrouded waters of the Gulf.

Suddenly there was light in front of them. It came from the door of a grounded lifter, and another Baernoi was silhouetted against it. The Baernoi holding Nalyvkina stopped, raised one hand in salute, then set her down with the other, as easily as if she'd been a doll.

"Greetings, worthy warrior," the second Baernoi said, in atrocious Anglic. "I am Behdan Zeg of Inquiry. Here we are enemy of your enemy. Hunters—" he used the True Speech word "—are Confraternity. Rest among us."

Nalyvkina had not had access to some unusual data for nothing, and this certainly looked like Behdan Zeg as she remembered his picture. He seemed thinner, and his clothing was more Ptercha'a than Baernoi.

"He speaks the truth," Ptercha'a said in Commercial Merishi.

"Are you Confreres?" was the first thing that came to the lieutenant's lips. It drew sharp looks and hisses. She put her hands together and bowed in apology, as she dragged together her knowledge of True Speech and Commercial Merishi.

"I thank you for rescue from my enemies," she said. "For this I call you friends. When it is safe for all of us, may I communicate with my own people, that they may come to me and take me home without danger to you?" She added a Scots Gaelic oath that Malcolm had told her meant, "May my road be muddy, the wind in my face, and my foes stronger than I, if I speak other than the truth."

Everyone apparently took that as a particularly potent invocation of the humans' gods. The first Baernoi pulled out his canteen and handed it to her. Without thinking, she took a good swig.

When she stopped coughing, she was lying on her back on the muddy ground. She was barely conscious of the dampness soaking through her clothes and into her hair, and vaguely thinking of poison. Then she remembered that Baernoi distilled liquor could run over 150 proof and she'd gulped several shots at once. With that comforting thought, she fell asleep.

Aboard U.F.S. *Shenandoah:*

Moneghan's flagship *Cavour* had just reached tight-beam range when Rose Liddell's communications display lit up. Something both COMMAND SECRET and PRIORITY ONE-PLUS was coming in.

She apologized to Moneghan and leaned back to wait for the decoding to finish. It seemed to take long enough for the shower she desperately needed. Her uniform seemed to be sticking to her like a commercial-sexer's skin suit in some places, in other places sagging as if she'd lost ten kilos. She probably had lost some; this kind of mental exercise took off weight faster than a workout but without putting anything in its place.

The message demolished most of what was left of her composure:

TO COMMODORE LIDDELL FROM MARSHAL BANFI. REQUEST YOUR CONCURRENCE AS SOPS IN APPOINTMENT OF MARCUS LANGSTON AS CG, LINAK'H COMMAND, IN PLACE OF MGEN JOACHIM TANZ KIA, WITH LOCAL RANK OF LTGEN. PROMPT REPLY STRONGLY ADVISED.

Liddell used words she seldom even thought. If her thoughts could have reached *Roma*, she would have probably been relieved on the spot for insubordination and fantasizing the murder of a superior officer. Longman's talent for leaving loose ends dangling and hitting Liddell in the face had reached the genius level.

Maybe it wasn't quite that bad. There'd been rumors that Banfi was planning to request Kharg's removal, or failing that, Tanz's, so that he could become head of both Federation and Administration forces on Linak'h. A drastic method of getting rid of Kharg—and one that apparently hadn't proved necessary, since Kharg was still running 222 Brigade and Tanz had died in harness.

Longman would have had to concur in Banfi's proposal. She'd been SOPS then, in fact the senior officer of Linak'h Command. No obligation to consult with either Uehara or Liddell—none imposed by law, anyway.

Liddell knew what her answer was going to be, and also that the "prompt reply strongly advised" meant that Banfi wanted an affirmative ten minutes ago. Well, the Marshal had regulations on his side, but Liddell was going to line up something more, like her three most trusted senior officers.

"Conference call, Liddell, Bogdanov, Moneghan, Fitzroy." Never mind that the chief of staff was reading the message over her shoulder and looking ready to start rolling his eyes and picking his nose at any moment. Banfi was about to learn that Liddell believed in leading, not driving. Although if that bothered him, he'd hardly be pushing Marcus into the ground job—

Two screened faces and one live one stared at Liddell, then at the message as it came up on their displays. Moneghan said something rude in Gaelic, but nodded. Bogdanov merely nodded. Liddell looked over her shoulder.

"Who the Hades else?" Fitzroy said.

"Good."

It went into the decoder:

LIDDELL TO BANFI AND LANGSTON. SENIOR OFFICERS OF LOW SQUADRON CONCUR IN PROPOSED APPOINTMENT AND PROMOTION OF GEN LANGSTON. WELCOME ABOARD, SIR.

About the time Liddell judged it must be on Banfi's screen, a familiar hand thrust a cup of tea in front of her. She turned, to see Chief Jensen clamping a tray of soup and sandwiches to the left arm of her chair.

"I am not going to kiss my steward. Will canonization be enough?"

"Are you planning on running for pope, Commodore?"

"Ask me about my postwar plans when we're postwar, all right?"

"Aye-aye, ma'am."

Twenty

News of the war on Linak'h spread even faster than news of the Confraternity coup.

On Charlemagne, Admiral Baumann and Admiral Kuwahara met with Foreign Minister Aung Bayjar, in Baumann's private sauna. They all gained security; Bayjar gained a chance to admire the Empress.

Intelligence was traded: what Aung Bayjar had learned in the Bureau of Emigration for what the Forces planned to do on Linak'h.

Kuwahara thought afterward that neither side had given or gained much. Bayjar's list showed more sins of omission than commission; intelligence from Linak'h and Victoria had already given the study group more than that.

Bayjar would know in advance about strategic objectives that were simple common sense. Regain command of space around Linak'h, reinforce Linak'h Command to corps strength, rearm the Administration Warband, and push the Coordination out of the Territory. Nothing subtle about it, in concept or execution.

They also exchanged views on the question of Confraternity reinforcements bound for Linak'h. Bayjar doubted that they existed. Baumann merely considered them unconfirmed.

Kuwahara was prepared to settle for their not being reinforcements for the Coordination.

In the Linak'h System, Joanna Marder and Charles Longman awoke aboard the Merishi-registered M.S. *Ged-Yauntzaff* to find that they had company.

Nineteen Ptercha'a ships, carrying three Legions from Chadl'hi, Oryng, and Pek, were closing with the four Merishi ships bound from Victoria in convoy with U.F.S. *Lysander*.

Before the two convoys rendezvoused, the Victorians

learned of another sighting. Light-hours from both Linak'h and the two convoys, somebody had fought a space battle.

Charlemagne:

Josephine Atwood climbed out of the swimming pool, pulled the plugs out of her ears, and wrapped a towel around her hair.

The attendant must have been super-alert; the robot with her clothes rolled up almost before she'd laid on the first coat of skin balm. She pulled on her clothes, used the cutter on her nails, and called "Weather" to the screen in her bay.

"Partly cloudy, temperature four degrees, wind from the NNW at seventeen km/h. Tonight's low minus two, with rising winds and fifty percent chance of snow. Tomorrow—"

"Bugger off," Atwood said. The Federal District was doomed by its midcontinental location to long, severe winters. By the calendar, this one was nearly over, but you only had to step outside to learn that it was retreating as slowly and stubbornly as a regiment of Baernoi Death Commandos.

Atwood, born in Dominion's tropics and educated in its temperate zone, did not consider herself doomed to enjoy that weather. However, she took out the overshoes and heavy jacket that she kept in the locker for weather emergencies during the winter (umbrella and poncho in summer) and pulled them on as she headed for the elevator.

She was tempted to cut back through the pool area, but there was the etiquette of not going into the pool area clothed on nude-swim days. Besides, she'd seen as much of that doctor's elegant posterior and well-muscled back as she needed to, unless she was going to have the chance to seriously chat him up.

Not bloody likely, not with another story to file by dinner time and the convention to pack for tonight. As the elevator door opened, Atwood wondered for the tenth time today what novelty she could extract from the modest amount of news available about the Linak'h War.

For the tenth time, she cursed the interstellar communications lag, which responded to her negative opinion no more than the weather forecast did. Twelve days for high-capacity communications to Linak'h meant that she was extrapolating from the situation as it had been two days after Rosie staved off sheer disaster.

But she'd already sung the praises of Commodore Liddell as much as Transrift was likely to care for, if not a bit more. Also, there was no law that said the Federation's luck couldn't have turned again.

Proclaiming victory too soon had ended the credibility and careers of more media people than Atwood cared to think about. She valued her career with Transrift; her connections with the Forces (specifically, with Sho Kuwahara through Captain Ropuski) were valuable but paid no bills.

What about taking it as a given that the outcome of the Linak'h War couldn't be known this soon, and speculating about troubles that might arise simply because the war had started?

That made sense. Quite a lot of sense. There was the communal situation on Asok—and the uproar when several off-planet Moslem potentates had offered to subsidize the emigration of any of their coreligionists who could not endure "Hindu oppression."

And there was the Kindred Worlds Empire. Six planets, nominally under the Emperor Carl III and his Viceroys, tolerated because they were harmless and in fact did more harm than good to the reputation of monarchies. But the long-standing policy of the Federation was summed up in the words of one Federation officer a generation ago (Marshal Banfi, wasn't it?):

"You can have your six planets. But if you try for a seventh, you'll have none."

Fine, or at least not unreasonable. But a dozen planets around the Empire were too weak to defend themselves from even its modest armed forces. Banfi's words needed Federation forces to uphold them. Those dozen planets needed massive doses of immigration to be independent of Federation forces.

There was a good starting point, at least. Although she'd better be careful in discussing emigration to the Kindred Empire area, so that she wouldn't give away even as part of the background any of the privileged information she'd been fed through Ropuski—

She realized suddenly that she'd been on the elevator longer than she should have been. Also, that she was alone in the car. If anybody had gotten on with her or been in before (likely enough), they'd gotten off. The indicator showed that she was already below ground level and heading for the service levels.

She thought of pressing the EMERGENCY STOP plate, then decided that would be overreacting. She would be setting off a full-scale rescue effort by panicking over something that was likely enough due to her own absentmindedness. At last she felt the elevator slow. As it stopped, she also felt a sharp stinging in her left buttock, as if someone had slapped a sheet of abrasive paper hard against her skin. She turned and discovered that the elevator was turning with her, which made no sense.

Then she knew she was falling, tried to break her fall with her hands, and knew just before her face slammed into the floor that she'd failed. The pain in her nose slowed but did not stop her slide into unconsciousness.

She was barely aware of the door opening and two large figures looking down at her. She neither heard nor felt anything after that.

Aboard *Shenandoah* off Linak'h, Commodore Liddell contemplated a generous supply of bad news and a limited range of options.

Longman had caught, fought, and destroyed the second Queen Bee and the last two Coordination cruisers. But two other hostile warships had escaped the battle, *Roma* had been damaged, and Longman herself badly wounded.

Admiral Uehara assumed command about the time he learned of the arrival of the Merishi and Ptercha'a convoys. They had to be protected, both from the Coordination and from each other. *Intrepid* microjumped for a rendezvous with the convoys.

She did not arrive. Admiral Uehara and four hundred Federation Navy people were gone. Rose Liddell was now the senior Federation Navy officer within many light-years, facing as many problems as her predecessors had faced, but she had fewer resources at her disposal.

There was no real alternative: *Lysander* alone could not guarantee the safety of the convoys. They needed a heavy-ship escort more than the Low Squadron needed a heavy-ship component.

As *Shenandoah* prepared to get under way, not even one

of Jensen's omelets could ease Rose Liddell's conscience. She doubted that anything would soothe Marcus Langston's or Emilio Banfi's tempers, when they looked at a sky where *Shenandoah* no longer rode as a shield against their enemies.

Charlemagne:

Josephine Atwood knew she'd been given an amnesiac as well as whatever knocked her out, when she woke up without remembering her name. However, the amnesiac must have been wearing off; her memory returned after she'd been awake for a while.

Exactly how long, she couldn't say and wasn't going to raise her frustration level by trying to guess. Instead she surveyed her quarters.

It was an almost perfect cube, about three meters in all dimensions. Beige padding covered floor and walls, including the door. No windows, but a steady, diffused twilight flowed down from ceiling panels. Marks on the wall suggested pull-downs. Atwood tried both, found a toilet and a water spout with a cup chained to it, and used both. She assumed that she was under surveillance, but knew that worrying about modesty was a guaranteed stress-builder in any hostage situation.

She would not have been surprised to be nude, but in fact she'd been stuffed into light trousers and tunic, besides having her battered nose packed and dressed. No underwear, bare feet, and the fabric was too light to make the clothes useful for either assault or suicide. Not that there was any place for her to hang herself from, even if she wanted to force her captor's hand by pretending to attempt suicide.

She wouldn't even pretend that until she had a better idea of who had kidnapped her and what they wanted. They might just decide to let her finish the job, or at least produce irreparable brain damage (if they had a seriously sadistic urge).

Odds were that the kidnappers were connected with someone who had been put in danger by the investigation into the emigration restrictions on Peregrine and the planets beyond it. But Captain Ropuski hadn't given out even the most tentative list of suspects, if in fact she had one. So suspecting why she'd been kidnapped wasn't going to help Atwood figure out who had done it.

On the other hand, it also meant that she didn't have any really dangerous knowledge about Kuwahara's study group. That cut both ways: her captors were unlikely to believe her denials and were more than likely to play rough trying to extract information she didn't have. However, she wouldn't have to swear mighty oaths to die before betraying her friends (*betraying Rosie, most of all*). That would happen in the natural course of events, if her hosts played rough enough.

She wasn't dead yet, though. She could play for time, although it would be nice to know how much she needed. She probably wouldn't be missed until she didn't show up at the convention and wasn't found at home, but that could have been two days ago. Not more than that; hair and fingernails hadn't grown enough to notice, and she was hungry and thirsty rather than starving and dried-out. Also, her nose still hurt.

She settled into the perfect position and slowed her breathing. She didn't have adrenaline or body fat to spare; yoga would take care of that without showing her fitness.

Of course, Josie, you may have already warned the bastards by not *going into screaming hysterics. But there's such a thing as self-respect, too.*

Twenty-one

Linak'h:

The TOC clerk took down the 1600 map print and replaced it with the 1800. Candice Shores sat at her field desk until the clerk had finished. The clerk was a reliable young corporal, but she'd lost a lover in the opening days of the war. Still reliable, she was now apt to jump at officers leaning over her shoulder.

The map neither showed any major changes nor cured Shores's boredom. Either the hostile troop movements of the past two days had ended or they'd dropped below the threshold of detectability.

Shores finger-combed her hair as she studied the map. Sixteen days into the war, only the stress addicts artificially sought out things to worry about. Everyone else had enough to go around.

The map told any soldier why. In the northwest, Kharg's 222 Brigade, down to three battalions, and three of the Administration's four Warband Legions. In the northeast, the Linak'h Brigade, four battalions with Shores's at its southern end.

Farther south still was the area they still hadn't officially named, around the old refugee camp and the Komarov house. At least the unit there had a name—Task Force Olufsdottir, for the CO of First/222 who was senior to the CO of Third/218. The two battalions had been cut off in the first two days of the war as Coordination ground troops flowed back and forth around them, taking more casualties than they inflicted but still leaving the Federation units inaccessible on the ground.

Holding Och'zem and the Zone, and stretching toward both Alliance and Merishi borders was the rest of Edelstein's 218 Brigade. One battalion and the last Warband Legion watched the west, the other three battalions guarded Och'zem, the Zone, and the training facilities where Confraternity militia were being field-trained as fast as cadre and supplies allowed. (There was one Confraternity cohort already in the field; there could be a Legion if the war lasted long enough.)

Throw in various odd units, and Shores was quite happy to be commanding only a single battalion. Even that command had given her the job of security for the Victorian expeditionary Battalion. Two hundred Vics had been caught in the Linak'h Brigade's AO by the start of the war. Three days later it was safe to move them—but by then Langston had decided to hold TF Olufsdottir on in place, which tied up a *lot* of air assets.

Tied up, not wasted—give Old Laser-stare that much credit. For three more days the Coordination made a major effort, with ground units at the end of their endurance and a few air strikes, to knock out TF Olufsdottir. They failed, and their casualties were impressive.

Meanwhile, though, a lot of Federation troops lacked the air assets to keep the pressure on Coordination units elsewhere. The enemy might have used this time to mass for new attacks or go underground for guerrilla warfare until they were reinforced or resupplied. The one thing Shores knew that they hadn't done was give up.

Shores sat back down and shoved a couple of print books off the desk to clear up her memo pad. One of them fell spine-up, *Wild Boers: A History of the Afrikaner Warrior*. Shores tapped the pad, saw the reminder to wash her underwear, and also saw that the screen was dimmer than it should be.

She swiveled in her chair and called Supply.

"Any progress on getting that quick-charger? It's getting so I can't even keep my memo pad up."

"Brigade has a bad case of *mañana,* I think," the Supply Officer replied. "I've exhausted—"

"Ah, Don Jaime, there are two kinds of supply officers, 'channels' and 'can do.' *Habla usted* 'can do'?"

"*Claro que sí.* I was thinking of a visit to TF Olufsdottir. The Third's supply officer was a classmate on the Logistics Course."

"Fine. You might also look up the Navy detachment at

the refugee camp. Start with Lieutenant Tachin. She's another can-doer."

"At your service, Colonel."

Better call Brigitte and warn her.

That would smooth the out-of-channels mission, always assuming that TF Olufsdottir had much to spare. The supply dumps established there might be half-rumor or entirely expended. But the task force was closer and lower than Forces HQ, and those quick-chargers were going to be needed before the battalion faced another round of heavy fighting.

The call might also confirm or deny those rumors about Brian and Brigitte having trouble. Not that Shores was going to ask outright, but she found that she cared. Cared, when she'd thought her attention might shrink down to her own battalion and the two children whom she prayed weren't waking up from nightmares and crying out for her.

But then, Brian and Brigitte were part of the military family. The only one that she'd ever really had—and now the only one she ever would have. Close family, too, after riding home from Victoria with them in *Shen*'s Bunkroom C-4.

For such, you *made* time.

"Reports from the patrols," came a voice from in front of her. Shores plucked the message forms out of the messenger's hands before she remembered to say, "Thank you," then flipped through them to find the one she wanted.

Good. Juan's patrol had sent in a double negative—no contacts friendly or hostile, no casualties friendly or hostile.

She scanned the others. All four patrols had the same strength—two Militia or Reserve scouts, either two squads of Regulars and a dedicated gunship or three squads, one with heavy weapons. Not to mention two SFO's with each patrol, which could call up additional firepower to the limits of available assets and ammunition, or start the reaction-force platoon off the pads in two minutes, the company in ten more.

Shores almost wished something had happened, other than a casualty-free sniping incident near the abandoned village of Molkussindan. But even if it did, it was the XO's turn to go out if a second company had to be put in; Shores would go only if things reached the point of coordinating units from two battalions.

That hadn't happened in nearly a week, long enough for the nights to become just enough cooler to notice and some of the leaves to show hints of color. *Wonder if that resupply run that's supposed to be on the way is carrying winter clothing?*

Linak'h:

The point squad clicked a contact report three minutes after Juan Esteva sent the double-negative back to battalion. He'd just warmed up to relay the report when the point squad clicked, "Halt and deploy."

Unobtrusively, Esteva watched the patrol leader. He was a Reserve lieutenant, leading a patrol for the first time. So far he'd done everything right, including not resenting the presence of Esteva and Jan Sklarinsky on a prisoner hunt. (Jan had been rude about that; snipers weren't the best prisoner-takers and "somebody with her head up her largest point of contact ought to have known better.")

A minute later, one of the Militia scouts came back from the point. They'd sighted one Coordination column, about three sixteens. No heavy weapons, and the tunics were cleaner than usual, except on one squad that seemed to be packing the electronics.

"Security precautions?"

"Standard."

"So. We'll assume their usual two flanking columns. We put one SSW up to the point, one with the CP aimed left, one with the right flankers. Esteva, tell our air to tree-squat until we shout, but come fast if we do. These Furballs may only *look* like they're coming in fat, dumb, and happy."

The patrol had been reinforced to three squads, each with an SSW plus a headquarters and air support. Esteva suspected that also had something to do with the planned prisoner-snatch. The Ptercha's habit of vigorously counter-attacking made taking prisoners hard and keeping them harder.

Their standard field formation reflected that habit. Where the terrain allowed, they would move in three parallel columns, and the center one wasn't necessarily the strongest. No matter which one you hit, it had someone to bring up to counterattack or at least fall back on.

That didn't make the Coordination supertroopers. The tactics had been used by light infantry for centuries; any smart Roman centurion could probably have worked it up in ten days once he learned about automatic weapons and shoulder launchers. It did prove that the Coordination was fielding pretty sharp light infantry, which so far meant what Esteva had expected: hard to kill and damned near impossible to really scare.

He looked up. Double canopy, peephole and redcones, with a lot of ferns and rotten trunks on the floor. This was mature second growth in an area probably first selectively logged about the time the planet was settled. Not as dense as what virgin forest the Great Fire had left farther north, but plenty dense enough to interfere with observation, lines of fire, medevac, and air strikes, to name just a few—

The SSW squad headed for the right vanished into the trees. Seconds later the SSW from the point opened fire. The interval between its first burst and the point pulsers joining in was just long enough to notice, which meant too long. Somebody trigger-happy, or something unexpected.

The patrol leader looked at his two sergeants. He stopped at a look, then hand-signaled his orders. The troopers broke alternately left and right, until everyone was belly to the ground and behind something. Not everyone Esteva saw had good observation, but not everyone had a good eye for terrain either, and anyway that was why you worked in squads, so that *somebody* was covering the approaches that you couldn't.

The SSW on the right let fly, and Esteva counted four grenade explosions, even farther off to the right. Friendly or hostile? It didn't matter. All by themselves, the explosions said that the enemy's flanking column was a lot closer than usual.

Esteva hoped the SSW aimed left was placed so it could swing and shoot right *fast*. He had a feeling it was going to need to.

Linak'h :

When the patrol's contact came in, Candice Shores had been in conference for ten minutes with Karl Pocher. He hadn't exactly made an appointment, but Shores had known he was in the area and probably why. She could help everybody by seeing him about what had to be on his mind: the future of the Victorians if Shores's battalion moved out and no longer protected them.

"We're only talking about two hundred ten, give or take fifteen, of our three hundred forty," Pocher pointed out. "The rest are back in the Zone or in 218's AO."

"I hope they'll stay there, too," Shores said. Pocher seemed to have a full set of data at his fingertips; a briefing beforehand or just the tidy mind of a conscientious leader?

"Do the Vics in the south still have their organic transport?" Shores asked. That had to give away the focus of her interest, but she didn't care much. Hiding it from somebody as shrewd as Pocher would be a waste of effort.

"They've all been assigned to stationary posts, mostly refugee and medical work," Pocher said. "I can give you a precise breakdown if you want."

"What I want is to know where the rest of their lift went."

As a Civil Action Group, the Vics had brought out a respectable force of civilian-type lift vehicles. They had made up the rest from purchased, leased, transferred, or possibly stolen lift from Linak'h. A motley collection, but in proportion to the strength of the unit the most complete lift outfit on Linak'h. Also one that the Vics were very reluctant to let anyone else (read: "Linak'h Command") touch.

Shores knew the logic of leaving the Vics alone: they were doing good work, and were so far the only sign of support from outside the Federation for the war on Linak'h. (The Be-Nice-to-Victorians movement had grown stronger since word of the abortive coup reached Linak'h In the process of saving themselves, the Vics had saved Linak'h from serious trouble.

She pulled the papers on her desk into a stack and weighted it down with the *Wild Boers*. "Where's the lift from the Teams in the south? Did Edelstein—?"

"It's all up here."

"I don't recall you're supposed to interrupt colonels."

"Oh, but I'm the official representative of the senior in-theater officer of an allied unit. That lets me interrupt anybody."

Shores couldn't help smiling. "Just how official?"

"Anything that doesn't get us dumped off on some other battalion or pushed into the Zone will pass with my boss."

"That's flattering to me, I suppose. Are you sure it's tactful?" She stared at Pocher again. "Or is there something else? Like your people wanting to fight the Merishi but wiser heads prevailing?"

Pocher's chair rocked back several cems before he caught himself. Then his head jerked. "We've got a lot of people spoiling for a fight. I've told them that if we jump the border with the Governance, we'll be going home in cells on an emigrant transport if we go home at all. If we work it off on the Ptercha'a, on the other hand—"

" 'No names, no pack drill.' " Shores explained the reference, and Pocher nodded. "Is everybody enthusiastic for combat, or just the veterans?"

"I haven't heard anybody who *says* they don't have a score to settle," Pocher said and added, "I agree—that means there are a lot of damned fools in the group."

"What about Merishi agents?"

"Not after the coup," Pocher said, in a voice that eliminated the possibility of argument. Shores didn't think that eliminated the possibility of Victorian security risks though. How to deal with that tactfully?

She fiddled with papers and displays that she hoped Pocher (who was dipping into *Wild Boers*) would think were the battalion TO & E. She had that in her head, where Pocher couldn't sneak a look at it; what she wanted was to *simulate* precision.

"The big question is when is your security unit that's coming in going to be down?" she said finally. "Once they've arrived, I think your people will be capable of self-defense where you are. Brigade can send in ground reinforcements or call air strikes. As long as you keep your transport intact, you can evacuate if things really get out of hand."

"That means informing Hogg."

If Pocher thought she was going to play this game with

only her own cards, he needed locking up. "I can't grab off all the extra lift you make available without checking to see if somebody else may need a slice."

"Colonel Shores—"

"This goes to Brigade, or you are trying to bribe a Federation officer, and the meeting is now over. Be glad you're not under arrest." She grinned. Judging from Pocher's expression, the display of teeth had the right effect.

"Sorry. You don't really think we were trying to hold on to the lift, so we could jump into any fight we liked?"

"Not really," *which counts as my Big Lie of the Week,* "but your CO is an amateur with guts. They don't always have the Big Picture." *A phrase which always makes my stomach turn when somebody uses it on me. Try again, Candy.*

But Pocher seemed to be made of reliable components. "And if the security detachment is understrength or late?"

"Then any lift Brigade hasn't borrowed is split between my battalion and the Vics. In return, we'll leave one company behind until we have a secure LZ at the other end."

"Good. Most of our lifters have got some armor or at least frag barriers inside. They're weak on guns, and none of them are worth much for air-to-air. I'll run that past the Group leader, then get back to you as soon as he replies or we have an ETA on the security detachment."

Shores nodded as Pocher rose. He was doing the sensible thing—having played his last card, he was taking advantage of her offer to get out of the game while he still had his shirt. He wasn't going to risk anything for the slight chance of finding out what Shores would do with the Vics if there was no secure LZ, for example.

(The Vics were going to be loaded aboard Federation lifters and flown straight to Task Force Olufsdottir, if the movement was south. In any other direction, they and their watchdog company—probably the Reserves, Shores decided—were just going to sit out at least the first battle. There'd be other chances for fur trophies.)

They were shaking hands when the report arrived that Juan Esteva's patrol was heavily engaged with a Band-strength force from a Coordination unit in an area where no such enemy strength had previously been detected.

Linak'h:

Jan Sklarinsky was already far out to the right on a snipe-and-snatch mission when the firefight got serious. Since she had several targets in the bad guy's flankers, she picked them off at the longest range the forest would allow, about two hundred fifty meters. For her, that was scattergun range.

The bad guys were good; they went to ground and returned fire with grenade launchers and one of their SSW's. Sklarinsky and her people needed all the concealment and all their skill in using it to get clear.

It helped that they weren't tempted to move fast. They all had heavy loads, extra rounds for Sklarinsky's rifle, grenades and carbine magazines for the security and observer. Grenades were good stuff if you had to break contact fast; they could do a lot of damage or raise a lot of smoke or both without revealing your position.

They reached their new position without having to shout or throw. Sklarinsky realized this was because their target column was trying to move in on the right flank of the patrol's position. With at least a sixteen in the column, they could do a lot of damage if they did.

"Time to stimulate an attack from the rear, people."

"What'dya mean, *simulate,* Sarge? Isn't this gonna be real?"

"Not as real as we want them to think. If they turn around and come at us, we haul off that way"—she jerked a thumb to their left—"and rejoin our people from the rear."

Sklarinsky's counterattack started off with two snipings and six grenades, two hand-thrown and four launched. The grenades would have done a lot more damage if the enemy hadn't already been moving forward. It looked to Sklarinsky like a frontal attack on the patrol's position. After she started shooting it really turned into one.

It also turned into a disaster for the Ptercha'a, as soon as the patrol had two SSW's firing. The Ptercha'a were good at using the ground, but a lot of them were hit in the first bursts before they went down. Then grenades flew in both directions at each side tried to force the other's people to move, and more bursts tried to hit them as they did.

All this kept Sklarinsky alternately moving in search of

a firing position, ducking friendly fire, and trying to hide from hostile eyes. She wondered if the Ptercha'a were trying the fairly standard tactic of light forces opposed to heavier ones with air support, a close grapple that would make air strikes too dangerous. If so, the only Federation force that close was her team.

Being under a friendly air strike can ruin your whole day.

Then from beyond *both* positions, a pair of Coordination SSW's opened heavy fire. Bark, needles, leaves, and wood chips sprayed from trunks at waist height; it looked as if the enemy gunners either didn't know how to elevate or were deliberately firing high.

More firing from the right, toward the front of the patrol, and a shout, "They're running."

A mucking lot of good that information's going to do if we can't follow the bastards.

Grenades now joined the hostile SSW fire, most of them smoke, laying a dirty white barrier between Sklarinsky's team and the patrol. Fifty meters long and ten meters thick, it blinded the patrol but not her team.

They moved cautiously since the SSW's were still firing, and every so often some Fed patroller lost patience and let fly. The security man took one round across his thigh; it missed all the grenades and hit on armor, so he only promised to poison the shooter's next beer and kept going.

The mix of friendly and hostile fire slowed Sklarinsky's team but didn't keep them from learning what the enemy flankers were doing. Or rather, had done. They'd been hauling away their dead, and from the number of blood trails and pools there'd been at least a dozen major casualties. All of them long gone, though—except for one stay-behind, probably looking for just such a target as the team.

The Ptercha'a found it, too. The observer had just shouted a warning when a bullet punched into his face and blew out the back of his skull. Sklarinsky and the security man both went down, rolling in different directions. The security man pitched a grenade; its blast drew both friendly and hostile fire.

It also moved the stay-behind out to where Sklarinsky had a shot at him. She used a solid slug for a leg shot to hold him, then two non-lethal grenades to take the rest of the fight out of him. Then she and the security man sprinted to the gasping, groaning Ptercha'a, snatched him up, and shouted, "Lively Legs coming in with a hostile POW!"

She hadn't used Juan's bed-name for her in public before, but she couldn't think of a better way of making sure she wouldn't be hit by her friends.

Linak'h:

Candice Shores had a busy five minutes after the patrol's report. She launched the reaction platoon, upgraded all the other Alert units, went over a list of air assets with the air liaison, and put in all the appropriate requests.

By the time she'd finished that, the patrol was either out of contact or too busy to update the brass. Each second that passed played on Shores's nerves, until she was afraid they were going to start snapping like overtightened guitar strings.

At least she hadn't lost the ability to send people into danger. She'd been afraid that losing her father and Ursula and then having to dump the children on the mercy of Linak'h Command while she went off to war might affect her that way. Grief reactions were like a pattern of cluster bombs; you couldn't be sure which way you'd be hit or how badly.

She'd come to accept that the matter of the Komarov house was a lot of little mistakes, some of them hers, rather than a crime with a specific culprit. She couldn't remember if she'd made that fully clear to Nieg before he disappeared into the black hole of the north. She wished she could; either guilt or satisfaction would be more definite than this perpetual doubt, itching like a heat rash in power armor.

What would happen if somebody else close to her went west—like the Juan and Jan Show—was another irritating uncertainty.

Barbara Hogg's call was a welcome break from that irritation. Shores wouldn't even have minded Hogg's micromanaging if she'd stayed on the circuit long enough for the patrol to win, lose, or haul ass. (Although with three enemy and one friendly ground unit and air at least on the friendly side, these possibilities weren't mutually exclusive.)

"How are you set for lift if we have to move your battalion into the area?"

Shores looked at the updated TO & E and Status Chart now pinned to the corner of the 1600 map, then mentally edited the figures. She didn't want to even think loudly about the deal with the Victorians at this stage, but on the other hand if Hogg was going to be openhanded and Shores's battalion wound up with a double surplus of transport, somebody else might wind up going short just so the Vics could have fun. The battalion commander responsible for this situation would have something else, as soon as Brigade learned about it.

"We're in the same status as we were. I can improve it some if we defer all non-essential maintenance. That should give us another ten percent for each lift."

"Do that. In fact, I'll make it an order for Brigade. Oh, not for general circulation, but it's official. *Shen* is heading out of orbit, to escort those Ptercha's whoever-they-ares and the Merishi with the Vics."

"Escort or referee?"

"Wherever did you get that idea, Candy? A certain Intelligence colonel?"

"Background only. I haven't seen Nieg since the war began. I don't even know where he is."

"Ah, this is also not for general circulation or even attribution. He's with the Rangers who are locating the Coordination's supplies and AD. I hope that's not your fault."

Shores didn't snarl. She counted to ten before memory cut in, reminding her that Barbara Hogg was old enough to be her mother and had been a captain when Shores was in OTC.

"You're my Brigade Commander, not my family's matchmaker."

"Seems like your family could have used one."

Shores was so completely speechless for so long that Hogg finally said something vaguely resembling an apology and cut off. Almost the moment she did, the patrol came back on-line, with Juan's voice delivering a brisk report.

It sounded as if they'd done better than good, even if they had two KIA and three WIA. Juan also mentioned "vital intelligence" in a way that made it clear nothing and nobody would make him discuss it over the air.

Simple solution to that: bring everybody in.

"Break contact in Blue or Red quadrants and proceed to coordinates 890654. We'll put the ready platoon down there to make a safe LZ and ground perimeter, and lift you people and your intelligence out in one go. If there are any bad guys left for the reaction platoon, they can have a party. If not, they can go out in the next lift."

"Gold One to Huntress," Elayne Zheng's voice broke in. "What about using the perimeter as a temporary FAOB? If you send out a fuel and weapons load for a few attackers, we can quick-charge them in the air. Then any bad guys who show up trying for the reaction platoon will have the sky fall on them."

Shores suspected this was one of Elayne's own brainstorms, but she called TacAir anyway. They were amenable, but left the final decision to the SAO on the spot. That probably meant Commander Shauli. When Shores considered what he might have to listen to from Zheng if he hesitated even a nanosecond, she decided that she herself had got off lightly with Barbara Hogg.

Another pass by the light attackers was drowning out Esteva's voice when Gold One came back on the air. "Affirmative to the plan as suggested, Huntress. We will implement and keep you updated."

The voice was Shauli's, and was it Shores's imagination, or did he sound a trifle subdued?

Linak'h:

It had been some time since the loudest sound in Fomin zar Yayn's underground post was the dripping of water in the cave down the tunnel to the right. There had in fact been noise for long enough that he thought his assistants owed him an explanation.

"Bad news is best served fresh" was a quotation attributed to half a dozen ancient warriors. Zar Yayn did not doubt that all of them had said it; all had been wise in war. But it was such ordinary common sense that he also suspected it had been first uttered by some warrior too ancient for the attention of the historians. Perhaps some clan chief had said it when he discovered that his ten best warriors had raided the wrong village, stolen the wrong stock, and slain blood-kin of his first, second, *and* third wives—

"A message from Third Twisdanaran Cohort, Senior," a voice said behind zar Yayn's ear.

He swiveled in his chair, to see one of the young assistants—what was his name? He was of Tribal stock, and some Tribal customs had left their marks on the way he stood and on the hints of dye in the fur of ears and tail, unhidden by his entirely Warband tunic and shorts.

Third Twisdanaran was one of the five Tribal Cohorts attached to zar Yayn's Legion Six-Seven. It was in fact bringing up the rear of the secret march, with the other four Tribal Cohorts and one from the Warband well out in front of it the last time all reported their positions.

"Have they found their supplies?"

"They did not say, but they have encountered the enemy." The assistant put the message form in front of zar Yayn; the senior read it three times, feeling his ears twitching harder at each reading.

"My reply is that they are to give greatest value to hiding from the enemy, until Father-rise of the day after tomorrow. Second value is finding and issuing their supplies. Only third is attacking isolated forces of the enemy, except in self-defense, and then they are to break off the action as soon as they can without leaving dead or wounded behind.

"The enemy does not know that our Tribal Cohorts are so far into his territory. The longer he remains ignorant, the better our chances for victory."

"As duty bids me, Senior." With that old-fashioned salutation, the assistant vanished. Zar Yayn looked at the message again. It mentioned dead and wounded; it did not mention having recovered all of them. Was this omission because they thought he would take their performance of duty for granted and not ask about possible failures?

Not impossible. However, he could not disgrace either the Warband or the Tribal leaders of the cohort by publicly asking them if they had failed in their duty, dishonored their fallen comrades, and given to the enemy knowledge that might do the Coordination's plan some serious injury.

Nor was his reluctance to ask entirely from concern for their honor. He had no doubt anymore that the moment he gave them any excuse, those seniors who listened too closely to the Masters would prove what good Servants they were by removing him from command of Legion Six-Seven.

That would be foolish, and Muhrinnmat-Vao would say so. But fear of lesser menaces than the Confraternity had given birth to greater follies, and might do so again if it led to the dismissal of Muhrinnmat-Vao.

It must be close to Fatherset now, and his stomach was reminding him that he had not eaten since both suns were in Linak'h's sky. He had best not forget eating so long too often, or he would return to Jillyah looking as if he had been careless of his health. Breeding women or new mothers were often of uncertain temper, and even at her gentlest she had little patience for that sort of thing.

Linak'h:

The patrol was home and dry (except for those who were using the showers). The dead Ptercha'a (a second body turned up on the left flank, along with fragments of others; air strikes were hard on evidence) and captured equipment and supplies had been inventoried, photographed, and analyzed to the limits of a battalion's capabilities.

What else happened was up to Brigade and higher levels, although as Shores watched the gunship courier lift off, she wondered if she could have made her own letter stronger. There was a fine line between recommending so little that you were slaughtered for lacking courage and recommending so much that you died for lacking respect to your superiors.

No, the recommendation she'd sent would do as much as anything could. "The apparent presence of both Tribal and Warband personnel from Legion Six-Seven suggests a major reevaluation of its location."

It also suggested a major reevaluation of the allies' ability to detect and prevent infiltrations or detect and prevent dangerous concentrations of the infiltrators. *Shenandoah*'s departure wasn't going to help there.

That departure made the newly arrived heavy cruiser *Justice* the heaviest ship in orbit. Her people didn't know Linak'h as well as *Shen*'s, and the cruiser's captain reportedly didn't think he had to defer to Mad Bill. He had done good work bringing his ship in crammed to the overhead with nine hundred high-grade reinforcements for Linak'h; that wouldn't keep him out of trouble if he ignored Moneghan's local knowledge.

Juan Esteva and Jan Sklarinsky strode up, in step and in

clean fatigues. When they saluted, Shores knew something was up. She examined them minutely, but they didn't blink, and she learned nothing except that both of them were well scrubbed, probably by each other.

"Permission to request your presence in the mess, ma'am."

"I'll consider it requested. I was thinking of taking a nap while the Higher Authorities decide what to do with this particular hot potato. It may be a long night."

"Yes, ma'am." Neither of them moved.

"Well?"

"We repeat the request."

Shores put her hands on her hips. "You almost make it sound like an order."

"Sorry, ma'am," they chorused.

"This is not Newlies' Day at OTC," Shores said. "Speak as if you knew me before today."

"Yes, ma'am!"

"And if you salute me again, I'll break both your wrists!"

Sklarinsky grinned. "Bargain, Colonel. We don't salute, you come with us."

Shores followed, resisting the temptation to put a hand on her sidearm. She followed them into the mess tent, half of which had been curtained off. As she turned, the curtain fell, a dozen voices shouted, "Happy Birthday!" and she saw thirty candles blazing on a large cake.

In ruddy-gold icing around the candles someone had written, "CANDY IS DANDY."

She closed her eyes. Her throat closed by itself. By the time she could say anything, someone had shoved a chair under her, someone else had shoved her into it, and somebody else had brought up a small table already laid out with a piece of cake, tableware, and a glass of brandy.

"I'll be damned," she finally got out.

"I never debate theology with a superior," the XO said. Roger Duboy looked positively cherubic. Shores couldn't take the smile off his face no matter how hard she glared. She finally gave up and returned the smiles.

"You're two days early, you know."

"Maybe Juan was using a Hunter calendar," Sklarinsky said. "They're hard to interpret."

Esteva stepped close. "I've also heard that there's a lot of stuff coming down the pipe, and we're standing at the bottom end. In two days we may be hip-deep in it. We thought you might want to—"

"Eat, drink, and be merry, for tomorrow we—" Her throat closed. She picked up the brandy glass.

"To absent friends!"

Twenty-two

Charlemagne:

Captain Ropuski was so upset over Josephine Atwood's disappearance that Admiral Kuwahara thought briefly of asking her to stay offscreen while he talked to Lieutenant Pfalz. She blamed herself for going along with using Atwood as a controlled leak and thereby making her a target.

Admiral Kuwahara blamed himself and Admiral Baumann a good deal more. The Empress had had the original idea; he had chosen Ropuski to implement it. She had done so, with great skill. None of them (and that presumably included Atwood) had thought the situation might lead to media people being targeted for terrorism. That hadn't happened at all on Charlemagne for nearly fifty years, and there'd been only isolated incidents since the Alliance Secession another two generations back.

None of these truths about everybody's mistakes improved anybody's disposition, and Kuwahara wasn't inclined to discuss any of them with the Federal District Violent Crimes officer. He was even less inclined to insult Lena by keeping her out of the discussion. He and his XO being on bad terms wouldn't revive Atwood if she was dead or rescue her if she was alive.

"I'm in charge of the case," Pfalz concluded. "We are treating it as political terrorism, so that will bring in the Federal Security Bureau, the Investigative Divisions of both the JAG and Intelligence, and the Military Police."

"I'll see if we can persuade either Intelligence or the JAG to bow out," Kuwahara said. "Both ID's on a single case has led to territory fights." This was not something normally discussed in public, but Pfalz's service stripes meant eighteen years as a Federal District law-enforcement officer. It was hard to imagine that the Forces had any real secrets from him.

"I'll try to keep the peace between them," Pfalz said.

"Do you think you can?" Ropuski said. Kuwahara did not look at her. Pfalz not only looked, he glared.

"Are you questioning either my competence or my authority?"

Ropuski and Kuwahara looked at each other. It was a reasonable but hardly tactful suspicion. A lieutenant like Pfalz might have been put in charge of the case because the District police weren't taking the Atwood case as seriously as the Forces.

"Neither," Ropuski said.

Kuwahara stifled a sigh. Good for Lena if she turned away the wrath; she was likely to do most of the day-to-day work with the investigation. With the situation on Linak'h now a full-scale (although probably winnable) war, Kuwahara had to delegate right and left in order to play expert. Half a dozen divisions and committees wanted him, with no regard for his need to eat, sleep, and go to the bathroom. (His family was achieving the status of mythic beings out of a remote past.)

"I'm sure you'll do your best. But we were thinking we might save you some trouble with the people over whom we do have authority." Pfalz looked skeptical. Ropuski grinned. "Remember that Admiral Kuwahara has direct access to Admiral Baumann."

"What about the rest of Forces Command?"

"We have it or can get it," Ropuski said. "If all else fails, we can go straight up to the War Council, again through Baumann."

"If you can buy me and my people some time, I won't refuse it," Pfalz said. "Sorry about the temper. I admit it looked a bit odd, but Inspector Gorshin said that I already knew all the people involved. Anybody else would have to learn the territory before they could be effective, and that would give other agencies time to gain squatters' rights."

They agreed that in addition to an apology to Pfalz, they all owed Inspector Gorshin a round of drinks, and then they ended the call. Kuwahara massaged his temples until he knew that wouldn't do anything for the migraine, turned down Ropuski's offer of a second try, and asked her to bring him his medicine.

The incipient migraine was fading even before the medicine kicked in. Kuwahara wondered if the massage had worked after all. Some of it certainly was knowing that the investigation was in good hands, so they could if necessary turn their backs on it and face a media community likely to be less than happy over losing one of its own people.

Linak'h:

The screen chime sounded. Brigitte Tachin keyed it on without interrupting her dictation, then said, "Hold," and turned to the screen.

"Rumor Central here. We top any tale. No, I am not the Official Tail. Oh, hello, Rafael. What brings you to scenic Linak'h?"

"I volunteered for Linak'h and came out in *Justice*. Meanwhile, somebody threw darts at a list of names and the dart for 'Naval Party in—' what do they call this place anyway?"

"Would you believe 'Komarovsk'?"

"Yes, if you'll explain why."

"Can it wait? Or can you come over here? If you're calling from the ASP, you're ten minutes' walk from Shore Party HQ."

"Always assuming no interruptions from the Furfolk."

"If you don't mind, Rafe, nobody uses that term. And we haven't had any serious rocket or missile attacks for two days."

"Very well. Twenty minutes?"

"More than long enough."

It almost wasn't. When Tachin played back the requisitions, she discovered two badly scrambled paragraphs. By the time she'd unscrambled them and put the requisition on-line, three more items had surfaced, screaming for attention. And when she'd finished those, who should limp in but Mort Gellis, with a report that the quick-charger for Candice Shores's battalion was loaded and would be on the way in ten minutes.

"Br—Lieutenant Commander Mahoney could have reported that."

"He was tied up."

"With what?" She almost said, "With whom?" but that would have been groundless and disloyal.

"Crating and loading the charger." Gellis avoided her eyes. "He's turning into a darned good loadmaster, if I'm any judge."

"You're not."

"Well, it's not just—"

"Mr. Gellis. I suggest keeping your tongue between your teeth and your nose out of my personal business. Or has something happened that I should know about?"

"No. I just—I just came over, because with the way the commander was acting up, I was in the way. The medics have told me to get more exercise anyway."

Tachin stared at her blank screen. She had stared at everything else since the war began, and even talked with a few people about Brian's situation.

Still blaming himself for the horror at the Komarov house, Brian was trying to do everybody's job as well as his own. Tachin didn't know if he was trying to drive himself to exhaustion or prove his versatility. It didn't matter. Talking to him was getting to be like talking to a robot with a sophisticated but rigid program.

"Well, if I can't find something for you to do, you'll be in the way here." She looked at him, feeling almost maternal impatience toward all socially incompetent men even though Brian was fifteen Standard years older and Gellis three or four.

"I haven't forgotten Brian, and I know that you'd rather wrestle Hunters barehanded than be around when he's in a mood." *So would I, or we wouldn't be quartered separately now.*

"What about calling Colonel Shores?"

"What about her? She has a battalion to run." *Not to mention having already done her best, with her father's death fresh in her mind.*

Gellis sighed. "All right. It was a thought. Maybe a substandard one. People are still beginning to notice how much has to come to you and how little gets done through Commander Mahoney."

It appeared that the NCO beervine was as infallible as ever. "When I get any ideas, I'll run them past you. Fair enough?"

"Fair—oh, excuse me, sir, I was just leaving."

Rafael Morvan slipped into the tent. Gellis vanished as Tachin stood up to grip Morvan's outstretched hand.

"Welcome to Komarovsk, Rafael. It's named after Nikolai Komarov." He sat, and she summarized what she had learned about Candice Shores's father. At first she tried to remember what she was supposed to know and what she'd learned unofficially. Then she gave up. Past bed-friendship gave Rafe no special claim on her, but she'd be damned if she was going to be a slave to "need-to-know." What could they do if she threw in extra details? Send her to a combat zone?

"Now, what did they tell you about Task Force Olufsdottir?" she asked.

Rafe played back the official briefing, but with a twist at one corner of his mouth that kept threatening to turn into a mocking grin. He finally broke off when Tachin couldn't keep her own face straight.

"Have I left anything out? Or have they?"

She pointed toward the front of the tent. "See that hole? That's the shelter entrance. Go down there and tell me what you see."

Tachin was standing at the tent door when Rafe climbed out of the hole and finger-combed clods of dark earth out of his hair, then pulled a broken length of root out from under his collar. With the help of one moon, the Red Child was giving its usually eerie light, and the night breeze carried the usual odors—ozone and exhaust fumes, fuel and lubricants, latrines and their chemicals.

(No more smoke or unburied Hunter bodies, praise God. They'd policed up the dead from the last major ground assault, and the patrols were fighting far off and usually downwind.)

"You must have been working the refugees like indentured immigrants."

"What do you mean, the refugees?" She held out her own hands. He contemplated the calluses, the dirt under the ragged nails, and the sprayspot over one blister that had become infected. She thought he wanted to hold her hands and realized that she wouldn't mind if he did.

"Everybody who wasn't on the firing line was ducking or digging for five days. If you haven't lost your hand as a masseur, you can probably set up a side business and retire after this tour."

He shook his head. "I'm going to sign on for a permanent commission. What about you? You've just about completed your first six, haven't you?"

"Yes, but I'm staying in too. I—it's not just saving the family money anymore. Would you believe I'm going to apply for the Advanced Weapons Course when we finish up here?"

"Hm. Maybe we'll be on campus together. I've applied for the Civil Action Medical, and I *think* they still give both of those on Riftwell."

She couldn't detect anything unreasonable in his voice, and surely her strained relations with Brian weren't so public that he'd have learned about them? Although she had to admit that Rafe had filled out a little since they were last close, and his rather colorless hair had turned a sleek light brown . . .

Three lifters droned up from Pad Four and formed into a triangle. A gunship dropped from high patrol to become their escort. Tachin's eyes followed all four out of sight.

As their shadows blurred into the night, red and yellow light danced far off to the west. TacAir putting down fire in support of a ground unit, it looked like, but that far off probably not even in TF Olufsdottir's AO.

She shivered, and remembered that this far inland, the nights balanced on the edge between summer and autumn. She went inside for her jacket. When she came out, Rafael Morvan was gone.

Charlemagne:

Josephine Atwood bent slowly backward until her hands touched the floor, then lifted herself until she was balanced on toes and fingertips. She held that position for a twenty-count, then bounced to her feet and picked up her tunic to wipe off the sweat.

Since her confinement hadn't included sensory or any other kind of deprivation, she'd quickly decided to keep up her exercise regimen. Maybe even increase it a notch and of course do it in the nude, putting on a show for the hidden cameras.

The show probably wouldn't affect anybody or anything, if the kidnappers were professionals. (And if they weren't, she might learn the hard way, but learning would still beat ignorance.) She couldn't do much more than send a message of total indifference to what they might see; she would go on with her life even if they put her in a cage in the Palace Square on Baer.

Besides, the psych profiles were right; she *did* have an exhibitionist streak (although she hadn't been the only one, back at Thatcher College). She also had something to exhibit, and the whole act was improving her morale even if it wasn't affecting that of her captors.

She ended by wiping herself down with the napkin she'd hidden for use as a washcloth—they didn't provide utensils, but the paper bowls of stir-fry could be emptied quite handily if you didn't mind messy fingers. Then she pulled her clothes back on and assumed the perfect position.

Yoga seemed to trigger some innate time sense in her, although it applied only to the time she was actually meditating. Twenty minutes was enough for her to reevaluate her situation.

Balancing meals, eliminations, appetite, and sleep cycles, she estimated this was her third day here. Where was here? Almost certainly on Charlemagne. It would be an exceptionally well-equipped terrorist group that could adjust gravity and atmospheric pressure in their hostage quarters.

Suppose it wasn't a mere terrorist group? Maybe she really had been captured by the Baernoi, or at least turned over to them? (She'd worked out the scenario of getting a kidnap victim off well-policed Charlemagne and all the way to Baer on the second day, as mental exercise. She'd concluded that it would be a good deal more than mental exercise for anybody actually trying to do it, and therefore probably was not being done.)

She decided to let the previous conclusion stand. On Charlemagne, and no doubt by now being vigorously sought by every agency with jurisdiction and a few without it. Nobody could resist the pressure her colleagues would be exerting, vigorously if not always intelligently. (She hoped they all remembered that the Federation's "no negotiations over hostages" rule was strictly applied only to *military* personnel, and not accuse Forces Command of either wantonly violating it or wantonly endangering her.)

If she hadn't been personally involved, she would have regarded the kidnapping as something of a victory. One kidnapping wasn't likely to create a panic, if the Linak'h War hadn't. It was in fact likely to focus even more attention on all the problems Admiral Kuwahara's study group was handling, or at least on all those he would be allowed to discuss in public. (There all Atwood could do was cross her fingers and toes and hope Baumann would allow Kuwahara's basic good sense to prevail.)

That situation was a two-edged sword, though. Lots of attention and a massive law-enforcement effort could force kidnappers to flee, after first destroying the evidence—i.e., the hostage. Being avenged might be nearly as complete a victory as being rescued, but not nearly as enjoyable.

Linak'h:

Marcus Langston was fond enough of the Ptercha'a to have begun calling them Hunters, but he'd found that fondness being severely tested in his two weeks as CG, Linak'h Command. He suspected that Marshal Banfi felt the same, since it was the Marshal's job to mediate the quarrels among the Hunter members of the Senior War Directorate. (Banfi didn't say so; he had no objections to being technically subordinate to an officer four grades and seventy years his junior, but he drew the line at confiding Confraternity secrets to Langston.)

Tonight's argument was mostly between Isha Maiyotz and Boronisskahane. Maiyotz was favored starting the reply to the Coordination's troop movements (Legion Six-Seven and its Tribal auxiliaries above all) immediately. Boronisskahane favored waiting until the incoming spaceborne Legions either declared themselves friendly or could be neutralized.

"By whom?" Maiyotz said. (This was the first time Langston had been a member, let alone chairman, of a strategy conference conducted entirely in Commercial Merishi. He hoped the common belief that it was adequate for sophisticated military subjects proved correct.)

"If necessary, *Shenandoah*."

"If?" Banfi put in. "What does the Administration have to put in her place? If it has nothing, and *Shen* does the work, then who is calling for the Hunters to hide behind human cloaks?"

Hunter fur did not allow visible blushes, even in ones as elderly as Boronisskahane. He showed every other sign of embarrassment, however, and for almost the first time that Langston could remember.

"The intelligence we have gathered from our prisoners makes it clear that the Coordination's Seniors are reluctant to ask their warriors for vigorous attacks on fellow Hunters," the chief of staff (or First Assistant, as the Hunters called him) said. He was a middle-aged, almost aggressively moderate Warbander, with an obvious aptitude for staff work and an equally obvious reluctance to offend any faction or senior.

If I was as uncertain as he is who'd be running things after the war, I might be the same. This thought damped but did not eliminate Langston's irritation at hearing obvious conclusions recited for the third time.

"What does this imply in terms of our reply?" Langston asked.

"Attacks will come against the Federation," the chief said. His claws tapped the display in the center of the conference table. "Against Kharg, against Task Force Olufsdottir, or possibly against Fourth/218 watching the Alliance frontier.

"So we should contemplate having our mobile reserve able to land on or in the rear of Coordination forces attacking any of these three. A more self-contained mobile reserve than we have been planning, not requiring air support or more than tactical lift, once it has landed."

He continued, laying out details with the care of a Senior Staff Course graduate. Langston was impressed; Banfi looked both impressed and flattered. Very likely the chief of staff had decided that Marshal Banfi's goodwill was most important; if that led to sound tactical planning, so much the better.

"We still have to consider what will happen if those Legions are not friendly or the Coordination has effective ships," Boronisskahane said. "I am not an expert in war—"

Langston would have sworn he heard Isha Maiyotz mutter, "Refrain from stating the obvious."

"—but it seems that until they know we are not, we should not weaken any of our positions to form reserves. The Confraternity militia is ready to take the field."

Not against Coordination Warbanders or Tribal Cohorts with their tails up, you fur-brained commissar!

"If we had to worry about those Legions, I might agree with you," Banfi said, with the grin he used to conceal particularly big lies. It made him look like an aging tree-tiger, pretending to be fit only for lying in the sun.

"But I have received a communication that indicates we have nothing to worry about. It has told me the name of the senior Legion commander."

"If this is so important, why was it not sent to me?" Boronisskahane snapped. What was left of his ruff was up and his ears were vertical, ready to swing forward.

Because three independent Hunter planets didn't send their best Legions to be your errand-runners, Langston thought. Maiyotz started so that he wondered if she'd read his mind.

Banfi laughed. "Do you remember a certain picture, of a Confraternity flag flying over a battered building on a planet I need not name?"

Everyone either did or was unwilling to admit a lapse of memory. Boronisskahane was the only one who spoke.

"Of course. The Confraternity has not forgotten your courage, or the weak spines of your seniors."

"Neither has Egobar Shorl. He is the one standing on my right, with a bandage where one ear used to be. Well, the leader of those Legions coming to Linak'h is Sarfas Shorl, Egobar's son."

"I did not expect you to fall into the human habit of seeing the Hunters as furry children, with a child's loyalties." Boronisskahane growled.

Isha Maiyotz glared, but Banfi spoke first. "Would you say that to Shorl? I doubt that your years and rank among the Confreres would save you from a challenge. Sarfas Shorl will not be putting his Legions between the Administration and the Coordination out of loyalty to me. He will be doing it out of loyalty to his father, to the Confraternity, to the Planetary Republic of Chadl'hi, and to good sense."

Boronisskahane lowered his head and made the claw-scrabbling gesture of submission. It left marks in the table-top. Langston wondered if Maiyotz would otherwise have assaulted her colleague. Her face would certainly have done well as a model for a battle-demon mask.

Friendly Legions removed one worry, but they'd had two. If Coordination ships appeared when *Shenandoah* was off herding the reinforcements safely planetward, what then?

Charlemagne:

Josephine Atwood's next meal was like the previous ones. Stir-fried vegetables (she recognized a combination she'd had twice before), bits of meat (this time what might be synthetic chicken, but highly seasoned), rice crackers, fruit juice, water. Adequate and well balanced, even to providing enough fiber. She could live on these meals for months, although it might be years afterward before she could step inside an Asian restaurant.

As before, they turned off the lights when they opened the slot to deliver the food. Her eyes couldn't adapt to the darkness fast enough to let her glimpse who was outside the slot. She couldn't even tell if it was an organic being or a robot, although faint mechanical noises suggested either a robot or machinery in the corridor outside.

What happened shortly after dinner was a break in the routine. The lights went down again, the empty containers vanished back through the slot (this time she was almost sure she saw a jointed arm, but it could have been a robot's waldo or a human's augmented prosthetis), and this time the lights did not come back on.

Instead, a portion of the wall slid open. The lighting outside was so bright that Atwood was dazzled. She threw up one hand to shield her eyes, then heard a male human voice (or a simulation of one) say:

"That would not be wise."

Before she could guess what "that" might be, the door closed and the cell lights came back on. They showed her a clearly human figure, wearing a totally anonymous coverall, low half-boots, and a belt with a trio of gas grenades hooked to it.

Atwood decided not to reassure her visitor that she hadn't been planning an attack. Any attempt to placate him would imply that she thought placating him would do her some good. Neither her training nor the facts of the situation led her to believe that. Instead she assumed the lotus position.

"Aren't you going to strip?" he said. Definitely male, or

else a sophisticated voice mask. Possibly built into his face mask—those features were too regular to be natural, unless he'd had major reconstructive surgery.

His hands were bare, though, and the backs showed fine dark-brown hair. Other things about him couldn't be disguised, either—he was medium height, stocky build, excellent condition (to the point of being potentially attractive, under other circumstances), and carried himself in a way that said "military" to Atwood.

Military or police, she corrected herself.

"Well?"

She realized he'd been seriously waiting for an answer. She thought for a moment of taking something off, or even everything, making a joke of it. Then she decided that his tone hadn't been humorous.

"I have a guest. A hostess follows her guests; preferences. You seem to prefer clothing."

"I prefer not to have my people wondering if you are available." *Anglic is his native language, and somewhere he's learned to speak precisely.*

"If you are using people who confuse being comfortable while exercising with availability, then I suggest you are employing a very poor grade of staff."

"You might not care to learn their qualities firsthand."

"If you have your people under proper discipline, I will not be in any danger unless you give orders to have me raped. Then you will be adding a second capital crime to your first, kidnapping. If your people are not properly disciplined—"

"Shut up!"

For a moment Atwood thought he was about to strike her. That seemed possible. The other threat seemed less credible.

If she was an asset, it would help to keep her alive, healthy, and witness to as little as possible. If she was expendable, then she would consider herself a dead woman who still breathed, and stopping her breathing might be an expensive proposition for her captors.

Then Mr. Mask would have discipline problems if he hadn't had them before, and he might need those gas grenades after all.

Atwood was looking so ostentatiously at the ceiling that she didn't see the men leave. She only heard the door hiss shut. Then the lights went off. She thought she heard raised voices, but at the same time the temperature started dropping.

Highly sophisticated, quick-acting temperature controls, she mentally noted, as if she was editing an interview. Which, come to think of it, was exactly what she had to do, to make sure it was fixed in her mind for afterward.

Linak'h:

Two Hunters took their places on either side of the motorized pallet. A third tapped control buttons in the rear. The pallet whined and rolled out the rear door of the lifter, down the ramp, and into the trees.

At that point it vanished from Brokeh su-Irzim's sight, but shadowy figures, the clink of tools, and the pop and crunch of crating material coming off indicated that the working party was at hand. He looked at the time. With no miracles and only a little good fortune, in a half-watch the Baernoi Territory's Hunter Field Force would have satellite communications.

Strictly speaking, they would be space-relay communications; *Perfumed Wind* was not a satellite and F'Mita ihr Sular would probably extract barehanded the tusks of anyone who said so. But names mattered little, compared to capabilities. With the newly delivered antenna on the ground, the Field Force could now link to the ship, the Inquirer headquarters, and even the Governor.

Su-Irzim picked up his field bag and slung it over one shoulder, then followed the antenna down the ramp and into the trees. The lifter had whined off into the darkness before he caught up with the antenna.

He skirted the working party, looking for either Sarlin or Zeg and seeing neither. He did see Solidessouf, surrounded by half a dozen armed Hunters and watching the night forest in a way that hinted of many more hiding close by.

To su-Irzim's surprise, the twin rose and saluted.

"Commander Zeg is leading a patrol toward the shore. He thinks the next battle may bring more fighting over the Gulf."

If the battle was half the size everyone seemed to be

expecting, it probably would. Between the allies' air-rescue services and the cold waters of the Gulf, no other stray pilots had washed up on the Baernoi shore. Even Zeg had so far drawn the line at actually taking his Field Force into the Governance.

"It is well to keep the Scaleskins' hirelings looking behind them," su-Irzim said. "What of Commander Sarlin?"

"He is with our guest."

"How does she?"

"Well enough. Our food sits well enough on her stomach. I also think she has begun to understand what our allowing her to go armed means. Indeed, she lacks for nothing except a male of her own race."

"I am sure her present situation has taken away her interest in such matters."

"Oh, be not so sure of that, Commander. Pilots are a special breed. I remember one my brother and I met—"

Su-Irzim listened to Solidessouf's bedchamber memories as long as he thought politeness dictated. It was really quite an unbending by either of the twins, to talk so with him, never mind bearing messages. Sarlin must have found something important to discuss with Lieutenant Nalyvkina, to turn Solidessouf into a messenger to an Inquirer with little field experience.

Respect deserved to be repaid by respect. He would not before now have trusted the Assault Forcer with this message. He might not have done so now, if it had been going to Zeg instead of Sarlin. Zeg was still a trifle slow to obey su-Irzim. He acknowledged that the Inquirer was effectively chief of the Inquiry mission now, but preferred to have orders come through his half-brother (in itself a miraculous improvement over a year ago).

The two People found a discreet thicket where they could be out of hearing of everyone except the work gang, who were making too much noise as they enthusiastically dismantled the station's packing.

"I hope those furry gentlefolk will know where to stop tearing things apart," su-Irzim said.

"Oh, they have two or three Confreres from over on the Wild Continent with them. One of them maintains that sort of equipment for a living."

"I thought the Wild Continent had none."

"He did not say that he worked on the Wild Continent,

just lived there." Su-Irzim must have looked as bewildered as he felt, because Solidessouf shrugged. "I think as does Commander Zeg. We do not even know yet how little we know about the Hunters."

This might be an explanation but could not be an excuse for the Governor's message. Su-Irzim took a deep breath.

"The Governor wants you to turn Lieutenant Nalyvkina over to him."

"The Governor has gold between his ears as well as on his tusks," was the mildest thing Solidessouf said. The forest returned to silence only after he ran out of breath. "I suppose the goldtusk knows *something* about Federation laws and traditions with hostages?"

"He might. But I think he has it in mind that if all we ask for is information, those laws and traditions may not hold so firmly."

"With a Marshal commanding the Federation fighters?"

"Marshals have more discretion than lesser commanders."

"That does not mean fewer wits."

"Perhaps not. But let us apply our own wits," su-Irzim added. "Suppose we obtain everything the Governor wishes and again allow him the honor of presenting it to his superiors? We will of course send it as well to the Office of Inquiry, so no one will lose anything."

"Except skin, if the Federation holds firm."

"Our skin is at the disposal of the Khudrigate, by oath."

"That goldtusk is not the Khudrigate."

"Show some charity, Assault Director Solidessouf. If he had not pulled in all his fighters to protect the capital, he would not have closed four outposts. We found the satellite station in one of them."

"Anything else?"

"When I have seen Commander Sarlin, I will give both you and him a list." Solidessouf's eyes narrowed. "Come, Lawbound. Some are born good thieves, but that does not mean that no others can learn."

Charlemagne:

Josephine Atwood's second meal after the gang leader's melodramatic visit included soup as well as the usual ingredients. The soup was a clear broth, but it looked as if something was floating in it.

She fished out a strip of transparent message form. Or rather, it had been transparent. As she watched, it started darkening. She hastily dropped it back into the bowl and held the bowl close under her nose, where nothing in it would show on the invisible monitors.

Words took shape:

WHEN YOU FINISH THIS MEAL, YOU WILL FALL ASLEEP. WHEN YOU WAKE UP, PRETEND TO HAVE RECEIVED AN AMNESI-AC/COMEALONG COMBINATION. YOU MAY ALSO BE BLIND-FOLDED. WHEN THAT IS REMOVED IT WILL BE A SIGNAL TO JUMP INTO THE GRAY SOAKO DIADEM LIFTVAN ON THE PAD. THEN YOU WILL BE AMONG FRIENDS.

Atwood's immediate reaction was a desire to flush the message down the toilet and the rest of her dinner with it. A little reflection suggested that the drug had probably already entered her system.

Trusting these unknown friends was therefore the only sensible course of action. If she missed whatever opportunity they might have given her, both she and they might not have another.

Of course, the whole message might be a trick, to bring about her being "shot while attempting to escape." That would not help the kidnappers if they were caught; it might help keep them from being caught at all, or with their superiors.

If any—although it was likely that her visitor had some outside or higher-up assets, if only to cover the tracks he left diverting resources to support his gang. This operation might have been laid on at short notice; she suspected that people and supplies had been laid in well in advance.

Besides, there was that Soako Diadem. A hundred million stellars for one—no, a hundred thousand; if she'd said a hundred million she must be dreaming—and in fact the room was beginning to look like something in a dream or maybe when she hadn't had her morning tea—

She had just the energy to stagger to the toilet and drop the rest of the soup and the message into it. Then she fell to the floor, fortunately in reach of the flush plate. She had just enough strength to press it and just enough awareness to hear the toilet flushing.

Her last thought was that maybe she should have made herself vomit.

Linak'h:

The orders for Shores's battalion came at 0230. She was awake at 0231, dressed by 0235, and at Battalion HQ by 0240.

By 0245, she'd learned that everything was well in hand and the best thing she could do for her battalion was to stay out of the hair and gross anatomies of the people responsible for that situation. She hoped she wasn't rationalizing; this was the condition that every battalion ought to reach but few actually did.

She did have to make a decision at 0252—the position of her command lifter in the battalion column. It would be three rifle companies, the heavy weapons, and elements of the supporting units. More elements than would have been possible without the support of the Vics— they'd already sent in ten lifters and were supposed to have twenty-two more on the way. Shores reminded the Operations and Supply people to be sure that the support units got priority for the Vics' civilian-type lifters, then went out to the pads.

The LI of A Company was staying behind, to secure the area until the Vics were through it and act as a reserve for the Linak'h Brigade's right flank. They had one platoon suited up, and Shores spent her first ten minutes at the pads giving them hasty inspection. She listened to some good-natured grumbling about sitting out the big one and reminded a few people who she knew were up for decorations that they'd already been in some big ones. Did they want to be accused of hogging the glory?

She didn't quite get the last word out with a straight face. Even the armored platoon showed stains and patches, battledress had faded and frayed (for that matter, she was wearing her own last set of clean underwear), and even two weeks of war had given a few people the thousand-meter stare.

She wondered what she looked like, then remembered

the words for it. "Warriors for the working day"—Henry V's army at Agincourt. But there weren't any finely armored opponents to set against her plain-clad people. Nobody anymore believed in trying to make a battlefield less hideous by dressing up the corpses in fancy uniforms. She supposed this was progress of a sort.

She walked out beyond the LI positions into the cleared area between them and Pad Three. Maybe that wasn't perfectly smart, but the snipers were long gone, the crazies would get her when and where they pleased, and none of her ghosts would talk to her in the light and chatter of the company position.

She started as a shadowy figure slipped across from the supply dump toward Pad Three. She had a moment's feeling that she'd thought a little too loudly about ghosts. Then the figure reached the pad, and cockpit lights in one lifter showed a human face, young, thin, and male, and a box being handed in through an open window.

The sentries' challenge alerted the Victorians. By the time Shores had identified herself, the cockpit lights were out. She still remembered the lifter's position, and strode along the line until she came to the right one.

There was enough light from the powered-up displays to show her a couple of faces she knew. Kathy McGuire, who with her father had rescued Elayne Zheng from the Roskill Mountains on Victoria, and BoJo Johnson, war hero on Victoria and stowaway to Linak'h aboard *Somtow Nosavan*.

"Johnson. What the Hades are you doing here?"

"Riding scattergun." He seemed to mean that literally; there was one across his lap, and the mysterious box was strapped into the seat beside him.

"What's that?"

"Some spare equipment," McGuire said. "I thought we were authorized—"

"That depends on what it is," Shores said. "There's also the matter of an underage—"

"Hey, they weren't checking ID's at the pad," Johnson put in. "You have a problem with that?"

Shores mentally reviewed the alternatives to having Johnson forcibly removed from the lifter, including doing the job herself. In a pinch, she could sacrifice her dignity to preserve BoJo's; the kid had guts if not much sense.

Or was it senseless, if you had a score to settle and were

old enough to hitch a ride to where you could settle it? BoJo wouldn't have to sit out the battle wherever they had Sophia and Peter now that the next round was coming up. He wouldn't be at the mercy of strangers; he could fight and if that was the way it worked out, die, among his own people.

"I heard about your father, Colonel," McGuire said. "We're sorry."

"Not half as sorry as those furry—" Johnson began.

"BoJo, shut up," McGuire said. The affection didn't sound quite maternal; Shores wondered if BoJo had continued to have an eye for older women. Although McGuire was—what, something like twenty-three Standard?—and from the perspective of Shore's thirty they both seemed barely pubescent. Or was it not her thirty years but just the last twenty days?

"All right. Trade. You show me what's in that box, Johnson, and you go."

He must have been expecting this, or else started unpacking. The lid came off, showing a under-barrel Mark 108 grenade launcher.

"It's supposed to fit most twelve-gauges," Johnson said. "I figured I might want something with a little more range."

"Spare me the details," Shores said. She wanted to rest her forehead against the night and dew-chilled hull of the lifter. "I suppose you also stole some grenades."

"Our load's half ammo," McGuire said. "Want to see the forms one of your Supply people filled out?"

"Since I'm sure you have them, no," Shores said. She fixed Johnson with her best imitation of Marcus Langston's laser stare. Either it wasn't very good or he was impervious to authority that couldn't really *do* anything to him.

Probably both. I wish my father was around to hear about this. He'd laugh his head off.

"Go ahead. You're illegal, immoral, and probably untrained. If you kill yourself with that launcher, no problem. But if you kill any of my people with it, I'll personally shove it up you all the way to the tonsils, *then* fire it."

Johnson made a mock-delicate gesture of disgust. "Oooh, how messy!"

Shores started to laugh. The urge died when a corporal

ran up. "Colonel, the rest of the Vic lifters are coming in. So is a flight from Brigade Support."

"We're not going to sit and nurse—" Johnson began, then McGuire put a hand half-caressingly over his mouth.

"Yes, you will, if that's the order," Shores said. "Anything else, Corporal?"

He motioned for her to move away from the lifter, then lowered his voice. "They've got a report of an unidentified ship inbound. Close, big, and fast."

Charlemagne:

Josephine Atwood was in an elevator with at least three other people. A small, slow elevator—but she'd never thought she was being held in a tall building. Charlemagne's cities were well policed, and with the manhunt that had to be on, too dangerous for her kidnappers.

That was all the blindfold let her know—that, and the fact that she'd been dressed in a coverall and shoes. Both were light but better than the paper-thin tunic and pants and bare feet of the prison cell.

Did that imply she was in Charlemagne's tropics or even its southern hemisphere? The planet's axial tilt was enough to give it Earth-like seasons, but the tropics were largely ocean and the southern hemisphere less heavily settled. No outlaw colonies, not on the Federation's capital, but a lot farther to walk to the nearest law-enforcement station or even the nearest communication box!

Maybe she'd better be careful before making a break. Know what she was breaking into, as well as out of. Unless it was life or death, and in that case she'd rather die in the wilderness than be slaughtered like a gourmet chicken. They couldn't dispose of her body if they didn't know where it was, either.

The elevator stopped. A rough hand in the small of her back pushed her forward. She was glad of the blindfold. It made it easier to pretend to be under the influence of the drugs (somebody had switched them; that much of the message was true) and also to hide her feelings. Right now her eyes would be showing a desire to bite that intrusive hand off at the wrist and shove it down its owner's throat.

The elevator door opened. She stepped out into the

open, feeling a cool breeze (early spring, not late winter) on her face, also sunlight. She smelled water and vegetation—lots of the second, and both close.

The breeze blew hard enough to distort voices, but she thought five or six more people were standing around her. Two of them were women, one was her visitor.

She was shoved forward again, but this time a second hand gripped her arm as the first one withdrew. Then a hand reached up toward her blindfold.

As fingers closed on the fabric, someone shouted. It was wordless, but she heard fear and uncertainty. Then the visitor's voice shouted. It held command, and also words.

"Keep it on!"

In two seconds Atwood fought one battle to control legs and bladder, a second for decision. Somebody was suspicious.

If she acted undrugged, they would be sure. If she let them increase the guard on her, she would be helpless.

Her hands leaped up and pulled the blindfold up. A stungun thumped close behind her, but the rounds *spatted* on somebody or something else. She needed one look to find the Soako Diadem, another to see that half of the people around her seemed to be wrestling with the other half. Only one gun out, that stunner, and the woman holding it didn't have a clean shot at anybody.

Except Atwood. She remedied that by diving into the nearest door of the Diadem and slamming it behind her, then slamming all the other doors and windows shut. Stun rounds whacked into the body and one smeared across a window but didn't touch her.

Get this bird into the air and escape that way? A moment told Atwood that the controls might have been beyond her even if they hadn't been locked down. Whoever was supposed to be in the Diadem to help her hadn't made it.

The only control accessible and unlocked was one that by law had to be—the emergency beacon. She slapped the plate for that, saw displays light up, then heard both the whine of the beacon and the shots of something more lethal than a stunner. A window starred and the passenger door dimpled inward.

The pilot's side window showed her a way out. The Diadem was parked on the very edge of the pad. Beyond the edge was a ten-meter drop to a stream, and the far bank of the stream was brushy up to the crest of the hill, where virgin forest began. Virgin or mature second growth (this was no time for botanical niceties) and looking as if spring was farther along than in the District—

Which means I may not die of hypothermia from going through that stream.

Atwood popped the door as one window blew inward, bringing a shower of fragments and a stream of curses. Someone stuck a pistol-wielding hand through the gap, and Atwood snatched up the largest fragment and slashed. She cut her own fingers but also the wrists in the window. Someone was screaming as she dove out the open door.

She was in midair before she remembered that the stream might not be deep enough to do more than kill her quickly by breaking her neck. Then she hit the water, going in much too deep to have that worry, so deep that she began to worry about ever seeing air again.

Her head broke surface, with the far bank almost within arm's reach. She tensed, anticipating a beam or round between her shoulder blades, but nothing happened as she staggered to her feet.

Nothing happened as she dashed up the brush-clogged slope either, tearing skin and clothes, losing one shoe, and yanking her hair several times on passing branches. The amount of shooting behind her was a possible explanation, but by the same token the farther she got from that amount of firepower, the better.

She stopped just inside the forest, because her breath was gone and she needed to massage a cramp out of her left calf. So she saw the Diadem lift off, wobbling as if it were damaged or people were fighting over the controls. She saw someone run to the other lifter, a military-surplus model she didn't recognize, and come out with a sinister-looking tube.

When that tube hurled fire, the Diadem plunged out of the sky.

Atwood ignored the remains of the cramp and the hot sand in her lungs and lurched to her feet. She couldn't tell who'd won the fight among the kidnappers. If it wasn't her friends, her visitor and his hardheaded crew might still be after her.

It wouldn't make sense. The emergency beacon might have survived the crash and would certainly have been picked up. Somebody would be showing up, possibly not with the muscle to fight these people but certainly with a radio to call for help. They would surely find an incriminating number of dead bodies and other things that made police people suspicious.

If her visitor had sense, he and his friends would be exiting the area in a heavy attacker and looking for a fast ship out-system. If they didn't have sense, they might hang around to try adding her to the body count.

Linak'h :

"Processor to all units. We have confirmed the incoming ship as hostile. Repeat, the incoming ship is a confirmed hostile contact. Standard deployment until we know their target. ETA to engagement distance for Processor is one-two-five minutes. Repeat, Processor will be engaging in one-two-five minutes."

Elayne Zheng acknowledged for Gold One with an electronic pulse. She knew the dry mouth would pass, with time or even a cup of water. Right now she couldn't have spoken if a Baernoi Fleet was launching missiles from orbit.

Speaking of missiles . . .

Gold One had taken on a fresh, mixed load. More air-to-ground than air-to-air, but they'd had their laser trued and toned aboard *Shen* the last time they docked for maintenance. Also, some of the air-to-grounds could be switched, and there'd probably be targets for the ones that couldn't be.

This ship had to be coming in as part of a coordinated (sorry about that) offensive, a second try at crippling the Federation forces on Linak'h. Was that Pussy convoy coming in also part of it? If so, they were late, and anyway they'd have *Shen* watching them for so much as a twitched tail.

Shen could keep the newcomers honest, if they needed it (and Zheng still wasn't prepared to bet much on the honesty of live Catpeople). Her own job was senior EWO of the attackers who were the last line of defense for the ground-pounders, if they needed it.

Zheng hoped *Justice* would prevail. To the gods of all her five ancestral strains, she prayed respectfully that both she and *Shen* would have a very dull night.

Twenty-three

Charlemagne:

Josephine Atwood heard no signs of pursuit, even after the firefight behind her died away. She did hear two lifters taking off. As far as she could tell, both went the same way and neither came over the forest.

She still went to ground until the last whine of their fans faded into the wind. Then she started moving roughly northwest, as far as she could tell from the sun, climbing steadily toward the crest of the hills. She avoided the open as much as possible, not only for safety but to stay out of the wind.

The tunic and trousers didn't seem as heavy as they had, and the wind seemed both stronger and colder. Of course, part of it had to be her being soaked to the skin. (She would have given ten years of her life right now for dry socks and her oldest pair of hiking shoes.)

The crest of the hill was open. She found a ravine that a spring had cut as it flowed downhill and crossed most of the crest hidden in its shadows and brush. She occasionally looked up, but saw only blue sky, with streamers of cloud to the south and no air traffic.

A look down from the boulders around the spring showed Atwood at least three farms. Probably hobby or vacation farms, on this kind of ground, and it was too late for winter vacations and too early for summer ones. The best she could hope for was being able to break into one and find food, clothing, shelter, and maybe even communications (assuming her former captors weren't waiting for her to reveal her location—paranoia was even more functional in fugitives, she decided, than in media work).

She was less than a hundred meters from the sensor border of the nearest farm when a young woman stepped out from behind a clump of wickbranch. She was young enough to be Atwood's daughter, which would have been more reassuring if she hadn't been pointing a police-grade stunner at the fugitive.

"Identify yourself, please." The tone also had a police flavor to it.

What was there to lose?

"Josephine Atwood, Forces Command correspondent for Trans-Rift Media."

"Himmel!" the woman exclaimed. Then she appeared to speak into a throat-mike-and-earplug com set. No, she did speak, but in what Atwood recognized as Germanic without being able to understand more than three words.

Atwood stood silent, carefully keeping her hands in sight. She couldn't help thinking that the rest of her was also in sight from the air, as well as exposed to the wind. Also, in properly suspensful dramas, the first person to help the fugitive always turned out to be in the pay of the villains—

"My grandmother—" the woman began, then started and whirled to the left, so violently that Atwood wanted to fling herself on the ground in case the stunner went off.

"Tonia, du bist einer . . . !" Atwood couldn't follow the rest, but doubted it was complimentary.

A red-haired girl about eight Standard appeared from the underbrush, wearing a coverall, boots, and a totally unrepentant grin. "Excuse me," the woman said. "Tonia was not supposed to follow me or anyone else guarding Grandmother's boundaries. We could not be sure who might come from the old hospital, after we heard the news of your kidnapping."

Atwood's face must have conveyed exaltation mixed with confusion. The woman shifted the stunner's aim without slinging it, and kept her eyes roaming about the landscape as she stepped forward.

"Forgive me. My name is Yeda Dobusch, and this is my grandmother's summer home. She sent me and my brother Dieter up here when she heard of the kidnapping. She suspected the people at the old hospital, but could not convince the new Prefect to investigate.

"Prefect?"

"Of Police." Yeda's description of the area meant nothing to Atwood, but she felt weak with relief at the mention of "police." Although if the present Prefect didn't get along with his predecessor, Yeda's grandmother—

"I would like some dry clothing and a hot drink, if you can manage those," Atwood said. "Also, I would like to talk to your grandmother, and have her call Forces Command without calling anybody else."

"You think—?"

Atwood shrugged. "I'm almost past thinking. It's more of a feeling. The fewer people outside Forces Command who know where I am, the better. At least until we get trustworthy reinforcements."

Something like a battalion of Light Infantry, with a few heavy attackers to chase down those lifters.

Linak'h:

Candice Shores lifted off with the third flight of her battalion, a few seconds before 0325.

At 0400, with false dawn in the west, the incoming ship was positively identified as hostile (or at least the troops in the fields got that word). Almost before Shores had time to assimilate that, the next order came: all troop movements were to cease within ten minutes. Troops outside established secure areas were to ground and establish their own.

Shores cursed. She was certain the same tension was producing the same results in other lifters throughout the battalion. It was SOP and even common sense to ground lifters and disperse their troops when an air-space battle threatened. In the air, troops were a concentrated, vulnerable, high-value target. On the ground, they could use the infantryman's oldest weapon, the shovel, and the oldest ally, the earth itself, against anything, including fusers.

Neither of these might be enough if your battalion came down all over Hades's half-hectare, most of the people not knowing where they or anybody else was, with the possibility that the enemy was present, with anything from snipers to long-range rockets, possibly able to get between the troops and their lift with anti-vehicle weapons.

One risk balanced another—and what Langston and Banfi had worked out said plainly where they thought the greater risk lay. They might even be right. The incoming ship was unlikely to get down low in range of Federation ship-killers. If it disrupted allied AD over even a limited area, however, the Coordination's remaining TacAir would surely take advantage of it, and a lightning raid that caught a battalion in the air could give the Coordination a morale-boosting victory.

Shores wanted to piss on the Coordination's morale, preferably from a great height, not boost it. She ordered her battalion to assume the best tactical formation they could in five minutes, spend three more scanning for possible hostile presence, then ground. At nine minutes fifty seconds, Shores's command lifter was on the ground on the edge of a field of overgrown gene-tailored rye.

She was the first out, but waited until everyone else had exited the lifter before she joined the march into the tree cover. She'd just nestled into a pair of tree roots when the Assistant Operations Officer came up.

"You forgot this, Colonel." He handed her the personal bag she vaguely remembered packing back at base. It held *Wild Boers,* a well-packaged piece of her birthday cake, and a flask of brandy decorated with a satirical self-portrait of her father.

"Thanks."

That was just like Captain Iqbal. He looked like a beautiful boy, too young to be out after curfew on many planets, but Linak'h was his third campaign. If there were medals awarded for working eighteen hours a day to keep the Operations section running smoothly, he had earned one several times over.

"Oh, I do not recall you ordered electronic silence."

"I didn't. Get to the point."

"D Company reported heat signatures about two kloms from their intended LZ position, bearing two-eight-oh. They moved the LZ back to four kilometers except for one squad that landed on the original position. They have deployed sensors and were being reinforced by a platoon with an SFO at last report."

"I trust you told them to go ahead."

"Oh, yes. We had no orders not to investigate anything we could reach on the ground, that I heard."

Shores hadn't heard any either. But it might not be too useful, making contact with the enemy when you couldn't take to the air yourself, and if he did your own TacAir might be too busy to deal with him!

Aboard U.F.S. *Shenandoah*, the Linak'h System:

Fifty-one hours out from Linak'h, *Shenandoah* and her escorts made their rendezvous with the incoming merchanters.

Two hours later, the combined convoy started for Linak'h. *Shenandoah* rode in the center of the whole formation, surrounded by the four Merishi ships. In a larger globe were the nineteen Ptercha'a ships, a motley collection if ever sensor readings told truth. *Lysander* was well out in front, four attackers formed a square around the globe, and four more hull-rode *Shenandoah,* ready to launch on five minutes' notice.

It was a non-standard formation, but in the Linak'h war, the word "standard" had been vented out the wastewater pipes many days ago. It had the advantage that Merishi and Ptercha'a could easily avoid collision or interference, but could not easily shoot at each other without hitting *Shenandoah* (which the Ptercha'a certainly would not risk) or being easily hit by the battle cruiser (which the Merishi would be equally careful to avoid).

There was also the matter of the rearguard. Some coverage of the rear hemisphere was provided by the four Federation outriders. But Liddell wanted long-range coverage; any hostile moves were likely to be from the rear.

Shen could have taken that position, but her sensor signature would have been detectable 200,000 kloms away. With that much warning, nobody but an improbably foolish enemy would be sucked in.

Liddell didn't want merely a passive watch against the Coordination's remaining ships, she wanted to read serial numbers on their debris. Apart from Linak'h and the convoy, there was *Roma,* limping home lightly escorted, possibly a match for a heavy cruiser, possibly doomed to be the next Federation capital ship lost in this campaign if she ran into any serious opposition.

Instead, the Merishi transport *Ged-Yauntzaff* with the Victorians aboard brought up the rear, sweeping the rear hemisphere with her own sensor suite. The sensor signature confirmed (not that Liddell needed it) that at least one Merishi merchanter carried warship-grade sensors.

Anything the Merishi sensors picked up, however, was relayed to *Shen* through the Victorian party, particularly the *Somtow Nosavan* command ground now justifying their return to Linak'h.

It helped that Admiral Longman was no longer in the chain of command. Admirals of vast seniority and limited combat experience might object later to trusting the convoy's safety to Merishi sensor operators relaying data through such an odd couple as Marder and Longman. But they were far away and their objections far in the future; the Golden Vanity could have objected more effectively from closer up.

Liddell thought she saw what the Merishi intended. They could cooperate with the Federation, but by having the data relayed through a human liaison, their cooperation became deniable. If Space Security's wrath loomed over them, they could always point an accusing claw at the treacherous behavior of the humans they had hosted aboard their *very own ships*.

The Merishi merchant princes, Liddell decided, might actually aspire to rule inhabited space. But, wiser than their own Space Security, they had apparently realized that with the Ptercha'a emerging as free agents, it would be well to be ready to meet their price. *No doubt from their point of view it is only a logical revision of the original practice of hiring Ptercha'a mercenaries.*

Meanwhile, there was a fifty-plus-hour voyage to Linak'h and twenty-three nominally friendly ships to bring safely to the end of it.

"Pavel?

"Commodore?"

"Message to all ships. Federation vessels will be at Alert Two until we reach Linak'h and unload the Legions or all hostile ships are accounted for. Ships in convoy can maintain whatever Alert status they please, unless we are attacked.

"If they don't go to maximum Alert then, I will not be responsible for their safety in space. And if I meet them dirtside, I will put laxatives in their drinks!"

"Understood."

Linak'h:

Candice Shores heard D Company's firefight before she heard about it. First her command lifter's acoustic sensors picked up small-arms fire. Then signal rockets and tube rounds lifted above the horizon, blazing in bursts of red and orange and trails of green and yellow. Finally, three secondary explosions rippled off in rapid succession, the last one so violent that Shores's first thought was that some fool had finally popped a fuser.

Everybody was already on Alert One, so Shores reported the sightings to Brigade, got an acknowledgment and an update on the ETA of the hostile ship (now about forty minutes), and promised to send more when she had it.

That took only five minutes, before D's CO figured out what had happened and reported—"an improvised composite of what I've heard from my people," as he put it. (Shores thought of reminding him that he could have been up forward seeing for himself, but Militia patrols no longer needed captains to hold their hands any more than the other troopers did.)

Apparently a patrol had been out linking up the two halves of the company by scouting a ground route over the three kloms between them. It ran into the point of a hostile troop movement, escaped detection, went to ground, and waited until the main body showed up.

It was worth waiting for—a number of ground vehicles, three up to six wheels, and some modified lift pallets that could be hand-towed under tree cover. The pallets also seemed to have onboard sensors; their escorts spotted the patrol and opened fire.

The patrol returned the fire. At the same time, the reinforcements they'd called for showed up, including a squad with heavy weapons. The heavy weapons killed four vehicles and produced the three secondary explosions, and in the confusion after the explosions all Company D units successfully broke contact, taking their three casualties with them.

"Good work," Shores said, and meant it. Three kloms in the dark across unknown territory in the time available was excellent going. Even if they'd cheated and used a lifter, doing it without alerting the enemy showed solid competence.

"We're going to pull the company into a single perimeter," the CO went on. "Or at least we will unless the enemy's reaction is so fast that my people will have to E and E. That'd take the company out of the battalion OB, and I imagine you don't want that right now."

Two companies plus the Vics, even well supplied and with plenty of lift and sensors, were not a promising proposition against a Coordination force large enough to have hidden out both ground and lift transport. *Call it a cohort-plus.*

Shores ordered the D Company CO to execute and got back to Brigade with the promised update. They were grateful; they also had bad news, which Barbara Hogg at least had the decency to deliver herself.

"We're going to have to cut back on that promised extra lift," she said. "Forces just told me to be ready to jump a Coordination formation from across the border. Not to jump the border, you understand, just be ready to hit them the moment they move out. I'm putting in OP's in the critical areas. Supporting them is going to take some of what I had hoped to spare for you. Making three battalions do the work of four is going to take the rest."

"No problem," Shores said. "Just as long as you don't need A Company. I need those LI to build a mobile sensor-and-snipe net linking my companies."

"They're yours, Candy, but I can't move them for you."

Shores looked at a map and a clock. Wiser heads at Forces Command had modified the tactical-movement freeze; it was no longer the total kind that let the AD people engage any aerial movement at will. Shores thought those were a resort of lazy AD people and maybe CO's who were more scared of casualties from friendly fire than they were of disaster to immobilized infantry.

"We can improvise, although the timing's going to be close."

"Don't cut it too fine. If you do have a couple of cohorts there, you can be damned sure they'll have air support the moment it's safe."

"We'll be good *and* careful."

Knowing that Karl Pocher was the field leader of the Vics didn't make it easier to reach him through the venerable Victorian communications gear. He finally went off the air for three minutes, then came back on over a much better set, that Shores could tell had both scrambler and burst capability.

"I'm using McGuire's lifter," he said. "They've improvised a slightly more sophisticated com and sensor set than some of the others." Shores was tempted to ask if BoJo Johnson had a hand in this, but she resisted the temptation.

She outlined the Vics' job—dump all their embarked supplies, then divide their troops into two groups. One would be security for an LZ around the supplies, to which the reset of Third/Linak'h would retire as soon as feasible. It would be centered around an old but secure Coordination base in caves under one of twin hills, Heights 349 and 380.

The other Vics would take the lifters back to the old battalion base, pick up the LI, and return to the new LZ. The LI would deploy from there, depending on the tactical situation.

"Let's call it LZ Ursula," Pocher suggested.

"I'm not sure—" Shores began.

Pocher cut her off. "Your father's lady was one Hades of a good soldier. Why not?"

Why not indeed?

"No problem. But get started on that unloading. If you're done before the Coord ship comes in, you can start for the pickup as soon as the space fight's over."

Linak'h:

"*Justice* reports five minutes to engagement," Captain Moneghan's voice said in Elayne Zheng's ears. "Enemy ship is identified as a *Bzeryni*-class cruiser, with a nonstandard sensor suite."

A throat-clearing, then:

"There may be other nonstandard goodies aboard that ship, so I don't want any of you in brainlock until she's turned into orbital debris. *Justice* may prevail. She may leave some work for us.

"We're also getting scattered AD contacts all around the compass. I have a nasty feeling Intelligence was right. The Coordination hid more than supplies when they went to ground at the end of the first week. How much more, I expect we're about to find out.

"The good part is that if they shoot that off, it's likely to be their last shot. The bad part is there is going to be a lot of target-rich airspace in sight of everybody's AD people. Check your IFF, and hang a flag out the window besides."

Zheng checked for hostile contacts that needed interpreting or communications relays that the computer couldn't handle. Her job tonight could turn from satellite surrogate to AD coordinator to SFO and back again in a five-minute cycle.

Nothing in either category showed up. She switched to the tactical display. The tally of hostile activity was mounting, and the map showed a concentration in the south and east. That meant good hunting for somebody; she hoped the hunters included Candy Shores.

Then the sky flamed bright and angry.

Justice's captain had deferred to both Moneghan's local experience and his combat record, if not to his junior rank. He had carefully stayed over Administration territory or over the ocean, at worst over the Wild Continent. Attackers substituting for satellites kept him plugged into the communications net.

They did not warn him against the covert missiles left in orbit around Linak'h by the Coordination's dead satellites. Some of them remained inside the hulks. Others had drifted clear of disintegrating orbiters. Some of these had been picked off as orbital debris or become too inert for even the incoming cruiser's signals to reactivate them.

None of them had been recognized for what they were. They were too heavily shielded and otherwise disguised for that, short of being boarded and physically dismantled. Both scaled and furred, the weaponeers who installed the missiles had done their job well, even if that job took them to the edge of the law. Planting mines in free space in peacetime was clearly prohibited by everything from the Kirov Convention on down. That these satellites became minelayers only after war began was a technicality.

The Coordination was not interested in the courts; they wanted a hard kill on *Justice*. Twelve missiles received the incoming ship's signal. Eight of them got under way. *Justice* detected four and picked off three, but the fourth detonated, swamping the cruiser in an EMP that temporarily wiped out her sensor capability.

It was the wrong time for that to happen. Three of the missiles were accelerating from a lower altitude, masked against the planet (where Coordination EW stations were now jamming hard). They were also too nearly in line with *Justice* for any of her friends to get a clear shot, except the two attackers on low escort.

The two from high escort were maneuvering to give *Justice* a clear field of fire and evade the enemy ship. They were out of missile range, one had her laser down, and the EMP was scrambling the sensors of the other too badly for a laser shot.

So *Justice* was not only blind but naked when the three missiles closed. She remedied the second condition immediately, raising her shield, but that blocked her own missile launches and didn't block the enemy cruiser's laser.

It speared through shield and hull, to disrupt the internal power grid. Not for long, five seconds at most, but that was enough for electrical surges to ruin some equipment permanently. Also, lasers, sensors, and shield all went down for those same five seconds—and the leading missile needed only four seconds to close the distance.

It had a light warhead (missiles small enough to be hidden in a satellite and still have high performance had to cut corners somewhere), but two kilotons so close that the fireball touched *Justice*'s hull was enough. Penetration plus transmitted shock wave killed most of her crew with merciful speed; those who died slowly in isolated compartments of internal injuries, burns, or radiation overdoses were a minority.

Those unlucky ones were also revenged before they died. The two low attackers came up at high speed, one to either side of the dying cruiser. They hid in the EMP of the fatal hit and trusted that it had also fratricidally disarmed the warheads of any other hostile missiles.

It had, but the Coordination cruiser didn't know it. She locked on to the two friendly missiles that came racing past her target, lasered them both—and couldn't switch targets fast enough when the two attackers themselves closed to laser range.

The Coordination crew didn't have time to raise their shield before the lasers hit, and after that it didn't matter because their shield generator had taken a direct hit. They were trying to control venting air and water from the other hit when both attackers salvoed a quartet of short-range shipkillers.

From the number of hits they obtained, two apiece would have been enough. Unlike *Justice,* now drifting in orbit around Linak'h, the Coordination cruiser had been driving straight at the planet. When power, controls, and crew all died, she kept right on going.

Orbital surveys found the crater where she hit the side of an unnamed mountain on an unnamed island to the south of the Wild Continent, It was as well that she didn't hit the ocean; a forty-thousand-ton meteorite could have added tsunamis to the troubles of Linak'h's inhabitants. As it was, she obliterated most of a mountain.

Elayne Zheng had about two minutes to live after Moneghan announced the double kill. Like all the tactically assigned ships, Gold One headed for the deck when the serious space fight began. If the Coordination cruiser wanted to engage Federation air, she would have to come low and slow while Moneghan was still alive above her, or else fight her way through his cruisers first.

Gold One's dive leveled her out at the head of a valley with a name hard to pronounce even for one fluent in True Speech. In the Coordination's files, however, it had been conveniently labeled "Forward Air Eight."

Seven light attackers took off the moment the orbital missiles started moving. Their weapons loads varied, but Taidzo Norl's was about average—two air-to-air missiles, two air-to-ground rockets with cluster warheads, and a scrambler pod.

Also about average was the fact that only one of the air-to-air missiles launched when he came up the valley and saw a Federation attacker practically filling his windshield. Ten days in the wilderness was even harder on weapons than it was on warriors—and Norl would have wrestled *quljins* for a chance to return to civilization, or at least hot water.

The missile that launched barely accelerated to full speed before it hit. It struck Gold One from below and to starboard, penetrating the hull, sending the blast of its warhead almost vertically upward. In the path of the flame lay Elayne Zheng and her station.

The flame burned her, her own consoles crushed her, and fragments gutted her. She died quickly, but not too quickly to scream.

Charlemagne:

Admiral Kuwahara had come to the office so early that he'd skipped breakfast, and nerves had his stomach so tight that he couldn't have eaten anything even if the Delivery Menu had anything he liked.

Two consolations so far: Captain Fraziano wasn't in, and Fumiko didn't know about his skipping breakfast. The second might not be a problem, unless his reaction to stress moved permanently from his head to his stomach.

Then the first consolation and the stress both evaporated together as Fraziano burst into Kuwahara's office.

"The Empress is on the line to you," Fraziano shouted. "They've found Josephine Atwood!"

Fraziano wasn't cleared for even an edited version of what the study group was doing with Atwood, but the man only simulated a fool. Even off in one corner studying the other dual-sovereignty planets, he couldn't have helped noticing that Kuwahara and Ropuski, at least, were on edge over Atwood's disappearance.

There was also the little matter of some segments of the media who thought Atwood had been kidnapped *by* the Forces, for a variety of exotic reasons (at least three fantastic hypotheses per mediacrat was Kuwahara's estimate). They had everybody at Forces Command nervous over questions being asked in the Senate.

Kuwahara nodded dismissively. His screen came up as the door closed behind Fraziano.

"Good morning, Admiral."

"It almost deserves the name, Sho."

Baumann looked almost indecently well rested and relaxed. Kuwahara was quite sure she hadn't written off Atwood as merely an expended pawn. Her concern had gone as deep as his. Possibly vanity helped; the Empress was notoriously vain about aging well, and uncontrolled stress added years rapidly.

Kuwahara listened to a summary of Atwood's first debriefing. "Any leads on the mystery leader?" he asked, at the first break.

"None, but we're lining up a list of people whose alibis Pfalz can start checking."

"Is Pfalz still on the case?"

"The FSB is taking overall jurisdiction to coordinate everybody else, but for the moment they're leaving Pfalz in tactical command."

"Who are they trying to bribe?"

"The District police, or possibly nobody." Suddenly Baumann looked less sleek. "There's also the possibility that they don't like where this trail may lead. They want to leave Pfalz at the head of the line for rolling heads if something goes seriously wrong."

"I trust they're at least securing the safe house and searching the area. One or both of the factions in that shootout may have left more than dead bodies behind."

"They are, but I'm positioning a Ranger Team that will deal directly with the local police. That will solve the jurisdiction problem; they'll be deputized for work in the area until this is over."

What Kuwahara would have liked to do was send down a battalion of Light Infantry in full armor, have half of them stand shoulder to shoulder around Atwood until her kidnappers were caught, and have the rest search under every rock, leaf, and twig in the area for the kidnappers. Euphoria at the woman's rescue was battling with fury at those who had put her in danger in the first place.

Which includes you.

I didn't kidnap her.

No, but you kept her in harness after it became obvious that somebody was ready to play rough.

Kuwahara told his conscience to call him some other time.

We'll have to talk sometime.

This evening. Deal?

Deal.

He turned back to the screen. "How much publicity are we going to get over this? For that matter, how much do we want?"

"We'll get more than we want," Baumann said. "The danger level is if Aung Bayjar decides to pull out."

"I've come to think better of him than that."

"So have I. I even begin to wonder about that charge of graverobbing. But honest men also have their limits, and a day's no longer for him than it is for us. He may simply be too busy to help us."

"So we need to find a way to get the last man out on our own?"

"I didn't know you played baseball, Sho."

"I haven't had a bat in my hands for thirty years, and nobody ever asked me to turn pro when I did. I wasn't a hopelessly bad infielder, though."

"Keep your eye on the ball, then, Sho. This game's not over."

The subject shifted, to the confirmation of Ptercha'a Legions, an "Intervention Force," on their way to Linak'h. Baumann's tone didn't change; it said clearly that the FSB would not be the only body looking for heads if something went disastrously wrong in these last days of the Linak'h crisis.

Linak'h:

Since Gold One didn't go down, Candice Shores had committed her battalion to action before she learned of her friend's death. The process took place in stages.

Stage One was the Vics finishing their unloading and what had been christened the Transport Section taking off. They were going to fly an indirect route, by way of Komarovsk. The stop would let them recharge en route and maintain a higher cruise speed in the air, making up for the time lost by the dogleg, which was needed to keep them in known friendly territory. (The most direct route led back over an area which Shores would have assumed to be swarming with Coordination troops even if Brigade hadn't told her so.)

Stage Two was Karl Pocher's Security Section of the Vics settling in to hold LZ Ursula, reinforced by a platoon from B Company.

Stage Three was the tactical movement of Shores's three companies back to the LZ. The rifle units went on the ground, the support units by air. Also airborne was a unit of six lifters under Shores's personal command, acting as AOP's and light TacAir.

She knew she might be moving her people out of the way of the enemy, instead of concentrating them in the enemy's path. She considered the risk of looking overcautious more acceptable than the risk of having her battalion shredded in detail.

She wouldn't be able to form a serious blocking force until she got her LI company, several hours from now. Even then she couldn't fall back and bring in the heavy firepower until the heavy firepower became available.

From what she was hearing on the radio, that might take a while. The Coordination was putting everything in the air that would fly—and using the term "flying" very loosely. Some of the sightings reported were of machines that had no business being in combat at all, let alone by daylight over enemy territory.

The convoy of support units droned overhead, steering a wobbly course to the east. Just below the clouds, Shores thought she caught a glimpse of a heavy attacker. Heavies meant friend, but not necessarily a friend with eyes, weapons, and time to help her.

B Company reported moving out, then C. D reported being ready to move out, but it had a problem.

"A patrol went out at first light, to check some debris we sighted as we moved in last night."

"So?"

"A sniper hit them on the way back. Just one, the patrol leader thinks, but he has two WIA already and one can't walk."

Shores did not approve of being pinned down by single snipers, but Hunter snipers might be better than even seasoned militia could handle.

"Leave a squad behind with heavy weapons, to pin down the sniper and let the patrol disengage. Everybody else, move out. I'll bring the Flying Squad over your way and look things over. Give me coordinates on a good LZ, so I can lift your people out after we get the sniper."

Regulars could have climbed rope ladders or even ridden out in Kim harnesses. That was a little much for the Vics or the militia. The integration of four different companies into a single working battalion was good, rather than perfect. The addition of a variable number of enthusiastic Vics made a complex situation more so.

"Yes, ma'am. Oh, the patrol did reach the debris, but it

was too far out in a stretch of marsh to be examined. They say it might have been pieces of the first cruiser."

Intelligence had been on everybody's backs since the first night of the war, to produce wreckage from *Shenandoah*'s victim. Unfortunately the main hull had fallen at least fifty kloms inside hostile territory. Bits and pieces kept turning up, doing the same thing to Intelligence as appetizers or foreplay—making them want *more*.

"Get any pictures?"

"Yes."

"Tell the patrol, 'Well done.' "

Aboard U.F.S. *Shenandoah*, the Linak'h system:

Fifteen hours from Linak'h.

It would have been eight hours or maybe even six if the warships had been cruising alone. The convoy's speed had to be adjusted for the Ptercha'a ships. Some of them had to be Hive War veterans, and the Ptercha'a had less expertise at keeping old ships as sound as new ones.

Commodore Liddell patted the nearest console for luck, then remembered that it was from *Shen*'s latest refit. She reached a little farther, patted a century-old bulkhead, and returned to her scrutiny of the tactical display.

Almost time. It had been two hours since the trailer showed up, an hour since repeated refusals to obey requests to break off got it classified as hostile. Liddell knew it was possible she was about to make an excruciatingly terrible mistake. It couldn't be as bad as putting three friendly Ptercha'a Legions in danger.

The matter would have been as simple as algebra if they hadn't needed a quick victory. That ship had to be kept busy from the moment the shooting started, too busy to hit the convoy. It also had to be destroyed before it could shout for help or divert *Shen* long enough to let other ships hiding somewhere out there get at the convoy.

Pavel Bogdanov would be the star, whoever got the credit officially. His shiphandling and his assessment of the convoy's expertise were both essential. Space was big, ships were small, but nevertheless, several hundred people died each year in space collisions.

"Alert One," Liddell said. At the same time, her hand

slapped a plate on the communications board. A prere-corded code flashed out, heading for *Ged-Yauntzaff.*

On the intercom screen, Pavel was already watching the controls. At the transport's acknowledgment, he spoke quickly into his throat microphone.

Shenandoah shuddered and lights dimmed as Commander Fujita fed all the ship's power into bringing her to a dead stop in space. Everything and everybody was still intact and working when the battle cruiser shot past *Ged-Yauntzaff.* If Charles Longman had been standing at a port, Liddell thought, she could have seen what kind of earrings he was wearing today.

Then the battle cruiser was in open space, rapidly closing the distance to the trailer. Bombarded with nothing but words for hours, he'd grown overconfident, closing to less than a thousand kloms.

That was a distance now closing in minutes, as the trailer came racing up toward *Shenandoah.* Liddell watched the display, knowing that whether the other captain shot, fled, or decelerated, he could not do the one thing that might save him—raise his shield.

The other ship began to slow. As she did, *Shenandoah* launched her four hull-riding attackers, eight buses, and a cluster of proximity-fused short-ranged missiles to act as mines. Liddell knew that Zhubova would also be hovering over the laser controls.

The other ship suddenly had her sensor suite and her captain's mind overloaded with multiple rapidly approaching threats. A laser stabbed out, hitting one of the buses, killing its power but not destroying it. The ship maneuvered to pass through the sector that had been covered by that bus, apparently believing it safe.

The mines were waiting. Five of them went off, laying a disk of junk space across the ship's course. By now *Shen*'s telescopes were putting the ship up on Liddell's screen. So she saw the open launcher bay start hurling missiles into space. She saw one of them explode prematurely, and others tumble wildly out of control, victims of fratricidal fragments.

She even thought she saw the mine debris slam into the open bay, detonating the ready missiles inside. She certainly saw a long pennon of gas and debris spew out of the launcher. The ship's shield flickered, held long enough to generate impact-sparks as more debris hit, then died.

Liddell listened to a long string of negative readings as *Shenandoah* closed to within fifty kloms of the ship. Some of her crew might still live; she might even be repairable. As a weapon for this war, she was finished.

"Flag to Weapons. Well done. Pavel, get the backup attackers off. Does the boarding party have full armor?"

"Yes, and multi-species medical kits."

"Good." Law, ethics, and the potential intelligence gains all dictated boarding the ship if there was any chance of doing so safely. The other attackers could get the buses under control, retrieve any usable missiles and detonate the rest, and generally tidy up after a battle cruiser that still had a convoy to bring safely to Linak'h.

Linak'h:

Company D's troublesome sniper vanished before Candice Shores could reach the battlefield. He also vanished without inflicting any further casualties on the two squads engaged.

Win some, lose some.

She slapped down one pilot who wanted to spray "the sniper's most likely line of evasion." They might have friendlies or civilians in the area. They surely didn't have ammunition for anything other than confirmed targets.

Shores concluded by assigning Trigger-happy the job of hauling the two squads back to their company. She was tempted to have him haul them all the way to LZ Ursula, to keep him out of the fighting until he cooled off, but that meant one-sixth of her aerial firepower would be out of circulation for too long.

It was an hour after they finished grounding in rotation for a lunch and sanitary break, that they finally gained firm contacts. After that the Flying Squadron was seldom completely out of contact with the enemy until Fatherset. Sometimes it was only one or two lifters, but once it was all six and several times it was five.

Power charges ran low, but TacAir now had attackers to spare; air-docking and quick-charges kept the lifters flying. Ammunition ran low, but before it did the Vics had returned to Task Force Olufsdottir with their load of LI.

Splitting the LI into two lifts let the Vics bring a resupply of ammunition to LZ Ursula. After that it was a matter of sending one lifter at a time back to the LZ.

Energy and fluid levels ran low, and there was nothing to do about that but prayer, pills, and canteens. Shores let Konishi do most of the piloting; she was stretching the limits of her duty by personally leading the Flying Squadron at all. But this close to the enemy, and airborne, she was also getting a firsthand impression of their strength, morale, and weapons, and of the terrain over which they'd be advancing.

It was all air-to-ground work. The Coordination's forward-based TacAir had either died, fled north, or gone back under cover. Konishi muttered into his fruit juice over this. If he was going to be flying an ACP, couldn't some nice Catman obligingly present himself for an air-to-air kill?

"Like the one who hit Gold One?" Shores asked.

They generated more secondary explosions and drew more ground fire as the afternoon dragged on. Either they'd strayed over an enemy base area or the Coordination was pushing up supplies and heavy weapons to its advanced units.

One lifter died just after 1730, when late afternoon was beginning to turn into twilight. A missile killed its power, but low altitude and soft ground saved the crew. Shores led three of the Flying Squadron in circling the crash until the fourth lifter could land and rescue the crew.

A fused charge in the remaining rockets turned the lifter itself into useless wreckage. Calling in a pickup for the lifter would have meant committing substantial forces in the face of unknown enemy strength, with night coming on.

Brigade called right after Shores's decision to blow the lifter. Hogg was briskly approving.

"You've got your people where the enemy can't ignore them *or* overcome them," Hogg said. "Keep them that way. Oh, by the way. You are now Task Force Shores."

"Any other developments I should know about?"

"Ah—you may be on your own for a couple of days. We're fully committed along the border, and getting results too. Edelstein is largely tied down for now, preventing an attack on the Confraternity militia."

"I thought the Coordination was trying to avoid them."

"The Coordination aren't the only people on Linak'h trying to make trouble for us," Hogg said.

Linak'h:

A face with freckles under tan and dirt poked itself into the steam bath.

"Somebody to see you, Colonel."

"Tell him to come on in," Colonel Nieg said.

"It's a her, and wouldn't it be nice if she did?"

"I didn't know you were two-way, Sven."

"I'm a good Ranger. I love having secrets."

"Well, I'm a Ranger too, and I don't like being kept waiting. So somebody is female."

"Female, Afroam—"

"—about five cems taller than I am, light for an Afroam, and full-figured?"

"How did you guess?"

"That's one of *my* secrets, Sven."

It was Major Morley, as Colonel Nieg had suspected. He led her to his quarters with a towel tied around his waist and his clean fatigues over his arm.

"Any particular reason why you came out to interrupt my R and R?"

"I didn't come, I was sent."

"No problem with the supply-dump data, I hope."

"Quite the contrary. One of the things they asked me to bring out was thanks, to you and all your people."

"They were Ram Daranji's people, really. I just went along to help around the edges." *And felt more useful than I had in months. Or at least less worried about things out of sight and out of my control.*

"That's not what I heard."

"Never mind what you heard. What else am I supposed to hear?"

"You're wanted at Command HQ for a covert mission."

"What's the support?"

"None. This is more diplomacy than anything else. You're supposed to go in solo."

Nieg untied the towel and started pulling on his clothes. Either Forces Command had gone collectively insane, or else they'd discovered something important enough to justify using Major Morley as messenger and escort.

"What have they decided makes me uniquely qualified?"

"How well do you know Behdan Zeg?"

"Does this have something to do with his Hunter mercenaries?"

"It might. Apparently they've been keeping the coast of the Baernoi Territory clear of their Merishi counterparts. That's how they rescued Lieutenant Nalyvkina."

Nieg dropped his pants. His jaw was already sagging.

"Rescued?"

"She's armed and free to move around their camp. The estimate is that if we send somebody with rank in to escort her home, the Baernoi may talk more freely."

"Talk? You mean negotiate, don't you?"

Morley shrugged.

"I wonder if Marshal Banfi is behind this. It's stretching Federation law about hostages to rescue his aide's lover, you realize?"

Morley's face took on an expression that increased Nieg's respect for Herman Franke's courage, if not necessarily his sanity. Right now, he felt naked being in the same tent with her without a sidearm.

"Say that to Colonel Davidson or the Marshal, after you've asked yourself what you would do if Candy was in the same position." Her tone suggested mayhem deferred rather than rejected completely.

"I see what you mean," Nieg said, after a moment.

Morley looked at him as if he was something she'd had to scrape off her boot. "Do you? Have you told Candy you care that much?"

She took Nieg's silence as the answer. "Then I suggest you do it, or she can geld you with a dull knife and I'll hold her coat." She turned briskly. "I'll be at the pad. We're lifting in ten minutes."

Linak'h:

It was the left forward fan of Candice Shores's lifter that finally threw a blade. The blade hurtled into Konishi's side window. Fragments spilling loose from the inside gouged his cheek. He clapped a hand over the wounds, blinked to be sure he had vision in both eyes, then started adjusting both lift and fan power.

As he did, the left rear fan also went out, and displays flashed and squealed irritably with alarm signals. Konishi swore.

"Fragment damage must have taken out the power feed. I'd better set her down."

Shores nodded. The sour taste of frustration was in her mouth, not the hard-edged taste of fear.

The lifter settled down a few meters from a thicket of yin-thorn, with Shores already unstrapping herself. She switched the gun turret to emergency power and swung it in a complete circle. Behind them, the communications people already had the rescue beacon on and were breaking out the emergency gear. The gunner was doing the same with the carbines and ammunition.

"Anybody out there?" Konishi asked, reaching under the displays for the medical kit. One eye looked bloodshot, but he could apparently see out of both.

"Negative on visual contacts, and I didn't power up the other sensors."

The radio squawked. "Flyboy Three to Huntress. What's your situation?"

Shores nodded at Konishi. "We're down two fans. I have to check for further damage. Keep us company, will you?"

"That's a—"

Light like a flare poured over them. Shores shut her eyes to save her night vision. When she opened them again, she heard nothing but static on the radio. Konishi had cut off all power; as she groped her way toward the door she also heard the crackling of flames.

"Somebody gave their power pack a jolt with a heavy laser," Konishi said. He now had part of his cheek dressed, and was holding a second dressing in one hand. In his other he held two carbines.

"Thanks," Shores said. She grabbed one, checked her own sidearm's ammunition supply, and leaped down to the ground.

All five of the lifter crew were professionals; they spread out but moved toward the thickest cover. Lasers were line-of-sight and easily detectable. The one that killed Flyboy

Three had to be on the move already if its crew had any sense.

No lasers didn't mean no threat, as they discovered a moment later. Shores's barely restored night vision vanished again, as unboosted launcher rounds rained out of the sky. Flares joined them, but the yin-thorn caught fire and provided all the light they needed to see the lifter's destruction.

Or would have needed, if they hadn't been too busy scrambling uphill to look behind them. Before they stopped, they'd covered three hundred meters horizontally and climbed high enough to overlook the crash site.

They also saw the sky, and Shores caught her breath at the sight. Darkness on the ground did not mean darkness in space, for ships outside the planet's shadow. Moving up from the southern horizon, in a miraculously clear sky, was a constellation of ruddy sparks. Ships, lit by the Red Child, moving into orbit around Linak'h.

One larger spark seemed to hang from the zenith itself.

"Shenandoah," Shores said.

Konishi shook his head. *"Roma,* I think. There was something about her hitting orbit, about sixteen thirty.

Shores couldn't remember that. She did remember that she was now definitely away from her post.

Another thing she deduced, from the amount of firepower used against the two lifters: she was in the middle of the biggest enemy concentration yet.

Final conclusion: the rescue force should have a heavy escort. They might need it, to fight their way through. They also might just be able to use it, to catch the Coordination troops.

"Chief?"

She summarized her thoughts for Konishi. Dried blood flaked off his face as he raised his eyebrows. "Any of us an SFO?" was all he said.

"No, but we can have them drop one, or at least the equipment."

Shores sat down and started counting the magazines in her slice of the ammunition. The gunner handed her a pair of night goggles. She looked up to take them, and saw the communications people bent over their gear, checking connections and status displays.

Charlemagne:

On the screen, Lieutenant Pfalz looked as if he hadn't slept for days. Possibly he hadn't. Admiral Kuwahara had managed to sleep almost normally while Josephine Atwood was missing. So why did he feel as weary as Pfalz looked now, when Atwood was safe?

It was statistically improbable to the far side of fantasy that anyone Kuwahara knew would be the mystery man or even connected with the kidnapping. That wasn't the real point, however.

The real point was that the Forces' role in the whole Linak'h situation had slipped over the edge, from impropriety to crime, if not to outright treason. Admitting that had been painful. Giving it publicity was going to be worse.

It was also necessary. Washing dirty linen in public was always bad. Pretending that it wasn't dirty in the first place was worse. That was a lesson that should have been learned a long time ago, in the case of that Colonel Dreifuss or some such name who'd been accused of treason just for being a Protestant in a Catholic army. Or had he been a Moslem in a Christian army?

Anyway, if your linen was dirty, you turned on the washing machine, and didn't care who knew it.

Kuwahara realized that he had been contemplating historical precedents while Pfalz tried to stay awake. "Yes, Lieutenant. Do you have—?"

He'd been about to say "anything important." If Pfalz was calling at all—

"I think we have a chance to identify the mystery man. We have a description, fingerprints, and a recording. They don't match anyone in our files. The FSB says they're trying a match, but it may be in File Eight-nine."

Kuwahara nodded. "File 89" was code for the secure Forces Personnel file. The District Police did not have access to it. Technically the FSB did, but sometimes they just mentioned it, as a signal to the Forces to do their own investigating.

It was now the Forces' turn at bat.

"How secure is your data link to Forces Command?"

"Not enough for this. If you don't mind sending a messenger—"

"Would Captain Ropuski do?"

"How well known is she to the mediacrats, other than Atwood?"

"She can be over there in half an hour. The media can't react that fast. Not unless they have this office monitored or an agent on our staff."

"Don't bet the family fortune on that," Pfalz said. "All right. I'll expect the captain in half an hour. Two suggestions, though.

"First, give her an armed escort. Second, keep Forces personnel away from the Palestra Health Club."

Kuwahara frowned. "Wouldn't it be simpler to just close it, if you suspect—?"

"I may be out of line even mentioning that. Anyway, it's one of those situations where we want to leave—someone in business, at least for a while. They may leave a trail we can follow to somebody bigger."

Twenty-four

Linak'h:

Candice Shores had only minutes to fret at being so far from her post. Unaided vision, never mind night goggles, showed substantial enemy ground movement almost before her squad was settled in place.

She briefly regretted that she hadn't had more time to settle the future of the children or talk to Nieg. Both would survive without her, but in this case death did not settle all debts.

Ten minutes after the crash, Shores's night goggles detected movement around the crashed lifter. A minute later, the turret gun opened fire.

"I thought you pulled the plug on that," she told the gunner.

He shrugged. "Not far enough, I guess."

"Any charged rounds?" Those were doctored 22-mm rounds that would blow up in the gun's breach, disabling the gun if not blowing the gunner's head off.

"I don't like 'em. Put a good ID on them, the bad guys know what to look for. Leave if off, and half the time you load 'em yourself when you're in a hurry."

So the Coordination had a usable heavy weapon. Right now it seemed to be shooting more or less at random, as if the enemy didn't know where the fugitives were.

That comforting situation didn't last long. All three people with night goggles detected more movement, adding up to a reinforced sixteen deploying across the foot of the slope. A range check gave a figure of three hundred meters, long for carbines.

Also, some of the murky figures visible in the goggles were carrying grenade launchers. Three hundred meters was not long range for them.

Shores turned to Konishi and the communications people. "You three, divide up the emergency gear and hide. Stay on the air to Battalion. We have to be inside their heavy-weapons perimeter at least. If we're not back in twenty minutes—"

"We?" Konishi asked.

"He and I are going to sneak around to the right and enfilade their firing line," Shores said, looking at the gunner. The man nodded.

"Right. In twenty minutes or if those people get too close, you hide or evade, whichever looks best. As soon as you've broken contact, get back on the air to Battalion."

"We have better observation up here," one of the communications people said.

Shores looked at her. "Dead soldiers call in no supporting fires," the colonel said. "Now is this a tactical emergency or a study group?"

That got everybody moving almost fast enough in approximately the right directions. Shores herself regretted giving up the excellent observation that the position allowed; it promised a real slaughter when heavy weapons or TacAir came through.

However, the observation went both ways, and a strong enemy force downhill was a new datum. New data equaled new tactics, in every war since tribes brawled over who got the best cut of the mastodon.

The sixteen was joined by a second while Shores and her partner were on the move, but they didn't advance. The Coordination didn't advance or detect her movement. They were either short of training or short of energy. Acute Ptercha's senses were no help if you didn' know what to look for or were too tired, hungry, and footsore to be alert.

Stands of brush, stone walls from a long-abandoned farm, and an old drainage ditch took Shores and the gunner nearly all the way to their goal. Fifty meters short of the lifter, she knew they'd have to fight the rest of the way. The enemy flank was stretching farther right, while some of the left flankers were beginning to drift up the hill.

Come on, you idiots! Shores addressed her battalion TOC and heavy weapons. *We're not only in trouble, we're in the middle of a target-rich environment! Maybe you want to get the Old Lady wasted, but why mess up your kill count?*

She signaled the gunner. "On the count of three. One, two—three!"

Both carbines opened fire at the same instant on completely unsuspecting targets. The range was barely thirty meters, and two bursts took out a couple of fours. Then the gunner leapfrogged forward, while Shores provided covering fire.

The lifter's turret swiveled toward the intruders—*one goal achieved,* Shores thought. Its burst of 22-mm sailed overhead, though. The gun couldn't depress enough to compensate for the angle of the grounded lifter.

More fire came from the enemy to the left. But it was mostly wild, aimed only by eye and tracer. No grenades— the Ptercha's had the sense not to use area weapons that would have endangered their own surviving right flankers.

That discipline worked against the Ptercha's. It let the two humans rush the last few meters to the lifter undetected. A wild round still caught the gunner in the leg. He sprawled, digging a trench with his chin. Shores stopped, ran back, and heaved him to his feet. They covered the rest of the distance three-legged.

As they reached the lifter, the Hunters inside seemed to notice the visitors. Squalling war cries sounded and tracer sprayed from the cockpit. Shores would have leased her soul for even a concussion grenade.

Instead she reached up, grabbed the muzzle, and thrust the weapon sharply backward. A Ptercha's howled, and another came sailing out of the rear door. The gunner shot him. A second leaped out, on to the gunner's back. The gunner rolled until he was on top of his attacker, while Shores jumped on the enemy soldier's outstretched arm. In battle gear she weighed ninety kilos; she heard light Hunter bone crunch.

The gunner lurched to his feet, blood now streaming from his neck as well as his leg. "Patch yourself up," Shores said. "I'm going to get the turret."

The bad luck over the grenades turned out to be good luck once they got inside. Except for a stunned Ptercha'a with a mashed nose and swollen eye, the lifter's interior was empty and intact. Shores scrambled into the turret basket, cranked it around, and fired by eyeball. The iron sights worked without power and gave her all the accuracy she needed.

It helped that the fight around the lifter had apparently gone unnoticed. The rest of the enemy infantry weren't precisely standing up gaping, but they weren't under cover from 22-mm rounds at pointblank range, either. After four bursts, the Ptercha'a were either dead or withdrawing.

Not running, though. The one grenadier kept at work, and if Shores had been in the open he might have avenged his comrades. As it was, the light grenades only popped against the lifter's armor, except for one that finished demolishing the cockpit windows.

The gunner had finished dressing his wounds; they probably ought to be sprayed too, but that would mean undoing the dressings. The leg one was almost solid red, and there was a bigger red patch than Shores liked in the middle of the neck one.

"Can you handle the com gear?"

"Have—to, don't I?"

"Unless I grow a third arm, you might."

The gunner gripped the back of one of the communications seats, and pulled himself to his feet. As he did, the ground heaved, the lifter lurched, and the chair twisted enough to break his grip. He fell back with a curse and a groan.

Shores stared out the window. To the north, it looked like all the Dia de la Federacion fireworks displays of her childhood rolled into one.

What she saw to the west was less comforting. A firefight was erupting along and behind the crest of the hill—behind the other three crewmen she'd left there. She hoped they'd have the sense to evade downhill now—and that she could get the lifter into the air long enough to pick them up.

"Forget the com gear," she told the gunner. "We're taking off for a pickup. Can you get on the gun?"

The gunner didn't answer or move. Shores checked his pulse; he'd fainted rather than died from loss of blood.

Now, how to steer this bloody thing at bushtop height with only two fans?

Aboard U.F.S. *Shenandoah,* off Linak'h orbit:

Liddell managed six hours' sleep out of the fifteen it took for Linak'h orbit. That was enough to keep her combat-effective and let her work out a basic tactical plan.

The convoy would stay beyond AD and mine range, escorted by *Lysander* and assorted light craft. More assorted light craft, led by Moneghan, would engage the highest-priority targets. *Shen* would provide tactical command, communications relays, high cover, and mine clearance if necessary.

Liddell would have been proud of this simplicity if she hadn't known that a second-year cadet could have evolved the plan. That same cadet, however, might not have thoroughly memorized the maxim "No battle plan survives contact with the enemy."

This one was no exception.

The first change was learning that *Roma* was in Linak'h orbit. She had a working shield and was taking out mines and any other suspicious objects, using her lasers with targeting data provided by Moneghan's attackers. Admiral Longman had died of her wounds two hours before the flagships reestablished contact.

The second change was the arrival of a detailed map of enemy supply dumps and support facilities in the northern Administration. Liddell recognized Ranger work and suspected Colonel Nieg's hand. She would have recognized a high-priority target even without Colonel Blum's prompting.

"If they're able to move the stuff south, they can put more muscle in the offensive there," Blum said. "Both Task Force Olufsdottir and Task Force Shores are about to be heavily engaged."

You think. And what the Hades is Task Force Shores, or do I really want to know?

"If they stay put, they can mount a third attack, on Kharg's rear and the Administration Legions. If they're able to evacuate, they can claim they weren't defeated in the field. Also, the Coordination Warband can put up a much better defensive fight."

"I didn't know we were planning on crossing the border," Liddell said.

Blum studiously ignored the probe. "There are too many civilians in the area for missile work. We'll need heavy beams, from low altitude."

Liddell found nothing wrong with that suggestion except the implication that she needed a lecture on naval tactics.

She used the first few minutes after Blum cleared circuits to revise her tactics.

Now it was *Roma* for high cover. Moneghan with at least four cruisers and as many attackers as possible, running interference for *Shen*. *Shen* doing the sweaty killing with her lasers.

Then a third change. Sharfas Shorl, the senior leader aboard the Intervention Force transports (rank equivalent to lieutenant-general) had two cohorts ready to land immediately, even by Combat Assault. It would be valuable to put them straight into the battle in the north, and *Shen*'s operations against the enemy bases would be ideal cover for their landing. Was this feasible?

Liddell would have said a resounding "No!" if she hadn't been sure that the suggestion came with the permission or even the support of Banfi and Linak'h Command. She thought of confirming this, then decided against such an obvious delaying tactic. Like the Vics, the Intervention Force wanted in on the fighting and would not be grateful to anyone who caused unnecessary delays.

Revise plan again: have *Roma* assigned specifically to provide top cover for the CA, as soon as a mine-free descent trajectory could be established. *Roma,* the Intervention Force, and Linak'h Command to coordinate directly; *Shen* was going to be busy.

There was nearly a fourth change. The Merishi sent a message through Captain Marder (who, to do her justice, had trouble keeping a straight face in the process), asking for permission and assistance to start landing their cargoes.

"Are any of their shuttles armed?"

Marder shrugged and hand-signaled, "I doubt it.'"

"Permission denied. They will remain in formation with those Intervention Force ships not engaged in the CA. We will not be responsible for the security of their ships, personnel, or cargoes otherwise."

"They claim humanitarian motives."

"Motives make no difference in the dead."

Liddell wanted to add an explicit suggestion as to what the Merishi could do with their cargoes, particularly the industrial abrasives. She refrained. Bad timing was not the same as criminality, even in Merishi.

"Tell Mr. Longman I'm sorry about his aunt," she concluded, and shifted her screen to Bogdanov.

"Pavel?"

"I've been studying the pattern of the enemy bases. I think we want most of the attackers low, to hit enemy forces trying to escape."

"That will put them close to where the Interventionists are going to come down."

"If the Interventionist shuttles have reliable sensors, that should be no problem. In fact, our attackers may draw fire that would otherwise go against the shuttles. Do we have a TO and E for the CA force?"

"No."

"Captain Moneghan and I will try to develop a plan that allows for anything short of all the Intervention shuttle pilots' being drunk."

Bogdanov delivered that rare flash of wit with a straight face. Liddell wondered if he sensed the same thing she did: they couldn't lose now, but people could still die unnecessarily.

Two hours and forty-one minutes from entry into Linak'h orbit, *Shenandoah* took position over the southern edge of the main part of the Big Burn. Two minutes and ten seconds later, her main lasers stabbed down through sixty kilometers of atmosphere.

Thirty-seven seconds of laser fire generated the first secondary explosions.

Linak'h:

Candice Shores lifted out into thirty seconds of stark terror and half an hour of anticlimax.

As she lifted off, the ridge line sprouted figures. The firefight escalated; grenades and Rockets were joining the tracers, and not nearly enough non-lethals. The first few bursts went miraculously wide, but that luck couldn't last long, and there was no cover or concealment for the lifter anywhere that she could reach before the enemy got lucky—

Then she realized that the tracers and the two rockets that followed them were hitting the enemy positions. The figures on the skyline were Federation LI in armor, and that flare going up was a signal for heavy weapons and air support to avoid the ridge line; *friendlies up there.*

A minimum-size power suit was the first to reach Shores after she grounded the lifter. She wasn't surprised to see KAPUSTEV on the chest. The next arrivals were a pair of medics, who stormed into the lifter as if she'd personally offended them by getting the gunner hit. In another five minutes, while the fire mission hammered enemy targets, Shores learned what had been happening while she fought her duel with the Coordination sixteens.

Iqbal was duty officer at the TOC when the report of the lifters' going down came in. He immediately scrambled the ready platoon of armored LI and lined up another whole company to go, in successive waves as necessary.

Meanwhile, the other three lifters of the Flying Squadron each dropped off three of their crews to secure an emergency LZ. They picked one just to the west of the ridge where Shores had crashed. So her three stay-behinds established contact with the nine newcomers about the time Shores was shooting her way through to the lifter.

That contact had to be suspended for a while, because another enemy sixteen came tramping up hill, past the nine, apparently heading for the ridge line. Meanwhile, the three lifters had been playing AOP, ridge-hopping to stay clear of any more missiles, building an impressive body of data on enemy positions.

At a time coordinated by Captain Iqbal, the LI dropped, the heavy weapons and a flight of attackers came down on the enemy positions like a lead boot, and the LZ team opened fire on the rear of the ridge-climbing sixteen. Then the lifters formed a firing line over the LZ and provided direct covering fire as the LI climbed the ridge to finish off the enemy.

"Which we did, to the count of twenty-two bodies and five prisoners," Kapustev concluded.

It couldn't have gone quite that smoothly, Shores knew. Still, even allowing for a proud officer's telling a good tale—

"Beautiful, Lieutenant. Absolutely beautiful."

"Thank you, Colonel. Ah—it's captain now."

"Is it?" Shores realized she must have sounded insultingly skeptical. "Well, congratulations, then." *If that's a compliment for the battalion from Linak'h Command, we can take a lot of them.*

Then she shook her head. "Tell me one thing, people,

any of you. *Why the Hades didn't you talk to me?* I nearly got a man killed taking out those sixteens."

Kapustev's face was unreadable through his faceplate. "It seems that a couple of radios malfunctioned."

"A couple?"

"At least. Also, poor reception—this area seems to be famous for it. Finally, Colonel, you were always telling us to take advantage of opportunities first and tell our superiors later."

That was as close to a direct quotation as made no difference. Shores sat down and put her head in her hands, wondering if she was going to laugh or cry. Then she looked at Kapustev.

"I suppose you also thought that if I did get killed, I couldn't complain about not being told?"

"Perhaps."

Shores jumped up and shook a fist under Kapustev's plex-armored nose. "Tell me another! Have you ever heard of the *rusalka*?"

"The murder victim who tries to cling to life by draining the energy of the living?"

"You know your Russian folklore too, I see. Well, just consider having me on your trail as a *rusalka* the next time!"

Linak'h:

The artificial lightning and thunder in the north had died by the time Brigitte Tachin stepped out of the Navy HQ tent. If the hammering of Coordination bases there was still going on, it was low-powered from low altitude.

The cool night air dried Tachin's sweat, saving her from mopping her face. She decided that when she got off watch she'd see if she could improvise a sweatband from her kit.

A Hunter with a box slung on his back waved to her. "Drink, Leader?"

That seemed to be all the Anglic he knew. Tachin was just resolving to try out her Commercial Merishi when another Hunter stepped out from behind a tree. He had a shovel over his shoulder and a sidearm on the other hip, and pointed his free hand at the drink-seller.

Tachin never learned the details of the one-sided conversation that followed. She only saw the results: the drink-seller marching off in the wake of the other (who wore a Confraternity armband and improvised sixteen-Leader insignia), presumably to join the latter's work party.

Komarovsk was largely rising (or digging in) on the backs of Hunter labor, although neither the refugees' self-defense units nor the Confraternity militia were technically labor troops. They were armed and organized, and some of them were even trained for combat, but they hadn't actually had to shoot lately. Infantry attacks anywhere in Task Force Olufsdottir's AO had been rare for a week.

She wished she could have bought one of those drinks before the sixteen-Leader confiscated the vendor. It was a hundred meters to the water point, for a canteen full of chemical-tainted, lukewarm fluid. How the Hunters were getting their stuff in was a mystery she was willing to let lie, if she could just buy some of it!

"Brigitte?"

It was Rafael Morvan, a welcome surprise. Also an outright miracle: he was holding two drink packs. Tachin could even see the condensation obscuring the logos.

"Forgive me if I was encouraging the black market. The vendor seemed to be under arrest, but they were letting him sell off his stock. I suppose the sergeant was getting a cut."

Tachin smiled. "Just putting the man to honest work." Morvan put a pack into the hand she held out. She opened it without reading the label. The first few swallows were a taste of Paradise.

"You coming off watch?" Morvan asked, when they both could speak again.

She shook her head. "Just a CO's privilege of taking a break."

"A CO? Are congratulations in order?"

"We got a message from *Shen* about half an hour ago. The Navy shore party and *Shen* are both sending people over to *Roma,* to help fill slots and make repairs. All three people senior to me are on the list." She did not add that Brian Mahoney was one of those seniors, and he hadn't even telephoned, let alone come over to say good-bye.

At least Mort Gellis is staying, praise the Saints.

"And you—?"

Thunder cracked down across the sky. An interminable

rumbling followed. Just when Tachin thought it would go on forever and was waiting for the alarm gong and alert flares, she saw lights stream across the sky. Dozens of lights, in fast-moving clusters.

The lights vanished into the ruddy clouds to the north, and the rumbling died away at almost the same moment. Tachin and Morvan stared at each other, realized that both were gaping, and laughed.

"I am getting nervous in my old age. They did warn us that the Intervention troops were coming down. I never expected them to land in parade order."

"A demonstration, maybe," Morvan said. "Any idea where they might be landing?"

Tachin shook her head. She didn't know, but she also realized that suddenly having a CO's responsibility was making her closemouthed. Or was it force of habit, after weeks of being unable to talk to Brian and being unwilling to unbend with anyone else? Elayne Zheng's death wasn't helping either, not when she hadn't yet been able to go off and cry decently for her friend.

" 'Loose lips blast ships,' " she quoted. "If you're off-shift—"

"For about another twenty minutes," Morvan said. "And in that time I have to eat, get over to the Catacombs, and scrub."

The Catacombs was the nickname for the tunnel complex under the Komarov house. Rumors about its length and treasures abounded. They spoke of ten kloms of tunnels, vast quantities of supplies stored there since the Hive Wars, and a fortune in Nikolai Komarov's artwork (or was it art collection, and had Herman Franke evacuated it, confiscated it, or stolen it?).

"Busy?"

"Not unless Task Force Shores has sent us some more casualties. The last shift cleaned out the last batch, both Fed and POW."

"POW's?"

Tachin found her throat drying up again as Morvan described what he'd heard of the battle along the ridge. "Is Candy safe?"

"Safe and back at the head of her battalion. But she and the Vics are apparently surrounded by a good part of a Legion."

"That Legion's in trouble," Tachin said. *Along with another friend of mine. And speaking of friends ...*

"Have you heard? Elayne Zheng was killed aboard Gold One."

"No!" Morvan's face confirmed another rumor: he and Elayne had been lovers on Victoria. *Probably at her bidding,* Tachin thought. It was the first time since the news came that she'd been able to think about Elayne and then smile.

"I'm sorry." Impulsively she hugged him, resting her cheek against his, hoping they wouldn't *both* start crying now, although Elayne deserved the tribute—

It was at this point that malignant fate or negligent saints allowed Brian Mahoney to come by. Tachin got a last look at the man over Morvan's shoulder. She saw Mahoney's eyes widen in a face even longer and thinner than usual under far too much dirt—and his hair was shaggy too—saw his lips twist, then saw him turn his back and walk off without a word.

Morvan felt her tension, also turned, and looked ready to go after Mahoney. Tachin gripped his arm.

"No. It's not your fault. Nothing happened that wouldn't have happened anyway."

"You—thank you for considering my feelings."

"It's the truth."

It was also true that she almost wished Mahoney had done something dramatic or disgusting. But that was a wish for him to make the decision about their future for her. If she lacked the courage to do that, how was she any better than he was?

She forced a smile. "I'd invite you in for that meal, but the people going up took all their own snack stashes and stole ours too."

"Naturally. The vendor's probably sold out by now, too. Either that or the sergeant has confiscated the rest of his stock for his own friends. I'll get by."

Linak'h:

The cave complex where Task Force Shores had its headquarters had several disadvantages, in spite of a lot of work by the Confraternity and, more recently, two Teams of Victorians. (They were too big to be platoons and too small to be companies, so the original name stood for now.)

One was the smell of a set of temporary Coordination tenants. All were dead; not all had been found. Burial under a pile of rocks in a distant tunnel was as decent as a soldier usually got, but it was hard on the people trying to do work in the same tunnel.

Then there was the lack of space. Ninety meters of rock made vital facilities and personnel fuser-proof. To get that much shelter had meant a lot of doubling-up. Shores's own quarters and office (decently veiled behind a hung ground-sheet), Intelligence, three supply dumps, and a water puri-fier all occupied different corners of one cave, and that wasn't the most crowded.

Have the surface checked for other access, she reminded herself. *If the bad guys find some and drop serious chemi-cals down here ...*

Finally there was the problem of not being able to hear the howl of the incoming rockets and rounds, the cheers and obscenities when they missed, and the screams and obscenities when they hit.

That one's easily solved, at least. Get this mite-ridden briefing over with and get back out in the open.

Shores looked at the men and women in front of her. Every section of the battalion staff was represented, and so were all four rifle companies and the heavy-weapons and support units. Three officers headed by Karl Pocher repre-sented the Victorians, all three looking as if they'd been digging ditches with their bare hands.

The map of the battalion's position probably told nobody anything new. Companies B, C, and D were arranged in a rough triangle, each with their quota of well-positioned (she hoped) heavy weapons. The Victorians and A Company (minus one platoon, with another platoon suited up) pro-vided the central reserve.

The map also showed current intelligence about enemy deployments around the battalion. Mostly guesswork; the map might as well have displayed calligraphed "Here Be Dragons" instead of the symbols for coordination units.

"All right," Shores said. "We are in position. We are going to stay in position. Where we are, the Coordination's troops in the area can't ignore us, can't bypass us without throwing off the whole timetable for this offensive, and shouldn't be able to overrun us.

"We, on the other hand, can hit them everywhere they show themselves over quite a large area. How large may change from day to day, depending on how far they stick their heads up.

"One warning. I expect everybody to take seriously the doctrine of having three alternate, ranged-in positions for each squad and each heavy weapon. We are not defending ground. We are killing enemies. I have done everything but a nautch dance for Command HQ to make sure we have plenty of ammunition. Not as many non-lethals as I wanted, but plenty of regulation mines and booby traps. I won't even think about the other kind, which I understand the Vics have been making in large quantities, and without blowing themselves up—yet."

That got a laugh. "I hope the enemy won't be happy with them either," she concluded. "Any questions?"

"How much lift are we keeping in the perimeter?"

"Enough to support patrols, medevac casualties, and re-supply the firing line. Anybody who thinks we've cut the quota too fine, see me after the meeting. Just remember that for a couple of days a lifter in the open may be a high-value target instead of a means of mobility. Yes?"

It was the Company D XO, half political appointee, half first-class trainer. Little combat experience recorded, some combat aptitude demonstrated, definitely a big mouth.

"Why is the LI armored platoon positioned behind my company?" At least he had the tact or sense not to add, "Do you think we're the weak link?"

Shores hadn't made up her mind either way. The Militia were superb as individual soldiers and squads and had been getting better as a company. But sitting, taking it, and then giving it back was a type of warfare they hadn't faced.

"With your permission, Colonel Shores?" Captain Iqbal said. Shores nodded. "You have the most rugged ground behind you. That lets us hide the LI most effectively. Like lifters, they are a high-value target. Far from protecting you, you are more likely to be protecting them."

The Militia officer shrugged. At least he knew when he'd reached the limits of discipline.

"Thank you. I won't quote any potent words from Command or Brigade—"

"God be praised," somebody said, and others laughed.

"—because both Langston and Hogg have the sense not to say any. Good luck, good hunting, and good having you in the battalion."

Linak'h:

Senior Warband Leader Sharfas Shorl had come to Marshal Banfi's headquarters with an escort of elite troopers. Never mind that Banfi didn't know what the Chadl'hi Warband called them or what unit their shoulder patches indicated. They had the indefinable quality that distinguishes the warrior who has chosen to step out ahead of the rest, farther into danger, farther from the civilian life and mentality.

The half sixteen stayed outside when the meeting began, but Banfi hoped they didn't hear anything that sounded like a danger to their leader. He had visions of their barging into the office and shooting Boronisskahane dead in his seat.

That or something else had Boronisskahane more subdued than usual. The old Hunter had withdrawn into an invisible lair these past few days, snarling at anyone who entered his personal space.

Banfi wondered if it was victory being in sight without the Confraternity being able to take the field properly that was upsetting Boronisskahane. If so, Banfi did not have much sympathy for him.

If the Confraternity hadn't moved for their coup, Sirbon Jols might have carried out his. Defending an Administration that didn't want to be defended would have been impossible for the Federation, politically or militarily. The Confraternity militia hadn't won any battles in the open field, but as support and security troops they'd been invaluable to both Warband and Federation. Without the work of Boronisskahane and his like over centuries, three Hunter worlds would hardly have been in a position to send Legions unopposed.

Boronisskahane, Banfi decided, had to be the kind of revolutionary who only counted it a victory if *his* revolution won. Here in Linak'h, everybody seemed to want to join the party, even the Federation! All the Confraternity's previous work no longer seemed to matter.

Banfi realized that Langston was looking at Sharfas Shorl and that the translation computer was on-line. They were using it to spare Confreres the need to use Commercial Merishi and to allow Langston, the nominal chair, real-time knowledge of what was going on.

"This strategic planning session is convened," Langston said. "The first item is a report from Sharfas Shorl."

The Hunter delivered his report without notes or hesitation. Two of his cohorts were already moving to contact, with reconaissance by their own scouts and also by suited human LI. The strategic strikes by *Shenandoah* had crippled the Coordination units facing them; reliable and valiant air support was doing the rest.

A moment of silence followed, as everyone remembered the cost of that "valiant air support." The Coordination hadn't touched *Shenandoah,* but they'd hurled their remaining air power against the low-altitude operations. Between them the Administration and Federation had lost half a dozen attackers, making sure the cohorts landed safely. *Cavour* was now in orbit, an abandoned, radioactive cripple. Half her people had survived; Mad Bill Moneghan was among those who hadn't.

The next cohort was on the way down and would make a secure-area landing. Shorl directed that the fourth and fifth cohorts, almost ready, be landed behind the first three to create a secure rear.

Banfi took his cue from Langston's nod. "In the name of the Administration Warband, I accept these proposals."

Nobody of any race, service, or allegiance dissented aloud. Shorl turned in his chair and drew a leather portfolio out of his case.

"I wanted to present this with more ceremony, but I had to reckon that I might not live until there was time for it. So I brought it with me."

Boronisskahane's ears twitched. "Instead of going with your cohorts?"

"The three cohorts have enough seniors for two Legions," Shorl replied. "Also, if I waited, the man we called Farsight might have earned his name again and learned the secret."

Banfi started at hearing his old Hunter warname from Shorl's lips. Of course, the leader would have heard it from his father—and if he had heard more, or *received* more—

The Marshal's heart thudded in his chest in a way that his doctors would not have approved.

Shorl laid the portfolio on the table, opened the seal, and drew out four envelopes, made of something with the sheen of silk that Banfi didn't recognize. Each of them had a signature in one corner, in the archaic ideographic writing, a second in modern writing in another, and a seal in a third.

The fourth corner was drawn tight with cords, which Shorl unfastened with a care that seemed ready to drive Boronisskahane to a stroke and did nothing for Banfi's heart. Sweat was trickling down his forehead when Shorl finished laying out the contents of the envelopes.

Four pieces of cloth lay there, four square pieces that among them made up a Confraternity flag. Banfi looked at the stain in the upper-left piece and knew it was the flag that he and Egobar Shorl had raised over Klykh'sam.

"We thought of tearing it into more pieces," Shorl said quietly. "That would have made a better story. But my father and his comrades were all warriors. We knew that the more who had a piece of the flag, the greater the danger that some would die without trustworthy kin to carry on the duty until the flag could be raised again.

"I would like to be among those who raise this flag again," Shorl went on. "But two here have rights ahead of mine. Marshal Banfi and Boronisskahane. The Senior among the warriors, the Senior among the Confreres."

For a moment Banfi could not see Boronisskahane or anything else clearly.

"Confrere?" Isha Maiyotz said softly.

"Oh, yes," Boronisskahane said. "Yes. How—how could it be otherwise—?"

Marcus Langston held up a hand, with an expression that Banfi had come to know meant trouble. The Marshal's first suspicion was resentment that Linak'h Command was being left out.

"I just received a message. Task Force Shores is under attack by Coordination Warband and Tribal units. They've identified the equivalent of a full Legion."

Shorl wasted no time in calling for a map display and his First Assistant. In a far corner of the conference room the two Hunters put their heads together briefly, then returned.

"Do we hold the air around Task Force Shores?"

Langston nodded.

"It is too late to make a battle-array landing of the next cohort. But we can bring down one of the next wave in the rear of the attackers. Perhaps both."

Langston nodded. "Near enough to close to contact on foot?"

"If you hold the air, very likely."

"Good," Langston said. "Because if we don't need to move your people, we'll have lift assets to spare. We can move maybe one of Edelstein's battalions and oh, a couple of cohorts of Confraternity militia. You come down north of Shores, we move up from the south, and we can bag everybody and everything the Coordination has in the area.

"That could end the war. It will certainly shorten it."

This time it was Boronisskahane's turn to put his head in his hands, and Banfi mentally awarded Langston a medal for strategic diplomacy.

Twenty-five

Linak'h:

It had been a good night, if a tiring one, for Juan Esteva (he and Jan had found just enough privacy for just long enough, apart from everything that needed doing on-duty). It hadn't been such a good morning, and the afternoon was beginning to look like one you wanted to send back to the factory.

C Company had the northern side of the perimeter. They also had an aggressive CO who pushed them a little too far down the slope, into the double canopy. So when the main attack came in, it was hard for the heavy firepower to keep track of who was where. That went even for the task force's own stuff; when the air people showed up, they tore their hair out, from what Esteva heard over the radio.

The Coordination got in behind the company and onto the slopes. This cut both ways; they nearly had the company surrounded, but they were out in the open. Everybody could hit them and did, and by the time the hitting was over the attackers were mostly out of the fight. (More dead than prisoners, unfortunately; non-lethals were getting tighter every day.)

The attackers were both Warband and Tribals, but you couldn't tell from the weapons or from the way they fought. Also, all of them looked as if they'd been living lean and rough for a while. Those wrecked supplies were beginning to take it out of the Coordination's troopers.

The company had a good many casualties, though not a lot of fatal ones. Coordination infantry weaponry was light, and Federation body armor saved lives unless you got it in the head or at close range. They retreated into new positions, and between the casualties and the new positions being full of dead Hunters, they were a bit shaken when Esteva came down to join them.

He brought reinforcements, a Team of the Vics with their own weapons and gear and an extra load of ammo, water, and medical supplies. He was using a map print to position them when Jan Sklarinsky came scrambling up over a boulder.

Jan's camouflage cream was smeared, and she'd need to shave her head to get her hair back in order. *Might not look bad that way, either—*

"Better get your people in and down fast, Juan," she said. "They're moving up heavy stuff down there, and I don't think we can get at it under the trees. They've thickened up on the ground, too, so I've pulled my own teams back. Even the air's going to have to—"

The Hunter "heavy stuff" proved her right in the next moment. A cluster of heavy rounds came in, all unguided, two of them duds. Esteva flattened himself on the ground, Jan on top of him, and they waited for the rumbles to die and the screams to begin.

Both happened on schedule. Esteva rolled over, got on the radio for a medevac, and heard an acknowledgment. By the time he did, Jan was over on the other side of the boulder, crawling downhill.

"You wait there, Juanito," she called. "I have to check that all my teams—"

The next salvo was only three rounds, and one of them was a dud, a second a smoker. The third went off fine, at least if you were a Ptercha'a gunner. Esteva had another opinion, when he crawled out and saw Jan lying on her back.

She didn't seem to be hurt, when he crawled up to her, and she was holding on to her pulser. But she had one hand over a bloody patch on her right hip, and was swearing softly. He also noticed for the first time that she had a field dressing on her neck, and fragment holes in her battledress shirt.

No blood; they must not have got through her armor.

"I guess I'm going to have to sit the rest of this one out, damn it," she said. "Contact Sergeant Pares and tell him that he's—unnhhh!"

That last was from a combination of Esteva's trying to move her and the shock wearing off. The shock of *two* baddies, Esteva realized. Something big had chopped through her right boot and halfway through her right ankle.

No more of those ten-klom runs at dawn and then back to bed, for a while.

Lifter whines sounded behind and overhead. Gunships popped up first, salvoing rockets into the tree line. They drew enemy heavy weapons, but not heavy enough to kill them, and marked the locations. TacAir came in—from out of nowhere, so it had to be a heavy attacker firing with the gunships spotting.

However it happened, the tree line erupted in smoke and flame from the payloads, more smoke and bigger flames from secondary explosions, flying trees and parts of trees, and flying Hunters (mostly in pieces). Enemy fire superiority over C Company was suddenly history.

The air support had walked the warheads from just ahead of B's outposts into the trees, so a lot of blast and fragments blew back into the Federation positions. Esteva spat out bark, rock dust, and what he hoped wasn't a wad of fur, and saw that everybody had kept their heads down.

Everybody, that is, except the people from the medevac lifters, two of them freshly grounded barely twenty meters behind Esteva. He hadn't heard them come, but he couldn't have heard the Last Trumpet in the middle of the air strike.

One was Federation, one was Vic, and he thought the Vic's crew was that wild kid BoJo Johnson and his lady friend. No, there was the kid coming down the slope with a scattergun across his back, a sidearm on his hip, and a big medkit in one hand.

He was carrying it for somebody else, thank God. Esteva had problems with the idea of the kid being a qualified medic. Johnson was riding scattergun on the real medics, who grabbed the medkit and spread out, spraying, sealing, pumping fluid loads into people whose hearts were about to stop from low blood pressure, and doing all the rest of the medics' good stuff.

Johnson unslung the scattergun and looked downhill, then to either side. His mouth twisted, but then it usually did; from what Esteva had heard, he hadn't had a lot to smile about in his life. But he didn't look like he was going to throw up, no matter how many dead bodies he counted.

"You legal for this sort of thing?" Esteva asked.

"Got a courier ship to spare?"

"Run that one past me again."

"I mean, I got enrolled along with everybody else, by order of President Gist and General Parkinson. You got a complaint, take it up with them, only they're on—"

Esteva thought he heard the word "Victoria" as everybody dived for cover. This time it included the medics, because the Ptercha'a who were shooting were doing it from close in.

Must have been a squad that went to ground when the rest of their people got chopped.

At least one of them had a rocket and sent it streaking up, blowing in the canopy of a gunship and sending it down. It hit the slope, somersaulted, and landed upside down.

The power pack began discharging, and everybody around it began clearing the area. That got some of them hit; the Hunters still had personal weapons and good eyes. They even popped a couple of people trying to rescue the gunship's crew, or at least recover their bodies.

Esteva ran around the medevac lifters, pounding on the windshields and pointing his thumb upward. The reply was another digit, also pointed upward. Then he saw that Johnson was following him.

He cursed medics. He cursed adolescent soldiers. He cursed the Hunters for being such decent people that you hated to kill them but such good soldiers that when they wanted to fight you had to.

He also saw where the Hunter squad was, when they opened up on Johnson but missed. Johnson was down and out of the way, besides swearing too loud to be hurt, when Esteva loaded a grenade into his launcher. Then he deliberately fired it to the left, so as not to give the Hunters the idea he knew where they were.

Bait them into being careless.

The Hunters shot back, aiming at a prone Esteva. They ignored Johnson, who suddenly opened up from farther up the slope. Two of the Hunters lost their nerve and broke cover. The second gunship hosed both of them, and Esteva put two more grenades right into the position of what he hoped was the rest of the squad.

It was the rest of that squad, at least. But there were more live enemies on the slope. Esteva dealt with the first two, Johnson shot the third, and one of the others threw a hand grenade as he went down.

It was going straight for the hatch of the Victorian lifter when Esteva jumped and caught it in midair. He heard the hatch slam behind him as he threw the grenade back.

The fuse ran out when it was three meters in front of Esteva. Small fragments made a ruin of his face and chest. A larger piece pierced one eye into his brain, which kept him from feeling much pain before he died.

Charlemagne:

The identification of the leader of Josephine Atwood's kidnappers arrived during a late snack. His service record arrived during desert.

Kuwahara had eaten, so it was as much a full stomach as a nervous one that kept him silent as Baumann absorbed chicken, coffee, sinfully rich cake, and incriminating data. Halfway through the second run of the service record, Baumann called, "Stop, highlight Lines 26 and 37."

Kuwahara stared at Line 26 and felt his eyebrows rise of their own will. Lieutenant Colonel David Crawshay had served as junior aide to General Szaijkowski when Mighty Max commanded the Eighth Army, his last assignment before coming to Charlemagne to rise the rest of the way there.

"Two years, too," Baumann said. "Unless all the other stories about Max there are lies, Crawshay would have been the general's chief procurer as well."

"Oh."

"You needn't be ashamed of being at a loss for words, Sho. Mighty Max has never stepped across the legal line, and he's both charming and I understand, good at it. But another adjective commonly used to describe him is 'insatiable.' Some aides distance themselves from his activities. Others think that procuring helps their careers."

"So somebody was blackmailing Crawshay?"

"Possibly. Possibly his lack of scruples was simply getting more blatant. Or possibly he simply used assets he'd developed independently to do what he thought his superiors might appreciate—create a big noisy diversion, like kidnapping a prominent mediacrat.

"This will certainly help our dealings with Mighty Max.

He will have to be more cooperative with our approach to this matter if it involves a former aide."

Kuwahara took a deep breath. "What is going to be our approach to this matter?"

"Charging Crawshay with kidnapping, terrorism, and possibly treason. That depends on whether any of his network was selling information outside the Federation, and whom they were selling it to."

"That will make a scandal."

"Of course. But only one scandal, that Forces officers tried the various things we have evidence they did. Not two scandals—that they did it and that their superiors tried to hide it."

Kuwahara let a breath out. It couldn't be the same breath, because he couldn't hold his breath that long.

It was good to know that the Empress also believed as he did: the best way to get the Forces left alone to handle their own affairs was to prove to their civilian superiors that they could be trusted to do so.

"Something bothering you, Sho?"

"I was thinking that if you were going to propose a cover-up, I would have to resign my commission."

Baumann frowned. "I should be insulted. Don't worry about that. But you might want to consider reassignment. If you stay on here, you'll be associated with the wrecking of quite a few careers before we've cleaned house.

"If you move out, you can probably have a Battle Group command or even a Fleet Deputy slot. Your three stars will become permanent either way, but I suspect you might have a better chance at four if you move on."

Kuwahara appreciated the frankness, and he knew his motives for staying on were complex. (Fumiko would not care to move again so soon, for one thing.) But he was sure of one thing: the more hands on the detail, the more thorough the cleaning job.

Linak'h:

Candice Shores heard of Juan Esteva's death with the same degree of emotion that she would have heard of a tax lien on her father's estate. (Which there probably was, although if Nieg and Franke between them couldn't handle the Ministry of Revenue neither of them was worth what she'd thought they were.)

She was just too bloody *busy*!

The attack in the north seemed to peter out after the diehards who killed Esteva (and others—she reminded herself to get an updated casualty list). Even more serious trouble was developing elsewhere.

The Reservists of B Company to the west had to fall back, across Height 349. They came back in good order, bringing everything and everybody, but they came nonetheless. Too much pressure from too many enemies.

More trouble to the south. The D's had the ground on their side, but numbers heavily against them. Mostly light infantry, either intended that way or reduced to that level by too many days' campaigning with too few supplies.

So. Don't worry if Height 349 wound up temporarily outside the perimeter. The best way of protecting the support units was to kill so many Coordination troops that the survivors wouldn't be up to the job of holding anything except each other's field dressings, antiseptic sprays, and hands.

Hold the crest with the armored LI, in an X-formation that would give them ambush capability (just enough cover up there for people in suits to hide from an enemy with no air recon). Let the B's retreat through the LI and across to Height 380—the valley in between was barely visible from the air.

Then wait until the Ptercha'a had massed for an attack on 349 *and* as many heavy weapons and as much TacAir as you could find were ready to hit the crest. Pull the LI back, draw the Ptercha'a forward, and hit them with everything but the drain stopper! (You could work heavy weapons in closer to suited LI than to anybody else; the suits helped against blast and fragments.)

Get another platoon of LI suited up, or as many as you had working suits to fit. Keep the rest of the LI and the Vics as a reserve—if the perimeter shrank, mobility wouldn't be so critical. Fieldcraft would be, and the Vics weren't as bad as you'd expected—Linak'h offered five times the cover and concealment of most battlefields on Victoria.

Oh, yes—move a temporary TOC out to the crest of 380, and take that post herself. Shores had the feeling that the

Mark I eyeball was about to become the Task Force commander's most useful sensing device.

Linak'h:

"How soon do you expect the actual transmission of material to begin?" Rahbad Sarlin asked.

Colonel Nieg had stopped being surprised at the sophistication of the translation computer, able to carry subtle intonations and shades of meaning. Instead he had become relieved that it was here, out in the coastal forests within twenty kloms of both the Braigh'n Gulf and the Merishi border. Clearly the Inquirers' presence here had official sanction, or at least a lack of official opposition.

The only point on which he had been more relieved was Lieutenant Nalyvkina's good health and (within limits) spirits. He suspected that her spirits would decline when she learned that she would definitely be barred from further combat flying.

Just not attending these meetings wouldn't be enough to clear her. She knew of the existence of the Baernoi-led Hunter mercenaries. That was just too big a secret to let fall into unknown hands. Fortunately, it would be Colonel Davidson's job to break the truth to his friend.

"Getting the Federation's agreement to the principles of this exchange of intelligence has taken a while," Nieg said. "I hardly think you expect me to reveal how long."

Only two hours, good time even if the 'Federation' so far consists of Marshal Banfi, General Langston, Commodore Liddell, and Governor-General Rubirosa.

"No," Behdan Zeg said. It was an actual word, not a grunt. "You are as generous as a beggar."

"One must play the beggar at times, in order to play the goldtusk at others," Nieg said. "If that is not an old saying among either of our races, it should be."

Zeg said something untranslated and probably untranslatable. He did not seem inclined to discuss comparative folklore.

Truthfully, neither was Nieg. Getting agreement in principle to an exchange of intelligence about Merishi troublemaking was as much as he'd expected, maybe a little bit more.

He was unlikely to have a chance for more. The pretext for this visit was the—rescue? extraction? retrieval?—of Lieutenant Nalyvkina. She was waiting in the next tent, personal gear packed, sidearm on and loaded, flight gear ready except for the helmet. In twenty minutes she and Nieg would be in the clearing for the pickup, and no human would voluntarily be on this side of the Braigh'n Gulf until the war was over.

But there had to be something more he could do—or at least say.

Inspiration came. Nieg normally distrusted inspiration; it led at best to people like Nikolai Komarov. Unfortunately he had no time for systematic analysis.

This is the hand; play it the best way you know how.

"I can give you one piece of intelligence, although not about the Merishi Governance. The four Simferos Associates chartered ships are urgently trying to sell their cargoes."

"How urgently?" the third Baernoi (Brokeh su-Irzim was the name Nieg remembered) asked.

"They will bargain—"

"What Scaleskin could resist bargaining, even if you were cutting off his potency?" Zeg snapped. "Tell us something we do not know."

"Easy, mother's son," Sarlin said. Nieg managed not to raise eyebrows as Zeg shrugged instead of snapping or snarling louder.

"They will bargain," Nieg repeated, "but I think you are better able to meet their price than is the Administration. Unless they have Confraternity funds at their disposal, and I do not know about that. I reveal no secrets to you when I say the Confreres do not reveal all theirs to us."

All three Baernoi laughed, then su-Irzim looked toward the door and rose. They went out, without Zeg trying to push ahead of his half-brother. Nieg decided this was worth noting. The two formidable Inquirers would be still more so if their long feud had ended, while Brokeh su-Irzim seemed to be parlaying his success on Victoria into leadership elsewhere.

It was no more than five minutes before the three Baernoi came back. As the tent door opened to admit them, Nieg caught a glimpse of the Ptercha'a sentries. They seemed to have thickened their cordon around the tent since the meeting began.

"We will be prepared to approach the Merishi concerning the purchase of their cargoes. Do you have a list with you?"

"No, but it was not transmitted to us in confidence. I am sure I can be authorized to send it as soon as I return to Och'zem."

The three Baernoi looked at one another again. Then su-Irzim stared at Nieg. "A rumor has reached us that the cargoes are very suitable for rebuilding after a war. Or building on a new world. A new world such as Peregrine."

Nieg's self-control had seldom survived such a rigorous test. Had someone been talking, or was this rumor pure bluff?

He couldn't do anything about rumor-spreaders back in the Zone while he was over here. He could reply to the bluff with one of his own.

"If so, it would not be surprising. Simferos Associates had some notions of what was about to happen on Linak'h. They would not have loaded the ships as if they were voyaging to a pleasure-planet for goldtusks."

"The Lords know this tree-furred pile of [untranslated] is not that," Zeg muttered.

"I think we can all agree on that," Sarlin said. "You know nothing of any plans for Peregrine and its sector?"

Only those plans of shortsighted Federation officials which made the folk of a dozen distant worlds desperate enough to indenture themselves to the Merishi. But General Kharg's files were hardly public property, although his cooperation in their examination and his combat record so far would mean he retired with a second star.

"Nothing. Nor would I be able to discuss them with you if I did, without authorization from the highest levels in Linak'h Command."

"Of course. We know about civilian superiors," Zeg said. He sounded almost as if he was reassuring a sick comrade, a tone that Nieg had always doubted the Inquirer could use.

Nieg also knew about civilian superiors. If the Inquirers' were anything like his, they would take Nieg's equivocation of any Federation plans for Peregrine as evidence of the existence of such plans. Plans in such an advanced stage, moreover, that they required immediate contact with the settlements of the Peregrine sector.

Which of course would promptly touch off a race among the major spacefaring races. Instead of restraining emigration, the Federation would find itself subsidizing immigration to Peregrine and its neighbors.

Possibly starting with some of those private armies on Victoria. If they have so much energy, let them work if off on wilderness or bandits.

An elaborate invitation to stay for a meal was given, as elaborately refused. Nieg and Nalyvkina rode pillion on Hunter-driven roadriders to the clearing and had less than five minutes to wait for their attacker to appear.

Nalyvkina sweated all the way across the Gulf; she seemed to be one of those pilots who hated to ride in the back seat. As they crossed the coast, they had to evade a convoy of Hunter shuttles coming down, and an exchange of messages identified them.

Two cohorts of Pek's Legion Five-Three were landing, to relieve the pressure on Task Force Shores. The Task Force was entirely surrounded by Coordination forces, and in serious danger of being overrun if help did not arrive soon.

Nieg was not the only one sweating by the time the attacker landed in the Zone.

Linak'h:

Candice Shores warned the support people in the cave not to try being heroes. The Coordination probably wouldn't use any lethal chemicals, not against an enemy who held the sky and could make it fall on them in retaliation.

"But if they ask you to surrender or they'll KM you, don't assume it's a bluff. Surrender and be alive for the victory celebration." Then she led her field TOC (Captain Iqbal and three sergeants, all armed to the teeth) out into the sunlight.

A blazing afternoon sun, the reek of death and explosives, and short water were beginning to peck away at morale by the time Shores reached the top of Height 380. She didn't promise miracles in order to restore it; she simply pulled out her display, incorporated a few updates from the ten minutes her trip took, and went to work.

Thicken up the snipers in the Militia sector was the first note she decided to act on. This prospect ended when she learned that Jan Sklarinsky had been medevaced and the other sniper teams were tied down in the C sector.

"We have extremely determined people against us up there," Iqbal said. "They are hiding in the ruins of the forest and sniping at our perimeter, so naturally our snipers must keep them down."

"Naturally," Shores said, hoping that Jan would be in the hospital before she learned about Juan.

Lucky woman. She can relax and let it hurt for a while before she has to do anything.

Random small-arms fire and an occasional, still more random heavy round plucked at the troopers on the summit of 380. But the medevac lifters kept up their steady work, sometimes flying directly out from the pickup point instead of relaying them to the aid station in the caves.

That would have to change in a few minutes. The X-formation of LI was in place, and B Company was coming back through them on schedule. In fact, she could see about a platoon of B's on the opposite slope, passing a stretch short of cover but staying well dispersed. Using her binoculars, she saw that the SSW's and shoulder launchers were in position to cover both the open ground and the flanks of the LI.

A whine swelling to a howl drew her attention upward. A gaggle of light attackers and gunships was racing up from the south, the lowest barely ten meters off the ground. Dirty, streaked with smoke, one showing a patch, they must be the Confraternity reinforcements she'd been promised. But if that was the best the Confreres' new air arm could do—

The gaggle—five, Shores saw now—sprayed flame. Solid black shapes separated from them, some falling free, others growing more tails of flame.

A bloody Coordination air strike.

The B Company weapons crews knew they were the target before Shores did. They stuck to their weapons, shot down one enemy so that more smoke and flame plumed where it fell, then died under the strike.

The platoon crossing the open ground went down. Not

all of them got up again. Some of those who did were shot down by Coordination infantry appearing on either flank of Height 349. The LI on the crest were cut off, and the mouth of the cave would be in a few minutes.

"Get those tubes on to the near face of 349," Shores told the heavy-weapons CO. "If they aren't hitting it in two minutes, you won't live to be court-martialed."

The CO must have been keeping his eye on the ball; the first round answered Shores's tirade within seconds. But messages poured in, building up a picture of too many threats coming in from too many directions.

The pressure in the north eased off for the moment. Nothing in the east. To the south, aimed fire up to SSW level building, mostly aimed at pinning down D Company. To the west, all Hades breaking loose, even if the 120-mm rounds were spraying the two enemy columns with flame and fragments.

Iqbal was calling for air support and tighter air cover, and the gunships and even some of the medevac lifters were up and shooting. But the really heavy air, it seemed, was off chasing the survivors of the enemy strike. That diversion of Federation air assets might do more damage than the original strike had.

Shores had the feeling that in a few more minutes her mind would be numb from data overload.

Decide now, Candy, while you still can. Stand where you are or shift around for a counterattack?

If she counterattacked, it would probably have to be with the Vics. Her LI would be wild to rescue their comrades, but they were also her best reserve. Taking them would leave a perimeter with one company chewed up and another sector held only by the militia.

It didn't take her long to reach Karl Pocher. He understood immediately.

"I'll strip out the people from the lifters—" he began.

"No. We need them for the wounded and ammo resupplies."

"We'll only be able to put up about eighty—"

"If we can't do it with eighty, we'll need eight hundred, which we don't have and aren't going to get until it's too late." The reports of reinforcements might not be true; the channel certainly wasn't secure.

"Understood, Huntress. We're on our way."

"Yusuf," she told Iqbal. "If I don't come back, you're running things on the hill. We're supposed to be getting all kinds of help, probably too late for more than vengeance. But the longer it takes our furry friends to kill us, the longer they have to hang around in the open."

Iqbal nodded. Everybody seemed to understand her so clearly today, or was that just an adrenaline-induced illusion?

By the time she met the Victorians, she was down off the crest, out of sight of what was happening on the south face. She wasn't out of sight or contact with the battery, though—she could practically throw her orders into their CP wrapped around a rock.

"Maximum depression you think is safe without hitting our own people, four rounds per tube into the face of 349," she ordered. "I trust your observers." She hoped that made amends for her threats earlier.

"Roger, Huntress."

The first rounds left the muzzles as Shores turned to the Victorians. Karl Pocher had command presence, otherwise you couldn't have told that they had a command structure. But they all had weapons in their hands, ammunition, and grim expressions. Armies had swept fields with no more.

"Move out."

They didn't move far before the sixteen rounds were done. That was enough to raise a wall of smoke shrouding the dip, hiding each side from the other. Shores didn't see an opponent until the smoke eddied and she saw a few Coordination infantry—Tribals, she thought—shooting at the cave entrance.

They died before they knew that an enemy had their range. The Vics had four SSW's, probably acquired as irregularly as their lift. One weapons squad from the LI had been ordered along, but two had come. Plenty of firepower to pin the enemy down until the friendlies got off the slope and the air support came back. If they were careful with ammunition—

What sounded like three or four firefights all at once blasted Shores's ears from the left. She turned, seeing Coordination troops swarming toward her and soldiers of both races falling.

She didn't need long for an analysis. Her first thought

was the Militia had given way. Then she realized that they'd done the opposite: held so firmly that the Coordination assault lapped around their—it would be around their right flank—and was coming into the dip without knowing there was anybody there to meet them.

Mutual surprise looked like it was leading to mutual slaughter.

Nobody really had time to build up a base of fire before the two lines collided. Shores swept a half-circle to her flank with her carbine, noticing that many of the enemy had nearly empty pouches and belts. Empty stomachs, too, and for quite a while. This *had* to be their last effort—and if desperate enemies used the tactic of getting in too close for heavy weapons to count, it could be their most dangerous.

The nearest SSW team was down, or at least not firing. Shores hadn't made records with an SSW, but she'd kept up her proficiency rating on one. Old LI habits were too tough for even juicy staff appointments or schools to kill.

The first enemy soldier she killed with the SSW was so close she could have bayoneted him, if the SSW had had a bayonet. The burst of slugs nearly decapitated him, and completely spattered both friends and foes with his brains and fur.

Shores followed by swinging in another half-circle, holding the firing stud down as she did. That exhausted a magazine, but somewhere in the last few seconds the tube crews had seen the new threat and retargeted.

One hundred twenty-millimeter rounds ripped the rear of the enemy attack. Ptercha'a flew high or fell lifeless; most of those who remained on their feet were bleeding. Most of the wounded were still firing, though, and kept on firing until they went down or ran out of ammunition.

The ones with empty weapons threw them down, drew knives, and came on.

Unarmed combat against Ptercha'a was supposed to be impossible for humans. But that had to be qualified. If the human was combat-trained, loaded with adrenaline, and wearing body armor, and the Ptercha'a were wounded, tired and hungry, and less well-protected, the odds in a one-on-one were about even.

Except that Shores had at least five Tribal levies coming at her.

It was amazing, she realized, how the knowledge of certain death speeded up one's reflexes. She popped the empty magazine off the SSW and threw it. It struck a Ptercha'a in the face and knocked him down.

One.

She used the SSW like a quarterstaff, a weapon she enjoyed, and knocked a knife out of an enemy's shattered hand.

Two.

She whirled, catching the next enemy between the muzzle of the SSW and a boulder. She couldn't have heard his skull crack, because weapons, people, and for all she knew the gods were making too much noise. But he—no, she—went down.

Three.

The other two got inside the swing of the SSW. One of them slashed at Shores's face; she felt flesh open and blood flow, but no pain. Another tried to rip her thigh open with claws and teeth.

She chopped at the knife wielder's throat. Ptercha'a reflexes almost saved him from the muscle-corded hand striking like an axe blade. He flew sideways and landed limp.

Shores whirled again, with the last attacker clinging to her. The claws and teeth had found their way through to unprotected areas, but that damage hadn't started hurting either when Shores swung the Ptercha'a against the boulder.

This time she did hear the skull crack, because none of the heavy weapons were firing and there were fewer shouting fighters on either side. She wondered vaguely if they were dead or just out of breath.

Then hands reached down from the top of the boulder and hauled her up to the top, over, and down the other side. She started to fight, and then she realized the hands had neither claws nor fur.

Then she screamed, because her wounds started hurting, and also because a noise like the end of the world tore at her ears. She thought she was flying, and knew that if she didn't stop soon she would rise so high she would kill herself when she landed.

Unless she grew wings on the way down? She waved her arms, but something was holding both of them, and they seemed heavier than normal instead of lighter. She looked to see if she could at least grow feathers, but she couldn't see anything. Not even her normal arms in dusty, bloody battledress.

She realized then that she was dying, and this was how it felt. *How silly, to go to all this trouble for knowledge that I'll never be able to put to any practical use.*

Linak'h:

Karl Pocher limped up the slope to the gun pit, favoring both his wrenched ankle and his dislocated shoulder.

The Yellow Father seemed closer to the horizon than it had when BoJo Johnson came for him. That was impossible; it wasn't that late in the day and BoJo had come only five minutes ago.

Pocher looked at his watch, found a bare wrist, and remembered that he'd lost his watch rescuing Colonel Shores. That and the dislocated shoulder were the results of hauling Shores over the boulder, and he twisted the ankle carrying her to the medevac lifter.

Not a bad score for a battle that had left both Heights in the condition he'd heard described but never seen—so thick with bodies that in some places you couldn't set foot to the ground. Not very many places, and not large, but where the Coordination troops bunched up and the heavy weapons caught them—

Pocher didn't believe in a God to thank, but he had to admit that circumstances had been with him and his people. His eighty Victorians had been down to sixty by the time Shores was rescued. Only minutes later air strikes and long-range artillery came down on all the attackers who were still in the open. Task Forces Shores pulled its head in and its collar up and waited out the barrage before going out to mop up.

They didn't have to do much of that, either. Friendly Ptercha'a from some planet he'd only vaguely heard of came in from the north. Confraternity militia came up from the south. A crowd of Federation support troops, in every degree of usefulness from medics down to public relations, came down from the sky.

Graves Registration had to police up the bodies of both sides simply to provide room for the sightseers.

Finally some senior officers arrived to modify the confusion. That eventually brought BoJo Johnson down the hill to Pocher's fighting hole with a message.

"Some brasshats up in the gun pits want serious words with you."

"Why the Hades me?"

"Don't know."

Pocher's breath *whuffed* out. "Am I the CO around here?" If so, he'd been horribly neglecting his duty—

"Nope. There's Iqbal, Kapustev, and at least one company boss still on their feet, and Duboy's not hurt bad. But the brass have talked to all of them. Now they want you."

"All right."

Pocher struggled to his feet. Johnson looked at him sympathetically. "Need a painkiller?"

"Probably."

"Sorry, I gave all mine to Kathy."

"Is she—?"

"Just nicked in a couple of places. But sore. Anyway, I can stop by the medics' on the way up and do a little trading." He hefted a bulging Coordination field pack.

"What's that?"

"Souvenirs. Coordination carbines and single-hands, dud grenades, empty magazines, a couple of knives. I never yet met the support-service type who wouldn't give their back teeth for a genuine battlefield souvenir."

Johnson slung the bag and unslung the scattergun, keeping the muzzle down and well clear of any living target but never keeping his eyes still for a minute. His feet seemed to find level ground without help from those busy eyes.

Both of them, Pocher realized, had finished turning into soldiers here on Linak'h. It wasn't what either of them had come for, and it remained to be seen how useful it would be in the long run. It also didn't prove anything other than the Second Law of Thermodynamics, although the rate of increase in the disorder of the universe did seem to vary.

Then they were at the top of Height 380, and Pocher realized that Johnson hadn't been joking about "brasshats." General Langston was there, with a small, lean, Asian-looking colonel who had to be the legendary Nieg.

Pocher managed a left-handed salute; Langston's return of it was embarrassingly more precise. Nieg merely nodded.

"Everyone we've talked to speaks well of your leadership," Langston said.

I suppose it's too much to ask, that you talk to our dead.

The general lowered his voice. "We wondered if you were—ah, satisfied with the role the Victorians were allowed to play in the battle."

The brass, Pocher decided, was not only on Langston's hat. It was in his balls, for asking that kind of question.

"If you want to spread anything I say to the media, let me talk to my people before I say it," Pocher said. "If this is a private conversation—"

Langston turned his laser stare on several officers who had been hanging too close and looking shocked at Pocher's *lèse majesté*. They gave ground reluctantly.

"Now, between soldiers—?" Langston asked.

"I think Colonel Shores did the right thing, all the way from when she arranged for the Vics to join her movements. We had orders to help, we wanted to fight, and we got our chance.

"As for her tactics—I'm not an expert ground-pounder. But they made this much sense. If she lost the Vics, she'd still have the LI to repair the damage. If she lost the LI, she'd only have us, and we might not have been able to do the job.

"As for leading us herself—"

Langston held up a hand. "Thank you. We will ask for a complete official report as soon as you've talked to your people. Right now, I'll just repeat the thanks. Colonel Shores is not in a body bag right now largely because of you. I'm grateful. Colonel Nieg is grateful. We'd like to show it somehow, without waiting for any official procedures."

Pocher had a brief vision of taking up his Navy career again, with an array of ribbons on his dress whites that would turn heads wherever he went.

For about a Standard year, maybe, and how many of the heads I turned would have anything in them?

"Give Victoria first priority for subsidized emigration to those planets out beyond Peregrine. Half of them are better than Victoria, from what I've heard."

Nieg was supposed to be totally imperturable, but he was now doing a remarkably good imitation of a man trying to pick his jaw up off the ground. Langston was doing equally well as a superior trying not to laugh his head off at a junior's expression.

"Who's been talking?"

"A lot of the people *Somtow Nosavan* brought back talked to Captain Marder and Mr. Longman before you got to them, Colonel. Both Marder and Longman passed a certain amount of it on to me. Did they violate any rules?"

"Quite a few," Nieg said. He sounded resigned rather than angry. "But I suppose prosecuting the people who helped save Victoria from a pro-Merishi coup for security violations would not look very creditable."

"It would make the Federation look like a bunch of vindictive assholes," Pocher said. "I thought you were trying to improve Federation-Victorian relations, which is why I made that suggestion about the emigration subsidies."

Nieg said what had to be rude words in several languages that Pocher didn't know, then shrugged. "All right, Captain Pocher. That particular promise is not something I can keep without those official procedures we were trying to avoid, or maybe even with them. But what I can do—"

"What *we* can do," Langston said.

"What the people who owe you a lot can do, will be done," Nieg concluded. "Now, if you will excuse me . . . ?"

He scrambled down the hill. Fifty meters away he was joined by a stocky figure, still in combat gear in spite of bloodstains and field dressings. Sergeant Major Timberlake had been nicked and near-missed a good many times today, and was technically on light duty. Apparently escorting visiting brass was considered light enough.

Probably hopes Nieg will put in a word for her getting back into the field right away. We've won this battle, but damned if I can see that we've won the war.

Linak'h:

Candice Shores knew she was wounded and in the hospital, but couldn't feel or see anything that proved it. It was all intuition and maybe a little reasoning; the pain and the drugs hadn't completely scrambled her wits.

What she saw was faces. Mostly faces that couldn't be here—her father and Ursula Boll, her mother (still on Quetzalcoatl five hundred light-years away), her brother Erik (flying a courier ship out toward Jumpoff, even farther), Juan Esteva (who at least didn't look angry).

Then the impossible faces went away and she began to see ones that might be real. Two doctors, Major Feinberg and somebody South Asian who didn't have a name in her mental file. Nurses, Nightingale Khan and at least one other (female, she thought).

Finally came faces she hoped were real. Sophia and Peter, looking so anxious that she decided to treat them as real—except that when she tried to talk, all that came out was a croak.

"Here." Nightingale Khan's face swam before the childrens'; she felt something cold on her lips.

Crushed ice. I take back half the bad things I've ever said about the man.

She sucked and licked until she could move her lips without their cracking, speak without her throat clogging.

"Hi, kids. Have they been treating you all right?"

"We missed you," Peter said, and was it just her imagination that he came out as clear as a bell?

"I missed you, too," she said. She hoped saying inane things like this was just the medication. She hadn't landed on her head; that she remembered.

She tried to reach up and touch her head. Her arms wouldn't work. Just like when she thought she was dying, they were as heavy as hull-plate.

Then she tried to hug the kids. That didn't work either. She decided to look at her arms, to see if they were at least still there.

No, what she felt wasn't phantom pain from amputated limbs. Both arms were there, bandaged and braced. One had a tube into it.

"I guess I'll have to hug you after I wake up. Promise." She wondered if Nightingale Khan had loaded that ice with something, because suddenly her eyelids were threatening to snap shut like a helmet faceplate.

Just before they did, she saw another face come up behind the children's. It was small and neat, with expressive dark brown eyes set against a darker brown complexion.

She hoped Nieg was real too.

Twenty-six

Linak'h:

The Battle of LZ Ursula wrecked Legion Six-Seven, its Tribal Cohorts, and its supporting units. It lost virtually all the warriors and equipment it had brought to the battle.

It also lost Fomin zar Yayn. Confraternity militia found his body in a crashed lifter thirty kilometers east of the battlefield. No allied action could account for its destruction, and rumors of Merishi assassination squads were in circulation before Fatherset on the day of the body's retrieval.

"By all means let them circulate," Taidzo Norl told Colonel Nieg. Norl had been taken prisoner by Interventionist scouts from Pek, after leading the last air strike on Task Force Shores. His captors' knowledge of his intelligence value led to his being turned over to the Federation.

"Only do not spread the tale that he died by his own hand," Norl added.

"I thought that was a death held in good repute among the Hunters," Nieg replied.

"Not by my sister's mate," Norl said. "Nor is this any secret. Say he slew himself, and few will believe you. Say he died in battle, and it will be to his honor. It may even be true.

"Say the Merishi murdered him, and you may put poison under their tongues or perhaps some more painful place."

"That also may be true," Nieg said.

Whatever the truth about Fomin zar Yayn's death, the rumors led to a mutiny among the Hunter levies in the Merishi Territory. (Nieg later learned this was a great disappointment to Behdan Zeg, who had been planning to lead his fighters across the border if the war went on.)

Meanwhile, the Coordination launched a series of probing attacks against 222 Brigade, Task Force Olufsdottir, and the isolated Fourth/218 on the Alliance frontier. Any of these attacks might have been converted into a serious one, if Task Force Shores had gone down, if hoarded supplies hadn't been destroyed by *Shen* and Hogg's troops, or if the Interventionist troops hadn't landed.

As it was, all the elements were present for allied victory and Coordination disaster. On the fourth day after LZ Ursula, a Confraternity delegation that included Boronisskahane met with the Council of Coordinators. Muhrinnmat-Vao was among the Coordination representatives.

On the fifth day, the Coordination asked for a cease-fire and offered peace on the basis of evacuation of all territory, return of all prisoners, and recognition of the Confraternity as a legal political party in the Coordination.

Colonel Nieg summarized the case for acceptance.

"The only thing we're not getting that might have been desirable is turning over all the surviving Merishi-trained terrorists to us. But those survivors may be a handful, they probably don't know anything we haven't learned elsewhere, and the Coordination may not even have them on its territory anymore. We should be prepared to take covert action against the terrorists on the basis of intelligence received through the Confraternity, but otherwise I think we can say that the war is over and we won."

Three days after the Coordination's request, Linak'h Command, the Forces of Intervention, and the Administration jointly granted it.

By this time the first brigade of Federation reinforcements was in Linak'h orbit, ready to land. Fortunately neither wave of reinforcements had brought with it an officer senior to Marcus Langston in his new rank of Lieutenant General or to Rose Liddell in hers of Acting Vice Admiral. So Linak'h Command's old warriors saw matters through to victory without being second-guessed by newcomers.

They even had the pleasure of stripping 199 Brigade of most of its lift, for the repatriation of Coordination POW's and the distribution of relief supplies. (The Baernoi used their own transport to land and distribute their purchases from Simferos Associates.)

Charlemagne:

The detailed report of the cease-fire and Linak'h Command's recommendations for awards and special promotions reached Admiral Baumann's office at the same time as an estimate of the sequence of events in the Atwood kidnapping.

Aung Bayjar studied the estimate with growing amazement. After reading it three times, he flung the papers down and said, "I do not anticipate problems with the War Council being indiscreet about this. The problem I anticipate is their believing it in the first place."

Admiral Kuwahara understood, even sympathized. Baumann, either short of sleep or more experienced in the ways of the Baernoi, did not.

"What's so incredible about a Tusker presence in the Federal District, or at least on Charlemagne? They've operated on at least twelve of the Old Starworlds in the last generation, so why not go for the brains?"

"Nothing is incredible about that," Bayjar said. "Where belief begins to falter is the rest of the—"

"If you say 'story,' you'll never visit my sauna again," Baumann said.

Bayjar had the grace to lower his eyes. Then he made a disgusted sound. "Very well. Then I will believe that the Merishi found an agent at the Palestra, who then turned or was turned by the Baernoi. So when Colonel Crawshay panicked and thought his friends would benefit from having Atwood kidnapped, both the Merishi and the Baernoi knew about it immediately, because Crawshay used *their* agent for *his* plans.

"Is that right so far?"

Both admirals nodded.

"The Baernoi then used one of their own people, unknown to anybody else, to split Crawshay's team into factions. Hence the fight that allowed Atwood to escape and the freedom with which the prisoners have been talking."

Baumann nodded. Bayjar grimaced.

"Stop nodding like a sleepy snake and tell me one thing more. Why should we believe the Baernoi wishing us well, to the point of exposing one of their own agents?"

"They haven't exposed anything they can't afford to lose

in the interests of furthering an exchange of intelligence," Kuwahara pointed out. He wondered how much of Nieg's report he should discuss, looked at Baumann, and saw one thumb raised but bent ninety degrees.

General picture, no details.

"We have reason to believe that the Inquiry mission on Linak'h had two objectives. One was to increase Baernoi contact with the Ptercha'a. The other was to decrease the danger of the Baernoi being exploited by the Merishi militants as they were on Victoria."

"In other words, to make sure that if we and they get into a fight, it's for our own objectives and not the Scaleskins'?"

Baumann inclined her head graciously. Bayjar tried to smile and almost succeeded.

"I may need more details on the Linak'h situation before I can offer that hypothesis to my masseur, let alone the War Council."

"I can offer one detail," Baumann said. "The sponsor of the Inquiry mission on Linak'h was Fleet Commander F'zoar su-Weigho. The man we believe is the chief of Baernoi intelligence on Charlemagne is now a respectable import-export merchant.

"However, at one time he was a Fleet officer. In fact, he was a classmate of su-Weigho's, and served as his executive officer in at least two Fleet ships. So I think assuming a connection is a reasonable hypothesis in this case."

"I wish we knew how many more cases there will be," Bayjar said. This time his smile was less strained. However, you are admirals, not soothsayers. I will go do battle with the War Council with the arsenal you have given me. You finish your fight for the honor of the Forces with what I have given you."

He bowed himself out, without letting go of the hard copy of the intelligence report or even loosening his grip.

"It's going to be badly wrinkled and he'll have cramps in his hand if he doesn't let go before the Council meets," Baumann said. She signaled for her steward, who appeared with two robots exhaling appetizing scents and a tray carried personally. The tray held two Baernoi *uys* glasses and a bottle of brandy.

Baumann filled both glasses and raised hers.

"To honest warriors."

Kuwahara drank, but half his mind was reviewing the unfinished report on the crimes and misdemeanors in the Forces that had led to the crisis. Honest warriors deserved toasts; the other kind deserved punishment, depending on whether they'd been criminal or stupid.

What they would actually receive depended on a good many factors, starting with the War Minister. His reasons for foot-dragging had become obvious when the list of suspects emerged; one was on his personal staff and three others had been appointed with his support. (Kuwahara suspected that there lay the explanation for the disappearance of the data from the interrogations of the mercenaries captured on Victoria, and possibly of the mercenaries themselves.)

Mobilizing for war on Linak'h was over. Mobilizing to fight for the integrity of the Forces might just begin.

Baumann nodded when Kuwahara suggested making the extradition of Colonel Crawshay a condition for any intelligence exchanges with the Baernoi. She frowned when he suggested bringing Langston, Liddell, and Nieg back from Linak'h.

"They'll need to come in starsleep unless you want to yank them out of there before their jobs are done," Baumann said. She slathered sweetspread on a muffin and munched vigorously. "Aren't you going to eat?"

"I'm just barely hungry."

"I'm closer to starving. I was up half the night with this *verfluchtig* estimate, then slept through breakfast."

"About our friends—"

"Well, I know that Captain Ropuski deserves a good tumble, which she'll get when Langston returns. I assume you are planning on reviving the Japanese custom of the second wife with Rose Liddell—what's it called?"

"It's no longer practiced, even on Yamato."

"Very good. But as I recall, Nieg's major interest is still on Linak'h."

Kuwahara couldn't manage a straight face anymore. Baumann watched him for a moment, then smiled.

"All right, Sho. You eat something, and I won't make any more rude remarks."

"I would call them lewd myself."

"As you wish."

Linak'h:

Fifty days after the cease-fire, the long-hidden Confraternity flag finally rose into the sky of Linak'h.

It rose over the newly dedicated cemetery at LZ Ursula, where five thousand bodies or parts of bodies lay, according to the rites of their various faiths or the customs of their skepticisms.

Boronisskahane protested strongly against having such a historic flag associated with a place of death, where it would not even fly alone. His mission to the Coordination had exhausted his body but strengthened his will.

His protest met a united resistance. Sharfas Shorl, Marshal Banfi, Isha Maiyotz, the Administration Warband, and all the senior officers of Linak'h Command protested even more strongly. Boronisskahane might have gone on to suggest not raising the flag at all, but he learned that this might persuade the Linak'h Confreres to vote him out of office.

Faced with that final humiliation, and offered the honor of bearing the flag if his health permitted it, Boronisskahane followed the example of the Coordination, conceding defeat while it could still be done without loss of honor.

So now the flag whipped in the autumn wind over the cemetery, along with the flags of the Federation, the Administration, the Coordination, and the three worlds of the Intervention. The Coordination flag had been sent; it was not yet time to allow the Coordination Warband to hold ceremonies in Administration territory.

The wind brought tears to Marshal Banfi's eyes as he walked down the hill. The scars of battle on the earth were still visible; it was too late in the season for even Linak'h's lushness to bring quick healing.

Without the wind, he would have been dry-eyed. He had seen too many deaths in too many wars, most of the deaths and wars far more vicious, stupid, or both than this one on Linak'h. It had taught a lesson which should not have needed teaching but had, and now had been taught more cheaply than it might have been otherwise. The Confraternity held and would not lose the position it should have won at least a century ago.

Serving the Federation while it honored that stupid ban on the Confraternity had always preyed on Banfi's conscience. Now his conscience was as clear as his service to the Federation was complete. The doctors had made it plain: this was his last war, if not his last year or two in the material Universe.

So be it. I can always come back and haunt people, if they drag their feet on finishing off the ban.

It had been more than fifty years since Hunters or humans died for supporting the Confraternity, at least on most civilized planets or without Merishi intervention. But before then, and even more recently at Merishi hands, the dead had included some of Banfi's comrades-in-arms.

They had taught him a good deal about haunting, which he would enjoy putting to use when the time came.

One of Isha Maiyotz's aides was standing in the path. Seenkiranda? Yes, and as might be expected, Emt Desdai was just behind her. It was good to see them both alive and together.

"Senior Maiyotz wishes to know if you will accept the hospitality of her flier," Seenkiranda said, using the most formal diction.

"Mine is as close," Banfi said. It was also better heated than Hunter craft. This brisk autumn weather was warm enough to let Hunters sunbathe. It gave him pains in obscure joints.

"Ah, but Cohort Leader Davidson and War-Flier Nalyvkina are already in it."

"What are they doing? Mating?" He had not actually had to drag them out of bed with a winch after Olga's return, but they had been a trifle preoccupied with each other.

"Only discussing whether to pair-mate, I think," Desdai said.

Aboard R.M.S. *Perfumed Wind,* the Linak'h system:

Brokeh su-Irzim contemplated the screen view of Linak'h. It now showed a complete disk, and even that was visibly shrinking. F'Mita ihr Sular had plenty of power under her thumb-plate, and she was using it to get clear of the still-debris-laden space around the planet as quickly as possible. She was also prudently climbing straight up from the plane of the ecliptic. The center of Linak'h's disk was the northern polar cap, with the sea ice already stretching far south of where it had been when the war began. Snow whitened land areas that had been gray and brown, and some that had been green.

As an experiment, su-Irzim tried to cover as much of the area of the war as he could with his thumb. Within a hundredth watch, he could cover all of it except the burns from the Great Fire.

Oh, and the Merishi Territory. The last public meetings before the election should be starting about now, if the display showed the right time. It had been inevitable that there would be an election, after the success of the one in the Administration and the disastrous failure of the Merishi-sponsored war.

It had not been inevitable that the Confraternity would win; it still was not. But the People's giving most of their purchased relief supplies to the Confraternity had done no harm.

If the Confraternity won, the next move would be the merging of the Merishi and Baernoi territories. (Su-Irzim doubted that the Merishi-governed Hunters would want to join the Administration, and he knew the humans would hardly allow it; the Territory still had to be infested with Merishi Inquirers.) That would be even more expensive than the purchase of the Merishi cargoes, and the Governor's banking connections would hardly generate the funds for it.

(For that matter, su-Irzim still kept making obeisance to the Lord of Wealth, that the Governor had been honest in raising the money for the cargo purchase. He probably had, and no doubt the Merishi would hasten to speak if he had not. It was what they might say that worried su-Irzim.)

If the merger passed, the combined Territories would need ground-fighters. What better foundation for that host, than Behdan Zeg's Hunters? And could Behdan Zeg lead them as well as they deserved without the help of his half-brother?

All of which explained why cabins that had been assigned to Zeg and Sarlin were now occupied by two Merishi Inquirers. Both seemed to be Special Projects, one a woman named Ezzaryi-ahd and the other improbably named Kep-Fah.

Who the woman represented, su-Irzim did not know and hardly cared. Kep-Fah, it appeared, represented Simferos Associates.

Footsteps on the worn carpet (*Perfumed Wind* had worked hard since Victoria) made su-Irzim turn. Zhapso su-Lal stood there, staring at the screen with a prayerful look on his face.

"Still worried about Zeg challenging the Governor?" su-Irzim said.

"Less so than I might be," the other said. "He listens to Sarlin now, which I would have thought incredible a year ago."

"A year ago Sarlin had no thought for Zeg's pride," su-Irzim said.

"You think that explains it all?"

"Enough to satisfy me for now, at least."

"You seem easily satisfied. But if you are explaining matters, explain this mission that has us rushing across the stars as swiftly as jewel-bearers to a Khudr's crowning."

"Not that swiftly," su-Irzim said. "*Perfumed Wind* is no courier's—"

A cough interrupted them. "Do you wish the brief pleasure of insulting my ship, at the price of loosened bowels the rest of the voyage?" F'Mita ihr Sular had her hands across her chest and a faint smile on her face.

"*Perfumed Wind* is a splendid vessel, worthy of carrying noble warriors," su-Irzim said. "The commander is a paragon of all the virtues of her—"

"The noble warriors have courtiers' tongues," ihr Sular said. "Very well. Your bowels are safe unless your tongues wag again. Now I had better see to the visual inspection of the cargo."

She withdrew briskly, su-Irzim gazing after her. He doubted he'd heard the complete truth; *Perfumed Wind*'s cargo monitoring and inspection gear had been completely overhauled since the war. Her departure would still let him and su-Lal talk more freely.

Or perhaps she was telling the truth. Her ship had received as a free gift a cargo of everything from the Merishi vessels that would be useless on Linak'h. Things that needed to be seen, touched, or even tasted might be among them.

Su-Irzim realized that he could hardly imagine what part

of a Merishi cargo might be useless to the Hunters of Li-nak'h but useful elsewhere. And he an Inquirer!

(It was true that Inquirers need not have merchants' skills. It was equally true that this might be about to change. It might have to change, indeed, when one considered how little the People knew of any of their rivals except the Smallteeth.)

Su-Lal was looking at him with humorous curiosity. "Who are you dreaming of now?"

"A beer."

Su-Lal pointed. "Under the counter, just below that dreadful—ah, *traditional*—painting of the Great Khudr's gun line."

The beer was excellent. After a second one, so was su-Irzim's mood. He could hardly complain about either the mission—assisting Fleet Commander su-Weigho in a secret meeting with the Merishi, to consider joint penetration of the Peregrine sector—or find any excuse for avoiding it.

Linak'h had given him unique knowledge. It could also dispense with his further services. He could even be spared the return to Petzas with his knowledge; no doubt messenger ships would be waiting at the rendezvous with su-Weigho's vessel. (Best begin organizing his final report at once, with a first version as soon as possible.)

The beer did not erase one nagging doubt. Zydmunir Na'an was representing Simferos Associates in person, for all that he was as old as su-Weigho and had led a much less active life. Did this serve the agreed purpose of the meeting?

Or did Na'an presume to draw the entire People into his personal battle to avenge his son? A great presumption, if so.

Not, however, one entirely dangerous to the People. Na'an's enemies were in the Governance Space Security. They could be a formidable ally for the People against the humans. They were also the home of many who wished to use People and humans against each other to the gain of the Merishi.

As long as Na'an helped the People move into the Peregrine sector, the People could justly be asked to help him against his own Fleet. A hand's worth of flourishing Baer-noi colonies within a single Passage of Peregrine would do more for the Khudrigate than Space Security ever would.

Su-Irzim poured another mug of beer. His insight, he felt, was complete. His mood, he knew, was excellent. This beer had nothing to do with either. It would merely taste good.

Aboard U.F.S. *Shenandoah*, off Linak'h:

The screen that had been showing Rose Liddell a view of *Roma* suddenly went dark.

They used to trip over themselves to keep my electronics running. Now they're unplugging them to reduce the power drain.

She quelled her irritability. It really didn't make any difference how much more she saw of the ship that would be taking her out-system in another two hours, along with Marcus Langston and Liew Nieg.

(In a starsleep capsule on the way to Charlemagne, the Lord be praised, not in the flag quarters, still less in the bed where Admiral Longman had died. She had been moved there from sick bay as soon as she knew that she wasn't going to make it; Liddell still hadn't been looking forward to sleeping in the bed.)

For the last time, she heard a door slide open behind her. For the last time, she turned and saw Pavel Bogdanov.

"My last tea aboard *Shenandoah*?" She pointed to the steaming cup in his hand.

"Look at the firsts, not the lasts, Commodore."

"Such as my first posting to Charlemagne? That could also be my last, you know."

"I do. But the War Minister can hardly dismiss Admiral Baumann. The uproar would bring him down."

"He can refuse to reappoint her next year. Or he can make so much trouble for her that she won't accept a second term."

"I won't say I know Admiral Baumann better than you do, even if I have served under her and you have not. I will say she has never struck me as one who would retreat from a fight without a better reason than a Minister's harassment."

Liddell nodded. Bogdanov wasn't finished. "Admiral Kuwahara won't abandon her, and you won't abandon him. So unless the War Ministry falls into the hands of madmen—"

Liddell held up her hands. "I understand. I—I haven't felt like this since the first day of my first command."

No, there'd been a Navy routine to help her through. It was more like the day she reported for induction, to learn that routine in the first place and leave the academic world behind.

I have been at home two places in my life—the University and Shenandoah.

She stepped aside from two robots carrying a table and looked at herself in the full-length mirror. She still looked almost as colorless as she felt, except for the blaze of gold on either shoulder.

Three stars. Permanent ones now. I didn't know that EDP promotions came in flag-rank sizes.

She drank the tea Bogdanov held out to her, then gripped those large, sure hands for the last time. He smiled down at her.

"Who's out there?" She pointed toward the exit from flag quarters. "I thought I heard drums and chanting a little while ago."

"Maybe you did. The Confraternity was supposed to be sending up a delegation."

"Who else?"

"Everybody off-duty, or who could claim their duty took them through here. People from the Army—I haven't seen Nieg—"

"He has other places to spend his last hours here."

"Merishi. Assorted Victorians, led by the Odd Couple—"

"How does Longman look?"

Bogdanov shrugged. "Bearing up."

"Help him if you and Jo Marder think he needs it."

Charles Longman had received a final message from his aunt that had made him guilt-stricken and gloomy, the night he and Marder dined with Liddell. But the commodore had watched Marder gently reminding him of his aunt's mixture of faults and virtues, his own duties, and her caring, without saying a word that couldn't have been broadcast on the media.

They'll spend a lot of time healing each other, that pair, but they have a lot of time. It was a shock to realize that Marder, who had to be past forty Standard, had begun to seem young.

"People from every ship I knew was in orbit and a few I had not. Oh, and Brigitte Tachin."

"With or without—?"

"Without. Not without a companion, however."

The end of the saga of Junior Officer's Bunkroom C-4. Elayne Zheng ashes on the way back to Agamemnon. Charles Longman prospering perversely as a merchant spacer. Brigitte Tachin reassigned to *Roma* (over the protests of Commander Zhubova, who had to be reminded that *her* Weapons Department wasn't shorthanded). And Brian Mahoney . . .

Trying to cling to his foothold in the Navy and to Brigitte and losing both?

A harsh, but probably not inaccurate judgment.

If Mahoney does go down this time, he can bloody well lie there until he gets up himself!

She put the empty teacup down and a robot made a dash at it. Another last.

No, not quite.

"Excuse me, Pavel. Before I go out and face this mob scene, I have to visit the head."

Bogdanov threw back his head and raised echoes with his laughter. Then he bent and kissed Liddell on the forehead. More than a brother's kiss, less than a lover's—a comrade's kiss that was exactly right for the occasion.

A first and a last in one gesture.

Linak'h:

Candice Shores was packing. She was five days from shipping out, and in order to go with the children was returning to Riftwell by way of Victoria. The survivors of the Victoria Expeditionary Battalion would be riding with her; she hoped the inevitable war stories wouldn't be too hard on the children.

The old division: cabin versus hold. Why did it seem so hard to make it now?

It wasn't drugs. She'd been out of the hospital for nearly six weeks, and would have been out sooner without the concussion and the first regen on her face wound. Everything else had been the Coordination trying to maim her without succeeding. Even that dying Tribal who'd chomped down on her thigh had missed both "important place" and major blood vessels.

No pain, therefore no painkillers, and the tranquilizer was a mild one. Memory loss was *not* supposed to be a side effect.

She sat down on her low bed and started sorting through the things on it. If she couldn't make decisions now, she could at least gather the stuff on which the decisions were already made.

The half-finished "Young Queen." Somebody had suggested that as her official portrait; regulations required one now. Hang it on the bulkhead and maybe she could decide by the time they reached Victoria.

The handmade flag-rank insignia. Keep with her, not because she expected to be wearing them any time soon, but because the silver in them was worth a good deal. Not all baggage handlers were honest.

The socks she'd been wearing when she was wounded. She'd thought of packing them, but now she decided they could go in the donations box.

Wonder of wonders. I've made a decision.

An elegant black leather portfolio. She hesitated a moment before opening it.

One side held an eight-pointed silver star with a ruby heart, hung from a thick purple ribbon. She remembered a randomly acquired statistic: two-thirds of all awards of the Federation Star were posthumous, and half the surviving winners had to take medical retirements.

She was alive and on-duty, one of thirty-eight active-duty Star winners out of nearly twenty million Forces personnel.

The idea had not lost its power to give her vertigo. Neither had the citation lost its power to make her laugh. It was official parchment, official calligraphy, and official jargon that made her wonder if the Board of Awards and she were really talking about the same two days' fighting.

"Outstandingly innovative tactical deployment of troops under her command," for example. She would have called it "letting my support units' area be overrun so thoroughly that I had to take it back with a scrambled attack by a bunch of amateurs." Who had died like professionals in saving her and her battalion.

The ones who had died. They had begun to balance in her mind, the ones she had sent or led to death and the ones who would live to remember LZ Ursula. There were a lot more of the second kind than the first. The letters to next of kin had begun with Juan Esteva's mother; they had only seemed to go on forever.

List of wounded—cabin baggage, so it can be checked for any omissions or necessary updates. The unloading of the hold baggage at the Riftwell end might take days; baggage handlers could be slow even when they were honest.

The decisions came swiftly now. By the time Shores had everything in the piles she intended, it was nearly 1600.

Bath, I think. Then I can take the kids out to dinner. Also Lu and Herman, if they aren't too busy trying to family-proof their contract. Marriage to a daughter of one of the old aristocracy of Monticello, it seemed, had ramifications that would make a Hunter inheritance mediator throw up her hands in disgust.

Shores walked into the bathroom and stripped. The only places she still wore light dressings were thigh and cheek, and cheek only because the regen work was underway. The thigh dressing was a standard spray; the cheek one was something with a long technical name that she wasn't supposed to get wet.

She would give another fingernail besides the one she'd lost to be able to take a hot shower. But baths it was, at least as far as Riftwell—and that meant sponge baths aboard ship; no tubs on converted emigrant transports.

She'd run the bathtub full when a familiar shadow crept across the bathroom floor from behind her.

She turned around.

"Hello, Liew."

"I wanted to see you before I left."

"Well, what do you call this?"

"The Young Queen with her armor off."

She couldn't manage a reply to that, so climbed into the bath instead. Nieg pulled up the stool Peter used for brushing his teeth and sat down beside the tub.

"I've sent a message to a friend of mine in the Family Registration Office on Riftwell."

"Liew, I don't—hold one. What did you ask?"

"If your application for guardianship of the children is granted, could she expedite the processing?"

"Consider me honorably bribed. I can use the extra time

to set up a trust for the children, if Herman comes through with that network of art dealers he claims to know."

"If he doesn't, somebody at the Kishi Institute will. If I might offer a word of advice—"

"Liew, how long before you have to be aboard?"

"A couple of hours, at least."

"Not long enough to waste talking around your point." She reached up and tousled his hair. "Right about there. Don't go bald, and nobody will notice. Besides, I like to run my fingers through your hair."

Nieg let her fingers roam across his scalp and down over one ear to his neck with an expression rather like a cat being stroked.

Does he think he's forgiven? Is he right? Does the concept of forgiving have any place here, now, between us?

Candy, you're a soldier, not an artist, and before god never a philosopher! This time she heard laughter in her father's voice.

"Very well," Nieg said. "After Riftwell, what?"

"Apply for a family-duty post, someplace with civilized care centers, decent educational networks, and so on. I'm a full colonel with the Star at thirty, Liew. I can afford a low profile for a few years."

"Can the children afford you?"

She didn't bristle; she'd asked for plain speaking and could hardly complain if she got it. "You've seen them with me. I didn't do anything to make them think I was the most stable place in a crazy world. Or at least nothing I wouldn't have done anyway. What's happened, has happened."

"Including major traumas for all three of you."

She nodded. "I wake up crying some nights. They wake up screaming other nights. It helps if we're all in the same room. Not so far to go, to realize that you're not alone."

The word seemed to trigger a flood of words from Nieg. "That makes sense. But family-duty posts aren't all they're supposed to be. An officer with stars in her future who takes family duty gets curious looks when the promotion boards meet. It's not gender problems, just the shortage of good people. *Really* good people.

"Besides, even a post that's intended for a family week can change overnight. With a few years and therapy, school and care centers can take over where you have to leave off. Right now—"

He can't be planning to testify against me, can he?

Outside on the road, two ground vehicles came violently together. Shores started. She scanned the bathroom, fixture by fixture, then brought her gaze back to rest on Nieg's face.

He means something completely different.

"Liew?"

"Candy, you could use a partner, and not only with the children. Although it would help if he was somebody—somebody the children already knew, and—"

Water splashed as Shores tried not to laugh. Liew wouldn't understand; he might be humiliated; if she humiliated him when she could see on his face what he couldn't put into words, she'd be (literally) a damned fool!

"Liew, ah—if this is a proposal—and if it isn't, could you say so—?"

Damn, now I'm doing it?

"Yes."

"Yes."

Somehow she found herself out of the tub, still naked, dripping on everything, including him. He was standing on the stool, and on it he was just tall enough that she could rest her head against his shoulder.

It was a novel sensation. Also an agreeable one. She would have to figure out ways of experiencing it again.

"What about your career, my friend?" she said finally.

He seemed to find the pose quite as comfortable as she did. It was a while before he said anything.

"Liew?" she prodded.

"People who look at my file do not see someone to be put to working miracles. They see a classic Intelligence cowboy, who ought to keep a low profile for a few years.

"Those years are going to be busy in our relations with the Alliance and the nonhuman spacefarers. Anyplace I appear, all four will immediately start looking for Federation plots.

"Intelligence people are the opposite of Young Queens. For us, the less exposure the better."

Grips tightened. In the mutual comfort, Shores knew that things remained to be settled. Children of their own, for a start. With Nieg's background, he would probably want them, preferably at least one son; that meant a multi-term commitment, twenty-one Standard years at least. Maybe longer, if they had to wait until Sophia and Peter could cope with the new half-sibling.

But they had time. Thirty wasn't as outrageously young for having children as it was for being a full colonel (in what was technically peacetime, at least).

"Liew, I'll say yes. But if you change your mind between now and when Forces Command lets you return to Riftwell, for any reason or none—"

He tipped her head up with a hand under her chin and kissed her. Instead of being angry, he had such a beautiful smile that it made her giddy. She knew this giddiness was not medication.

"If one Intelligence officer can stand a little exposure—"

"I believe the phrase is, 'Help me out of these wet clothes'?"

He hopped down from the stool and she put an arm around his waist. He grabbed a towel as they left the bathroom, and she dried herself while he stripped.

"Dear God," she said softly. "You are beautiful."

He smiled again. He gripped her hands, to draw her gently down onto the bed. He kissed her on the lips and the throat, then started working down—

The door alarm rang. The air turned color with unrestrained curses. Then Shores laughed.

"Just the kids coming back, Liew. It won't be the last time they interrupt, either."

If you and/or a friend would like to receive the *ROC Advance*, a bimonthly newsletter featuring all the newest and hottest ROC books and authors, on a complimentary basis, please fill out this form and return it to:

ROC Books/Penguin USA
375 Hudson Street
New York, NY 10014

Your Address
Name _____
Street _____ Apt. # _____
City _____ State _____ Zip _____

Friend's Address
Name _____
Street _____ Apt. # _____
City _____ State _____ Zip _____